IN THE
NAME
OF
LOYALTY

IN THE NAME OF LOYALTY

CYNTHIA COPPOLA

The Russos

Salvatore Russo
Anna Ricci Russo
Tony Russo
Ruth Klein Russo
Bob Marino
Louisa Russo Marino
Bobby Marino
Sophia Marino
Rena Russo Trovato
Dominick Trovato
Janet Russo Obremski
Ryan Obremski
Nancy Russo Lewis
Richard Lewis
Anthony Russo
Susan Rubinetti Russo
Mia Trovato
Gabrielle Obremski
John Russo
Julia Obremski

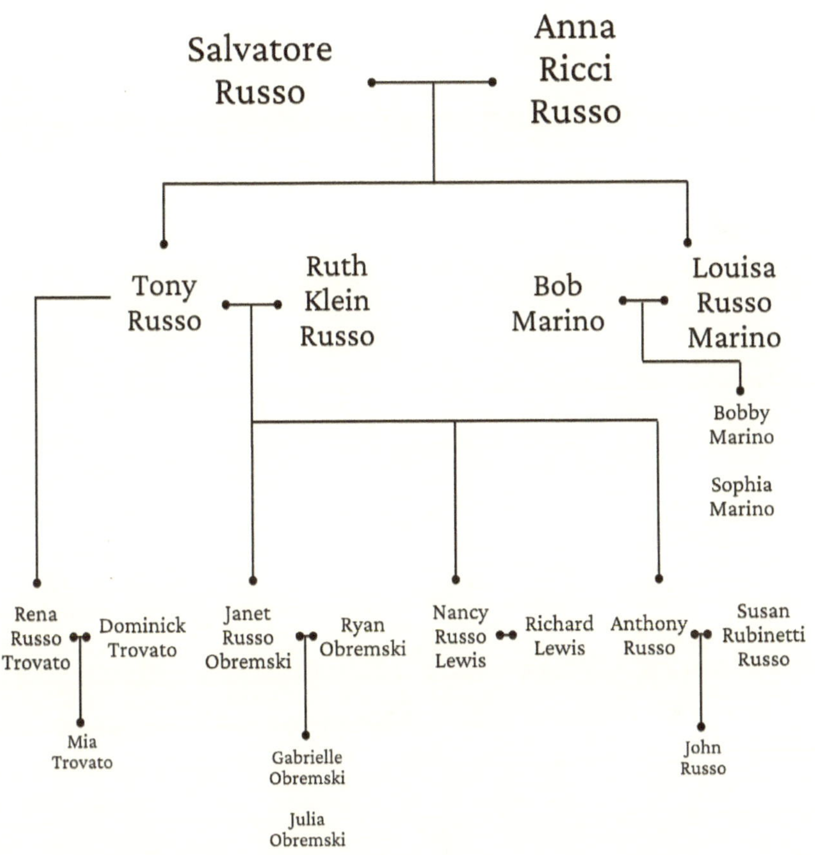

The Bocelli Family

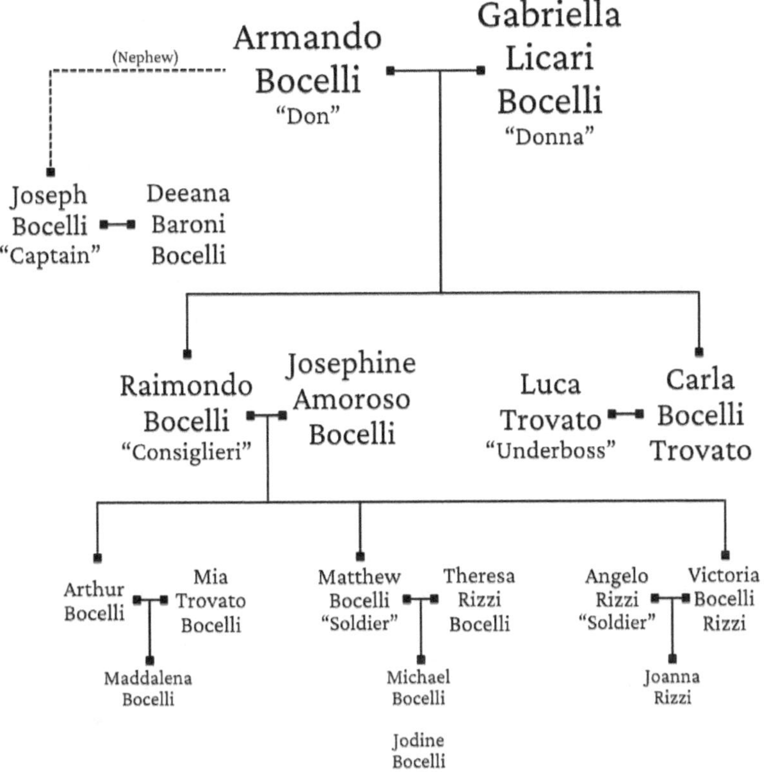

The Esposito Family

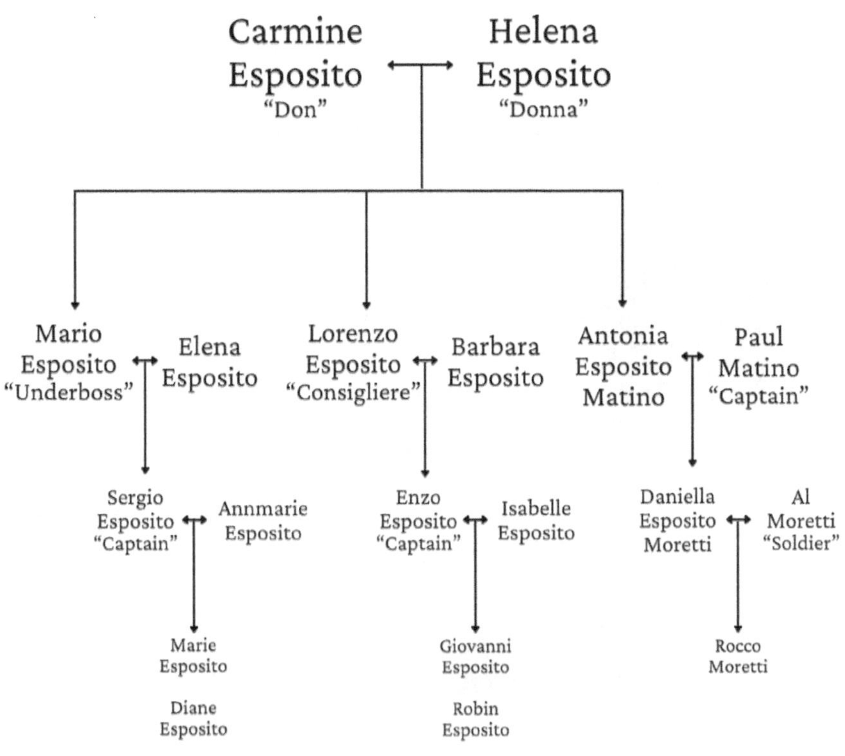

SWEET BEGINNINGS

ONE

MIA HELD HER breath as she stood frozen on the stairwell. She didn't have to strain to hear her grandparents arguing in their bedroom. It had been a long time since they'd had a disagreement this heated, and she never meant to cause a fight, but she knew it was inevitable.

"I won't have it!" Tony slammed the closet door shut.

"Tony," Ruth reasoned, "let's talk about this rationally."

"There's nothing to talk about. I've made up my mind. How can you even entertain the idea of her spending the summer with *those* people."

"*Those* people are her family. There's nothing we can do to change that. I understand how you feel, but remember, Mia is confident and strong. Let's face it, she's coped with turmoil her whole life as she saw her mother go through depression, alcoholism, and addiction that can be directly attributed to her father's death. Although Rena's been gone for two years, Mia's still trying to process it. She needs answers, Tony. She has questions about her father and his relationship with her mother that we can't answer. She feels that if she could get some insight on Dominick, she can start design school in September with a clear mind."

Tony's tone softened. "We've protected her all these years. I will not lose her to them just as we lost Rena. I can't go through that again. I just can't."

"Mia is not Rena. We won't lose her, I'm sure. In fact, I think the best way we can protect her is to be supportive. She's eighteen now, and doesn't need our permission, but she wants our blessing."

"Yes, eighteen. The same age Rena was when she ran away with Dominick."

"You're right. Don't forget, Mia not only has a good head on her shoulders, and a great plan for her future, but, unlike Rena, she knows beyond a doubt how much we love her." She squeezed his hand. "Now it's time to trust her."

"Ok, Ruthie," he whispered, "I suppose you're right."

"I worry too, but she's only going down the shore. She'll be back before we know it."

"Eight weeks is a long time. A lot can happen."

"We'll send her off with a nice big family dinner on Sunday. We'll remind her of the value of loyalty and trust in the Russo family."

Mia heard the squeak of the bedroom door and started to descend the stairs.

"I suppose you heard everything?"

"Not everything, Grammy." Mia looked down, ashamed that she got caught eavesdropping. "I could tell Poppy wasn't happy."

Ruth joined Mia in the middle of the stairwell. She brushed Mia's hair behind her ear and together they sat on the step. "No, Poppy wasn't happy, but he's not angry either. He's concerned about your safety. We both are, but I convinced him that you should go."

Mia smiled. "Thank you. I guess I can understand your concern, but I need to know who my father was. All I've ever heard from you and Poppy was that he wasn't good for Mom. All Mom ever said was how much she loved him. But I don't know anything about him. What made him the dynamic person that Mom loved so much and the appalling person you hated so much? You've all told me the stories of your experiences, but I need to know what made him who he was. The only people who can tell me that are his family."

"You know the people you'll meet and spend time with down there may be dangerous?"

"I *do* know that. But I also know that Uncle Luca wouldn't let anything happen to me, and probably the safest place I can be is at his home."

"There is a very strong possibility you'll meet Carmine Esposito."

Mia's face turned red and her grip on Ruth's hand strengthened. She nodded quickly. "I thought of that," she said blankly.

"I'm sure he'll know who you are but avoid him if you can." Ruth took Mia's face in her hands and looked her straight in her eyes. "You must not speak to him about our family, and, Mia, by all means, stay calm. Do *not* show him your anger."

"I won't. I know it won't change anything." She stared straight ahead. "He killed my great-grandparents, possibly my father, and indirectly, my mother. Nothing I say to him will matter. He's too evil to care."

"Yes. I. I, suppose you're right."

Mia's face softened and she kissed Ruth's cheek. "Don't worry, Grammy. My goals this summer are to sunbathe on the beach, read a bunch of books, and learn about my father so I can come home and start school feeling refreshed in September. I won't let anyone get to me."

"Okay," Ruth nodded slowly. "We'll have an extra-special dinner Sunday night."

"Does that mean you'll make Eggplant Parmigiana?"

"Absolutely."

TWO

AS SHE DROVE down the Garden State Parkway Monday morning, Mia turned the volume up on the radio and at the top of her lungs sang along to Bette Midler's latest song, *The Rose*. She loved that song because it reminded her of her mother. The past two years were tough for Mia as she navigated finishing high school and adjusting to life without Rena. She often felt guilty thinking of her mother's death as somehow a blessing. It was no secret that Rena had a difficult life, and her story was a sad one. Mia understood Rena's attraction to Dominick and why she fell in love and ran away with him so young. Quite simply, her father gave her mother the love and acceptance she felt she didn't have throughout her life, and having Mia made her feel complete. But Dominick was killed shortly after he was arrested for drug distribution. There were rumors that Carmine Esposito had Dominick killed to prevent him from testifying in court, but Dominick's family said that wasn't true. They claimed Dominick had no intention of ratting out Esposito, and that his smart mouth and cocky attitude was what got him in trouble in prison. Rena had told Mia that the five years they were married were the happiest of her life, and during that time she and her father, Tony, had made great strides healing their relationship. Mia knew that her grandfather never really accepted her father, but with Ruth's encouragement, he was able to remain cordial within Dominick's presence. When Rena got the news of Dominick's death, she spiraled down a black hole that she was never able to pull herself out of. In spite of all the love and support Tony and Ruth gave her, Rena's depression led her to be institutionalized for a short time, and she battled with it for the rest of her life.

Mia's eyes welled up as she recalled her mother's death. She was in a terrible drunken state and had told Mia that loyalty and love was not something to be taken lightly. She made Mia promise that she would keep her distance from her father's family. Rena had warned that there were a lot of things Mia didn't know. She had passed out before Mia could ask any questions. Although Mia had disposed of the vodka, sometime during the night Rena had washed down multiple pain pills with another bottle she must have had hidden somewhere. Mia found her lifeless body the next day.

She tried to sort through her mixed feelings about spending the summer in Mantoloking. She barely knew her aunt and uncle, and part of her didn't believe she could trust them or would be comfortable surrounded by people she barely knew. She was content at home with Ruth and Tony, their simple pool, and quaint backyard, but her final conversation with her mother haunted her and she knew she had to go despite her mother's warning to stay away from her father's family. She was determined to learn more about her father, and the only way to do that was to surround herself with his people. She needed to see for herself what drew her mother into that world, and what caused Rena to sink into the depths of hell after Dominick died. Rena had often told Mia that Dominick was the greatest love of her life. She spoke about the fabulous parties and dinners they would attend and how dangerous his job was. But at the end of every story, Mia's heart would break for her mother as her face would cloud over. Rena would then shake her head with fury and warn Mia, "Don't get so captivated by bait that you don't see the hook." As a young child, Mia couldn't understand what Rena was trying to tell her, and now she was resolved to find out.

She turned off the radio, took a deep breath, and pulled up to the gate that secured entry to the property. Before she had her window down, she heard a gravelly voice say, "Yeah, can I help you?"

She hesitated, leaned in closer to the box where the voice came from, and said, "Uhm, I'm Mia?" After a few moments of silence she added, "I … I'm staying with my Uncle Luca and Aunt Carla this summer?"

The gate eased open, and Mia quickly shifted her car into gear and drove down the gravel lane that led to the house. To her surprise, the large stone mansion that appeared before her seemed inviting. As she approached the circular driveway, the double glass-paned doors opened and Carla appeared, standing between two large white columns looking even more regal than Mia had remembered. She pointed toward the five-car garage and followed behind Mia as she parked her 1975 Pacer next to a brand-new, shiny, red BMW convertible.

"Mia, sweethcart." Carla cooed, "Welcome to paradise." She held her arms out wide and embraced Mia with a strong hug and a kiss on each cheek.

"Hi, Aunt Carla, It's good to see you again," Mia said awkwardly.

"I'm just thrilled that we get you to ourselves this summer. Now don't worry about your bags, I'll have James come out and get your things and bring them to your room."

Mia tentatively looked back at her car as Carla put her arm around Mia's waist and led her to the front entrance of the house. As they entered, Mia felt overwhelmed. She wasn't used to such grandeur and wide-open living spaces. She marveled at how bright the house was, not only because it was decorated in various shades of white and seafoam green, but also because she could see straight through from the entryway to the back of the house where the kitchen and living area were. The imposing windows along the entire back wall gave Mia the feeling that she was actually on the beach.

Carla studied Mia's face closely, "Don't worry, sweetheart, you'll feel at home here in no time."

Mia let out a long breath, nodded her head, and whispered to herself, "We'll see about that," as she followed Carla into the kitchen.

"Gina," Carla sang out as she glided into the kitchen. "I'm famished. Is lunch ready?"

"Yes, Mrs." Gina, stood in the kitchen holding a tray with a pitcher of iced tea and glasses.

"Very good. I think we'll eat lunch inside today. The humidity is starting to kick up. Unless, Mia, you'd rather the patio?"

"Oh no, inside is fine with me." Mia tried unsuccessfully to make eye contact with Gina.

"Where's my manners." Carla chuckled. "Mia, this is Gina. She and her family have been with us since Uncle Luca and I married. They're a part of the family."

"It's nice to meet you, Miss. If there's anything you need, please let me know," she said with a thick Italian accent and a smile. Mia was touched by the warmth in her eyes. She had seen that same warmth in pictures of her great-grandmother, Anna, and knew instantly that Gina was sincere.

Carla gently took Mia's hands. "I've given Gina strict instructions to make sure you're comfortable. She's taken the liberty of stocking up on some snacks we thought you'd like, but after you're settled, you'll need to sit down together so she can get to know your likes and dislikes."

She led Mia to the table and motioned for Gina to serve the lunch.

"You'll meet Gina's husband, James soon enough. He is the head of our security team." Carla shrugged her shoulders. "I've tried to convince him to spend some more time at home on weekends with Gina, but he's very loyal. Especially to Uncle Luca."

Mia wondered if she felt comforted or alarmed over the fact that they had a security team.

Carla continued. "Mia, I truly am thrilled you agreed to spend the summer with us. Your uncle and I both had wanted to be a bigger part of your life all these years. But what's done is done. You're here now." She nodded to Gina, who placed a large Cobb salad and breadsticks on the table.

"I'm happy to be here too," Mia looked out at the ocean trying to contain her emotions. "I don't really know much about my father, and my mom, well, she'd been sick for so long. It's just been tough, that's all."

Carla took Mia's hand, "Yes, I'm sure it has been."

"Don't get me wrong, Poppy and Grammy are the best, but I have so many unanswered questions and emotions that even they can't help me with."

"Your Uncle Luca and I were grateful that if we couldn't raise you ourselves, that it was Tony and Ruth who did. But I'm sure they aren't so thrilled about your spending the summer here with us."

"They're just protective. That's all."

"Hmm, protective. Yes, I can understand that." Carla pat Mia's hand, "People fear what they don't understand. It's human nature. But we are family, and I assure you, there is nothing you will ever have to fear. Hopefully, by the end of the summer you'll have some answers to your questions, and you'll have a better understanding of your parents and who *you* are."

Mia felt a pang in her heart. She sensed that spending the summer with her aunt and uncle was going to be life changing. "I hope so, too."

"I have many wonderful things planned for us. This summer, I'm going to cut back on my appointments, and I made it a point to clear my schedule every Tuesday so we can really get to know each other. You know, Uncle Luca doesn't come down here until the weekends, so it will be just us girls during the week."

"He doesn't?" Mia was surprised. The only time she had ever known her Poppy and Grammy to be separated was when Grammy stayed with her sister, Janet, to help out when Janet's son, Gabrielle, was born. Even then, Poppy was at Janet's house every night and only went home to sleep.

"Oh no," Carla said casually. "During the week it's easier for him to stay in the house up in Alpine so he can tend to business. You'll see. It's pretty quiet here during the week, but when the men come down on the weekends, it's another world entirely."

Mia nodded and wondered to herself, what exactly was Uncle Luca's 'business' that he tended to. She knew he was very powerful and worked for Aunt Carla's father, Armando, the head of the Bocelli Family. As his underboss, Uncle Luca was next in line to be the head of the family should anything happen to Armando. But Mia was curious about what he did every day. Was his life really like the movie, *The Godfather*?

"I made appointments for us at my favorite salon tomorrow, so we can kick the summer off right. I'm treating us to a full morning of pampering from head to toe, lunch at a nice little spot on the water, and then of course, we'll have to update our summer wardrobe at the boutique."

"Aunt Carla, you don't have to do that. I'm fine just spending the day at the beach," Mia said as she ran a piece of breadstick across her plate, soaking up the dressing.

"Darling, I insist. When was the last time you had a day of pampering?"

"I painted my nails the other day before I came."

Carla took Mia's hand and inspected her nails. "Very well done. Good choice of color."

Mia blushed at the praise, and said proudly, "Thank you."

"Have you ever had a professional massage and facial?"

"Not professionally. Sometimes I do my own face mask on Sundays, though."

"You do have a lovely complexion, but trust me you will love a high-end facial and massage. They're just divine."

"Well, Okay, if you *insist*."

"I do insist, and it's not often that I'm refused." Carla smiled at Mia, placed her napkin on the table, and stood. As she breezed out of the room she waved her hand in the air and said, "Gina, go ahead and show Mia to her room."

THREE

SUMMER, 1980

THE NEXT TWO days were a whirlwind of shopping and lunches at Carla's favorite spots throughout the shoreline. At first, Mia was skeptical of her Aunt Carla's intentions, but the more time she spent with her aunt, she came to realize that she was actually a generous person. Mia watched her closely as she interacted with Gina and her family, and noticed that Carla was not just kind, but she genuinely cared about them and their wellbeing.

On Thursday morning, as Mia descended the stairs, she found Carla on the patio sipping coffee. The more time Mia spent with her, the more she came to admire her. She was the epitome of class and held herself with such confidence and grace. Whenever they entered a shop or café Carla was treated like royalty. Yet, she never came across as condescending. While her demeanor set her apart, she was genuine and always took the time to chat with everyone from the shop clerks, busboys, and wait staff to the shop and café owners. She knew everyone's name and showed a true interest in their lives. In turn, they seemed to light up when she entered the room and were happy to be in her company. Mia assumed that Carla would be feared due to her being Don Bocelli's daughter, but nothing could've been further from the truth. It was clear that the community embraced her not from fear but from respect.

When Mia got to the bottom of the stairwell, she was taken aback by the commotion of people scurrying around cleaning and cooking, and Gina quickly shuffled over to her with a tray of coffee and croissants.

"Good morning, Miss. The Mrs. would like you to join her outside for breakfast."

"Good morning, Gina," Mia said as she looked around. "What's going on?"

"We're preparing for tomorrow."

"Tomorrow?"

"Yes. Every year Mr. Luca and Mrs. Carla host a Fourth of July party. It's very grand." Gina turned toward the patio door and added, "Is there anything special I can get you for breakfast?"

"That's right! Tomorrow is the fourth. I almost forgot about the party," Mia said as she tapped her hand on her head. "You know what, coffee will be just fine for now. Thank you." She wondered if she would ever get used to having a maid cater to her.

"Ah, good morning, my niece," Carla said brightly as Mia sat at the table. "How did you sleep?"

"I've never slept better. The bed is so comfortable."

Carla nodded, "That's the white goose feather and down bedding. You will have a hard time sleeping with anything else from now on, I'm afraid." She took a sip of coffee and continued. "As you can see, the house is in preparations for our annual gathering. I thought you might like to join me down on the beach this morning to get some sun. I like to make myself scarce while the family sets up. We've been doing this for so long, they know exactly how I like everything."

"The family?"

"Yes, Gina's family." Carla said casually, and then reached over and put her hand on Mia's arm. "I'm thrilled because this will be your opportunity to know *your* family better. You can see us as we *really* are. A loyal family." She tapped her hand a few times and reached for a croissant. "But I can only afford to spend a few hours with you today. As the hostess, I, too, have a lot of preparations that I need to take care of." She then looked around, leaned in closer, and whispered, "I also need to follow-up and make sure all of the preparations are done properly."

AFTER SHE FINISHED her breakfast, Mia packed her beach bag and quickly changed into one of the new bikinis Carla insisted she couldn't live without. This was the first day since she arrived that she would get to sunbathe, and she wanted to spend as much time as she could in the sun. She loved everything about the beach. Some of her best times were when she and her sister, Nancy, would drive down the shore to Seaside Heights. Sometimes their brother, Anthony, would join them, and they would spend all day on the beach and most of the night on the boardwalk eating large, thin slices of pizza and Kohr's custard, playing Skee-Ball in the arcades, and going on the rides. The smell of the ocean and the sounds of the amusements were always exciting. As she walked down the stone path and along the pristinely manicured grounds toward the beach access, Mia felt like she was on her own exclusive island. It was quiet here in Mantoloking. Seaside's beach was packed with families whose blankets were so close to each other you could hear everyone's conversation. The beach in front of Carla and Luca's mansion was private and peaceful. She took a deep breath and welcomed the smell of the refreshing sea air.

She shouldn't have been surprised that her Aunt Carla had an umbrella, cooler, and a table set up for her comfort, but she wasn't used to such luxurious living. Her idea of a good day at the beach was lying down on the hard sand on top of an old sheet that had her shoes, towel, and beach bag on each corner to keep it in place.

"I think I can get used to this," Mia said in wonder as she made herself comfortable on a lounge chair.

It was a beautiful day. The sky was a rich, royal blue with pure white clouds that looked like cotton balls magically suspended in the air. Mia lifted her face toward the sun and enjoyed the pleasant breeze that was just mild enough to be refreshing.

Within a half-hour, Carla joined her wearing a large pair of sunglasses and a burgundy kimono covering a matching one-piece bathing suit.

"Hello darling. How do you like our little beach?"

"I love it. I think I saw some dolphins."

"Yes, I'm sure you did. You'll start to see them more frequently as the weather gets warmer." Carla pulled out a bottle of Coppertone from her straw bag and applied it on her legs. "What's that you're reading?"

"A book from V. C. Andrews, *Flowers in the Attic*. I just started it, but so far, I like it."

"I've never been much of a reader," Carla said. "What's it about?"

"Actually, it's about a family and their secrets."

"Hmm." Carla raised her eyebrows. "You know, every family has secrets. It's just the way it is. You can look at a family and think that they have it all together and everything is wonderful. But behind closed doors, you never truly know what's lurking. And deep, deep back in any family's history, there's always some untold truths buried." She turned and looked out on the ocean. "Of that, I'm sure."

"I don't know about that," Mia said casually. "My mother was very honest about our family history. I can't imagine that there's anything she's hidden. She shared some pretty dark truths."

Carla nodded, tentatively, "You know Mia, Uncle Luca and I always wanted to have kids of our own." She sighed. "But sadly that wasn't to be. When you were born, we were thrilled that your parents asked us to be your godparents."

"Godparents?" Mia's eyes grew wide.

"You didn't know?" Carla said putting her hand over her mouth.

"No. I didn't." She shook her head at the revelation and realized that maybe there were, in fact, some secrets that her mother had withheld.

"Yes, sweetheart. We are your godparents. There was a small christening at Our Lady of Mt. Carmel Church."

"Really?" Mia's breath caught in her throat.

"It was the first time I met your grandparents. They were lovely under the circumstances. We never blamed them for being upset over Rena and Dominick running away together, and we actually shared the same sentiments that it was a bad idea. We all thought your parents were rushing into things and that perhaps Dominick might not have been the best choice for sweet Rena."

"Really?" Mia's head was swimming with questions. "Why wouldn't he be the best choice for her? She always said how much she loved him."

"Yes, she did love him very much, and I do believe he loved her also. But Dominick had a strong vision of what he wanted his future to be, and we were afraid that his eagerness to obtain his aspirations quickly would cloud his judgment in making good decisions."

"And is that what happened? Did he make bad decisions?"

Carla hesitated. "Maybe Uncle Luca can shed a better light on that. All I know is that both of your parents loved you immensely." She shook her head. "It was clear how devastating your father's death was to your mother. Our hearts broke for her. Broke for you both, actually. We tried so hard to be a strong presence in your life. But Rena," Carla looked down. "Maybe she was so heartbroken she needed to distance herself from your father's family. I don't know. But she closed the door and limited our opportunities to see you." She looked up at Mia and said, "But, my darling niece, you're here now." She grabbed Mia's hand and said, "And I couldn't be happier."

Mia's head was spinning. Why wouldn't anyone tell her that her Aunt Carla and Uncle Luca were her godparents? This was an important detail that Mia felt someone should've told her. To be a godparent is an honor usually bestowed upon people who are not only very dear to the family, but who would also play a special and important part in the godchild's life. Mia couldn't figure out why Rena hid that from her. Granted, her family wasn't particularly religious, but they made it a point to go to mass every Christmas, Easter, and on the anniversary of her great-grandparents' death. Was it a casual oversight or an intentional secret? Why would her mother share the hard truths of her ancestry, like how Don Carmine Esposito had her great-grandparents killed for stealing money from his uncle before they fled Italy, and not share something as special as Uncle Luca and Aunt Carla being her godparents? It all made Mia more determined than ever to find out why her mother had been so adamant about Mia staying away from her father's family.

She snapped out of her thoughts as she heard a cheerful voice call out, "Ciao." She looked up to see a girl her own age waving her hand as she strode across the sand. She had a bright smile that lit up her face and when her flip flops got caught up in the sand making her stumble and almost fall, she let out a burst of laughter that was contagious. It was obvious that she was confident and didn't take herself too seriously. As she got closer, Mia admired her long black hair that was swept up in a casual bun and her natural beauty that she accentuated with only red lipstick.

"Victoria!" Carla laughed and turned to Mia. "This is my brother's daughter. Theirs is the house next door. Victoria will be starting NYU in the fall."

"You must be Mia! I'm so happy to meet you."

"Hi." Mia smiled. "That was a nice save. I'm impressed you didn't fall. I'm not sure I would've been able to recover like you did."

"Yeah, well, honestly, I've face-planted in the sand one too many times. Please, call me Vicky. Victoria is way too formal for me."

"Oh, my dear, you must be more formal if you're going to be a lawyer."

Vicky looked at Mia and rolled her eyes. Mia liked her instantly.

Carla stood and started to gather her things. "I'm going to let you two get to know each other. It's time I head up to the house and see to the preparations for tomorrow. Will your brothers be joining us this year?" She asked Vicky.

"Yeah. Matt came down last night. He's spending the day with Daniella, and Artie is coming down tomorrow morning."

Carla nodded her head. "Daniella, huh? I'm surprised they're still dating."

"I can't figure out what he sees in her." Vicky shrugged.

"Hmm." Carla nodded thoughtfully. "And Artie? What's going on with him?"

Vicky laughed. "You know Artie. He's very serious about his studies. I keep telling him he needs to get out there and date more, but he says he'd rather not waste his free time trying to impress a girl he's not interested in." Vicky shrugged and looked at Mia. "My two brothers couldn't be any different from each other. Artie is very academic and thinks through every one of his decisions. And Matt, well Matt would rather stick needles in his eyes than go to college and loves working for the family by day and partying by night."

Carla nodded. "This is true, but it takes all personality types to keep the family successful. Either way, I'm happy to have the whole family together this year." Carla smiled at Mia and waved as she started toward the house. "Enjoy the rest of the day, girls."

"Our aunt can be very formal, but once you get to know her, she's really special." Vicky plopped down on the empty lounge chair and took a floppy straw hat out of her bag and placed it on her head.

"I'm only just getting to know her better," Mia said.

"I'll tell you this. You're all she's talked about for weeks."

"Really?"

"Yup. She loves her family and always said the family was incomplete without you."

"Really?"

"Really!"

"Huh. Thanks for saying that," Mia whispered.

Vicky looked at Mia, cocked her head and smiled. "So, I'm just gonna say it. I'm not trying to be weird here, but I hate beating around the bush." She shrugged and put her hand on Mia's arm. "I'm getting a great vibe from you. I can tell already you and I are gonna be good friends." She leaned in. "Was that weird?"

Mia chuckled. "Nope not weird. I have the same vibe. I'm actually feeling relieved. I didn't really know what to expect about coming down here and staying with Aunt Carla and Uncle Luca, and I definitely wasn't expecting to meet anyone my age."

"Trust me, you don't want to do a whole summer down here without someone to hang out with. It can get pretty lonely."

"Have you had a lot of lonely summers?" Mia asked as she reached into the cooler and handed Vicky a lemonade.

"Yeah I guess I have. I mean it's always cool hanging out with my brothers when they're around. I've invited the few friends I have to come and stay with us, but of course, their parents didn't feel comfortable."

Mia nodded. She didn't want to ask why the parents didn't feel comfortable, but she assumed it was because of the Bocelli Family's line of work. "I'm no stranger to lonely summers either. My closest friend back in Lyndhurst always went to visit her family in Puerto Rico for the summer, and when my brother and sisters weren't around, I spent a lot of time reading."

"Wait? Brother and sisters? Aunt Carla said you were an only child."

"Technically I am. I was pretty much raised in a house with my grandparents and their kids. They're actually my aunts and uncles but I think of them as my sisters and brother. You can say I've had a complicated life." Mia took a sip of her lemonade. She never liked telling her life story. Most people couldn't relate and would either withdraw from her or start to treat her with pity.

"Okay girl, start talking. You tell me about your complicated life, and I'll tell you about mine."

Mia sat up and smiled. Maybe Vicky was the one person who might actually understand the events of Mia's life and not get freaked out by them.

"Deal!" She said and let out a long, slow breath. "Let me ask you first, what do you know about me and my family?"

Vicky flipped over onto her side and faced Mia. "I really don't know much. I know your father was Dominick, Uncle Luca's brother, and he died in prison when you were just a baby, and your mom didn't keep in touch with the family much after that."

"Yup, that's the basics. My mom, Rena, met my father, Dominick, when she was still in high school. I guess she liked the bad boy type."

Vicky nodded, "I can relate to her already."

"Well, my grandfather, Tony, didn't approve of their relationship. I guess he thought my father was too old for her. There was a lot of drama because of it, which led to a big fight that put my father in the hospital."

"You mean your grandfather beat up Dominick?" Vicky leaned in.

"Yup. It was really bad, and my mother really couldn't forgive my grandfather for it."

"I guess I could understand that. I'm lucky that my boyfriend, Angelo, is like part of the family, but if anyone sent him to the hospital, I'd be pretty upset. What did she do?"

Mia raised her eyebrows and rolled her eyes. "She ran away with him the day after she graduated high school."

"Ooh," Vicky said as she nodded her head.

"Yeah. My grandfather took it really hard. After he went out looking for her, he collapsed with a heart attack." Mia looked down and ran her finger along the edge of the beach towel.

"But he was alright though, right? You said you were raised by your grandparents," Vicky said softly.

"He survived. But life changed for everyone after that. He and my grandmother bought a house in Lyndhurst and moved away from Brooklyn. My mother tried really hard to smooth things over between him and my father, and although she was kind of successful, there was always some tension." Mia looked out on the ocean and pulled her knees up to her chest. "After my father died in prison, my mother had a breakdown. I went to live with my grandparents and their three kids while my mom had to go away for a short time."

"Oh, Mia, I'm sorry," Vicky said as she squeezed Mia's hand.

Mia nodded slowly. "I was just a baby, and in fact it was the best thing. My mom moved in too, but she was very unstable and depressed. She became an alcoholic and became addicted to pain pills. She really couldn't be much of a mother to me. Poppy and Grammy gave me a great life and raised me alongside their kids, Janet, Nancy, and Anthony. They were all there with me through so many ups and downs."

"And your mom? Aunt Carla said she died a few years ago."

"She overdosed." Mia turned toward Vicky. "I like to think she's in a place where she can finally feel happy."

"I'm sure she is," Vicky whispered and then perked up. "You know, I saw a picture of her once. She was absolutely beautiful. I guess you can say she was kinda like a rose with thorns. Very captivating, yet, painful if you're not careful."

Mia was taken aback. Vicky was not only completely unfazed by her story, but she understood. No one had ever been able to fathom the details of Mia's past, let alone grasp them as fully as Vicky did. "That's exactly right," Mia said as she looked at her new friend in wonderment.

"What are your sisters and brother like?"

"They are the best. First there's Janet. She's nine years older than me. She tends to be the most serious of the bunch and always looks out for me offering advice and encouragement even when I don't know I need it. She taught me how to swim. Then there's Nancy. She has one of those personalities that draw you in, and people always feel like they know her well, even after just meeting her. She got me into reading. All summer long we would sunbathe and devour books we would get at the library. Even though she's seven years older, we're really close and tell each other everything."

"I always wanted a sister," Vicky said dreamily.

"I can't imagine my life without them. They're the best when it comes to advice and fashion tips." Mia nodded her head. "Now my brother, Anthony, he's just a hoot. He's got the greatest smile and laugh. He's closest to my age and is only four years older than me. He's always been my partner in crime. We would sneak out of the house at night whenever we could and pull pranks like move Poppy's car or build a giant snowman right in front of the front door."

"Ha. That's funny. I never teamed up with my brothers to play tricks on my parents. We only targeted each other," Vicky said. "Like the one time Matt and I super glued everything to Arties's desk. He was so mad. He wouldn't talk to us for a week."

Mia burst out laughing. "Did he get back at you?"

"Yup. He washed what he thought were our favorite clothes in bleach. Little did he know, Matt's favorite shirt was already ruined with a large grease stain from when he slobbered pizza all over it, and he took my clothes from a pile that was going to the Goodwill." Vicky shook her head and smiled brightly. "He was so proud of his revenge. We didn't want to burst his bubble, so we pretended to be upset and let him think he got even."

"That's so sweet of you guys. Tell me more of your story."

Vicky chuckled and waved her hand. "I'm starting to think my life isn't that complicated after all." She sighed. "It wasn't easy growing up as a Bocelli. Once I got old enough to realize my family wasn't like most other families, it was hard to make and keep friends. I mean, I had a couple of friends throughout school, but I don't know how close you could say we really were. There was always some excuse as to why they couldn't come to my house for a sleepover and that kind of thing. But I always knew the truth."

"I get it. There were a few girls I got friendly with, but once their parents heard about my mother's issues, the friendships dissolved," Mia rolled her eyes.

"Right?!" Vicky shook her head. "Like how about getting to know me for me, and maybe even try to meet my parents and see for yourself that they aren't dangerous serial killers."

"Weren't there other kids within the Bocelli Family that you were friends with?"

"Yeah, some. But, I don't know, it always seemed like everyone wanted something. I found myself questioning if they were really friends with me because I was cool or were they trying to get an in with the family."

Mia nodded. "That's got to be tough when it comes to dating too, I bet."

"Forget about dating. The guys from school who weren't in the life didn't stand a chance around my brothers and my father. If they weren't scared away from their intimidating protection tactics, they were scared away from my say-it-like-it-is personality." Vicky threw her head back and laughed. "Besides, I'm more attracted to the bad boy types like your mom was. That's why my boyfriend, Angelo, and I are so good for each other. He grew up in the life, he's making his own way up the ranks, and doesn't want any favors. Not to mention that he's sexy and sweet at the same time."

"He sounds perfect!" Mia said.

"So far, so good," Vicky said and crossed her fingers. "My family loves him and are pushing for marriage already. Can you believe that?"

"*Marriage*? Really?" Mia raised her eyebrows and leaned in.

Vicky nodded. "Most especially the men in the family. They don't take my career choice seriously. They want me to marry and continue the tradition of being a wife and mother. But I want more, you know?"

"I get it," Mia said.

"I want to work alongside my father and break down the anti-quated roles that have been in place within families like ours for centuries," Vicky sighed. "Every time the subject comes up, Uncle Luca, my father, and my grandfather laugh and roll their eyes. But

I'll tell you this, Aunt Carla, my mother, and my grandmother light up with pride."

Vicky took a long sip of her lemonade and turned to Mia. "So, what about you? How's your love life?"

"Non-existent right now. But I'm not complaining," Mia answered. "I'm taking some time for me before I start school in September."

"Good plan!" Vicky said. "I think we'll just have to do all we can to have the best summer of our lives before we both start school in September."

Mia smiled at Vicky. "I like the sound of that."

FOUR

MIA SPENT MOST of the night restless and unable to clear her mind. Her thoughts ricocheted between the happiness over meeting Vicky and the prospect of having a fun summer together, the revelation that her Uncle Luca and Aunt Carla were her godparents, and the betrayal she felt over her mother withholding that information. By 5 a.m. she was tired of tossing and turning and decided she would get up and enjoy quiet time on the patio before everyone else emerged. She was hit with the beautiful sound of opera as she opened her bedroom door and made her way downstairs. In the kitchen she found her Uncle Luca in a navy, velvet robe waving his arms and singing along dramatically as he was preparing pancakes.

"Good morning," Mia said loudly.

Luca turned quickly. "Aah, Mia. Come. Come, give your old uncle a hug." He held out his arms but held onto a spatula in his right hand and a pitcher of pancake batter in his left. Mia saw that her uncle was on his way to aging gracefully. She could see small specks of grey scattered throughout his thick, black, curly hair, and his face had a few more lines on his forehead and around his eyes. But his dark, thick eyelashes and dazzling smile kept him as handsome as she remembered. She moved in quickly and found surprising comfort in his big, bear hug and the woody scent of his Polo cologne.

"Look at you." He put the batter and spatula down and turned her around inspecting her as if she was a rare jewel. "Bellissima! But, of course, you are beautiful. You are a Trovato."

Mia smiled, but she was also surprised by his statement. Throughout her life her greatest attributes and accomplishments have been praised because she was a Russo. This was, in fact, the first time anyone acknowledged out loud that she was a Trovato. She couldn't blame her grandparents for having pride in their family name and ancestry, but she again felt deceived by her mother. Rena always said Dominick was the love of her life so why wouldn't she be proud that Mia was a part of his lineage? What made her so bitter toward his family that she kept Mia from them?

"What are you doing up? My singing didn't wake you, did it?" Luca lifted his eyebrows and tilted his head.

"No. I couldn't sleep. I didn't hear you until I started down the stairs."

"You couldn't *sleep*? What's wrong? Is your room too hot? Too cold? Is it the bed? I can have a new mattress here within the hour."

"No. Please, no. Everything is fine. I've got a lot on my mind that I'm trying to figure out."

"Aah. I see." he nodded and began preparing more pancakes. "Why don't you put on a pot of coffee. I make pancakes and sing opera when I need to sort through my thoughts."

As she helped make breakfast with Luca, he took the time to explain the meaning behind all of his favorite arias. By the time the pancakes were done, Mia had developed a better appreciation for a style of music she felt she had never really taken the time to understand before. And by the time they had made the accompanying fresh squeezed orange juice, bacon and cheesy scrambled eggs, Mia's mood was lifted.

"Wow, this is a lot of food," Mia said as she and Luca sat at the table and filled their plates.

"I guess we had a lot on our minds."

"Yeah, I guess so."

"What's troubling you?"

Mia hesitated. There was a lot she wanted to talk to her uncle about, but she wasn't prepared to dive in so early in her visit. This was the first time she'd seen her Uncle Luca in a few years, and really the first time she had had the opportunity to spend alone time with him or Aunt Carla. When she first arrived, Mia was guarded and resolute on exposing the flaws that hurt her mother so deeply. But so far, Mia had become more confused than anything. She hasn't seen any hurtful behavior or attitudes, and she had begun to doubt whether her mother's feelings toward them really had any merit.

Luca put his hand on hers and said, "I know how hard the years must've been for you. It couldn't have been easy with your mom being sick and with her passing and all."

Tears sprang to Mia's eyes. "No. It hasn't been easy," she whispered.

"I always had great comfort knowing that it was Tony and Ruth Russo looking out and raising you. Good people, your grandparents."

"If it wasn't for them, I don't know what my life would've been like."

"Aunt Carla and me, we were fond of your mother too. I'm sorry to say she got a raw deal with my brother."

Mia snapped her head up. "What do you mean?"

After taking a long sip of coffee, Luca sighed and said, "Let me start by saying, I loved my brother. Always have and always will. But Dominick lacked, shall we say, patience. He had big dreams and big goals, and quite frankly an unrealistic view of how this life of ours works." He straightened up in his seat and leaned toward her. "I'm sure I don't have to tell you what the 'family business' is." He raised his eyebrows.

"I have a good idea."

Luca nodded. "Back then, Carmine Esposito's territory included parts of New York, New Jersey and Pennsylvania. I'm not certain as to what happened, but the Commission decided to give the New Jersey territory to Carmine's life-long friend and comrade, your Aunt Carla's father, Armando Bocelli. Armando quickly became a well-respected Don with my father, your grandfather, Antonio as his Underboss. May he rest in peace," Luca said as he made the sign of the cross. "As for Dominick and me, we were just coming up through the ranks, but he wasn't satisfied in learning the business from the ground up. He wanted to make a name for himself and establish his power quickly, so he chose to stay in New York and work for Carmine. I was happy to come to New Jersey and learn the business from our father." Luca took a sip of coffee and stared out the window. "Dominick was thrilled with the chance of working muscle for Carmine, and I suppose he got cocky when Carmine took him under his wing. Dominick thought he would gain power and respect quickly working for him."

Mia sat at the table staring at Luca, captivated. She had always been told her father's family were members of an organized crime family, but now she was finally getting a first-hand description of who her father and his family really were. She was afraid to interject and ask questions for fear of Luca losing his train of thought and forgetting something.

Luca shook his head. "We all tried to warn him. Me, our father, even Carmine himself told him to slow down. Things take time and he couldn't expect to rise through the ranks quickly. That's just not how it's done. You have to prove yourself, prove you can be trusted and are worthy of being a member of the family. This thing of ours is not like they show in the movies. It's a hard, conflicting life. Being impatient or overzealous could be catastrophic." Luca turned and looked at Mia. "I'm afraid your mother fell in love with your father and got caught up in his impossible ambitions."

"So, what really happened to my father?"

Luca began, "Dominick—"

"What's all this?" Carla fumed as she circled around taking in the mess.

"Good morning, Mi Amore. We made breakfast. Pancake?" Luca said brightly as he extended the platter of pancakes toward her.

"Pancakes?" She eyed him suspiciously. "No. There's no time for pancakes. Close to one hundred family members will be here by noon. Ugh. Gina will be here any minute and she will certainly pitch a fit when she sees this mess."

Mia interjected. "We've got it Aunt Carla. We'll clean it up. She'll never know."

Luca nodded sheepishly behind Mia and whispered, "We'll finish our talk soon."

FIVE

IT DIDN'T TAKE Mia and Luca long to clean up the kitchen, and within an hour, an army of workers had ascended onto the grounds bringing more food and alcohol than Mia had ever seen at one time.

"Mia, sweetheart, it's time we go upstairs and get changed. Everyone will be here before we know it. What do you think you'll wear today?"

"Gee, I haven't thought about it." Mia knew that it would be a mistake to wear her old peach bathing suit and terry cloth cover that she had brought with her. While they were comfortable, they looked worn, and she wanted to make a good impression.

"Why don't you wear that lovely black suit with the red piping and ruffle we picked up at the boutique in town? That'll pair nicely with the black cover up dress we found in Cape May." Before Mia could respond, her aunt stopped and took Mia's hands in her own. "Today's going to be a big day for you. You're going to meet many family members you've never met before, as well as the family associates. It will be a lot, and I'm sure it may be overwhelming for someone who isn't used to the family. If you ever feel uncomfortable, just find me, I'll help you through it."

"Thank you," Mia whispered. The truth was, she was already beginning to feel anxious. She wouldn't necessarily consider herself to be shy but meeting close to one hundred family members and associates that she had grown up hearing were dangerous, was intimidating.

Carla squeezed her hands before heading to her personal dressing room.

By the time Mia finished showering and dressing, the house and yard were unrecognizable. A large number of people were milling about, and tents had been set up with various themes. The main tent contained a dance floor with tables surrounding it boasting large floral arrangements of roses and tulips. In the far right, a small band was playing while a DJ was set up in the far-left corner. Close by, there were other tents filled with buffet tables containing clams, lobster, shrimp, and oysters encased in ice, and a variety of grills where a whole pig, various steaks, ribs, sausage, hamburgers, hotdogs, and vegetables were being cooked by people Mia recognized as Gina's family. Another tent contained everything anyone could possibly want to drink including punch fountains, beer, wine, soda, and various mixers. The pool was filled with floats and beachballs, while additional lounge chairs and umbrellas were set up along the perimeter.

The one thing Mia wasn't expecting to see was the large muscular men that were standing like giants along the perimeter of the house, along the beach access, at every door, and in every corner. Nothing and no one would ever get past those guys, Mia thought to herself.

But it was the faces that stunned Mia most of all. So many strange, yet familiar, faces had emerged. Everywhere she looked there were people who resembled *her*. Sure, she bore a likeness to the Russo side of her family, but it was at this very moment Mia realized she looked more like a Trovato than a Russo. She stood on the patio slightly breathless as she took in the sight of the family she was about to meet. She quickly found Carla in a group of women tilting her head back as she laughed lovingly touching an older, sophisticated woman on the arm. Mia had been captivated by her aunt's confidence, and today she held her head even higher and bore an air of royalty as she started to work her way through the crowd toward Mia.

"There you are. You look stunning. That black suit and sundress was a good choice."

"I thought it might've been too much," Mia said as she pressed her hands to her hips. It took her more than an hour to dress and fix her hair and makeup. She wasn't used to getting done up for a family barbeque, but knew she had to put in an effort today. Usually, she would throw on any old bathing suit and flip flops, put her hair in a ponytail, and just run a quick glide of lip gloss over her lips. She was glad she put in the extra effort because, as she looked around, she noticed that mostly every other woman at the party was stylish.

"No, it's perfect." Carla put her hand just under Mia's chin. "You are perfect. Now come. There's people you must meet."

Carla led Mia to a small table where two women were seated.

"Momma," Carla said with reverence. "This is Mia. Mia, this is my mother, Gabriella Bocelli."

Carla's mother raised her head and locked her eyes with Mia's. Mia knew she was being given the once over and shifted her legs slightly. Carla placed her hand on the small of Mia's back and tapped it ever so gently. Mia felt kindness in her touch and the gesture filled Mia with confidence.

"It's so very nice to meet you Mrs. Bocelli."

Mia reached out her hand to the woman, who took Mia's hand in her own as she stood. "Actually, it's *Donna Bocelli*. But for you, I'll make an exception."

"Oh," Mia said nervously. "I meant no disrespect."

"Mia, I'm sorry. I should've explained," Carla said. "In public, the head of the family is always addressed with the title of *Don*, and his wife with the title *Donna*."

"I understand you will be spending the summer with your Aunt Carla and Uncle Luca."

"Yes, ma'am."

"That's quite an honor. I do hope you enjoy the summer."

"Thank you. I'm having a lovely time already."

As Donna Bocelli nodded, Mia smiled genuinely, but her stomach clenched with intimidation. Gabriella Bocelli was the most striking woman Mia had ever seen. She was slightly taller than Mia and her short, full, silver hair framed her thin face highlighting her deep brown eyes and thin lips. She wore white, flowy silk pants with a matching blouse and jacket in a large navy flower pattern. Her presence commanded respect, and Mia was afraid she would offend her with any other mistakes.

"Mia," Carla continued. "This is my sister-in-law, Josephine Bocelli."

Josephine jumped to her feet, kissed her on both cheeks, and said, "It's very nice to meet you. You can call me Josie. I believe you've already met my daughter, Vicky?"

Mia instantly felt comfortable with Josie. "Vicky? Yes. We met yesterday."

"She had nothing but good things to say about you."

As Josie took Mia's hand, Mia noticed that she was wearing the same ruby ring that Carla wore every day on her right ring finger. She turned her head and noticed that Donna Bocelli also wore the same ring. The ring was stunning. Set in gold, it had a large oval ruby in the center, flanked by large, square rubies on each side that were turned 90 degrees to be in the shape of a diamond.

Surrounding the top and bottom curves of the oval ruby were smaller, round opals, and running down the shank of the ring were diamond baguettes. Mia had never seen anything like it.

"You're ring is just beautiful." Mia turned to Carla. "Does it have a special meaning? I notice all three of you are wearing it."

Donna Bocelli smoothly sat down as Carla and Josie locked eyes. Mia thought she detected a slight smile on each of their faces. "It's just a family ring. Now, let's get going. We have a lot more introductions to make. Let's continue over here," Carla said as they approached a table with burly middle-aged men and average look-ing women.

The men quickly jumped to their feet as Carla neared. "I would like to present my beautiful niece, Mia," she said with pride. "Mia, this is Big Al and his wife Bella, Nico and his wife, Camilla, and Dino, and his fiancé Cecilia."

"Hey, hey! Mia! Bring it in." Big Al removed the cigar from his mouth as he pulled Mia in for a strong hug. "It's about time you came around."

"Mia!" Camilla squealed and pushed Al aside to move in for a hug. "You're a beauty. Now let's make sure we have a nice long chat today."

"I will, thank you." Mia smiled.

"Madone! Let her be." Nico winked. "Hey, Dino pass that plate of moozadell. Here, sweetheart, try this. I made it fresh, myself."

Mia took a bite of the fresh cheese and nodded in delight. "It's delicious."

"Ha, ha! Now this girl knows what's what," Nico said and kissed her cheek. "I'm really glad to finally meet Dominick's daughter."

Carla continued to escort Mia throughout the crowd and introduce her to just about everyone. With each introduction, Mia reveled in the affection the family bestowed upon her. Everyone welcomed her with warm hugs, double cheek kisses, and delight at finally being able to meet her. It didn't take long for her nervousness to fade, and she was soon drawn into the camaraderie and pride everyone shared within the family.

"Well? What do you think?"

"Everyone was so warm and friendly." *They don't seem dangerous at all.* Mia thought to herself.

"Yes," Carla said with enthusiasm. "Of course they were. You're one of us, you're part of the family."

It took Mia a minute to compose her thoughts and emotions. She was beginning to feel proud to be a part of this family that she had never met before.

As Mia looked up, her Uncle Luca caught her eye from across the yard, he gave her a grand smile and nodded. She realized that her Aunt Carla didn't bring her over to the table of men he was sitting with.

"Aunt Carla, are you going to introduce me to that table?"

Carla paused. "Not today, sweetheart. We'll leave those formal introductions for another time."

Before she could question Carla further, Mia was spun around by two hands on her shoulders. "Hey!" Vicky enthusiastically grabbed Mia, kissed both cheeks and gave her a tight squeeze.

"Ah, Victoria, what a lovely greeting. It does my heart good to see you two are getting along so well. Can I count on you to introduce Mia to the rest of your clan?"

"Of course. I'd be happy to."

"Wonderful. I will leave you two girls to enjoy yourselves. Be mindful to stay hydrated." Carla turned and waved as she disappeared within the crowd of guests.

"I'm so glad you're here," Vicky whispered. "There's not usually a whole lot of females at these parties that I like to hang around with."

"Your timing couldn't be any more perfect. Aunt Carla just finished her introductions and my head's spinning." Mia was glad to have a new friend in Vicky. She appreciated her outgoing, bubbly personality and easy demeanor.

"Yeah, I saw. It looked like you could use some saving." Vicky stood on her toes to get a good view of the pool area. "Let's grab some lounge chairs before the old folks get comfortable and never leave. Then we can grab some food and eat poolside."

"That's a great idea."

"I told the boys I would save them a spot too."

"The boys?"

"Yeah, my brothers. I told you about them, didn't I? Artie and Matt?"

"That's right you did. Which one's which again?"

"Artie's the one studying to be a lawyer, and Matt's the one who isn't." Vicky laughed. "They're Irish twins. They were born only eleven months apart and they couldn't be any different from each other. You'll see."

"You'll see what?" Mia and Vicky were startled by the sudden appearance of what Mia assumed was one of Vicky's brothers.

"Mia. This not-so-bad-looking disheveled mess is my brother, Matt."

"Hey." Matt took the cigarette out of his mouth with his right hand.

"Hi."

"Matt!" Vicky snorted. "You're crumpled from head to toe, your breath stinks, and is that sand in your hair?" She reached over and tousled his hair. "You look like you slept all night on the beach! What happened to you?"

"I slept all night on the beach." He shrugged. Mia couldn't tell if his glassy eyes were from drinking, lack of sleep, or both.

"Did you have a fight with Daniella again?"

"No. You've gotta see each other to have a fight. We had plans, she never showed."

Vicky didn't try to hide her irritation. "*Again?* Matt, really! When are you going to give up on her?"

"Aaah." He waved his hand. "She's a good time when she shows up. Me and the guys made a bonfire and got hammered."

Vicky raised both arms in the air. "I give up. Did you see Mom yet? Does she know you slept on the beach?"

"No. I came up the beach steps to avoid seeing anyone."

"Why don't you get settled here and we'll get you some food?" Mia offered.

"I like you!" Matt smiled at Mia. "My sister was right for once. You *are* nice."

Mia blushed while Vicky retorted. "Of course, *I* was right. I'm a good judge of character." She playfully pushed his shoulder. "Let's go, Mia."

"Does that happen a lot with your brother?" Mia asked Vicky as they were filling plates with food.

"The partying? Well, my brother likes to have a good time, that's for sure, but when Daniella stands him up, he tends to drink more." Vicky leaned in closer to Mia and whispered, "He'd never admit this, but I think it's a blow to his ego. I personally wish he wouldn't bother with her, but you'll see. She'll snuggle up to him and wiggle her way out of it."

"Hmph. I know the type."

"Really?"

"Unfortunately." Mia took a small plate and started to fill it with fruit salad. "Eddie and I dated on and off throughout high school. Just when I thought things were going good, he'd start acting up. He'd be all distant and too tired to go out or talk on the phone. Then of course, I'd hear he was out with some other girl."

"What a jerk."

"Yeah, he was. Every time I was just about over him, he'd come slinking back as sweet as can be. I'd get all caught up again. We'd have a good six months or more and then the same shenanigans all over again. The straw that broke the camel's back was when he stood me up on New Year's Eve. We were supposed to go to a party, so I got all dressed up and ready to go. He never showed and never called. I called his house at least five times with no answer. I was devastated."

"I bet you were. Did you go to the party?"

"No. I couldn't bring myself to it. I went to my sister, Janet's, house and spent it with her and her husband."

"Oh, that sucks! What did he say when you finally talked to him?"

"Get this, he said he fell asleep getting dressed! Can you believe that? Of course, I was getting reports from all my friends that he was hanging all over another girl all night. That was it for me, so I gave him what he deserved."

"What do you mean?"

"I took a baseball bat to his Z28." Mia shrugged.

"You mean, you destroyed his *Camaro*? Did you get caught?"

"No one had proof it was me, but everyone knew. My grandparents weren't happy at all. They said my temper would be my undoing, then they grounded me for two weeks."

"Wow, you really are a part of this family." Vicky laughed and began talking about a guy she dated in high school, but Mia became too distracted to hear her. She noticed Luca sitting at a small corner table set off apart from everyone with the same men that her Aunt Carla didn't want to introduce her to earlier.

"Vicky?" She cut Vicky off mid-sentence. "Who are those men

with Uncle Luca?"

Vicky glanced at the table, her eyes went wide as she looked at Mia. "You don't know?"

"No. Aunt Carla said she would introduce me some other time when I asked her."

Vicky chuckled. "Okay so, the man sitting next to Uncle Luca is *Don Bocelli*, my grandfather and Aunt Carla's father. Next to him is *Don Esposito*, and the other man is my father and Aunt Carla's brother, Ray. They are the heads of the families."

"Oh." Mia barely whispered. "Do you mean that's *Carmine Esposito*?"

"Yeah, that's him." Vicky looked at Mia who had gone pale.

Mia found it hard to speak. "I've heard so much about him. He looks like a regular man."

"They're all just regular men, I suppose. What were you expecting?"

"I don't know." Mia shook her head to try to snap out of her daze and return to reality. But only a few feet away from her was the man whom she believed had her father killed and whom she knew had her great-grandparents killed. As if he could read her thoughts, Esposito raised his head and locked eyes with Mia. He cocked his head slightly and leaned forward, he then smirked and raised his wine glass in a toast to Mia.

SIX

MIA COULD FEEL her temper rise. Her grandmother warned her she would most likely see Esposito, but no amount of warnings could truly prepare her for the emotions that crept up when she saw him in the flesh. All this time she held onto the tales of Carmine Esposito, the mythical creature who was a great monster disguised as a human. Now that monster had the audacity to torment her! To *toast* her. A gesture for most that was friendly and personal, yet for Mia it was taunting. It was his way of acknowledging that not only he knew who she was, but he was aware that Mia knew exactly who he was as well.

"Are you okay?" Vicky saw Mia's face go from stark white pale to bold faced red.

"I think I'm going to be sick." Mia handed her plate to Vicky and pushed herself through the crowd of guests, into the house and up the stairs to the bathroom connected to her bedroom. She fell to the floor in front of the toilet and felt herself begin to retch. She laid her head against the cold porcelain and began to sob. What was she doing here? She should've stayed home in Lyndhurst. What did she think would happen when she saw Esposito? Did she think she was going to give him a piece of her mind? She caught her breath when she heard a gentle tapping on the door.

"Mia. May I come in?" Carla asked as she opened the door. "Oh, sweetheart." She helped Mia off the floor and walked her over to the bedroom. "Here, let's sit a bit, huh?"

Mia nodded in appreciation but was embarrassed for her aunt to see her like this. "I'm sorry. I hope I didn't make a scene."

"No, you didn't at all. Don't worry. I saw you run up here and Vicky told me you felt sick." She rubbed Mia's back. "It wasn't the food though, was it?"

Mia shook her head.

"It was Don Esposito, wasn't it?"

Mia nodded her head quickly as tears flowed down her cheeks.

"I was hoping your paths wouldn't cross today. That's why I didn't make the introductions. I know the history between him and your mother's family is not a good one."

"He had my great-grandparents *killed*."

"I know, sweetheart." Carla rubbed Mia's back.

"How is that okay?"

Carla was silent for a long moment. "I won't pretend that I understand or agree with everything that has happened, and the pain that you and your family have suffered is *not* okay."

"And what about my *father*? Did he have my father killed?"

"I can't answer that."

"You can't or you won't?"

"I just don't know, Mia. I'm not privy to most of the business. It's not my place to ask, and they wouldn't tell me if I did. That's how it works."

"I'm sorry, but he's a monster."

Carla nodded. "He does have a strong temper and a taste for revenge."

"How can you stand being a part of a family like that?"

"All I can say is that my father, Don Bocelli, and Don Esposito are two very different people who run their families differently. But I must respect Don Esposito's position even if I don't agree with his philosophies and methods."

"I understand," Mia whispered. She had a pretty good idea how things worked within the family organization. But understanding it and liking it were two different things.

"He doesn't come around often. He only makes an appearance at our annual Independence Day party." Carla took Mia's hand. "I'm sorry, sweetheart, I should've prepared you better."

"It's okay. I tried to prepare myself for when I saw him for the first time. But the scenarios I created in my mind aren't the same as reality."

"You're right about that. Did you speak to him?"

"No. He recognized me though."

"I'm sure he did," Carla snorted.

"I wasn't expecting him to be so ordinary. I pictured him to be a larger-than-life being." Mia shook her head. "Not a grandpa."

Carla chuckled. "He has aged. Back in his prime, he was a very distinguished man who would make a room go silent upon entering. But don't let his appearance fool you. He's just as powerful and daunting as he ever was."

"I noticed."

"Now, Mia, I promise you won't be in his presence again this summer. In fact, he has already taken his leave today. We are by no means a typical family. But we are loyal, and we are devoted. I don't ever want you to feel intimidated. If you ever do, you come to me right away. I will always protect you."

"Thank you." Mia reached out and squeezed Carla tightly.

"You are an important part of this family. I truly want you to see our family for who we *really* are, not who people *think* we are."

Mia perked up. "I have to admit, I've felt conflicted about that. No one seems to be like the rumors I've heard."

"You mustn't believe everything you're told. I don't mean you were lied to, I just mean that people often make mistaken assumptions without knowing the truth. Besides, rumors are nothing more than a bunch of tall tales that grow every time someone speaks of them." Carla stood. "What do you say? Do you think you're up to coming back to the party?"

"I'm so embarrassed by the way I ran out."

"Nonsense." Carla waved her hand. "By the end of the night, you'll see what embarrassment looks like after a few of the goombahs have had their fill of drink."

Carla walked Mia out to the pool where they found Vicky and Matt tossing a beach ball to each other.

"Hey, Mia. How do you feel?" Vicky asked.

"So much better," Mia replied as she looked at her aunt.

Carla put her hands on her hips and said, "I told you girls to stay hydrated. See what happens when you don't drink enough fluids? It's hot today, and if you're going to spend it in the pool, I suggest you all drink plenty of water. Gina will have her hands full cleaning up messes by the end of the night." She smiled brightly and shook her head. "Let's not add to it."

Vicky and Matt swam to the edge of the pool as Carla turned and waved.

"You look a lot better. Do you think it was really the heat?"

"I don't know, could've been. But now I'm really hungry. I think I'm going to fix a new plate. Can I get you something?"

"I could go for a sausage and pepper sandwich." Matt answered quickly.

Vicky shot him a look and said, "Matt, really?"

"What?"

Mia laughed. She found Matt endearing. "One sausage and pepper sandwich coming up."

Mia felt more comfortable now that she was over the shock of seeing Carmine. As she made her way to the food tents, quite a few people nodded at her like she was someone of importance. A refined man with silver slicked back hair stopped her. She thought his name was Tony or Tommy but wasn't completely sure.

"Mia! How ya doing? You need anything?"

"I'm good. I'm going to get some food."

He leaned in, touched her arm, and looked around as if he was about to share a deep dark secret. "Stay away from the gabagool on the plastic platter. Nickey Hands brought it from his goomar's family deli." He shook his head. "That's the cheap shit. The good stuff's in the mini fridge under the table." He raised his eyebrows.

"Good to know. What about the sausage?"

He pressed his thumb, pointer, and middle fingers to his lips, kissed them and spread his hand. "Now, you can never go wrong with Sally's sausage and pepper sandwiches."

"Hey, Mia." She was swept up in a hug by Joe, one of Carla's cousins. "Now don't listen to a word Tommy here is tellin ya." He released his grip on Mia and jabbed Tommy in the side. "Unless he's giving you a tip on a sure thing."

"No tips today, I'm afraid," Mia smiled.

"You any good at Bocce?" Tommy asked. "We're gonna have a match in a little while and I swear to God, I'll drop my son, Jackie, as my partner if you can bring the goods. I got five hundred riding on it."

"Oh, no. I'd stick with your son, then. I'm not really good under that kind of pressure."

"Hmm. Well, alright. Maybe just a game then, some other time."

"I'd love it."

Tommy tapped Joe on the back. "Don't look now, Joe. Here comes your misses."

"Ok boys, let's not keep Mia cornered." She took Mia's hand and pulled her aside.

"I know we met earlier, but I'm Dee. It's so hard to keep track of everyone's name in a family this size. Are you having fun?"

"Yes, I'm having a really good time."

"You know, I grew up with your father."

"You did?"

"I did! My father, Giancarlo, was Dominick's godfather. As kids, we were together every Sunday, and as we got older, we ran around with the same crowd."

"What was he like as a kid?"

Dee smiled brightly. "Honestly, he was the troublemaker in the group. But what fun we had! He didn't like the words 'no' or 'couldn't' or 'shouldn't'. If there was a 'no trespassing' sign, Dom was trespassing and bringing us all in with him." She shook her head. "He knew how to charm the girls too. There wasn't any girl around who didn't want to be around him, and when he set his sights on something he wanted, he didn't let up until he got it. Your dad? He was one of the most charming bad boys around." She paused a moment and looked down, her voice faded. "It was a shame what happened to him, really. There wasn't a dry eye at his funeral. And your mom? She held you tight and looked so lost. I didn't know her well, but it was clear she loved Dom, faults and all."

Mia nodded. "Thank you."

"You know, your dad was a lot of things, but he really was something special." Dee lifted her cup of wine. "Here's to you Dom." She gulped the drink, and her face brightened. "I was headed over to the tent to dance with the other gals. Wanna join?"

"I can't. I'm grabbing some food for Matt and me."

"Well, you can't keep him waiting." She laughed. "He can eat, that one. We'll talk some more another time."

As Mia continued on toward the food tent, she started to get an idea of the type of guy her father was. She knew the bad boy type. There were a few of them at school. Mia was never especially attracted to that type of guy, but she could understand the lure. She entered the tent and started humming along to the song *Shining Star* the DJ was playing as she fixed two sausage and pepper sandwiches.

"Good song, isn't it?"

Mia turned and gasped. "You look just like John Travolta!"

Artie quickly looked down and laughed. "I get that a lot. I'm Artie Bocelli."

"Artie! You're Vicky's brother! You know you really look like him." Mia couldn't help but stare. He was so attractive. His wavy brown hair, chin dimple, and wide smile made him look like the star's twin.

"You must be Mia. Vicky was telling me about you." He smiled at her and when their eyes met, he quickly looked down again.

"That's me," Mia said awkwardly and then instantly regretted her response.

"You must be hungry," he said as he watched her try to manipulate two plates of food.

"Yes, I am. I mean. It's not all for me. I just wanted something light. Like fruit, but your brother, Matt, he wanted a sausage sandwich and then I thought, I like sausage, so why not." She let out a high pitch giggle that she'd never heard come from her throat before.

"Sausage is good. I think I'll have a sandwich too." Artie said and reached past Mia for a plate.

She felt him watch her as she tried to walk away balancing the plates she had in her hands. After taking a few baby steps, she turned to look back and found him leaping forward to catch one of the plates.

"Hang on, tiger. Let me help you with that."

"Thank you." She blushed and felt a shiver down her back when his hands brushed hers.

"Anytime," he said still unable to look at her for long.

As they walked back to the pool together, Mia tried to come up with something clever to say him.

"Mia, are you sick *again*? Your face is all red!" Vicky hopped out of the pool as Mia and Artie put the plates on a table.

"No, no. I'm fine. Artie was just helping me."

Vicky took a step back and stared back and forth between Mia and Artie who was standing as still as a statue looking down at his feet.

"Artie was helping you?" Vicky smiled. "So, you met my other brother?"

"Yes, we like sausage." Mia rolled her eyes and couldn't understand why her ability to speak coherent sentences had left her.

"Is one of them for me?" Matt asked as Artie held out a sandwich. "You got your finger in it. What's the matta with you?" Matt shoved half the sandwich in his mouth with his left hand and smacked Artie in the head with the right.

"Matt! Get outta here with that. You're dropping peppers everywhere." Artie took a step away from Matt and smoothed his polo shirt.

"Come on, Mia, let's sit here in the shade while you eat." Vicky took Mia's plate and led her to a table on the other side of the pool looking back at her brothers.

Mia let out a large sigh as she sat, drank half a glass of soda, and looked up to see Vicky staring at her. "*What?*"

"What happened at the food tent? You can barely speak, and Artie can barely look up."

"Nothing. We just met. He saved Matt's plate from falling."

Vicky sat back in the chair and smiled. "Okay." They sat in silence for a few moments before she spoke again. "He's single. But very focused on his studies."

Mia sat back in her chair and smiled. "Okay."

"Hey guys. What's going on?" A deep voice called out.

"Angelo," Vicky squealed in delight as she lept from her chair and jogged over to the largest human Mia had ever seen.

"Who is that?" Mia asked Matt as he and Artie walked over to where she was sitting.

"That's Ange, Vicky's boyfriend," Matt said as he waved to Angelo.

"He looks like a giant," Mia whispered in amazement as she stood, craning her neck to get a better look at him.

Artie smiled. "Don't let him fool you. Underneath that mammoth exterior is one of the nicest guys you'll ever meet."

"Unless he's taking care of business for the family," Matt added. "You definitely don't wanna get on his bad side."

"Ange, this is Mia," Vicky said proudly as they approached.

"Mia. You're all Vicky's talked about. It's good to meet ya," Angelo said as he draped his arm around Vicky's shoulder.

"I was hoping I'd get to meet you today." Mia smiled. "Vicky said a lot of great things about you, too."

"How's everything going, Ange?" Artie asked as he held out his hand to shake Angelo's.

Mia marveled at the vast difference between Angelo and Artie. Angelo had a body builder's physique and was an imposing six feet tall, while Artie was handsome in a preppy, businessman sort of way. Mia felt herself get warm as she couldn't help looking at Artie's lean, five-foot, ten frame. She found his body to be much sexier than Angelo's muscular build.

Matt cleared his throat and locked eyes with Mia. He smiled at her slyly and nodded his head. She knew she'd been caught sizing up his brother.

"Who's up for a game of volleyball?" Matt winked at Mia before he took a running jump and did a cannonball into the pool, splashing water on Mia and Vicky.

"You're going to get it," Vicky announced as she jumped into the pool, followed by Angelo. "Come on in, guys," she called out to Mia and Artie.

"I'm game if you are," Artie said as he laughed and jumped in.

After almost an hour, Vicky cleared her throat loudly and pushed her head toward the other side of the pool. "Matt, it's for you."

Standing at the edge of the pool was an attractive young woman in a yellow, flowered sundress. Her long shiny brown hair fell just over her spaghetti straps and was pushed back with a large pair of white sunglasses. She pursed her full lips. "Hey Matt."

Matt shook his head at her. "Unbelievable."

"I'm sorry," she cooed.

"You're sorry!" Matt demanded.

"I was babysitting little Paulie and Rosie yesterday and the DeMarcos didn't come home until really late. I just couldn't meet you." She tilted her head and casually flipped her hair behind her shoulder.

"What? Did the phone break?"

"When I noticed the time, it was too late to call. I knew you wouldn't be home." She swung her hips ever so slightly. "Daddy picked me up after midnight and I couldn't sneak out to see you."

"What do you think I'm a stunad?"

"Of course not. You can ask my father if you want."

"No." He sighed. "I won't do that."

"I'll make it up to you." She blew him a kiss. "I promise."

"Well, alright. I was getting ready to get out of the pool anyway."

Matt swam to the edge and hoisted himself out of the pool. As he leaned in to hug her, she held him back with both arms and squealed, "Don't! You'll get me wet."

Vicky, Angelo, Artie, and Mia exchanged glances as they walked out of the pool together and grabbed their towels.

"I'm sorry, I don't think we've met." Daniella stepped closer to Mia and looked her up and down.

"I'm Mia," she said.

Vicky and Artie stepped closer to Mia.

"Mia?"

"Yes, Mia Trovato. Luca and Carla's niece."

"I know who you are. You're Dominick Trovato's daughter." She quickly turned her back on Mia and added, "Hmm that's a pity."

"Excuse me?" Mia spat.

Daniella looked over her shoulder, "It's a pity what happened to your father," she said. "No one should die that way."

"Daniclla!" Matt scolded.

"Not to mention, I heard your mother was a lunatic."

Mia leaned forward, picked up a cup of soda, and got ready to take a swing, but Artie grasped her elbow and Vicky managed to take the cup out of Mia's hand before she was able to throw it at Daniella.

"Now that's enough! What's the matta with you?" Matt grabbed Daniella by the hand and led her down the stairs toward the beach. As they walked away, Mia heard him say, "That was cruel. She's one of us."

Mia took a deep breath and slowly exhaled. "Wow!"

"I'm really sorry about her," Vicky said.

"Me too. You didn't deserve that," Artie added.

"It's not your fault, but you should've let me throw my soda at her. That might've taught her a lesson in manners."

Vicky and Artie exchanged looks. "Oh no, Mia. You can't do that. That would've been really bad," Vicky said as she put the cup down.

"And what she said wasn't really bad?"

Artie put his hands up. "It's just that there's ways of handling these things, especially for someone who's in the family."

"What was I supposed to do? Let her talk to me like that?"

Vicky took her hands. "Don't stoop to her level or lower. She'll do a good enough job of making herself look bad, and by keeping your cool, you'll make yourself look good."

"You're kidding right?"

"No, she isn't." Artie answered. "Look. Most of the people here have some pretty wild issues with each other, but they never show their anger or resentment. It's not our way."

"Are you saying I should let her walk all over me?"

"No. We're saying maintain your cool, have patience, and wait for your opportunity," Vicky said.

"Opportunity for what?"

"You'll know it when you see it," Angelo raised his eyebrows and shrugged.

Mia shook her head. "I still think you should've let me throw my drink in her face."

"There's almost always serious consequences when someone acts impulsively. Especially out of anger," Artie answered.

"Especially where Daniella's concerned." Vicky added.

"Why is that?"

"Because she's Don Esposito's *granddaughter.*"

SEVEN

THE NEXT AFTERNOON, Mia poured herself a glass of iced tea and decided to do some sketching out on the patio. Her thoughts kept drifting to Artie, and she found that she felt lighter and happier than she'd felt in years. When she heard her Uncle Luca come out on the patio, she quickly closed her sketchpad and slid it under her chair. He tossed a basketball hoop in the pool and threw a ball to Mia.

"First one to make five baskets gets to pick out a movie to watch tonight."

"Hah! You're on!" Mia threw the ball from the lounge chair, and it sunk right into the hoop.

"I think I'm in trouble," Luca said as he picked Mia up and threw her into the deep end.

They laughed and splashed each other while playing basketball, and after Mia broke their four-to-four tie, she raised her hands in victory.

"Good game, Uncle." She held out her hand to shake his.

He nodded and shook her hand. "It was fun. You're a good player."

"I had a lot of practice. I was on the basketball team in school."

"Were you?" He smiled and then his smile faded. "I wish I

knew. I would've come out to see you play."

"I only found out recently that you and Aunt Carla wanted to spend time with me."

Luca grabbed a raft and pushed it toward Mia. "There's a lot you don't know, I'm sure," he said as he pulled over another raft and leaned on it.

She tilted her head, "Like what?" She said hoping she was going to finally learn more about her father.

"Your father was a complicated man. He was my little brother, and I saw the good, the bad, and the ugly with him. I tried to help him, guide him. Ever since he was a kid. But Dom, he never liked rules." He tapped his head. "Caparbio! He was so stubborn that he'd rather not graduate high school than participate in physical education class and get a passing grade." Luca shook his head at the memory. "Didn't wanna change his clothes in the locker room."

"He *failed* gym class? I thought he graduated."

"He graduated! Your grandfather went down to the school and worked it out with his principal."

"So, he fixed it?"

"Not in the way you're thinking. He didn't believe that anyone should get a free ride or special attention because of the family, and he especially didn't use intimidation to *fix* things like you were thinking. No. My father made Dominick go down to the school really early every Saturday morning and run laps around the football field until he ran a mile. He then had to mop and clean the locker room until it was spotless. He did this every Saturday for his entire senior year."

"How did they know if he really ran the mile?"

"Your grandfather paid the gym teacher out of his own pocket to supervise it all."

"My father must've hated doing that," Mia chuckled.

"He did, and it didn't matter what the weather was. Dom was out there running and cleaning every week. The locker room got disgusting during football season. Especially after a Friday night game. He found out rather quickly that his bad attitude and complaints added more miles to his run time." Luca laughed.

"He would've been better off just participating in class."

"You're so right on that. But, see Mia, that's the thing. I don't think he learned a lesson from it. His determination to make a name for himself and be a boss only got stronger along with his bad temper."

Mia sighed. "My grandparents say my temper will be my undoing."

Luca looked at her for a long moment. "Well, then, let's just make sure that doesn't happen."

Mia nodded. "Do you think it was his temper that was my father's undoing?"

"Yes. Yes. I do. Unfortunately, his temper made him a great muscle man for Don Esposito, and Esposito relied heavily on his muscle and thus your father. I have no doubt it was his temper that led to the incident between your father and your grandfather."

"Poppy said he tried talking to him and even reasoning with him, but Poppy has a temper, too."

"I'm afraid to say the altercation between Tony and Dominick was inevitable. I know how my brother was, and quite frankly I don't blame Tony one bit for what happened."

"You *don't*? I always felt like my mother never forgave him."

"Mia, look. If some punk from one of the families started showing an interest in you, I would be concerned. If he was disrespectful when I tried to have a conversation with him, I would be furious. If he picked a fight like Dominick did, I wouldn't have shown the restraint that your grandfather did."

"Restraint? I was told Poppy broke his ribs and injured his hand to the point where he could barely use it."

Luca nodded. "That's true, but Tony didn't break both of his hands, and Dominick recovered. He still could've had a good future within the family if he wasn't so impatient and reckless."

"What do you mean?"

"Your father was so eager to become a 'made man' that he tried too hard. He made some bad decisions and got involved with people he shouldn't have. He really thought Don Esposito would open his books and initiate him. The sad thing about it all is that he would've eventually gotten everything he wanted if he only had patience and respect."

"Did Don Esposito have him killed? I was told he was arrested for dealing and then killed in prison."

"He was arrested on drug charges, and he did in fact get killed in prison. I can't say for sure if Esposito gave the order. He's always said that out of respect for both Don Bocelli and my father he wouldn't have let it happen. Fact is, Dom might've mouthed off one too many times in there and paid the consequences."

Mia nodded her head. "I suppose it really doesn't matter who killed him, it's who he was that got him killed."

"You know, sometimes we get so caught up in talking about people's flaws that we forget to mention the good. I think I knew Dominick better than most everyone, and I can honestly say that as temperamental and indignant as he was, he was also charming. When he liked you, he showed it. And Mia he did have many friends and acquaintances that were proud to know him, and he would've done anything for them."

"That's really good to know." Mia sighed. "I've never heard that about him."

"I have no doubt he loved your mother, he wasn't really good at relationships, but he did the best he could." Luca took Mia's hand. "I will say the best relationship he's ever had with anyone was with *you*." Mia cocked her head. "He absolutely adored you. The day you were born he was so proud and happy."

Tears streamed down Mia's face. "Then why did he have to die?"

Luca shrugged. "I don't know, I suppose it was his fate."

"Dinner's on the table," Carla announced as she walked toward the edge of the pool. "Come, dry off and let's eat." She leaned in and locked eyes with Mia. "Are you crying? What's happened? Luca, why's she crying?"

Luca hopped out of the pool and wrapped a towel around his waist. "She's okay. We were just talking about Dominick."

"I'm fine, really," Mia said as she stood next to Luca rubbing her wet hair with a towel.

Carla nodded, but Mia caught the look she and Luca exchanged before Carla led them into the house and wondered what it was that they were not telling her.

EIGHT

ON SUNDAY, MIA learned that she was to help Carla and Donna Bocelli cook dinner. She wouldn't mind helping Carla so much as she was now feeling pretty comfortable around her and Luca, but Mia knew nothing about cooking, and Donna Bocelli was very intimidating. All morning, she worried about doing or saying the wrong thing, and the last thing she wanted was to insult anyone, especially Don or Donna Bocelli. By the time they arrived at the house, Mia's right eye was twitching.

"Poppa, I want you to finally meet Mia," Carla said as she put her arm around Mia's shoulders.

"Ah, Mia. Yes. I feel like I know you already," Don Bocelli said as he embraced Mia with a firm hug and kissed her on both cheeks.

"And you remember my mother," Carla added as she took grocery bags from Donna Bocelli's hands.

"It's nice to see you again," Mia said purposely not calling her by name for fear of making a mistake.

"Come, give me a hug." Donna Bocelli surprised Mia and she was comforted by her warm hug and the scent of her Youth Dew perfume. She turned to Luca and Don Bocelli and said, "Okay. It's time for you two to go get comfortable while we cook."

Luca chuckled. "There's a Yankee game about to start."

"Good. Go watch that." Donna Bocelli waved her arms, and the two men scrambled away quickly.

Mia thought it was strange that Donna Bocelli gave Don Bocelli orders with no reaction from him, but Donna Bocelli smiled at her and said, "He may be the boss of the family, but I am the boss of the home. Otherwise, he don't eat." She pointed at Carla and continued, "This one here needs to take some lessons in that."

Carla laughed and said, "Okay, Momma. Luca is very happy with Gina's cooking."

"Aah!" She waved her hand, took her apron out of one of her bags and started to pull out pots and pans.

Carla quickly followed behind her mother, and Mia stood still for only a moment until Donna Bocelli put her to work. She must've sensed Mia's nervousness and led her through every task. Mia saw the pride she took demonstrating how to chop onions, slice garlic, and how to make braciole.

"Mia, next weekend you do it by yourself. Hmm," She nodded.

"Next weekend?"

Carla answered, "Yes my parents come every Sunday for dinner."

"I don't know if I can make braciole myself by next weekend."

Donna Bocelli waved her hand. "Nonsense. You're a natural. Just cook from here." She tapped Mia's heart. "Not from here." She tapped Mia's head.

During dinner Mia enjoyed the casual conversation. She didn't know what she had expected, but she didn't expect Don Bocelli to be so down-to-earth. Mia marveled over the fact that the conversations about how the Yankees were doing this year made it seem like a regular Sunday dinner that anyone would have, and that Don Bocelli, the most powerful man in New Jersey, would lick his fingers after eating garlic bread.

"Mia," he said as he ran his bread along his plate. "Tell me more about you. What do you want to do now that you've graduated high school."

"I'm going to the New York School of Interior Design starting in September." She nervously lifted her glass of water and took a few sips.

"Interior Design? That's wonderful," Donna Bocelli looked delighted as Don Bocelli nodded his head.

"You must have a talent for creativity." Don Bocelli raised his eyebrows.

"Yes, I'd like to think so. I've gone to summer classes and workshops on art and design, and I really liked the interior design projects more than the others."

"And why was that?"

Mia realized that Don Bocelli was inquisitive and pointed by nature. Although it seemed like she was being interrogated, she could tell by his facial expressions that he was interested in what she had to say.

"I was able to transform a blank space into a work of art that was functional. I didn't get the same sense of satisfaction when I turned a blank canvas into a work of art." Don Bocelli leaned in seemingly intrigued with the conversation. "At first, I really thought I wanted to pursue being an artist, but when I learned more about interior design, I realized there is so much that goes into it. It's not just picking out nice colored curtains. I'll be able to work with architects and engineers to design a space fully and completely. The color and furniture details are just the fancy bow on top of the package, and I'll be the one creating the whole package." She smiled. "Besides there's a better future in it."

Don Bocelli pointed to Mia and nodded quickly. "Yes. That's right. You will be very successful. I can tell."

Mia felt proud to have Don Bocelli's approval. She was enjoying her stay with Carla and Luca more and more by the day and found a connection with this side of her family that she didn't know she had been craving.

"I would love to see some of your artwork." Carla said as she reached out and placed her hand on Mia's forearm.

"I have my sketchpad with me if you'd like to see it."

"Yes. Please," Carla said enthusiastically.

Mia quickly retrieved her sketchpad from her room. She considered tearing out some of the raw pieces that she had drawn during her dark times, but decided to leave them in. She didn't want to have to edit herself. She wanted them to see everything there was to see about her.

"Here it is." Mia handed the pad to Carla as Luca, Don, and Donna Bocelli shifted themselves around to look at it.

"I have to warn you, there is an eclectic mix of things in there. I tend to sketch with my emotions, and when I was going through a hard time, I did a lot of sketching."

"Of course," Carla said.

They slowly flipped through the book nodding and sharing their thoughts on the images and what emotions they invoked. Mia could tell when they got to the images she drew shortly after Rena died. Carla pulled her hand up to her mouth when they saw the sketch of Rena's lifeless image on the floor with foam trickling down her face. But when they got to the collage entitled "Assassino" in bold red letters with blood dripping down into images of two elderly people splayed out in a street, Donna Bocelli gasped.

She quickly turned to Don Bocelli and said, "Armando!" as a tear fell down her cheek.

Don Bocelli shook his head and stood up straight. "Mia," he whispered. "I don't know what to say. Your family suffered a lot. This thing of ours can be a brutal business." He looked down. "Some take it too far, and for that I'm sorry." He looked up and his wet eyes met hers. "I wish I could've changed things." He took her hands in his.

Mia nodded and hugged him. She knew how things worked, and actions had consequences, but hearing him say that he would have changed the fate of her family members if he could have, made all the difference in the world to her.

Luca broke the silence as he took the sketchpad and was inspecting it carefully. "Mia, what's this a picture of?"

Mia looked at the sketch and saw that he was looking at a drawing of a pink bicycle that had streamers flowing down from the handlebars and daisies on a white basket.

"That's my favorite bike in Poppy's garden."

Luca looked at it closely. "That's your favorite bike? When did you get it?

Mia laughed. "I got it one year for Christmas. Santa left it under the tree for me. I loved that thing. I rode it all over until I was too big to ride it anymore."

"Santa?" Luca smiled brightly.

"Yeah. Every year I get a gift from Santa. Even now." She shrugged her shoulders. "But the funny thing is Poppy and Grammy insisted they weren't Santa." When she looked at her uncle, her face turned serious. "Now that I think of it. None of the other kids got gifts from Santa after they stopped believing." She narrowed her eyes. "Most of my favorite gifts were from Santa."

Carla asked, "You mean like a Barbie Doll or an Easy Bake Oven?"

"You mean you?" Mia suddenly felt lightheaded and grabbed onto a dining chair.

Luca embraced Mia, "Yes, you've been our little treasure your whole life. We've loved you from afar and tried to make your

Christmases a little extra special."

"We knew how difficult your life was at times. Although you were in great hands with your grandparents, we knew you had a piece of your heart missing without your father." Carla patted Mia on the back.

"I don't know what to say. Except thank you."

Luca moved forward and hugged Mia. "You're very welcome. But you don't have to thank us. You've been a part of this family since the day you were born."

"And we are loyal to our family members," Don Bocelli added.

"Thank you, Don Bocelli," Mia whispered.

"What is this? What is this, Don Bocelli?"

Mia looked around confused.

"Here at home, I'm Nonnuccio," he said tapping his chest. "You only call me Don Bocelli in public. Yeah?"

"Okay," she replied and quickly looked at Donna Bocelli.

"Yes. In public I am Donna Bocelli. But here, with just us intimates, you may call me Nonnina. That is, if it's okay with you."

Mia quickly nodded her head as her heart exploded with love and pride.

The front door burst open, and Ray rushed in followed by Josie, Matt, and Vicky. "Ciao!"

"Ah, Ciao, Ciao." Nonnuccio walked over and greeted his son while Carla and Nonnina took pastry boxes from Josie and led her to the kitchen.

Deep down, Mia was hoping to see Artie walk in behind them, but he had said he was going to return to the city that morning for his internship.

"Hey." Vicky said brightly. "How was your day?"

Mia looked around the room and caught her breath as Artie walked in smiling at her. "It's getting better by the minute."

Vicky whispered in Mia's ear, "When I told Artie we'd be seeing you tonight, he immediately changed his plans and decided to go back up north tomorrow morning." She looked at Mia and raised her eyebrows.

"Hey Mia," Matt said brightly as he took a long gulp of soda and let out a long burp.

"Where's your manners?" Artie said as he looked at Matt in disgust. "I'm sorry for him." Artie shrugged his shoulders, and his face grew red as he locked eyes with Mia.

"Sorry, Mia," Matt said pulling Mia's eyes from Artie's spell.

"No problem, Matt," she chuckled awkwardly, and the three of them stood in silence looking back and forth at each other.

"Alright," Vicky said as she marched over to Matt. "Why don't you and I get some pastry before the good ones are taken."

"What are you talking about? We never run out of pastries." Matt protested as Vicky pulled his arm and led him to the kitchen.

Mia smiled at Artie. "I'm happy to see you. I thought you were going back to the city tonight."

Artie quickly looked down and then back up at Mia. "I was going to, but then I realized I didn't really want to."

"I'm glad you didn't," Mia said softly.

"I was thinking, if you don't have plans next Saturday, I would love to take you out. You know, on a date?"

Mia nodded her head excitedly. "Yes," she said louder than she wanted to, and felt herself blush when Vicky and Matt turned to look at her from the other room. She let out a large breath. "I mean, yes," she said calmly. "I would like that."

"Great," Artie said as he grinned.

"Great!" Vicky sang as she bounded up to them and put an arm on each of their shoulders. "Now that we got that out of the way, let's play Clue."

NINE

SUMMER, 1980

OVER THE NEXT week, Mia tried not to bring Artie up in every conversation she had with Vicky. She thought she had been doing well until Friday afternoon when Vicky reached out and put her wrist on Mia's forehead.

"What are you doing?" Mia asked.

"Checking for a fever. We've been floating in the pool for almost two hours now, and you haven't mentioned my brother once. You must not be feeling well."

Mia waved Vicky's arm away and began to chatter. "Have I been talking about him a lot? I tried not to. I guess I couldn't help it. I'm really nervous about tomorrow. What do you think I should wear?"

Vicky leaned in toward Mia and took both of her hands in her own. "Get a grip, sista. I don't know who's more nervous about this date. You or him."

"Him? What do you mean?"

"I mean, he's called me every night this week trying to sound casual and ask about how my day was, but what he was really doing was asking about you. We haven't spoken to each other this much since that time our parents took us camping and we had nothing better to do."

"He asked about me?" Mia's eyes lit up.

"Yes! And he's been grilling me on what he should plan to make the date perfect."

"What did you tell him?" Mia leaned in.

"I told him, what I'm about to tell you. I'm not getting involved."

"What?"

"Nope. I'm gonna let you two figure this out yourselves." Vicky smiled and tapped her pointer finger on Mia's nose.

"Oh, yeah, okay," Mia said, trying not to feel disappointed.

"Hah! Did you really buy that?" Vicky squealed as she hopped off her raft and tipped Mia's over, plunging her into the pool.

"Aah," Mia howled and pushed a wave of water at Vicky.

"You don't really think I'm not going to do all I can to get my new best friend and my brother together, do you? Especially, when it's so clear how made for each other you are!" Vicky laughed and splashed Mia back.

"Do you know what he has planned for tomorrow?" Mia asked.

"I do not. I suggested a nice restaurant on the water."

"That'll be nice."

"Ange and I went dancing on our first date. I suggested that to Artie too, but he didn't take to that idea so much."

Mia nodded thoughtfully. "All I know is that he said he'd pick me up at one and to wear something comfortable."

"If you were going out with Matt, that would make me worried. He'd have you riding a dirt bike through a swamp. But with Artie, that probably means something romantic like a long walk on the beach after a nice meal."

True to his word, Artie arrived at precisely one o'clock the next day to pick Mia up. She nervously descended the stairs hoping that the navy Bermuda shorts and pink cotton blouse was a good choice for their date. Her Aunt Carla beamed as she walked across the room and embraced Mia tightly.

"You look lovely," she said putting Mia at ease.

Mia looked over at her Uncle Luca who had one hand on Artie's shoulder as he leaned in whispering and pointing his finger on his other hand. Mia recognized that pose and knew that their uncle was giving Artie strict instructions on how to behave on their date. It was the same talk that her Poppy gave to every one of Janet, Nancy, and Mia's dates. The only difference was Mia felt profound embarrassment when Poppy delivered the talk to her dates, whereas it warmed her heart to see her uncle express the same level of concern for her wellbeing as her grandfather did. She smirked as Luca reached into his pocket to offer Artie money, and Artie waved him away.

When Artie turned toward Mia, his face lit up and he held out a bouquet of tulips. "These are for you," he said and took a step toward Mia.

"Thank you. Tulips are my favorite flower." She smiled brightly.

"I know. Vicky told me."

Mia handed the tulips to Carla and said a silent "thank you" in her head for having Vicky as a friend.

"Are you ready to go?" Artie asked.

Mia nodded and kissed her aunt and uncle before following Artie to his red Mustang convertible.

"I've got the top down. Is that alright?" He opened the passenger door for her.

"Yes," she said enthusiastically, and she reached into her purse, pulled out a band, and pulled her hair back into a ponytail.

"Where are we going?" Mia asked as Artie sped up on the highway.

"It's a surprise," Artie beamed.

Mia sat back and enjoyed the drive. It was a perfect day to have the top down on the car, and she loved the carefree feeling of the wind on her face.

Although the drive took a lot longer than Mia expected, she didn't mind. They talked about their favorite songs, and when Artie put his favorite mix tape in the cassette player, they both sang loudly, waving their arms to the music.

"We're here," Artie said as he pulled into a large parking lot.

Mia looked around and was baffled. The only building in the lot was a large roller skating rink. She strained her neck looking for a restaurant on the water, but there was clearly no water around. *Maybe there's a movie theater,* she thought to herself as she continued to look around. *Oh God. We're going roller skating,* she realized.

Artie held out his hand as he opened her car door. She tried to mask her concern as he beamed at her.

He went around to the trunk and grabbed two duffel bags. "You and Vicky look like you're the same size. I brought her skates along so you wouldn't have to rent any," he said proudly.

"Good idea," Mia said as she stared at the bags.

Artie looked closely at Mia's face. "Do you like skating?"

"I've never been," she said trying to sound cheerful.

"I thought this would be fun," he looked down.

Mia's heart broke when she saw the defeated look on his face. He was obviously so excited about doing something fun together, and she didn't want to make him feel any worse.

"You know what. Let's do it." She straightened her back and smiled broadly.

"Are you sure? We can go somewhere else if you want."

"Nope. I wanna try. Just be warned, I can be clumsy on a good day." She took one of the bags from Artie and nodded her head confidently.

Artie's smile lit up his face. "I'll help you. I'm pretty good at it."

Once inside, they sat together on a bench, and Mia was impressed that he remembered to bring a pair of socks for her.

"I love this song," Mia said as the S.O.S. Band's *Take Your Time (Do It Right)* began to play.

She hopped up from the bench and shrieked as she lost control of her balance, flailed both arms in the air, and fell to the floor with her legs splayed. Artie's eyes grew wide as he raced over and reached out his hand to help her up.

"Whoa," he yelped as he lost his own balance and landed next to Mia. They stared at each other as their shock and embarrassment transformed into howls of laughter.

"I … am … so … sorry," Mia tried to say as tears ran down her face, and she tried to regain her composure.

"No … problem," he managed in between taking breaths.

When their laughter subsided, Artie got to his feet and took a hold of the bench with his right hand while he helped Mia up with his left.

"Do you wanna leave?" He asked softly.

"No way," she mused. "I've got to at least make it once around the rink. But I think I'm gonna hold on to the railing as I go."

"That's probably a good idea," he said as he took her hand, and led her into the rink.

Mia gripped the railing tightly as she tried to find her balance. She felt awkward in the beginning, but it didn't take her long to gain a little bit of confidence.

"You're a really good skater," she said turning to Artie.

"I love skating. Me and Vicky were never athletic like Matt, so our parents used to take us to the Paramus Roller Rink every week. They said it was to get us to do some exercise, but really they loved skating as much as we did. They used to do all kinds of fancy dances together like the waltz and stuff."

"Really? I can't imagine that."

"You'd be surprised. Dad looks tough on the outside, but really, he's quite a smooth dancer in the rink and on the dance floor."

"Are you good at the couples dances too?"

Artie laughed and shook his head. "No. That was never for me. Vicky was starting to get into it for a while. But then she lost interest after she fell, and Matt teased her for two weeks about it."

"Yeah, I would probably lose interest too. Do you still go?"

"Not so much anymore. I miss it sometimes. There was a group of us kids that would go every week, and we would hang out together. But as we got older, everyone started to get involved in other activities. My parents still go as often as they can, though."

"It must be a nice date night for them, huh?" Mia smiled. She was having a better time roller skating than she thought she would.

"Yeah," Artie's eyes twinkled. "It *is* a good date night for them."

When Air Supply's, *All Out of Love*, started to play, Artie swung himself around, so he was skating backward in front of Mia. "You're doing really well. What do you say you let go of that railing?" He reached out both hands. "I'll hold you up."

Mia put her left hand in Artie's right and tentatively released her grip from the railing. As she clutched his hands, a warmth flowed through her own hands and up her arms. When she looked up at him, his eyes told her she could trust him.

"I won't let you go," he said tenderly and rubbed his thumb over her hand.

Mia could feel her face flush. She didn't want to unlock her eyes from Artie's, but another couple swooshed past them so quickly, the trance was broken.

"Do you take all of your first dates roller skating?" Mia flirted.

"Ha. No actually, you're the first. The other girls I've dated were nothing like you."

"Oh?" she tilted her head.

"Yeah. Like my last girlfriend. We met in the Chess Club at school. She was nice and all, but she was always so serious."

"And, serious is not good?" Mia was intrigued.

"I just think there's a time and a place for serious. But you also need to let your hair down a little and have some fun. Our relationship didn't last very long, there wasn't much laughter. You know what I mean?"

"I do know what you mean."

"It seems like all the girls I meet at school are very academic and competitive, and the other girls I meet outside of school are really superficial. You're different. You're refreshing."

"Refreshing? I've never been called refreshing before," Mia said liking the compliment.

"Yup." He beamed. "For example, not one of my other dates would've wanted the top down on the car. They wouldn't want their hair to be messed up. And there you were, ready to put your hair up and enjoy the wind."

Mia smiled. She had never been appreciated for just being herself before. She always had to try hard with other guys, mold herself into something that they were interested in. But with Artie, she felt at ease and could be her natural self.

"What about you? Am I like the guys you usually date?"

"Not at all! I dated my ex pretty much throughout high school. He was a football jock. When it was good, it was really good. But then his ego would inflate, and he would start acting like a jerk. By the end, my heart, my spirit, and my trust were spent."

"How do you feel now?" Artie asked.

"Actually, pretty good. I made a conscious decision not to let myself get caught up in that kind of relationship again. It's refreshing." Mia met Artie's eyes. "Just like you," she whispered as she blushed.

Artie looked down as his face turned red. When he looked up and met her eyes, his face was serene and his eyes tender. They skated along in a peaceful silence. After a few turns around the rink, he squeezed her hands and said, "Wanna get out of here and get something to eat?"

Mia nodded her head gently. "Yes," she said hoping he didn't hear her stomach growl.

When they returned to the car, Artie asked, "What do you think about a picnic while we watch the sunset?"

"I love that idea," Mia beamed.

"Cool. The best place to see the sunset is at the Barnegat Lighthouse State Park. I thought we could order dinner from Neptune's and take it with us."

Mia knew that Neptune's was one of the most elite fine dining restaurants along the Jersey Shore, and while she did want to try their food someday, she was enjoying how smooth and relaxing their first date was. "I have another idea, if you don't mind."

Artie scrunched his eyebrows together, cocked his head, and said, "Sure, what do you have in mind?"

"Burgers," she said confidently.

"Burgers?" He laughed. "I offered Neptune's, and you want a burger?"

"Yup!" She bobbed her head up and down once, smiling brightly.

He shook his head and shrugged his shoulders. "Refreshing!"

ARTIE LED THE way along a trail to a patch of beach that would give them the best view of the lighthouse and the sunset.

"Right here should be good," he said and gently spread a large blanket on the sand.

Mia carefully kicked her shoes off before placing the bags of food and vanilla shakes in the middle of the blanket. "This is a great spot," she said as she gazed at the water and the lighthouse. The sky was clear and the sun, a soft orange orb, hovered just over the horizon.

She felt Artie's hand slide around her waist, and when she turned to look at him, his skin glowed from the sun's reflection.

"Here, let me get this for you," he whispered as he ran his fingers across her forehead, brushing a strand of hair away from her face.

Her breath caught as he cupped his hand on her cheek, and they leaned into each other. She felt like she might melt, as his warm lips grazed hers. She raised her arm around his neck and entwined his hair within her fingers. He pulled her close, kissing her tenderly. Her heart thumped wildly, and her spirit came alive as his touch told her it was safe to trust again.

As the sky transformed through shades of orange, purple, pink, and red, Mia and Artie fed each other fries, sipped their shakes, and shared warm, gentle kisses. Artie held her tightly, and Mia let out a long, peaceful breath hoping that this most perfect date would never end.

"Matt and Angelo are having a bonfire on the beach tonight. Wanna head back and join them?" He kissed the top of her head.

"Sure, that sounds like fun." She turned her head and leaned into him for a last kiss before they packed up.

As they approached the bonfire in front of Ray and Josie's house, Mia felt like she was walking on a cloud. She loved how her hand felt in Artie's, and the protective way he said, "Watch your step," as they trekked across the sand.

"Hey, there's the love birds," Matt called out. "How was your date?"

Artie squeezed Mia's hand as she looked up at him. When she looked back toward Matt, she saw Daniella standing next to him, staring blankly at Artie. Knowing that more than likely their paths would cross frequently throughout the summer, Mia had decided she would try to be friendly to Daniella, in spite of her rudeness when they first met.

"Hi." Mia smiled. "It's nice to see you again, Daniella."

Daniella slowly moved her head in Mia's direction and fixed her blank stare on Mia's face.

"Hey Mia. There's all kinds of drinks in the cooler. Help yourself," Matt said as he put an arm on Daniella's shoulder breaking her eye contact with Mia.

Mia wondered what was wrong with Daniella. Was she shocked to see her and Artie together? Mia couldn't understand why Daniella was consistently rude to her.

"Oh good, you're here," Vicky cheered as she rushed over to Mia. "I set up some chairs over here for us." She took Mia by the hand and led her to a set of empty chairs around the fire.

Vicky plopped herself in a seat and grabbed Mia's arm. "How was it? Tell me everything."

"He showed up with a beautiful bouquet of tulips. Thank you for that, by the way," Mia smiled, glad for the distraction from Daniella's stares.

"Uh huh, good." Vicky nodded her head, seemingly pleased with herself.

"Then we went roller skating. Did you know we're the same shoe size?"

"Wait. What?" Vicky shook her head aggressively. "He took you *roller skating*? What kind of lame first date is that? Wait 'til I talk to him." Vicky looked around and when she saw Artie, she started to get up from her chair, but Mia put her hand on Vicky's arm to stop her.

"It was a *perfect* first date," Mia nodded her head. "Best one I've ever had."

"You've got to be kidding me. This is a joke right? He really took you to Neptune's and you took a long walk on the beach like I told him to do."

"Nope. I mean, he wanted to get dinner from Neptune's and bring it with us to watch the sunset, but I told him I'd rather have hamburgers."

"Hamburgers? I feel like I'm dreaming." Vicky shook her head again. "You went *roller skating*, and after that you had *hamburgers*?"

"Yes," Mia glowed.

"And this was a *perfect* first date?"

Mia raised her eyebrows and smiled brightly. "Yes."

"Oh brother! You two are more made for each other than I thought."

As Vicky let out a snort and laughed loudly, Mia and Artie caught each other's eyes across the fire. His slow blink and small nod sent chills down her spine, making her wiggle in her seat and smile back at him.

"Matt," Daniella squealed as she sat in his lap, rubbing her foot up Artie's leg as she did.

Mia saw Artie's immediate flinch and discomfort, and she wondered if Daniella had done it on purpose.

"Hey Vick," Angelo called out. "I love this mix tape you made." He turned up the volume on his boom box and raised his drink in a toast to Vicky.

"It took me forever to get that tape just right." Vicky rolled her eyes. "I wanted songs that I could dance around and sing to loudly when I'm feeling cranky.

"You made a lot of good choices," Mia said as Eddie Rabbitt's,

Driving My Life Away, ended and Blondie's, *Call Me,* began.

"If you like it, I'll make you a copy. Ange wants one for his car," Vicky said and grabbed Mia's arm. "There she goes," Vicky scoffed, "She puts on a show every time we're all together," she said pointing to Daniella.

"*Why?*" Mia was dumbfounded as Daniella danced provocatively in front of Matt and Artie.

"She loves to be the center of attention," Vicky said. "Scootch over. Here comes Artie with his chair."

"What's the matter Art," Angelo laughed. "Don't like having a front row seat?"

"She gets worse every time I see her," Artie shook his head and positioned his chair between Mia and Angelo. "It's much better over here."

"So Artie," Vicky chided. "*Roller skating*? What happened to our plan?"

"It didn't feel right." He shrugged his shoulders.

"And roller skating did?" Angelo asked.

"What can I say, I'm a hopeless romantic," Artie laughed and leaned over and clasped Mia's hand.

"We're gonna go for a walk," Matt announced as Daniella draped her arms around him.

"Wanna come?" She asked Artie, looking over her shoulder at him.

Artie shook his head in disgust. "You two have fun."

Vicky leaned in close to Mia. "You know what that means, don't you?"

Mia shook her head.

"They're gonna go find a place to have sex."

"And she invited Artie along?" Mia couldn't believe how inappropriate and crude Daniella was.

Vicky shrugged her shoulders. "She's drunk."

"What do you say, we call it a night?" Angelo looked at Vicky who nodded back at him.

Mia helped Vicky gather the chairs while Angelo and Artie extinguished the fire. "Hey Vick," Mia hesitated. "Did Artie ever date Daniella? I mean, it seemed like she was flirting with him all night."

"No they never dated, and to tell you the truth, I don't even notice her antics anymore. But I wouldn't be surprised if she did flirt with him." Vicky took Mia's hand and whispered. "Seriously, don't pay any attention to her. She knows very well that Artie is not and never will be interested in her. From where I'm sitting, he's fallen for you, hook, line, and sinker."

Mia knew girls like Daniella, and she knew she couldn't let her guard down whenever they were together. She smiled as Artie walked toward her, and she appreciated his respectful and refined nature.

Artie held out his hand. "I'll walk you home."

"Good night guys," she called over her shoulder to Vicky and Angelo as she and Artie walked toward their Aunt Carla and Uncle Luca's house. She bumped her hip into Artie as she said, "I had a great time today."

"I did too. Best first date ever! Maybe next weekend, would you wanna go to the movies? I heard *Airplane* is really funny."

"Yeah, I'd like that," she said as they reached the patio door. "But shouldn't you be spending your weekends in New York for your internship?"

"Nah. Last year I had nothing better to do, so I stayed up north doing a lot of grunt work for no money. But this year is different."

"Are you sure?"

"Mia," He ran his thumb on her cheek. "There's nothing keeping me in the city on the weekends this summer. My heart is here, now."

TEN

SUMMER, 1980

OVER THE NEXT few weeks, Mia fell into a nice routine and was enjoying her summer in Mantoloking more than she had anticipated. Every morning she and Carla would eat breakfast together and talk about anything and everything from family gossip and stories from the past to the latest movies. In the afternoons, Carla and Josie were often busy with meetings. Mia didn't know what type of meetings they were, but they sequestered themselves in Carla's library or they were out of the house meeting with other wives. Vicky said that that's the way it always was with them, and she never asked questions. But Carla made it a point to be home every night for dinner with Mia, and most nights they ate dessert on lounge chairs looking out over the ocean. On Saturday mornings she looked forward to making pancakes with Luca while listening to his favorite opera pieces. Sometimes they cooked in silence, lost in their own thoughts, and sometimes they had deep discussions about religion, politics, and when the Yankees might win another World Series.

Most afternoons, Mia and Vicky met at the lounge chairs on the beach, and they would spend their time alternating between sunbathing and swimming in the ocean and in the pool. On rainy or cloudy days, they would usually go into town to have lunch, shop, and get manicures and pedicures. Weekends were family time, and Carla's house often became a revolving door of family and associates.

Matt was usually around on the weekend if he didn't have to work or if he wasn't spending time with Daniella. Mia came to learn that directly after high school he oversaw the management of several restaurants and cafés in the northern part of the state, and now six years later, he was working closely with Luca to bid on and oversee construction of multiple hotels and casinos in Atlantic City. Mia was impressed with his business savviness far more than she was with his taste in women.

She and Artie spoke on the phone every night during the week, and he came down to the shore every weekend. She loved how he was different than the other guys she dated. He was sophisticated and polished, down-to-earth, humble, yet goofy all at the same time. She was falling for him harder and harder each time she saw him, but worried about how her family back in Lyndhurst would react to their relationship.

Mia put her book down on her lap and looked at her watch. Only fifteen minutes had passed since the last time she checked. Although she enjoyed spending the day with Vicky, the anticipation of seeing Artie made her restless, just as it did every Friday afternoon.

"I suppose Artie should be here soon," Vicky teased.

Mia smiled. "Will you be seeing Ange tonight?"

"Yeah, we're supposed to have dinner with his family. It's his uncle's birthday so they want to celebrate. What about you? Do you and Artie have plans?"

"Yup. We're ordering pizza and watching a movie," Mia said excitedly.

"And you're excited about that? The least he could do is take you out to the movies."

"We both love staying in on Friday nights. We're going to watch *Texas Chainsaw Massacre*." Mia sat up, "Maybe I'll have him get a box of Entenmann's Chocolate Chip Cookies too."

"Hey! Those cookies are our thing!"

Mia laughed, "You're right. I'd hate to have him see me polish off a whole box of them the way you and I do."

"Oh, brother." Vicky laughed. "Seriously, Mee, I've never seen Artie like this with anyone." She reached out and put her hand on Mia's arm. "He really likes you. I mean *really* likes you."

"Honestly?"

"Oh my God, yes!"

Mia smiled. "I *really* like him too. But I worry sometimes."

"About what?"

"My family back home in Lyndhurst. You know they didn't like my father, and I'm afraid they won't give Artie a chance."

Vicky raised her eyebrows and said, "You've just got to help them see that Artie isn't your father."

"How am I going to do that?"

"Slowly. When you call home, talk about Artie a lot. Slip into the conversation he's studying to be a lawyer, how you both like to stay in on Friday nights, and any other qualities of his that they'll like. They'll form a good opinion of him before you even have to tell them you're seeing him."

"That's perfect! What a great idea." Mia smiled and started thinking of different things she could slip into her conversations with her grandmother.

Mia and Vicky turned their heads as soon as they heard Angelo's tell-tale, high pitch whistle he made whenever he wanted Vicky's attention.

"Look who I found," Angelo said as he pointed to Artie walking next to him.

Vicky hopped up from her chair and took a running leap into Angelo's arms wrapping her legs around his waist. If Mia hadn't known better, she would've thought they hadn't seen each other for a week like her and Artie, but they had just had lunch with Angelo only a few hours earlier. Mia stood as Artie walked over to her chair. He took her face in his hands and kissed her lips tenderly.

"I missed you," he whispered in her ear.

Mia's heart started to beat double-time as she hugged him tightly, and said, "Thank God it's Friday."

"Vick, we need to get ready for dinner," Angelo said as he swung Vicky around in his arms and gently put her down on her lounge chair.

"So soon?" Artie asked. "It's only four o'clock."

"Have ya met your sister? Madone, it takes her forever to get herself all made up."

"I never hear you complain about the finished product." Vicky giggled as she threw her towel at Angelo and gathered the rest of her things.

"Hey, maybe later you wanna join us? We're thinkin' about going to that little club in Seaside after dinner." Angelo said as he took Vicky's beach bag from her.

Artie put his arm around Mia and looked at her. She gave him an indifferent look hoping he would realize she would rather stay in. "We'll see. Give us a call before you go."

Mia smiled inwardly because he had known exactly what she was thinking by looking at her face.

"Bye guys. Enjoy your movie," Vicky said as she and Angelo walked down the beach hand in hand toward her house.

Artie turned to Mia and said, "I'm sweating let's take a dip." Before she could answer, Artie whisked her up in his arms, flung her over his shoulder, and jogged into the tide.

"Artie!" Mia squealed. "Put me down. I'm too heavy for you." Mia knew she wasn't too heavy for him because she was petite at five feet, two inches tall and one hundred pounds.

"You're a lightweight," he laughed and threw her into the ocean before he dove in after her.

They laughed and swam for quite some time and when Mia started to feel tired, Artie took her in his arms, wrapped her legs around his waist, and they floated in the water together.

Artie lifted the chain Mia was wearing in his hand and looked at it carefully. "This is really nice."

Mia let out a small breath of air. "Thanks. It was my mom's."

"It must've been hard for you when she died."

Mia knew he wasn't trying to pry. She hadn't told him anything about her mom's death. It was a deep conversation that she hadn't wanted to get into before, but now, she found she was ready to open up to him about it.

"It was always hard with Mom. She had a difficult life, and just couldn't be the mother I think she wanted to be. Grammy was more like a mom to me than she was."

He kissed her cheek, and she draped her arms around his neck.

"My mom took my father's death really hard." Mia took a deep breath and looked down. "She was so despondent, she had to be committed in a psych ward and was given electric-shock treatments."

"Oh. Oh wow, Mia."

"After that she turned to alcohol for comfort, and it wasn't long before she started abusing pain pills." She looked up at him with tears in her eyes. "One morning, I found her. She had overdosed on vodka and pills."

"You mean, *you* found her?"

She nodded.

He squeezed her tightly. She knew he didn't know what to say. What was there *to* say?

"I'm sorry you had to go through that." He looked deeply in her eyes, and she could see his own eyes filling with tears. He raised his hand, kissed it, and pressed it against her heart.

She placed her own hand over his and smiled. "I've decided I'm going to live my best life and try to make a difference. I want to honor both my mom and Poppy too. I want to make them proud of me."

Artie nodded. "I have no doubt you will." He cupped his hand on her cheek. "I've always said I wanted to do some good in the world too. Try to help people who are in need. It's a hard world out there."

Mia felt a wave of peaceful relief flow through her body. It wasn't easy for her to open up and discuss her mother's death. Letting down the wall she had built around her heart and letting Artie in was a big leap for her, and his reaction proved he was as genuine and tenderhearted as she thought.

She pushed away the memory and kissed Artie's cheek. "So, what was it like growing up being a member of the Bocelli Family?"

"Aah, the family!" He rolled his eyes. "Growing up, I thought all families were like ours. But then I started playing with some of the kids on our block and realized that they didn't have a bunch of uncles coming in and out of their house at all times of the night to have private meetings with their fathers." He laughed. "And then I found out we were the only family that had security guards at family parties."

"Yeah, I have to admit, that was a little intimidating for me at first," Mia said.

"It's sometimes hard for me to picture the family as an outsider. You know, for a long time I had never heard my grandparents referred to as Don and Donna. As a kid you don't pay attention to those things. You just try to stay away from your parents as much as possible during parties so that they don't notice you eating so much junk food. I'll never forget the time when I was about seven or eight, Big Al scooped me up in the air and said, 'There he is, how's the little prince doin?' I must've looked at him like he was crazy, and I said, 'I'm not a little prince.' He laughed as he put me down and said, 'You're Don Bocelli's grandson, someday this'll be your kingdom.' I had no idea what that meant but I watched Nonnuccio all day and noticed how different he was around everyone else and how everyone showed him respect." Artie shook his head.

"When did you finally realize the truth about the family?"

"The next day, I asked my father about it. He waved it off and said Big Al was just teasing me. I didn't buy it, so I started sneaking around the house trying to spy on my father and his associates."

"You didn't?" Mia's eyes grew wide.

"I tried." Artie shrugged. "But I wasn't very successful. I kept getting caught. When Matt and I got into middle school, my parents sat us down and tried to explain things. They knew it was only a matter of time before other kids would start saying stuff to us and they wanted us to be prepared. They were sure to tell us that our family wasn't like the stories we heard about big time gangsters, and Nonnuccio was no Al Capone. The Bocellis avoided violence at all costs, and we were a family of loyalty and honor."

"Why did you choose to become a lawyer while Matt's learning the business from the inside?"

"Honestly, I really liked the section of my high school history class that covered the law, so I took a law elective and loved it. We always knew I'd be the one to go to college because I loved school and was really good at it. Matt always hated school, but he was super smart, and he had an innate mind for business."

Mia looked at Artie closely. His personality and demeanor were a lot like his father's. They both had a calm, trusting way about them. She could tell he was going to be a great lawyer.

He looked deep into her eyes and said, "What are you thinking about?"

"You're a lot like your dad."

Artie twirled her around making the saltwater fly up toward her face. "I am like him in some ways, but I actually think I'm more like my mom."

"You think?"

"Yeah. My parents say it, too. I have her nurturing empathy, and Matt has my father's indifference. Yet another reason why he's better suited for the family business."

"You know, now that you mention it. I can definitely see that. I guess I've fallen for the right brother."

Artie cocked his head. "You've definitely fallen for the right brother. Now if only I can find the right girl." He laughed and then dunked them both into the water, and when they emerged, he held Mia tightly and kissed her more passionately than he ever had before.

"Make no mistake," Mia said. "I am the best thing that will ever happen to you."

He looked into her eyes, ran his thumb across her cheek, and said, "Without a doubt."

ELEVEN

THE SUMMER FLEW by quickly, and it turned out to be the best summer of Mia's life. By the end of August, she felt like she belonged in the family. She came to understand that although their way of life was foreign to her, she appreciated their deep loyalty, love, and acceptance. Now that summer was almost over, Mia felt sad that the fun had to end. But she also knew her life had changed forever and that nothing would stop her from being a part of the family. When her Aunt Carla told her about a small party she was putting together in her honor, Mia was thrilled. She couldn't think of a better way to spend her last Sunday night in Mantoloking than surrounded by the key members of the family that she had come to love.

Artie planned a special dinner for their last Friday evening of the summer together, and Mia spent most of the afternoon getting ready. As she sat at the vanity applying her makeup, Carla softly knocked on the door.

"Hi, sweetheart. What time is your dinner with Artie tonight?"

"He made a six o'clock reservation at The Shrimp Box."

"That sounds lovely. Would you like me to put your hair in a French braid?"

"Sure. I never could learn how to do a French Braid on myself."

Carla smiled. "You know, Mia, I really loved having you with us this summer. I'm really going to miss not seeing you every day."

"I know. I feel the same. This summer was amazing. Thank you for everything."

"I hope that after you go home and start school, we don't become strangers again. We meant it when we said you are an important part of the family."

"I don't want that either. All I wanted from this visit was to get answers about my father, and I got them and so much more. I got a family that I didn't know I needed until now."

Carla nodded and kissed the back of Mia's head.

"But I'm left with some questions about my mother now, and I'm wondering if maybe you can help with that?"

"I'll try."

"My mother always seemed conflicted when it came to my father and his family. She would always talk about him being the love of her life and then by the end of the conversation she was bitter and warned me to stay away from his family. Did something happen?" Mia turned her head to look at Carla. "You can tell me the truth."

Her aunt was quiet for what felt like an eternity. She finished styling Mia's hair and sat on the side of the bed.

"Mia, your mother loved your father so very much. Sometimes feeling that much love makes us have blinders on and we cannot see the whole of the other person. We've told you how fixated Dominick was to have a position of power within Don Esposito's family. Well, he wound up doing some things that were hurtful to Rena."

"He *hurt* her?"

"Not physically. Although he did have a wicked temper, I don't believe he ever got physical with Rena."

"What *did* he do?"

"He did what many men in families like ours do. He started spending a lot of time away from the house and took up with women. Your mother expected a traditional marriage, and Dominick couldn't give that to her. He was all consumed with impressing Don Esposito and moving up. He got involved in situations that he shouldn't have, and unfortunately Rena started to see a side of him that she didn't like."

Mia looked down and started to pick at her nails.

Carla lifted her face so she could meet her eyes. "Mia, when your mother got pregnant with you, I know your father tried to be a devoted husband and father. He was enamored with you and would've done anything to protect you and keep you happy. I do believe he loved Rena deeply, but men like him are drawn to the excitement and the thrill of the life. Some wives are able to accept the way things are, and others cannot. I'm afraid your mother wasn't prepared to be a wife to a man like Dominick."

"I started to suspect it was something like that."

"Rena had come to me for advice after you were born." Carla's face softened at the memory. "We would have breakfast together every Saturday. The three of us. I would hold you and give you your bottle, and once you fell asleep in my arms, we'd put you down and spend the rest of the morning talking."

"What was she like back then?"

"Hopeful. She loved you and Dominick so much. She wanted nothing more than to find a way to make her marriage work."

"Were you able to help her?"

"I'd like to think so. I explained to her that men in this thing of ours often have a life outside of the marriage, but they're always loyal to their wives. Especially if they have a child together. I tried to help her understand that marriage dynamics change for everyone not just for people in our life, but loyalty means accepting and loving someone, faults and all."

Mia nodded. "That's really good advice."

"It was the advice my mother gave to both me and Josie before our wedding days, and it's the absolute truth." Carla sighed. "Rena and Dom seemed to be doing better, but then he got arrested, and well, you know the rest."

"But why did my mother want to keep me from the family?"

"I think she was so tormented over her loss that she blamed the family for Dom's behavior and her unhappiness."

"But that's just not fair."

"No, it wasn't. But Mia, don't blame your mom. What's done is done. She thought she was doing right by you, and I truly believe she wanted to protect you."

Mia sat quietly contemplating everything that Carla was telling her. She felt bad for her mother. Rena never found the happiness that she was searching for. But why did she think she was protecting Mia by keeping her away from his family?

"Let's focus on the future, hmm? We've got the rest of our lives to make up for lost time. Always carry your mother and father in your heart, and always remember how much they really did love you and wanted nothing but the best for you."

"I will. I'm so glad you didn't give up on me."

"Never. I fell in love with you from the moment I first held you in my arms." She kissed Mia's cheek and looked out the window as they heard a car pull up. "Your Knight in Shining Armor must be here."

MIA HELD ARTIE'S hand as they walked into the restaurant. His firm grip made her feel safe. She had tried to be more upbeat and casual than she was, but her mood was solemn after her conversation with Carla. Mia always dreamed that her parents' marriage was a fairytale romance, but somewhere deep down she knew that couldn't be true. She didn't have time to process everything Carla told her before Artie showed up for their date, and she could tell Artie noticed her mood. When they were seated at a small table by a window that gave them the best view of the water, Artie smiled at the hostess and slipped her a tip.

"Great view," Mia said casually as she put her napkin on her lap.

"Yeah, I thought it would be a nice spot to celebrate the end of the summer." He leaned in closer to her. "You don't feel like celebrating with me, do you?"

"It's not that," she said and put her hand on his. "Before you came to pick me up, I had a conversation with Aunt Carla about my parents. I guess I'm still thinking about it."

Artie blew a sigh of relief. "I thought, well, never mind."

"What? What did you think?"

"That maybe you were about to tell me you didn't want to see me anymore now that summer was over."

"You mean, that's an option?" Mia tilted her head and smirked.

Artie instantly relaxed and chuckled. "I would hope not."

Mia's mood lightened a little as she lifted her menu. "Not an option for me."

During dinner, they fell into a comfortable, easy conversation. Mia felt she could talk about anything with Artie.

"Do you want to talk about your conversation with Aunt Carla? You don't have to if you don't want, but maybe it'll help you sort through it."

"Yeah, I would. I'm sorry if it'll be a bit of a downer though." Mia looked down. "You know how I told you my mom never really had an easy life?"

Artie nodded and put his hand on hers.

"She didn't trust people easily. When she met my dad, she trusted him." Mia paused for a moment, "But now, Aunt Carla told me he wasn't very trustworthy."

"Yeah, from what I can tell, he was a typical cugine."

"What do you mean?"

"A guy who's trying hard to be made."

Mia nodded, "That's what I'm told." She leaned in closer to him. "Now I have a question for you. Do all the men in the family run around with women and disrespect their wives?"

Artie tapped his finger against her hand. "I'm not gonna lie. Many have a goomar from time to time. But the girlfriends, they don't mean anything."

Mia looked at him in shock. "I'm sure they mean *something* to the wives."

"I can't say anything about that, 'cause I don't know. I just know about what I see. In my house, if my dad had a goomar, I would've never known. There've been times when he was out overnight, but I really think it was because of business. When he'd come home, my mom would greet him at the door, make him food, and they would often spend a lot of time talking and whispering together. Sure, they've had some humdinger fights, but I never heard anything come up about other women."

"Hmm." Mia looked out the window in contemplation.

"Now, some of those other wise guys, the ones lower in rank, they don't hide a thing. I wonder if having a girlfriend and a bad temper make them feel important or something. But when it comes down to it, they stick with their wives and go to extremes to protect them and defend them."

"That's *crazy*."

"I guess it is. But you know, Mia, people usually behave according to their status. The upper level of the family, you know

Nonnuccio, my father, and Uncle Luca, they hold themselves to a high standard. You'll never see them behaving in any other way than dignified and respectful at all times. They're admired and respected for that. But people who are subordinates act like they're tough guys. It's how they try to get the same respect, but I don't really see it working well for them."

"And what about you? Will you ever have a position in the family?"

Artie chuckled, "I don't really want a position. I'll hopefully work for the firm that took me on as an intern."

Mia looked skeptical. "Are you allowed to do that? I thought you had to work for the family."

"No, my father and Nonnuccio gave me their blessings. Now Matt? He's not only expected to work for the family, but he wants to."

"Why? What's the difference between you?"

"I'm not really sure. I do know that Matt always showed an interest in the family."

"And what'll happen to Vicky?" Mia was interested to hear Artie's position on her career.

"I feel bad for her, really. She's super smart. Probably smarter than me. She could be a great lawyer for the family, but being a girl will prevent that from happening."

"So, she has to just get married and be a wife?" Mia could feel her irritation rise.

"I don't agree with it either. But it's what's expected."

"But can't that change?"

"I just don't know, Mia. The people that do business with the family wouldn't usually respect a woman in power. A lot needs to change before Vicky can be accepted as a powerful figure within the family.

After they finished their lobster dinners, Mia sat back and put her hands on her stomach.

"That was really good."

"It was. What do you say we take a walk on the beach and share some custard?"

"That sounds great."

As they drove to the boardwalk, Artie excitedly turned the volume up on the radio and said, "That's our song!"

Mia listened to Artie sing along to *Shining Star*, and she realized that his fear earlier might've not been so far-fetched. She was at the point in their relationship where she had to decide if she wanted to continue and consider a future with Artie or walk away before anyone got hurt. She always wanted a love like her grandparents had. They'd faced so many challenges together and made a beautiful life together. Mia knew it would be difficult for her grandfather to accept Artie, but maybe there would be a chance. He wasn't going into the "family business." He was going to be a lawyer at a very prestigious law firm, and he was nothing like her father. Artie was very respectful, personable, and had integrity.

"Perfect timing," Artie announced. The song ended just as he found a parking spot and turned the ignition off. He opened the passenger side door for her and together they crossed the boardwalk and entered the beach access.

"Artie, the sign says no one is allowed on the beach after dark."

"Then let's not get caught." He chuckled as he grabbed her hand and started jogging across the sand toward the water.

"Do you always follow the rules?" He chided.

"Yeah, most times," Mia answered as she looked up at him. "You?"

"Yeah, most times," he answered as he kicked water up at her.

Mia squealed in delight and together they walked hand in hand along the shoreline admiring the full moon against the dark sky. She held tight to his hand and wished the night would never end.

As if reading her thoughts, Artie stopped walking, took her into his arms, and kissed her tenderly and passionately. He cupped her face in his hands and looked deep into her eyes.

"Mia, I know we only met this summer, but I love you, and I'm hoping that you would consider a future with me."

"Artie," Mia started, but he cut her off.

"Shh. I don't want you to answer yet. There's a lot for you to consider and think about. I insist we both finish our studies and start our careers before we even think about the possibility of marriage. I also think it would be smart for us to really get to know each other's families better."

"Well, I—" Artie put his finger on her lips.

"Hear me out fully first. You've met and spent some time with my parents, but you need to really observe the family before you become a part of it. I need you to make sure you know what you're getting into. Even though I won't be working for the family, I'm still connected."

"I know—" Mia smiled as Artie shook his head.

"Nope, not yet. I want to meet your family, have your grandfather's approval. I want him to really see me. Know me for who I am, not who he may think I am. I know how very important your mother's family is to you, and that makes them important to me. If we marry, I want us to start off right. I want the kind of marriage that I see my parents and grandparents have. A marriage based on mutual respect and trust. That's how I think the love will last."

He finished and stared at her. "Are you going to say something?"

Suddenly, Mia knew Artie was perfect for her. She pushed up on her toes and ran her fingers through his hair. "I don't need time to think about my answer. We want exactly the same things." She wrapped her arms around his neck and kissed him deeply.

"Okay, then." Artie almost lost his balance. "Ice cream?"

They walked back to the boardwalk and Mia never felt more connected to anyone. He wrapped his arm around her as they walked, and in that moment, she knew they were going to protect and love each other for the rest of their lives. They sat huddled together on a bench looking out on the ocean as they ate their frozen custard. Their reverie was broken when Matt hopped over the bench and snuggled up to Artie.

"What's up buttercup?" He said as he took Artie's ice cream out of his hand and started to eat it.

"What's the matta with you?" Artie said as he reached for the ice cream.

Vicky, Angelo, and Daniella joined them at the bench. Mia noticed Vicky and Angelo were sharing a bag of zeppoles while Daniella looked on in disgust.

"Hey guys." Mia greeted them and couldn't hide her happiness.

"Having fun?" Vicky knowingly smiled at Mia.

"It's been a great night." Mia said and wished Daniella weren't there so she could talk privately with Vicky. Angelo handed Vicky the rest of the fried dough balls and walked over to the other side of the bench to talk to Matt and Artie.

"Mia, I hear you'll be going home?" Daniella asked as she looked around at the people walking by.

"Yes, I'm heading home on Monday."

"So soon?" Daniella asked snidely.

"Mia has to get ready for school. Don't you, Mia," Vicky replied proudly.

"School? Hmph. I didn't know you had to go to school to be a clerk at some store."

Mia whipped around toward Daniella. "What gave you the impression I was going to work as a clerk in a store?"

"I just thought it would only be natural. It's so hard to come up with tuition money these days."

"You are quite mistaken. For your information, I have a full scholarship to The New York School of Interior Design."

"Yes, they often award those things to the needy."

"What is your problem?" Mia stood up but took a step back after she locked eyes with Vicky, who quickly shook her head.

"My problem?" Daniella sneered. "I assure you, *I* do not have a problem."

Mia nodded and took a cleansing breath. "Okay, well, just to set the record straight. I *won* the scholarship at a major regional competition. Although, I would've had no problem attending the school without it. I entered for the prestige, and that award will open many career opportunities for me."

Daniella nodded casually and began looking around.

"What is it that you do Daniella? Do you work?" Mia tried to emulate the tone of voice she's heard when her Aunt Carla was talking to a waiter who had annoyed her.

"I work at a salon," she answered as she wiggled her leg.

"Nice. Are you a stylist?" Mia asked sweetly knowing Daniella didn't pass the test to get her license.

"No, not yet. I'm studying under one of the best in the business," she said and quickly added, "Matt, let's go. I'm bored."

"Of course," Mia nodded and smiled at Vicky who nodded at her.

The three couples started to walk along the boardwalk when a guy wearing a tight, white tank top knocked into Matt, looked back and thumbed his nose at him.

Matt quickly looked around and said, "Did you see that?"

"Yeah, I saw it. Wasn't that Enzo?" Angelo answered.

"Who?" Artie stopped walking.

"You know that dirt bag from the Marino crew." Angelo answered.

Matt nodded quickly. "Yup, that's him. What's his beef though?"

"Hey Matt. You got a problem?" Enzo called from the pizza stand.

"Yeah. Yeah, I got a problem. What's your problem?" Matt darted toward Enzo with Angelo following behind.

"Artie?" Mia touched his arm.

"Don't worry, I got this." He kissed her forehead and casually walked over to Matt who was pointing in Enzo's face.

Vicky grabbed Mia's hand as they held their breath watching the encounter.

Artie stood between Matt and Enzo and signaled Angelo to step back. "What's going on?"

"I got no problem with you, Artie." Enzo shook his head. "It's your brother here that needs to pay up."

"What are you talking about?" Matt answered in disgust.

"My numbers won, and I ain't seen my money yet." Enzo pointed at Matt.

"When did you hit?" Angelo asked.

"Last week" Enzo spat.

Matt and Angelo exchanged a look and shook their heads.

"Is this true?" Artie asked Matt and then turned to Enzo when Matt didn't respond.

"How much?" Artie asked Enzo.

"Two grand! And I want my money." He took a step closer to Matt.

"Look man, I don't know what happened. I don't manage that side of the business no more." Matt shook his head.

Artie looked at Matt, "Who's doing it now?"

"That would be Joey's turf," Matt answered with a shrug.

"Well, he didn't pay *me*. What, you don't have any control over your people?" Enzo asked in disgust.

Angelo took a step closer to Enzo and balled up his fist. Artie pushed his hand away. "Ok, this is not going to fix anything." He took money out of his pocket and pushed a couple of bills toward Enzo. "Here's two hundred. Tomorrow Matt'll make sure you're paid the rest."

Enzo looked down at Artie's hand. Artie pushed it closer to Enzo and he finally accepted the money.

"Ok, Artie. But if I don't get my money tomorrow, there'll be trouble."

"Understood." Artie nodded and shook hands with Enzo.

Mia ran to Artie and hugged him after Enzo walked away.

Artie turned to Matt. "Now you need to have a sit down with Joey. You may not operate that part of the business, but you do need to manage the people. That's what Uncle Luca depends on you for."

"Yeah, I know, Art. But I'm caught up spending long hours in A.C., and I can't micromanage everyone."

"Maybe you should talk to Uncle Luca about it. Get his take. I think you may have a real problem with Joey." He pat Matt on the back.

Matt looked around. "Where's Daniella?"

Vicky rolled her eyes and pointed. "Over there."

"Is there a problem?" Daniella asked sarcastically as she walked toward them eating cotton candy.

MIA WOKE UP the next morning feeling as if she was floating on air. Although this would be the last Sunday of the summer with her father's family, she was excited to go back to Lyndhurst and be with her mother's family again. After the incident on the boardwalk, Artie and Mia decided to go back to the house, and they sat on the porch long into the night making plans for the future. It wouldn't be too hard for them to see each other in New York because their schools were only about three miles from each other. Mia told Artie she would talk to her grandmother about him and together they could tell her grandfather about their relationship. Mia was hopeful that her grandfather would like Artie, and the sooner they got to know each other the better.

Mia was startled out of her daydreams when she heard a loud commotion downstairs.

"What's going on?" She asked as she ran down the stairs and over to Carla who was hugging Nonnina while Luca and Nonnuccio were huddled together whispering.

"There's been an incident," Carla answered. "They're in the hospital."

"Who? Who's in the hospital?" Mia started to panic.

"Matt and Artie." Carla whispered.

TWELVE

SUMMER, 1980

MIA FELT THE air rush out of her lungs, and she slumped onto the couch thinking she must've been dreaming, and this was nothing more than a nightmare. When she felt Carla and Nonnina sit beside her, she knew it wasn't a dream. She looked back and forth between Uncle Luca and Aunt Carla.

"What happened? How are they?"

"We don't really know what happened. All we know is that Matt's pretty banged up." Carla took her hand. "And it looks like Artie got the worst of it. They're worried about swelling on the brain."

"Oh my God. Oh my God." Mia rushed to Luca. "I've got to go to him. You've got to take me to the hospital."

Luca hugged Mia. "I don't think that's a wise idea right now. It could be dangerous."

"Dangerous?"

"Right now we have to stay put and sit tight until we know more."

"If you don't bring me, I'll drive myself." She pulled away from Luca and put her hands on her hips.

Carla reached out to her. "Mia, sweetheart, I know how you feel. God knows I do. But Uncle Luca's right. We don't know who did this and we don't know why. It could be a warning to the family, in which case we must all be very careful."

"I can't just sit around and wait." Mia shook her head and tears started flowing down her face. "I *can't*!"

Nonnina took Mia in her arms and sat with her on the couch as Luca and Nonnuccio went into Luca's office.

"Mia," Nonnina said with authority. "Now's the time for the women of this family to show our true nature. We are strong and we are brave. It will not help anyone if we react with our emotions and not our heads. We'll hear news soon, and we'll make the proper decisions then. You *will* see Artie. *I* will make sure of it, but we will not have any other member of this family put into danger unnecessarily." She leaned in closer to Mia. "Yes?"

As Nonnina was talking, Mia noticed at least fifteen large men go into Luca's office led by Gina's husband, James, who was Luca's head of security.

Mia nodded and said, "Yes." Deep down she knew it was a bad idea to jump in her car and run over to the hospital on her own, but she was so worried about Artie, and she felt helpless.

"Okay, we've got some news," Luca said as he and Nonnuccio entered the room followed by James and two other security guards. "Looks like Matt got into a beef about Daniella, and Artie got caught up in the middle. I wanna head over there now and check in on things, I'll take Mia and Carla with me."

Nonnuccio added, "It doesn't seem to be anything more, but to be sure, Gabriella and I will keep an eye on things here with James and his crew. I'm sending four men with you, Luca. I don't want to take no chances."

Within fifteen minutes, Mia was dressed and seated in the back of a large black car sandwiched between her Aunt Carla and Uncle Luca. All she could think to do was pray. Although she lost much of her faith the day her mother died, saying prayers during the ride to the hospital helped to keep her calm. They rushed through the corridors and found a waiting room that had two family security guards positioned at the door. Inside were Ray and Josie huddled together, Vicky pacing, and Angelo sitting in a chair nervously pumping his right leg up and down. When they entered, Carla quickly embraced Josie and Vicky ran to Mia while Luca, Ray and Angelo huddled in a corner.

"Jo, what's happening? How are the boys?"

Through her tears, Josie said, "They took Artie down for some kind of X-Ray test on his head to see if there is swelling or blood clots, and the doctors are in with Matt now."

"How are *you* doing, sweetheart?" Carla asked as she led Josie to a chair.

Josie shook her head. "I've been better, I can tell you that. I'm so glad you're here," Josie said as she reached out for Mia's hand.

"Do you know what happened?" Mia looked at Vicky who sat down next to Josie.

"We were able to talk to Matt earlier. He said he asked Artie to go with him to pay Enzo what he was owed. Apparently, they stopped for a bagel after and ran into this guy Mauro." Vicky leaned in and dropped her voice. "Mauro started talking about Daniella like he was dating her." Vicky shook her head. "Matt lost it because as far as he was concerned, *he* was dating Daniella and knew nothing about Mauro. Artie, of course, tried to step in and smooth things over, but some guy that must've been with Mauro came rushing out of the bagel shop and caught Artie off guard. Next thing you know, the four of them were going at it. Someone inside must've called the cops because when they heard the sirens, Mauro and the other guy took off."

"All this over a girl?" Mia shook her head.

"Not just any girl." Carla reminded her.

"That one! She's just like her mother." Josie shook her head, looked to her right, and made a spitting noise. "Puttana!"

Both Vicky and Mia exchanged looks just as Dr. Card entered the waiting room.

"Mr. and Mrs. Bocelli, you can go in and see Matthew now. He has a fractured tibia in his left leg, and we set the leg with pins and a brace for now. We want to look at it when the swelling goes down. We may have to put in a rod to help it heal properly. He also has a fractured radius, so we set his right arm in a cast as well."

Josie gasped and put her hand over her mouth.

Ray put his arm around Josie as Dr. Card continued. "We need to keep him here until the swelling goes down in that leg and we can determine the next course of action."

"Of course." Ray answered. "Any news on Artie yet?"

"Arthur is back from imaging, and we're waiting on the results. He's heavily sedated to keep him as comfortable as possible."

"Can we see him?" Mia asked.

"Family only at this time."

Josie straightened her back and took Mia's hand. "We're all family here."

Dr. Card nodded. "Both of your boys will need a lot of rest."

Ray nodded his head. "We understand." After the doctor left the waiting room, he turned to Josie. "Why don't you girls go in and check on Artie. We'll go in with Matt for now."

"Mom, there really is a lot of us here. I think I'll let you guys visit some more and I'll head back to the house."

Mia looked at Vicky and saw how exhausted and overwhelmed she looked.

Carla put her arm around Vicky's shoulders. "That's a good idea. Why don't you come back to our house with me. We'll prepare some food. It's going to be a long couple of days."

Josie hugged her daughter tightly. "That's a good idea, baby. You go."

Vicky nodded and walked over to hug Mia. "I can stay if you need me."

"No. I'll be alright." Mia shook her head, her voice cracked as she said, "I just need to see him."

"I know you do."

Luca cleared his voice and said, "Okay. Ange, I want you to go back with Carla and Vicky, and report back to Don Bocelli. Fill him in on everything. Ray and me, we'll go in and see Matt." He looked at Ray and pat his shoulder. "We need some more information about this Mauro character."

As everyone started to file out of the waiting room, Mia could hear Luca tell the security guards he wanted no one in and out of the hospital rooms except the nurses and doctors that were on a list he slipped them.

Josie grabbed Mia's hand before they entered Artie's room. "I need to warn you, this isn't going to be easy. Artie is in really bad shape, and you may not recognize him."

Mia nodded and squeezed Josie's hand. She felt her knees buckle and she had to lean on Josie as they approached him. Artie looked so small laying in the bed propped up by multiple pillows. Josie had been right. Mia couldn't recognize him, and if she didn't know better, she never would've believed it was him. His entire face was an amalgamation of red and purple bruises. His left eye was swollen shut while his right cheek and nose had turned a dark shade of purple so deep, they looked black. His lips had ballooned to three times their size, and Mia noticed blood seeping through the bandages that covered his right hand.

"Are you okay?" Josie whispered as she held Mia up.

Mia nodded. "But *this* is not okay."

"No, my sweet. It isn't." Josie led Mia to Artie's bedside and started to stroke his hair. "I'm here my sweet boy. Your Momma's here."

"Can, can he hear us?" Mia whispered wanting so badly to reach out and touch him but afraid to do so.

"I believe he can." Josie took Mia's hand and placed it on Artie's left one. "Look who's here." Her voice lifted. "Mia's here."

"Heyyyy," she said softly. "I'm here Artie. You're going to be alright."

Josie gave a slight smile to Mia and nodded. "That's right. You don't worry about a thing, you just rest and get better."

Mia and Josie sat by Artie's side taking turns holding his hand in silence. Mia was in awe of Josie's strength and tried to draw confidence from it that everything was going to be alright.

The consolatory silence was broken when a nurse barged into the room pushing a squeaky cart. "I'm sorry Mrs. Bocelli. We need to clean his wounds and change his bandages."

"Of course. You be gentle, now." Josie kissed Artie's head and walked out the door.

Mia held back for a moment. She gently squeezed Artie's hand, leaned over to his ear and whispered, "I love you my shining star." She kissed his head and left the room.

Mia bounded up to Luca, Ray, and Josie who were standing together outside of Artie's room. She pointed to Luca and demanded, "You get those guys who did this to Artie!"

"Don't worry, we'll take care of it," Luca answered.

Mia shook her head. "Don't let them get away with this." Her blood boiled with anger and the deep need for vengeance ran deep into her soul.

Luca put both of his hands on her shoulders and looked her in the eyes. "I promise you. We got this!"

THIRTEEN

DR. CARD ENTERED the waiting room holding what Mia assumed was Artie's chart.

"Mr. and Mrs. Bocelli. Good news. There is no swelling on Arthur's brain, and we cannot find any evidence of blood clots."

Mia felt her entire body loosen.

"Oh, grazie a Dio!" Josie stood and made the sign of the cross.

"Yes, thank God!" Ray hugged Josie.

"I'd like to keep him here for observation for at least a day or so. As you can see, he's pretty bruised up, but I have every confidence that he'll be just fine. I would like to strongly suggest that everyone go home and let Arthur and Matthew rest. Right now, sleep is what's best for them. We'll begin pulling back on Arthur's sedation through the night. By tomorrow, he should be in a better position for visitors."

"I don't know." Josie shook her head. "I don't want to leave them."

Dr. Card took Josie's hand. "Mrs. Bocelli, it's my professional advice that you can help them the most by going home, eating a good meal, and getting some rest also."

"It'll be alright Josie. Everyone's out at the house, and it might do you both some good to head back there with us," Luca said.

Ray and Josie agreed, and while Mia helped Josie gather her

things, Ray and Luca pulled the doctor aside. Ray leaned in close to the doctor's face. "I want a phone call immediately if anything changes with my boys. Do you hear me?" He leaned in closer and tapped his finger on the doctor's chest. "If their blood pressure goes up even a little, I wanna know about it!" The doctor nervously looked back and forth between Luca and Ray. "I don't want you leaving their side for nothin! Do we understand each other?"

"Yes, of course." Dr. Card nodded.

Luca handed the doctor a folded paper. "This is the number you call day or night." He raised his eyebrows.

"You have nothing to worry about. I assure you." Dr. Card bowed his head and scurried out of the waiting room.

Mia could see Ray and Luca giving the security guards strict instructions before they all left and returned to the house. Her relief over Artie's condition turned to disgust when she thought about the events that landed both him and Matt in the hospital. What was it about those Espositos that made it so easy for them to be able to cause so much heartbreak and strife in other people's lives? She had no doubt in her mind that Daniella was seeing Mauro while stringing Matt along. But why? What was she playing at? Mia had a soft spot for Matt. She could see he was smart when it came to business, but she couldn't figure out what he saw in Daniella.

When they got back to the house, Mia was relieved to find that Vicky and Carla had prepared a feast. Mia knew that cooking was a great way to cope with anxiety, and by the look of the many trays of food and the expression on the women's faces, their fears had been somewhat comforted. Now that she knew both Artie and Matt were going to be okay, she felt famished and fixed herself a large plate of food. She and Vicky went out on the patio to try to make sense of things.

"What's Daniella's story anyway? Mia asked bluntly.

Vicky rolled her eyes. "Nothing is good enough for her, and she's always looking for the next best thing."

Mia slapped her hand on the table. "Yes! She acts like a spoiled princess!"

"Yup. I mean take a look at the car she drives. I don't know about your grandparents, but mine never would've given me a brand-new Trans Am the day I got my license. She totaled hers within a week, and a day later she was handed the keys of a new one right off the lot."

"Do you think she's using Matt until the next best thing comes along?"

"Between you and me. Yeah, I do."

"But what does Matt see in her?" Mia leaned in.

"Artie and I have asked ourselves the same question," Vicky answered. "We've come to the conclusion that it's all about the chase."

"What do you mean?"

"She keeps him on his toes and keeps him guessing, right? If the day ever came when she was completely invested in their relationship, he might lose interest." Vicky shrugged. "The challenge would be gone."

"Interesting," Mia said thoughtfully.

"It had to have been hard for you to see Artie like that today."

"Yeah." Mia's eyes got wet. "He was barely recognizable." She looked down, and then she dropped her fist on the table in anger. "And for what?"

"Matt gets crazy sometimes when he feels he's being disrespected."

"No, Vick. I don't blame Matt. He's just as much a victim in this as Artie. Nope. This is on Daniella."

"You're right. But what can we do about it?"

Mia shrugged her shoulders. "I'll tell you what, someday she's going to get hers. I promise you that." She was quiet for a minute and then said, "I wonder what your mother meant when she said, 'she's just like her mother?'"

Vicky skooched her chair closer to Mia and whispered, "Rumor has it, Antonia has an eye for the men." Vicky looked around. "Especially *young* men if you know what I mean."

"But she's married, right?"

"Yup!" Vicky said as she popped an olive in her mouth. "But Paulie knows better than to do anything about it. Even though he's a 'made man' in the Esposito Family, he would have to answer to her brother, Mario, not to mention her father, Carmine. Paulie's not going to risk it, I'm sure. He probably has his own goomar on the side anyway."

"Let me ask you. How do you feel about the whole girlfriend on the side business?"

"I hate everything about it," Vicky scoffed.

"I don't think I could live like that. Knowing my husband is out and about with another woman," Mia said.

"You mean *women*."

"No!"

"Yup. Some of them have multiples. It's all an ego thing if you ask me." Vicky rolled her eyes.

"Unbelievable."

"Tell me about it." Vicky rolled her eyes again. "I'll tell you, if I find out Angelo is seeing anyone else, I'll stab him. I mean it!"

"Angelo adores you. I don't think he'd ever look at another woman." Mia tapped Vicky's hand.

"I really do love him," Vicky whispered.

"But?" Mia frowned.

"Sometimes I get conflicted. You know I want to be a lawyer and not just a wife."

"I don't understand why you can't do both."

"In families like ours, it's not the way. We come from a long line of old-fashioned thinking."

"Maybe you could try to change the thinking. How does Ange feel?"

"Actually, he said he'd be fine with the idea of me having a career." Vicky leaned in and whispered. "He'd never admit it to anyone, but submissive women turn him off. He likes a woman to take *control*." She smirked. "If, you know what I mean."

"Gotcha!" Mia laughed.

"I'm sure you've noticed, the family is very tightly knit. We don't trust outsiders, and we always have to be on our guard with who we let in and trust."

Mia nodded.

"It wouldn't be easy for me to be a lawyer on the outside unless I work for a firm that's connected. And like I told you, the men in our family don't really think a woman could possibly contribute. But *Nonnina*? She pretty much told me in no uncertain terms, that I was to go to college and get my law degree." Vicky shrugged. "So, here I am. Getting ready to work my butt off in college to get a degree I may never use."

"Girls come inside, we're having a family meeting." Carla said as she poked her head out of the patio door.

"I've never been part of a family meeting." Vicky said in alarm. "They're always for the men."

"Maybe things are changing." Mia patted her shoulder as they entered the house.

They sat down on the couch between Carla and Josie. Nonnina sat in an armchair sitting up straight and poised while Angelo sat in a chair brought in from the dining area. Luca and Ray both stood in the back corner with their hands crossed in front of them.

Nonnuccio stood erect in the front of the room and cleared his throat before speaking. "We can all agree that this thing that happened to Artie and Matt is troubling. We learned that this Mauro fellow is a part of the Esposito crew. Not high in rank, just an associate. The other guy is a friend of Mauro, a wannabe who's trying to get in with the outfit. Goes by the name of Tiny on the streets."

Nonnuccio paused for a moment while Ray shifted his legs and Angelo leaned in closer.

"Now you all know, I don't condone violence for the sake of violence, but we cannot just sit back and let this happen." Nonnuccio moved his arm and pointed to everyone seated. "An assault on *anyone* in the family is an assault on the *whole* family."

Nonnina nodded her head in agreement.

"Now I've spoken at length with Don Esposito, and while we disagreed on the cause of the incident, we did agree that Mauro and his friend took it too far and should've shown restraint out of respect for our family." He turned to look directly at Angelo. "Angelo, I'd like you, Silvio, and Rocco to take care of this tonight." He waved his hand. "Tiny is a nobody, so you do what you gotta do with him, but Mauro, he's connected. You send the message and leave it at that. I don't want anything getting out of hand."

Angelo nodded his head and said, "Understood."

"I want everyone to be on high alert. We don't know this Tiny or Mauro and hopefully they'll understand what a mistake it would be to take this any further." He waived his hand. "But you never know." He straightened his back. "Capisce?"

Everyone nodded and replied with murmured responses. "Okay good." He nodded, held up a glass of whiskey in a salute, then gulped it down quickly.

Vicky sprang to her feet and walked Angelo to the door. Mia smiled slightly as she watched the tenderness between the couple.

To her surprise, she was not only relieved they were going to make retribution for hurting Artie and Matt so badly, but she found comfort in that the family really were loyal to each other. It's one thing to say such things, but here was her proof that they were steadfast in their allegiance to each other.

FOURTEEN

VICKY CALLED MIA early on Sunday morning to tell her that she heard from Angelo and the payback was done. Mia was relieved and hoped that they could put all of this behind them and Artie could focus on healing. She quickly went downstairs in anticipation for her opera and cooking session with her Uncle Luca, and when she caught him singing at the top of his lungs while conducting with a wooden spoon, she started laughing so hard her laughter turned to tears. Luca dropped the spoon and folded her into his arms.

"I know, let it out. It's okay. It's all okay now."

All Mia could do was nod her head as her tears flowed releasing all of the emotions and anxiety she had bottled up.

Luca kissed Mia's head, and said, "You know these things happen. Idiots have been losing their heads and fighting over women since the beginning of time. It's just lucky that nobody pulled a gun out."

Mia groaned and cried harder, making Luca regret his last statement.

"I." Mia tried to form her words in between her tears. "I … Just … Worry … About … Everyone. I … Love … You … All … So … Much."

Luca pushed Mia back so he could look into her eyes and brushed her hair from her face. "Don't you start worrying now. Ya hear me? Nothing is gonna happen. I mean that." He held up the gold chain and horn that he always wore around his neck. "You see this? This is *my* protection, it keeps me safe so I can keep everyone else safe."

"He's never taken it off since I gave it to him on our wedding day." Mia turned to see Carla standing behind them. "And it's never let us down." Carla kissed Mia's head and took her hand. "It's true, our family is more susceptible to danger than most, but Mia, conflict can happen to any family at any time. We can't live our lives worrying about what could happen. Rest assured, the Bocelli Family is smart and savvy. We don't instigate trouble, but we do put a stop to it. There is a difference."

Mia nodded her head and wiped her eyes. She understood there was a difference between causing trouble and ending trouble and was comforted to know that her family wasn't as cruel as the Esposito Family were, but the idea of dangerous conflict still worried her.

"Do you have to put a stop to trouble often?" She looked back and forth between her aunt and uncle.

"It's been quite a while, I'll tell ya that. But, I don't want you to worry." Luca shook his head. "You let me do the worrying, yeah? Now let's make our pancakes."

Preparing breakfast with Luca relaxed Mia quite a bit, and by the time they sat down to eat, she was humming along with the music.

"I'm going to be sad to see you leave tomorrow." Carla said as she took a sip of coffee.

"I'm not going home tomorrow. I'm not leaving until I know Artie is okay."

Carla shot a look of concern at Luca.

"Mia," he started, "Artie's going to be fine. You heard the doctor yourself. You need to go home and get ready for school."

"You saw him, Uncle Luca, how could I go home with him like that?"

"Sweetheart," Carla said gently. "Artie will have Josie, Nonnina, and me looking after him. He's in good hands. Your schooling is *very* important."

Mia shook her head vehemently. "I can't. I just can't."

Luca took a deep breath and let it out slowly. "Okay. What if you and me go over to the hospital after breakfast. Check in on him and Matt. If he's alert and seeming better, you go home and prepare for school."

Mia thought for a moment, shrugged and said, "Yes to going to the hospital after breakfast, but no promises about going home."

Luca raised his hands in surrender. "Okay."

"What do you think we should do about our dinner tonight?" Carla looked back and forth between Luca and Mia.

"Actually, Aunt Carla, I was thinking about that. Do you mind if we keep it small tonight?"

Carla looked relieved and put her hand on Mia's. "My thought exactly. I'll make the phone calls while you both are at the hospital.

MIA STOOD OUTSIDE of Artie's hospital room and took a deep breath. She could hear Luca exclaiming, "Hey Slugger." as he entered Matt's room. Mia opened the door and inched her way into the room toward Artie's bed. He slowly moved his hand and wiggled his fingers.

"Stella!" He said softly.

"Uhm, no Artie, It's Mia." She choked, heartbroken at the sound of another girl's name.

"My Stella Splendente," he said.

Mia held back tears as she looked at him. "I. I came to see how you were. I can go. I should go." She turned to run out of the room, but he lightly grasped her hand.

"No. You. You're my Stella Splendente."

"No Artie. It's Mia, I'm *not* Stella."

"Stella Splendente! My shining star!"

"Oh, you mean me? *I'm* your shining star?"

"Yes." He whispered.

Mia laughed in relief and kissed his hand and his head. "How are you feeling?"

"Tired and sore." He said as he intertwined his fingers with hers.

"Do you need anything?"

"I got you. That's all I need."

"I'm not going anywhere. I'm staying down here until you're better."

"No."

"What do you mean, No? I'm not leaving your side."

"You need to go home. Start school. Bad enough I may not go back on time. But you," he tried to shake his head. "You can't delay."

"I can start next semester."

Artie tried to shake his head. "I'm fine. Just banged up. Doc says I can go home tomorrow. In a couple weeks, I'll be like new."

"I don't know," Mia started when a nurse entered the room.

"It's time for your ice packs again." She said brightly as she crossed the room.

"Can you tell her I'm okay?" Artie asked the nurse as he pointed to Mia.

The nurse smiled as she handed the ice packs to Artie. "He looks really bad. But he's going to be fine. The swelling will start to go down in a few days. You'll notice the bruising will take a few weeks to clear up, and we'll send him home with a small prescription for pain. Don't worry. He's tough, this one."

As the nurse was leaving the room, Josie burst in with a number of shopping bags.

"Artie! Mia!" She squealed and rushed over to kiss them. "I brought soup." She flitted around the room unpacking a thermos of soup, a linen napkin, and a soup spoon. "Let's get you up. You need to eat."

She pressed the buttons on the bed and made Artie's legs and head go up and down multiple times until Mia stepped in. "Here, let me help with that."

"You're such a dear." She tucked the napkin under Artie's chin and started spoon feeding him the soup.

"Thanks, Mom." He managed to say in between spoonfuls.

"Your father spoke with Dr. Card this morning. You're coming home tomorrow, but Matt will have to stay another couple of days until they know for sure about his leg." She wiped his mouth with the napkin and continued feeding him. "We'll stay down here an extra week or more and head up to Saddle River when we know about Matt's leg."

"See?" Artie looked at Mia. "I'll be fine," he said as he put his hand up to stop Josie from feeding him anymore.

She quickly packed up the soup and said, "I'm going to bring Matt his soup. Do you need anything?"

"No, Mom, I'm good."

"Get some rest." Josie kissed Mia and Artie on their heads and slipped out of the room.

Mia sat next to Artie and took his hand in hers. "It's nice how your mom takes care of you."

"She's a good mom." He tapped her fingers. "Go back and start school, please."

"Okay," she sighed.

"Good," he whispered sleepily.

"I hate to leave you, but you need your rest."

He nodded slightly. "I'll call you every day. I promise."

She kissed his hands and his head.

"I love you too, my Stella Splendente."

Mia's voice caught in her throat. "You heard me?"

"I thought I was dreaming." He managed. "But when I woke up, I knew I wasn't."

"It definitely wasn't a dream." She kissed him again and quietly left the room as he started to snore.

Mia was walking toward Matt's room as Ray, Josie, and Luca had come out.

"Is everything okay?" Mia asked nervously.

"Yeah, yeah. Matt fell asleep." Ray answered. "I need a smoke," he said as he pressed the elevator button multiple times.

"Me too," Luca said as he patted his shirt pocket to make sure his cigarettes were there.

"You two go ahead, we'll meet you down there." Josie waved them on. "Ever since I quit smoking, I can't stand to be around it," she said as she scrunched her nose up. She put her hand on Mia's arm. "I want to thank you for caring for Artie. The hardest thing for a mother is to see their son hurt, but two sons, madone! I know he'll always be alright when you're around. It's Matt I worry about."

Mia reached out and hugged Josie tightly. Her short, quick breaths told Mia she was trying hard not to cry, and when she broke away to get a tissue out of her purse, Mia rubbed her back.

"I'm sorry to say that Matt got them into this mess. That girl has a hold on him and she's, well, she's just not good for him."

"I agree. I think Matt can do better."

"I've noticed how close you and Artie have become, and I'm so very happy. You're good for each other. I can tell already. I pray Matt finds the same."

"I think he might."

Josie patted her eyes, put the tissue in her purse, stood up straight and said, "I hope you're right."

FIFTEEN

MONDAY MORNING CAME too quickly for Mia. She put the last of her things in her car and turned to face her Aunt Carla and Uncle Luca. "This was the best summer of my life."

"Ours too," Luca put his arm around her.

"Speak for yourself. Mine was the year you proposed to me." Carla jabbed him in the ribs.

"Okay. The best summer of our adult lives."

"This isn't goodbye you know, Mia," Carla said hugging Mia. "I do hope we'll be seeing each other more than once a year now."

"Definitely." Mia answered. "You know, when I agreed to come here for the summer, all I wanted was to learn more about my father. I never expected to feel like a part of the family."

"We will always be here for you." Luca squeezed Mia and kissed both of her cheeks.

"Now call us when you get home so we know you made it safely. We're going to stay down here to help Ray and Josie until Matt and Artie can head back north. I'll let you know when we are back up to Alpine, and we'll have dinner so you can tell us about school."

"I would love that." Mia gave them both hugs and kisses before she got in her car.

She could hear Luca whisper to Carla "We've got to do something about that car. That thing can't be safe."

"I love my car!" Mia honked and waved as she pulled down the driveway.

The drive back to Lyndhurst went smoothly, and Mia was glad she decided to wait until late morning to avoid the traffic. As she pulled into the driveway, Ruth rushed out of the house waving her hand.

"Mia!" She pulled open the car door. "Give me a hug. Boy did I miss you."

"Hey Grammy." Mia hugged her grandmother tightly and breathed in her usual scent of L'air du Temps perfume. "I'm home," Mia said tenderly.

"Let's go inside. We'll get your things out of the car later. Are you hungry?"

"You know, I could go for one of your tuna sandwiches."

"Coming right up."

After Mia called her aunt and uncle to let them know she was home, she and Ruth sat at the kitchen table talking over their lunch.

"Tell me about Artie." Ruth smirked and raised her eyebrows.

"Artie?" Mia stammered. "What do you mean?"

"He was the topic of most of your conversations." Ruth put her hand on Mia's arm. "A grandmother knows when her granddaughter is smitten."

"Smitten?" Mia couldn't contain her laughter. "Nobody says that anymore, Grammy. But, yeah, I guess you can say we're in a relationship."

Ruth nodded her head and took a sip of tea. "He sounds like a nice boy with a good head on his shoulders."

"But?" Mia prodded.

"But you know his family background."

"Yeah, but Grammy, he's not going to be working for the family. He's interning at a great law firm in Manhattan and once he gets his degree next year, he'll have the opportunity to work for them full time." Mia shook her head.

"Well, that's something. You know he'll have to meet Poppy before you go any further in this relationship."

"I figured. Can you help me break it to him? I think he'll really like Artie. He's kind, respectful, smart, and funny."

Ruth nodded. "I had a feeling this was the case, so I already started preparing him. At first, he wasn't happy, but I think I'm breaking through to him. Give me a little more time and we'll have Artie over for a Sunday dinner."

Mia was both relieved and grateful to have Ruth on her side. "Okay."

"Did you find the answers you were looking for over the summer?"

"I think I did. I think I came to an understanding of the dynamics of my parent's relationship. My dad was who he was." She shrugged. "He didn't like authority or following rules. I can see how Poppy and him would clash."

Ruth nodded. "Yes, they certainly did."

"And I guess Mom fell in love with his charm. But I also think she wasn't in love with his bad-boy ways."

"What do you mean?"

"I think maybe she thought once they were married, he would settle down and be the kind of husband she wanted him to be. But it turned out, he was the only kind of husband he could be. I don't think she realized he couldn't change. Who knows, she might've even still gotten depressed if he didn't die and their marriage wasn't how she pictured it would be."

"Hmmm." Ruth pondered. "You could be right. How do you feel about all of this?"

"It's a lot to process, but I'm getting there."

"Good." Ruth squeezed Mia's hand. "I was thinking, why don't we go to Willowbrook Mall this week and get you some new clothes and supplies for school?" Ruth asked as she started clearing the dishes.

"Grammy, I'm not in Grammar School anymore. I don't need new school clothes," Mia said as she handed her the lunch plates.

"Mia, you are starting The New York School of Interior Design in little over a week on a very prestigious scholarship. I want you to walk in there looking and feeling like a million bucks. I'm not sure last year's jeans and tee shirts will help you achieve that. Besides, you've earned and deserve a few new fashion-forward outfits."

"Okay, you win." Mia thought about her usual wardrobe choices. She really did feel more confident and attractive wearing the clothing Aunt Carla had gotten for her from the boutiques. Before this summer, she didn't really pay close attention to what she was wearing, but her grandmother was right. If she was going to be a successful Interior Designer, she really should start looking the part and ripped cut-offs and tee shirts wouldn't cut it."

"Do you mind if we get a makeover at Macy's too?"

"That's a lovely idea," Ruth nodded as she washed the dishes, and the phone began to ring. "That's the phone. Mia, could you answer it for me? It's probably someone just selling something."

Mia walked over to the phone hoping it wasn't a salesperson and would be Artie.

"Hello?" She said in anticipation.

"Stella!" Mia's heart lifted at the sound of Artie's voice.

"Hey you. How are you feeling? Are you home yet?"

"Yup. Mom and Pop just brought me home."

"You sound so much better than yesterday."

"I feel a lot better. Still sore, but a lot of the swelling went down."

"It's so good to hear you almost like yourself again. How's Matt?"

"His swelling is going down too, and the doc said he won't need a rod after all."

"That's great." She lowered her voice. "By the way, has he heard from Daniella? What's going on with that?"

"Get this, she came rushing into his hospital room yesterday. Tears flowing and everything saying Mauro was lying and none of it was true."

"You're kidding?"

"Nope! When I went to his room to say goodbye today, she was all on the bed snuggled up to him."

"I just can't get over her. She's something else."

Artie chuckled, "Yes, she is. But she's Matt's problem. So, how's my Stella Splendente?"

"I'm good now that I know you're home and doing better."

"I told you there was nothing to worry about."

Mia could hear Josie in the background. "Is that Mia? Let me talk to her." She heard Josie's bracelet jangle as she took the receiver. "Mia, my sweet. I take it you're home safely?"

"Yes, I got home a couple of hours ago. How are you? You must be happy to have Artie home?"

"Yes, I can take much better care of him at home than they do at that hospital. I'm sure you can tell his spirits are up."

"Yes, he sounds great."

"He's starting to look better too. It won't be long until our handsome boy is back to himself. I do hope to see you soon. When we go back to the big house, you must come for dinner, yes?"

"Yes, okay. That sounds good."

"Okay dear. I'll give you back to him. Ciao."

"Ciao."

"Dinner with my parents, huh?" Artie chided.

Mia chuckled. "You know, you'll need to come and have dinner here sometime soon, too."

"I'm looking forward to it."

SIXTEEN

FALL, 1980

FOR THE NEXT three weeks, Artie and Mia spoke on the phone at least twice a day. Mia called Artie every morning before school and Artie called Mia every evening. They talked for hours sharing how their days went, what their plans were for the next day, and how Artie's bruises were healing. It turned out Artie only had to miss the first week of school and he was back on track with his studies and his internship. They had been able to meet for coffee and an occasional meal, but Mia was anxious for him to meet Tony sooner rather than later. They both agreed that Artie should look his best when he met her grandparents, and they knew that couldn't happen until his bruises were all but gone. By the end of September, Mia saw that Artie looked healed enough to come for Sunday dinner.

"It was a good idea to have Artie come early so he could talk with Poppy before everyone else gets here," Ruth said as she rolled a handful of meat into a ball. "But, Mia, for God's sake, stop pacing. You're making *me* nervous."

"I can't help it. What if Poppy hates him?"

"He promised me he would have an open mind. I've been preparing him for this for almost a month now. As long as there's no surprises, I feel like it'll go well."

"Okay, okay."

"Here, make the salad." Ruth pushed a head of lettuce toward Mia.

Mia only got halfway through cutting up the lettuce when the doorbell rang. "It's him. He's here." Mia flew out of the kitchen and past Tony who was reading the paper in the living room.

"Stella!" He smiled at her as the door swung open. She melted when she saw his big smile. He wore khaki pants with a white polo shirt and a navy blue and white cardigan sweater. He kissed her cheek as he entered the house carrying a bakery box and a bottle of wine.

"Hey. You look great." She whispered and led him into the living room where Ruth was standing next to Tony's chair. "Grammy, Poppy, this is Artie."

"I'm very pleased to meet you Mr. and Mrs. Russo. These are for you."

"Lyndhurst Pastry Shop?" Ruth moved forward to take the bakery box.

"They have the best pastries around. We only get our pastries from there. I hope you like them."

Ruth laughed. "We love their pastries. They really *are* the best."

Tony stood and looked Artie in the eye, he stared for a few seconds, and then reached out to shake Artie's hand. "It's nice to meet you, Artie."

"Mia told me what your favorite wine was, so I had my mom pick up a bottle for you."

"That was very thoughtful. Thank you," Tony said as he accepted the bottle, read over the label, and nodded in approval. "I think I'll open it for dinner." Tony handed the bottle to Mia, who quickly placed it next to Tony's plate on the dining room table.

"Come, sit down." Tony gestured to the couch as Mia and

Ruth returned from the dining room. Mia nervously sat next to Artie while Ruth sat in the wing chair next to Tony's.

"I understand you're studying to be a lawyer," Tony said breaking the awkward silence.

"Yes, sir. I'm in my second year at NYU Law."

"That would make you, what? Twenty-four?"

"No Sir, actually, I'm twenty-two. My grades enabled me to graduate high school a year earlier than most kids my age, and then I went on to NYU and was able to get my bachelor's within three years."

"Really?" Tony was impressed. "How did you manage that?"

"Most semesters I took extra courses, and of course, I continued my studies throughout the summer."

"When did you have time for fun?" Ruth asked.

Artie chuckled. "I guess I didn't have much fun. Right now, school is the most important thing, and I want to stay focused on my studies and future career."

Mia took Artie's hand and nodded.

"So, you didn't spend the whole summer down the shore?" Tony asked.

Artie shook his head. "Not really. I was interning at Hornstein, Drakeford, and Brown this summer. I drove down to our shore house Friday night or early Saturday morning and returned early Monday morning."

"Hornstein, Drakeford, and Brown? That's quite a prestigious firm." Tony raised his eyebrows.

"Thank you. My mentor, Professor Stolpen, helped me to get it. They said that if I get a three hundred or higher on the law exam, I can have a full-time position."

"And what about your family? Wouldn't you be expected to work for your family?" Tony asked bluntly.

"Poppy!" Mia admonished.

"No, Mia, it's a fair question." Artie leaned forward as he answered Tony. "It was clear since I was a kid that I was going to be the one to go to college. My brother, Matt, really wasn't very good academically. I mean he's smart and all but going to college wasn't his thing. I'm really quite lucky because my father allowed me to choose my vocation. Both he and my grandfather gave their blessings and permission for me to study Business Law and work at a firm in New York. Matt will work for the family. He's always been drawn to the family business and that world. I would prefer to work in an office."

"I see." Tony nodded and stood. "Artie, come join me out in the garden."

Mia and Ruth looked at each other as Tony led Artie through the house and into the yard. They walked through the garden talking for over an hour, and when they came back in, they were laughing, and Tony was patting Artie on the back.

SEVENTEEN

"CONGRATULATIONS, MIA." Tony held up his wine glass in a toast. "We all know how very hard you worked these past two years, and I'm sure I can speak for all of us when I say how proud we are of you."

"Thank you, Poppy." Mia's eyes twinkled as she placed her hand on her grandfather's. "And thank you for putting your differences aside and coming together to celebrate my graduation."

"We're honored to be included," Carla said as she nodded at Ruth, who smiled warmly back at her.

"Yes, thank you." Luca added.

Tony took Ruth's hand and said, "We know how important you are to Mia, and how much it means to have her family attend her graduation."

"Even still, we know tickets for the ceremony were limited, and we really appreciate your giving us the opportunity to attend." Luca wiped his mouth with his napkin.

Mia leaned back in her chair and took a sip of coffee. She never thought she'd see the day when her grandparents would be sitting in a restaurant having dinner with her Aunt Carla and Uncle Luca. But here they were, and Mia was grateful that her grandfather mellowed some over the last two years. She never did learn what he and Artie talked about in the garden that day they first met, but Tony seemed to truly like Artie. The two of them often spent time together tending to the garden, watching sports, and even playing chess. When she asked Ruth about allowing her Uncle Luca and Aunt Carla to attend her graduation ceremony, Mia expected some pushback. Instead, Ruth was very agreeable and said she would talk to Tony about it. Mia knew that even though it was incredibly hard for both Tony and Ruth, they kept an open mind when they got to know Artie, and now she hoped the same would be true with Uncle Luca and Aunt Carla. She would like nothing more than to bridge the gap between them. Now that Artie was working full time at Hornstein, Drakeford, and Brown, and she had accepted an entry-level position at CL Designs, it was time for them to start seriously talking about the next step in their relationship. Mia really wanted harmony between the families. Including her aunt and uncle at her graduation was just a small step forward and the real challenge, Mia knew, was going to be uniting Artie's family and her grandparents. For now, Mia was happy to sit back and enjoy the success of the first phase of her plan she called Operation Family Unity.

Artie looked around and said, "This place is incredible. I've heard about Tavern on the Green, but never thought I'd get to eat here."

"Me too," Mia added. "Dinner was so good. I saw there were horse and carriage rides outside, do you think we can take one?"

"You know what," Luca said as he reached into his pocket and handed money to Artie. "Why don't you two go ahead and enjoy, while we finish up our coffee and dessert."

"No, Uncle Luca. It's okay. I got it," Artie said as he stood and held out his hand to Mia. "Your chariot awaits."

Both Carla and Ruth looked on lovingly as Mia accepted Artie's hand and they walked out of the restaurant arm in arm.

"He really is a good kid." Luca said.

Tony nodded. "Yes, I have to agree with you there." He shifted awkwardly in his seat.

"They make a lovely couple," Ruth added.

The two couples sat in silence for a few moments.

"Tony look," Luca started. "Now that we have some time to talk, I'd really like to make amends between us." He leaned in. "I know how you felt about my brother, Dominick. I don't blame you. Truth is, I tried with him. I really did. I tried to set him straight since we were kids. There was nothing I could do to calm him down, get him to act right, teach him some respect." Luca shook his head. "I want you to know that I'm sorry for everything that happened with Rena. She deserved better."

Tony looked down, nodded, and moved his dessert fork back and forth. "I appreciate that."

"Please understand, the rest of us in the family are not like Dominick. In fact, when you get to know Artie's parents, you'll see they're salt of the earth people. Real kind, humble, and genuine."

"After getting to know Artie, I have no doubt that is true. But the fact of the matter is your family business is quite unethical and dangerous. I lose sleep most nights worrying what that will mean for Mia." Tony sat back in his chair.

"I won't insult you by defending the family business. But Artie has himself a great job at a major law firm and wants to pursue his independence."

"I see what you mean, but their safety cannot be guaranteed. There are still dangers to being a Bocelli."

"Tony, you know yourself, there's dangers in all facets of life. Think about it, how many of your vendors at the restaurant you're with now are connected? I would say, probably all of them."

Tony smirked, "Yeah, you're right."

"That makes you more involved in a family business like ours than Mia and Artie are. Look, I'm not trying to minimize your fears. With everything that's happened to you and your family, I get it. But Artie and Mia are pretty serious about each other, and I have it on good authority he's ready to ask your permission for her hand."

Tony nodded slowly. "I knew this time would come."

"Listen, the Bocelli Family is *not* the Esposito Family, we're far more loyal and united. Artie would like you to meet his parents and grandparents before he does anything. He respects you and values your opinion. He wants to do things the right way."

"Alright, we can do that," Tony conceded as Ruth put her arm around his shoulders and shared a smile with Carla.

"Very good." Luca leaned back and smiled. "Why don't we have dinner at our place?"

"That would be lovely," Ruth said.

"I'll give you a call, and we'll set it all up." Carla gave Ruth a knowing smile.

MIA COULDN'T BELIEVE her ears when Ruth told her they were invited for dinner at her Aunt Carla and Uncle Luca's house in Alpine to meet Artie's family. She had gotten the impression that Luca wanted to talk to her grandparents when he suggested she and Artie go for a carriage ride after their dinner together, but she never thought they would've made dinner plans. The thought of the upcoming gathering both excited and terrorized Mia. This meeting was inevitable, but even after two years of being with Artie, it seemed like it had snuck up on her quickly. She wanted her grandparents to see the wonderful and amazing people the Bocellis were, but she wasn't sure if Tony could get past the fact that Artie's grandfather was *Don* Bocelli. For Mia, the word *Don* was only a title. In the two years they were together, Mia didn't notice anything out of the ordinary when it came to Artie's family. They seemed like most other families she'd been around throughout her life, with the exception of living in mansions and having security guards around all the time. In fact, one of her favorite memories was the snowy Sunday they spent at Ray and Josie's house playing Monopoly with his grandfather. Nonnuccio gave Matt a run for his money that day, but Matt eventually won the game.

On their way to the house, Mia warned Tony that he would have to announce them at the security gate and that there would probably be a few guys hanging around the front and the back of the house. She knew that made him tense when he became silent during the rest of the drive. Mia was comforted that Ruth, as always, seemed to be more relaxed than Tony, and the big burly men that greeted Mia with strong hugs didn't even phase her.

Carla met them by the front door and greeted them with her usual charming sophistication. "Hello, I'm so happy we're doing this." She gave Ruth and Mia both a large embrace and kisses on each of their cheeks. "Don't tell me these are from the pastry shop?" She asked as she noticed the bakery box in Ruth's hands.

"Yes. Artie had said the family loves their pastries." Ruth gasped slightly as she took in the rest of the house. "Your house is just gorgeous," she said in awe.

"Thank you," Carla said humbly. "I'll give you a tour."

Luca hugged Mia and Ruth and then rushed forward with his arms extended. "Tony!" He reached out and shook Tony's hand and patted him on the back at the same time. "How were the directions? Did you find the place alright?"

"Yes. No problem at all."

"Wanna join me in a scotch?"

"I'm more of a bourbon man, actually." Tony shifted nervously.

"Ahh so is my father-in-law. Let's get you set up." He turned to Mia and said, "Artie and the others are in the family room."

Mia took a deep breath and made her way to the family room. *So far, so good*, she thought to herself. She ran her hands down the skirt of her dress and wondered if they would ever stop shaking.

"Hey, babe." Artie popped up from the couch and kissed her cheek. "This is it, huh. Operation Family Unity in full swing."

"Yeah." She looked around anxiously. "I should go with Grammy as Aunt Carla shows her the house." She craned her neck to see where Aunt Carla and Ruth were. "Should I go?" She looked at Artie. "Maybe I'll give them time alone to talk." She nodded. "I think I'll go find them." She said and turned to walk away.

"Hey. Come here." Artie pulled Mia back and embraced her. "They're fine. It'll be fine."

"Mia!" Josie bounded over to them. "How are you, my sweet?" She pulled Mia out of Artie's embrace and wrapped her arms around her tightly. "Where are your grandparents?"

"They're here. Grammy is with Aunt Carla getting a tour of the house, and Poppy is with Uncle Luca getting a drink."

"Good. That means my Ray'll be getting a drink with them, which means they'll be best friends in no time. I'll go find the ladies and introduce myself. Nonnina and Nonnuccio will be here shortly, I'm sure." Josie called out to Carla as she made her way down the hall.

Artie took Mia's hand, kissed her cheek, and led her to the couch where Vicky was sitting next to Matt with her arms crossed around her chest.

"What's going on?" Mia looked at Vicky.

"She did it again. Stood Matt up on another date."

"Daniella?" Mia asked surprised. "I thought things were better between you two," she said as she sat on Matt's other side.

"So did I."

"At least you weren't thinking about asking Nonnuccio permission to marry her," Vicky scoffed.

"Wait, what do you mean permission?" Mia looked at Artie.

Artie waved his hand casually. "It's more like a blessing. You know, the guy always asks the parents for their blessings to marry."

"It's a little more complicated than that." Vicky interjected and gave Artie a hard look. "Who we marry is a big deal. The family must be able to trust the spouses. It's complicated if they're an outsider, and their whole family has to be vetted. If they're from another family, then it gets political."

"I didn't know that." Suddenly it hit Mia that Artie's choice of wife wouldn't be his own. Her head began to spin. He wouldn't be able to marry just anyone. Especially not an outsider. But *was* she an outsider? Daniella seemed to think so. But what exactly *was* an outsider? Would her bloodline automatically make her an acceptable choice for Artie? This dinner was far more important than Mia had realized. They were here so the family could scrutinize her grandparents and determine if Artie and Mia could marry. Mia began to feel lightheaded. It all made sense to her now. In order for her to marry Artie, approvals had to be given. Mia shook her head and willed herself to snap out of her thoughts. After all, the family was always so welcoming and affectionate to her. Surely, they wouldn't be if they didn't think she would be a good match, would they?

"Matt, I'm getting really tired of Daniella doing this to you. Don't you think it's time you cut her loose once and for all." Artie said as he handed Mia a soda.

"Every time she does these things, I get so pissed off at her. But then, you *know*." Matt shrugged.

"No," Artie answered. "I don't know. I really don't get it."

Matt lowered his voice and looked around. "She wiggles her ass and … Bam, we're in bed."

Vicky and Mia groaned as Artie smacked Matt in the back of his head.

"You've got to be kidding me! That's what it is? It's all about the sex?" Vicky scowled.

"I'm tellin ya. I've had my fair share of girls, and none of them can do what she does."

Mia took Matt's hand. "Matt," she couldn't help but giggle. "I'm sure she's very talented, but I personally don't think she deserves your time or attention."

Artie tried to keep a straight face as he added, "Mia's right, enough's enough, already. It's time you get a nice girl and think about settling down."

Matt held up his hands in surrender. "When you're right, you're right. I'll tell her I'm done tomorrow. But if she gives me that sexy pout thing she does with her lips, I can't make any promises."

"Fine, then we'll blindfold you." Vicky raised her hands in disgust.

"Who's getting blindfolded?" Nonnuccio asked as he and Nonnina entered the room.

"We want to blindfold Matt so he can break it off with Daniella without looking at her," Vicky said as she rolled her eyes.

"Pff." Nonnina spit. "It's time you move on from that one. Find yourself a *nice* girl." She reached out to hug Mia. "Mia, where's your Grandma?"

"We're right here." Carla announced as she led Ruth and Josie into the room. "Ruth, these are my parents."

"It's so very nice to meet you Don and Donna Bocelli."

"Ah," Nonnuccio waved his hand. "We're just family today. Please. Armando," he said as he touched his chest. "And Gabriella." He gestured to Nonnina.

"I prefer, Ella," Nonnina said as she took Ruth by the arm and led her to the sunroom with Carla and Josie following behind.

Mia watched the women walk away and noticed Nonnina and Ruth smiling and nodding as they whispered with each other. That had to be a good sign, she thought. She looked at Artie who raised his eyebrows and grinned back at her. They all turned their heads as they heard laughter as Luca, Ray and Tony entered the room.

Nonnuccio looked at Tony and reached out his hand. "You must be Tony. I've heard nothing but good things. Please, here with the family, call me Armando."

"It's good to meet you, Armando. Mia is quite fond of both you and your wife."

"As we are her. She's a charming young lady."

"Thank you. We're quite proud of her." Tony looked over at Mia and smiled lovingly at her.

Mia smiled back at her grandfather and let out a long breath. The reality that not only did she have to get Nonnuccio's approval to marry Artie, but she needed Tony's approval also made her feel queasy. She and her grandfather had different experiences when it came to 'families.' The level of pain and devastation Tony suffered at the hands of Don Esposito was unfathomable. Although there was a chance that Mia's father's death was at the hands of Esposito as well, she didn't have the same type of loss. It was different for her. She never knew her father. She couldn't have the same crushing heartbreak for a man she had never met. Mia had no doubt that Tony was fond of Artie, but she couldn't be completely sure if he would give his blessing for her to marry into a 'family.' Even if that 'family' operated differently than the Esposito Family. In Tony's mind, they were all connected. Mia's hands began to shake again, and she forced herself to try to concentrate on the here and now.

When Rosie, the weekend maid, entered the room and

announced that dinner was ready to be served, Mia hoped that sitting at the dining table would calm her nerves.

"Thank you, Rosie," Luca said. "I'll get the ladies."

When Luca was out of earshot, Mia overheard Nonnuccio whisper to Tony. "I don't know why they need maids and such. There's nothing like my wife's cooking, and I know my daughter can cook just as good." He looked at Tony's glass and added, "Bourbon, eh? Now you're talkin. Let's fill up our glasses. We can chase the wine with it." Mia hoped that it was a good sign that the two men that would pretty much determine her fate were bonding over drinks.

Artie was very attentive to Mia during dinner. He made sure to put his hand on her leg or her hand when he sensed her nervousness rise. It seemed that everyone was enjoying themselves as the conversation flowed smoothly and lightly throughout the dinner. By the time dessert was served, Mia began to relax, and she enjoyed the friendly conversation and warm feeling everyone seemed to share.

Vicky took a final bite of her Sfogliatella and announced, "Ange and I are going bowling, and Matt you're coming."

Everyone at the table fell silent and stared at her, then turned to stare at Matt who was dead silent. He wrinkled his face and said, "Bowling? I'm not going bowling. What are ya crazy? What do I wanna do that for?"

"Because they have cheap beer, and you get to throw a sixteen-pound ball down a lane to purposely knock something over."

Mia chuckled to herself as she noticed everyone at the table looked like they were watching an intense tennis match during the interchange.

Angelo nodded his head toward Matt and added, "Come on, man. You'll get your frustrations out. My cousins'll be meeting us there, and they're always good for a laugh."

Matt considered the proposition and said, "Okay, but you're buying the beer."

Mia walked with Vicky toward the door as Angelo, Artie, and Matt discussed the last time they had bowled and what their best scores were.

"Bowling?" Mia said looking skeptically at Vicky.

Vicky laughed. "Yeah. It was the only thing I could think of to get Matt out of the house and around Ange's cousin, Theresa. She's sexy and spunky and I just know Matt'll love her."

"So, you're setting Matt up?" Mia laughed.

"Shh. Lower your voice." Vicky looked over at the guys. "My brother is a mastermind when it comes to finances and business, he doesn't let anyone get over on him, and he could make millions selling sand in the Sahara. His only blemish is Daniella, and that's all about to change. I'm done with her shenanigans concerning my brother, and I think it's time Matt sees there's better options out there. The best way for Matt to get over her is to fall for someone who is just as lively as she is, but who isn't a manipulative shrew. Theresa is perfect for Matt. I just know it. She's gorgeous, confident, and classy."

Mia nodded her head. "Okay, I can see that. It could work."

Vicky lowered her voice. "No one knows my intentions, not even Ange. Matt would never consider any girl I tried to set him up with, and it's best if Theresa doesn't know either. It's all got to happen naturally. I just have to create the opportunities for them to be around each other."

"This is going to be good."

"Vick! Come on let's go, we're all waiting." Angelo called from the front door.

"Gotta go."

As they started walking back toward the dining room, Artie

grabbed Mia by the waist, turned her around, and said, "I think Operation Family Unity is going well. What do you think?"

"I'll know better during the car ride home. If Poppy doesn't talk, it means he's not happy. If he's chatty, then he had a good time."

They both turned their heads toward a wave of laughter coming from the dining room, "I'm thinking he's going to be chatty." Artie said as he kissed Mia on the cheek.

"What's so funny?" Artie asked as he led Mia back to her seat at the table.

"I was just telling the story of how you would run down the street in just your diaper calling after the mailman back when we lived in Wallington," Josie said still laughing. "Ray was working a lot back then, and this one took to calling the mailman 'Daddy'." She waved her arm. "Oh, what the neighbors must've thought."

Ray laughed and put his arm around Josie's chair, "Thank God the mailman was a redhead and pale as snow. Artie looked nothing like him."

Tony laughed and said, "My father used to tease my mother all the time about the butcher."

The room grew silent, and Mia noticed that Artie's family all looked down at the table. Tony continued nervously, "It was all in good fun. He didn't mean anything by it."

Nonnuccio nodded still looking down, and Nonnina turned in her chair so she couldn't look at everyone at the table.

"I can hear him clearly even to this day," Nonnuccio whispered. "Anna if I didn't know better, I'd think you were taking up with that butcher, Guiseppe. Why else would he give you the best cuts of meat."

Ruth gasped as Tony's mouth fell open. "How? How would you know what he said?"

Nonnuccio remained silent and slowly lifted his head to look at Tony. "We were friends."

"I don't understand." Tony shook his head.

"We were all friends. Us, Sal, and Anna. I wasn't sure if you remembered or even knew for that matter." Nonnuccio took his wife's hand.

Nonnina turned in her chair and sat up straight. "Your parents were our dear, dear friends. We'd play cards most Friday nights and go to dinner at least once or twice a month. She and I spoke on the phone every morning while we drank our coffee." Her voice broke. "Not a day goes by—" She jumped up and ran to the bathroom. Mia could hear her sobs grow with intensity as she closed the bathroom door.

Mia couldn't read the expression on both of her grandparents faces. She, herself, was shocked and didn't know what to say.

"How could you possibly have been friends with my parents?" Tony asked and just as the words left his mouth his eyes grew large. "You set them up! You told your buddy, Esposito, all about them and where they'd be." He slammed his fist on the table.

Luca walked over to Tony and put his hand on Tony's shoulder. "It wasn't like that, Tony. Hear my father-in-law out."

"No, it wasn't like that at all." Nonnuccio said shaking his head. "I had no idea about what happened to your family back in Italy. I knew your father from way back in our masonry days. We worked together and got to be friends, and then we got the wives together. Sal and Anna knew all about my life and the Bocelli Family."

"Now hold on right there. That I know is a lie. If there was one thing my father preached it was to stay away from people like Esposito. 'No good would come out of doing business with people like that.' He would say."

"You're right. Your father didn't trust Carmine or the way he did his business. He knew I was different and ran my family *my* way. Many, many nights we would sit together and share a bottle of chianti and top it off with Sambuca." Nonnuccio shook his head. "Your father sure loved his Sambuca." He waved away the memory with his hand. "We would often talk business together. He gave me a lot of good advice through the years on how to keep the focus on business and not violence." Nonnuccio refilled his and Tony's whiskey glasses as Nonnina returned to the dining room wiping her eyes.

"We were at your grand opening. Salvatore Brunos. We were there." She looked at Ruth as she spoke.

Ruth's face brightened as she remembered. "Yes. Now I remember. Ella and Manny. All night I kept thinking I knew you from somewhere, but I just couldn't figure it out. Anna was so proud to introduce you to me. She said you were her closest friends along with Vic and Mary." Ruth reached out and grabbed Nonnina's hand. "I remember her saying her day couldn't begin until she had her daily coffee and gab fest." She stood and the two women embraced.

Nonnina nodded. "Every day she would tell me all about what was happening with all of you. She worried about you when you first moved in, but she loved you like you were her own."

Ruth's eyes filled with tears, and she put her hand on Tony's shoulder. Tony turned to Nonnuccio. "Manny? *You're* Manny?"

"Yes, that's right." Nonnuccio nodded.

"My father always said, 'My friend, Manny, now that's a man of integrity and principles.'" Tony said in disbelief.

"It was Salvatore that kept me in check. He was my trusted advisor when it came to integrity and principles." Nonnuccio shook his head and looked Tony in the eye. "I didn't know. I didn't know what Carmine was gonna do." His eyes became glassy as he choked.

"I would've given up everything to save him and your mother." He looked down at his hands and balled them into fists. "When Carmine told me what he'd done, I lost it. I broke my hand punching him. He told me that was the first and last time he would ever let me get away with that, and if I loved my family and wanted to keep them safe, I would understand that it was just a business decision."

Tony sat back and rubbed his face with his hand.

"I got the message he was sending, and our friendship dissolved. We respect each other as associates, but I do not respect the man and leader that he is." Nonnuccio leaned in. "Since your parent's death, I've changed how I do business. I focus on construction and building. I won't get involved with anything that has to do with violence if I can help it. The Meadowlands? Atlantic City? That's our bread and butter. I don't like loan sharking, and I have a strict rule to stay away from the drugs and junk that's out on the streets. That's a personal vow I made to your father the moment I learned of his death."

"I just can't believe any of this," Tony said softly shaking his head.

"Your father's advice was accurate when he said nothing good comes from doing business with people like Carmine. But Tony, your father was a very pragmatic person. You can't be in the masonry or restaurant business and not have some business with at least one of the top New York families. Your father knew what was what and he saw and judged people for who they were. He was a smart and shrewd businessman, but he was also open minded to people's true nature."

Mia leaned into Artie as he put his arm around her. She could see all of the emotions that played across Tony's face. His glassy eyes told her he was reliving that horrible night they were killed, yet the serene smile he gave to Nonnuccio was warm and tender.

Mia looked at Ruth who still clung to Nonnina's hand while tears streamed down her face.

"That's exactly who my father was," Tony said as he nodded. "I've put a wall up all these years, and every once in a while I'll let in a memory, but tonight you've brought him to life once again. He spoke of you often. I didn't make the connection because he always called you Manny, and he never let on that you were *Don Bocelli*."

"I was *never* Don Bocelli to Sal. We were like brothers. I admired and respected him far more than any man I've ever known." Nonnuccio lifted his glass in a toast and took a long sip.

Nonnina said softly. "Their funeral was a wonderful tribute to their beautiful souls. We said our goodbyes to them privately at the cemetery after the service, and then thought it was probably best to give your family privacy. We didn't know how you would feel about us once you found out the truth, and we wouldn't blame you even now if you have reservations." She squeezed Ruth's hand.

"Sal and Anna spoke so highly of both of you, and they were both excellent judges of character." Ruth nodded. "I, for one, am looking forward to getting to know their nearest and dearest friends." She stood and the two women embraced. "Tony?"

Tony nodded. "I'll be honest. I feel like I've been sideswiped and quite frankly, am still in a bit of shock. But yes, I think I'd be open to seeing you through my father's eyes."

Nonnuccio nodded slowly. "Very good."

Luca and Ray both stood and lifted their glasses. "A toast." Ray said. "To family and friends, old and new."

"Here, here." Tony and Luca said in unison.

Mia locked eyes with Josie's and they both smiled as they used their napkins to wipe the tears streaming down their faces.

"Gentlemen, why don't we enjoy a cigar? Yes?" Nonnuccio said as he led the men toward the back deck. "Tony, I still smoke your father's favorites." He stopped and turned back toward Artie. "Artie, come, join us for whiskey and cigars."

Artie eagerly jumped to his feet and almost knocked his chair over. He smiled at Mia and said, "I gotta go with them. Are you okay Stella?"

Mia nodded and watched him as he eagerly made his way outside.

Ruth plopped down in her chair and let out a long breath and shook her head as Nonnina sat next to her and did the same.

"I can't believe you knew my great-grandparents," Mia said, looking at Nonnina. "Why didn't you tell me?"

"This was a conversation that Nonnuccio needed to have with your Poppy first."

Mia nodded. She understood the complexity of the situation. Her grandfather had spent many years feeling anger and resentment over his parents' murder, and she wouldn't blame him if he harbored those feelings toward Nonnuccio because of his relationship with Esposito. Mia had suspected that Nonnuccio wasn't as close to Don Esposito as they once were. She had not seen him at any family parties or gatherings other than the annual Fourth of July party each year. Even then, Esposito only made an appearance for a short time and was often gone within an hour. She now hoped that Tony would see Nonnuccio for the man his own father was friends with and not direct his resentment toward him.

"This is really quite overwhelmingly wonderful," Ruth said as she held up her coffee cup so Rosie could pour her a refill.

"It is wonderful," Carla agreed. "I remember your in-laws. Your mother-in-law's laugh would fill up an entire room."

"Yes," Ruth said fondly. "It was hard not to smile when she was around."

"I wish I could've met her." Josie added. "She sounds wonderful."

Nonnina looked at Mia. "She was wonderful. You remind me of her."

Mia sat up straight. "Really?" She looked at Ruth. "Grammy, you've said that too."

"Yes." Nonnina tilted her head, taking in Mia's face. "There are a few facial expressions you make that sometimes catch me off guard. It's as if I'm looking at her again."

Carla sat next to Mia and put her arm around her. "Mia, sweetheart, there's something we need to discuss."

Mia locked eyes with Ruth who shrugged her shoulders and returned the look of wonder.

Josie placed her hand on Mia's. "It's clear how much you and Artie love each other, and I have it on good authority he's outside right now asking for your hand in marriage."

Mia gasped as tears of happiness grew in her eyes.

"We all love you very much, my sweet, and there is nothing we would like better than for you to be Artie's wife," Josie continued.

Carla turned Mia's head toward her own. "But Mia, you need to think clearly about what it will mean to marry into the family."

Nonnina sat up straight and spoke in an authoritative voice. "While it is true Artie will continue to work at his present job, you will both still be *part* of the family." She paused and looked Mia in the eye. "The family will always be loyal to you both and will do everything possible to ensure your safety and innocence when it comes to the family business." She then turned and met Ruth's eyes. "Don Bocelli has already made contracts with the Esposito Family and the New York families that will keep you protected at all costs. We want you to have a prosperous and peaceful life together."

Mia's head started to spin. All she could hear was that Artie was asking for her hand in marriage and his family had already given their blessings. She didn't worry about what it meant to be a part of the Bocelli Family, in her mind she already felt like part of the family. She couldn't see any reason why she should be concerned about making it official.

Carla squeezed Mia's hand. "Mia, sweetheart, you have to know it's not always easy being a part of this life." She looked over at Ruth. "But the women of this family, Donna Bocelli, Josephine, myself, we are a council unified in ensuring that the family never forgets the integrity and principles that Don Bocelli holds dear."

"There is nothing I want more," Mia said choking back tears.

Josie reached across the table and took Ruth's hand in her own. "Ruth, we would like to ask your permission and blessing for Mia to join her life with Artie's and become a treasured member of our family."

Ruth released her hand from Josie's and put it to her chest. "I … I just don't know," she said slowly. "I have so many concerns." She shook her head.

"I'm sure you do." Nonnina leaned in toward her. "I vow to you that Mia and your entire family will be safe and protected from anyone. Most especially the Esposito Family."

"Our families will be united. I understand that you have to have some allegiance to Carmine Esposito, but we cannot."

"You will not have to." Donna Bocelli reassured her.

"I'm not sure you understand. My husband cannot even be in the same room as that man. It would kill him."

"Oh, my dear." Nonnina put her arm around Ruth. "I *do* understand. The men, well they follow the old traditions in showing respect by inviting the heads of the other families to major family events like weddings and christenings. But we, the women of this family, we make sure the troublesome ones do *not* attend."

"I'm not sure I follow you."

Nonnina stood. "The Bocelli Sisterhood is *very* powerful and *very* persuasive. Have no doubt, Anna Russo's tenacity and commitment lives on within me, and I promise you, you will *never* have anything to worry about."

Mia caught Ruth's eye and gave her a pleading look. Ruth stood and took Nonnina's hands. "Anna Russo was more like a mother to me than my own mother was. She considered her friendship with you and your husband as one of her life's greatest blessings next to her family. I think she would be honored for her great-granddaughter to become a part of your family."

Mia squealed in delight, jumped up from her chair and hugged Ruth. "Thank you, Grammy," she whispered in Ruth's ear. She felt a tap on her shoulder and when she turned around saw Artie kneeling on one knee holding an open ring box.

"Mia, I knew the minute I met you and we bonded over sausage sandwiches that you were something special. But I didn't know at that time how you would become part of my heart, part of my being. All that's good in my life is made better with you in it. Here in front of our families, I ask you, will you marry me, my Stella Splendente?"

Mia fell to her knees and hugged Artie, "Undoubtedly, yes! I'd be honored to marry you. You are all I need in this life."

Everyone in the room cheered, as Artie slid the most beautiful two-carat Tiffany engagement ring Mia had ever seen on her finger. Mia stared at her finger as tears streamed down her face. She had never been happier.

EIGHTEEN

TWO WEEKS LATER, Mia and Ruth were invited to Nonnina's house in Wayne for lunch and wedding planning. Ruth had surprised Mia with a pile of bridal magazines the night before and they sat together at the kitchen table making a binder filled with ideas for wedding dresses, bridal bouquets, bridesmaid dresses, and color schemes. Mia knew Ruth shared this tradition with both Janet and Nancy when they got married, and Mia was excited to do it for her own wedding. On the way over to Nonnina's, Mia and Ruth talked about Mia's new job at CL Designs.

"How do you like your job?" Ruth asked. "We haven't really gotten a chance to talk about it much."

"Grammy, it's amazing. I love the firm. It's really small. The owner, Carlo, he's the architect, then there's Angela she's the interior designer. She's kind of old, though, and I can tell that Carlo likes my ideas. I have a feeling she may be retiring soon and hopefully, I'll get to fill her shoes. Carlo's wife, Maria, is like the office manager. She runs everything."

"From what I understand, they are one of the most successful firms in New Jersey. My friend, Lydia, had seen an article in *New Jersey Monthly* that featured them."

Mia nodded. "Yup. Carlo opened his office in Montclair about ten years ago. Before that he worked for a firm in New York. And get this, he said maybe within a month or so, I can start meeting with clients by myself."

"That'll be wonderful," Ruth said as Mia pulled into the driveway. "Is this it? Is this their house?"

"This is it. What's wrong?"

"Nothing. Nothing's wrong. I'm just surprised. Carla's house was a modern mansion, and this house ..." Ruth hesitated.

"Isn't?" Mia laughed.

"I'm just surprised that's all. I guess I expected their house to be different."

"Nonnuccio and Nonnina had this house built over twenty-five years ago, and they said they don't see any reason to change it."

Mia got out of the car and took in the large white colonial with black shutters. She really did like it even though it was outdated. Every time she was there, she imagined all of the ways she could update it without losing its warm, comfortable charm. She especially liked the large front porch and the property the house sat on. It was set far off the road, and after passing through the iron gates, the tree-lined road led to a circular driveway with a fountain in the middle. In the back, Nonnuccio had put in a beautiful patio and garden complete with a fishpond and gazebo. She took the binder from Ruth's hand, and as they walked toward the house, she waved to Marco who sat in the guard house that was discreetly positioned between the driveway and the wooded area.

Nonnina greeted them as they walked along the path. "Good afternoon, ladies," she said smiling. "Ruth, thank you so much for stopping at the bakery."

"Of course, it's my pleasure," Ruth said as Nonnina leaned in and kissed both of her cheeks.

"I'm sad to say Carla couldn't make it today. She's tending to a situation that just popped up, but Josie should be here any minute."

As they walked in, Ruth complimented Nonnina on her house and the view of the backyard. Just as they got comfortable at the dining table, Josie had arrived carrying a calendar and a notebook.

"It's so lovely to see you again, Ruth," Josie said as she gave Ruth a warm embrace. "Mia, my sweet, how's everything?"

Mia gave her a large hug and a kiss on each cheek. "It's great. I think I already love my new job."

"Good, good. You'll have to tell me all about it."

"Ladies," Nonnina said brightly, "are we ready to get down to business?"

Josie and Ruth excitedly began to share their ideas as they flipped through the binder Mia and Ruth had put together the night before.

"Hello ladies don't mind me, I'm just passing through," Nonnuccio said as he stopped at the table and grabbed a cannoli from the platter. "How's the planning coming along?"

"We've just started," Nonnina said as she handed him a napkin.

"I know there's a concern about Carmine attending, but I must insist that he receive an invitation. We may not be friends any longer, but I cannot put the family at risk by offending him."

Ruth sat up straight, but before she could speak, Nonnina placed her hand on Ruth's arm and tapped it three times.

"Of course, darling. We understand. Now why don't you leave all the planning to us. Hmm?" She smiled sweetly at Nonnuccio, handed him another cannoli, and blew out a long breath after he was out of earshot.

"Ella," Ruth began, but before she could finish her sentence, Nonnina had tapped her arm again.

"There is no need to worry, Ruth, I assure you receiving an invitation and attending are two very different things."

"But you can't be certain he won't attend."

"Leave it to me." Nonnina said with authority as she opened her personal monthly planner and began to flip through the pages. "I've done quite a bit of research, and Mia, if you don't mind, the best date for you and Artie to marry will be Saturday, October 9th."

"But that's only four months away," Mia said in shock.

"Ella, I don't really think we can pull together a wedding in that short amount of time," Ruth added.

"Why October 9th?" Josie asked.

"I have it on good authority the heads of the New York families will be sequestered from October 8th through the 10th for their annual Commission meeting."

Josie nodded and pointed to Nonnina, "You're a genius." She turned to Ruth and said, "If you don't want Don Esposito to attend, it must be on the ninth. He'll be at that meeting." She then turned to Mia and took her hand. "Mia, my sweet, I know it's short notice, but I promise you, you will have the wedding of your dreams."

"Can we even get a wedding dress in time?" Mia said looking around the table.

Nonnina chuckled, "Oh my dear, a close friend of mine is the owner of the most famous bridal shop in Manhattan. She's assured me that if we get you in there by the end of the month, she'll make certain you will have any dress you want in plenty of time for your wedding."

Mia's eyes brightened and she turned to Ruth, "What do you think?"

Ruth smiled at Mia as she said, "A fall wedding would be beautiful. Why don't you call Artie and discuss it with him."

Mia jumped up from the table and ran to the kitchen to call Artie. She was relieved that he had answered the phone by the third ring.

"Hello?"

Without taking a breath, Mia began to ramble. "Hey honey it's me. Nonnina said we should have the wedding on October 9th. Your mom said we can have the wedding of our dreams. All I have to do is go to the city by the end of this month to pick out my wedding gown. It could be done on time. Don Esposito won't be able to make it that day. Nonnuccio said we have to invite him. What do you think?"

"Stella?"

"Yes, it's me. What do you think about the ninth for the wedding?"

"July 9th?"

"No! October 9th. Weren't you listening?"

"Ok, babe." Artie chuckled. "Can you start again, but slower this time."

Mia took a deep breath. "Nonnina said the best day to have the wedding would be October 9th so that Don Esposito wouldn't be able to go. But that's only about four months away. Your mom said it wouldn't be a problem, and we could have the wedding of our dreams. What do you think?"

Artie was quiet for a moment and then said, "I'm free October 9th. What about you?"

"Yes!" She squealed. "It's not too soon, is it? We're not rushing things, are we?"

"Stella, I knew by the end of that summer we met that I wanted to marry you. Why wait any longer?"

"I love you."

"And I love you, my Stella Splendente." Artie lowered his voice to a whisper. "Hey, not to change the subject or anything, but guess who's coming over to watch the Yankee game tonight with Matt."

"Daniella?"

"Nope! Ange's cousin, Theresa!"

"You're kidding?"

"I guess they hit it off. Vicky warned me to play it cool, and I really wanna tease Matt about it, but I don't want him running back to Daniella either."

"I agree with Vicky," Mia said. "Do you think it would be bad if we stayed in to watch the game with them instead of going to Houlihan's for dinner?"

Artie laughed, "You read my mind! Come on over when you're done there, and you can tell me all about our wedding plans."

Mia floated back to the dining room and walked in just as she heard Ruth ask about an engagement party.

"Oh Grammy, we don't need an engagement party."

"Nonsense," Ruth said. "Of course, you should have an engagement party, and a bridal shower too."

"You absolutely must have an engagement party and shower," Carla said as she entered the room.

"Aunt Carla, you made it," Mia exclaimed as she jumped up to hug Carla.

After everyone greeted Carla and filled her in on the details of the wedding, she said, "Mia, we want to celebrate you and Artie's love and the joining of our families. I insist we have the engagement party at my place."

"Thank you," Mia said humbly. She then hesitated and added, "Can I ask a favor? My sister, Nancy, is starting a catering business, and she really is a great cook. Would it be okay if she catered it?"

"That's a great idea. She's family. I'll call her and we can plan everything together."

Nonnina and Josie were huddled together looking at their calendars. "I believe Saturday, July 11th, might be a good day for the engagement party." Nonnina said as she winked at Ruth.

"That'll work just fine for our family," Ruth nodded and gave Nonnina an understanding, grateful smile.

"Now, I just have to inform Helena Esposito that she will need to reschedule her great-grandchild's christening to that day."

"Wait, what?" Mia said. "I don't want to cause any trouble."

"It's no trouble at all." Nonnina stood. "In fact, Mia, why don't you join me in the office while I call her. It will be a good opportunity for you to see how to handle situations such as this."

Mia followed Nonnina into her office and sat down next to the antique mahogany writing desk. Nonnina moved the phone closer to Mia and started to dial. "In situations involving other families, you must always maintain authority and dignity. Never, ever reveal your emotions. I admit that can be hard, but you must learn quickly."

She sat up straight and spoke into the receiver, "Helena. Hello Darling, I understand congratulations are in order. A granddaughter is such a blessing."

Mia could hear excited chatter through the phone but couldn't make out what was being said.

"Robin really is a beautiful name even though it isn't from the old country." Nonnina raised her eyebrows as she looked at Mia. "Helena, we need to discuss the christening. I'm sure you'll want the ceremony to be sooner rather than later. Might I suggest July 11th?" She nodded her head. "I realize the invitations have been printed, but you see, I'm afraid I'm going to have to insist that it be that day. Our Arthur just got engaged to Mia."

Mia was mesmerized as she took in Nonnina's charm and authority.

"Thank you, yes, we're thrilled. But we have a dilemma. Of course, we would love for you and Carmine to attend the engagement party, but you remember the terrible events that occurred with Sal and Anna Russo? I would like to prevent old wounds from blistering, and the only way I can prevent that is if little Robin's christening is on that very same day." Nonnina winked at Mia. "You understand, I'm sure."

Mia then watched Nonnina tilt her head slightly.

"Now Helena, I know the kind of pull you have within St. Alphonso's, especially with Father Bonelli. Perhaps a nice donation could persuade him to change the date to the 11th due to some, I don't know, unforeseen church business? Otherwise, I'm afraid an Esposito family secret you hold near and dear might accidentally be leaked out. It would be a shame, really, after all that was done to maintain Antonia's reputation."

Mia sat back in her chair and wondered what kind of secret the Esposito's had that would be big enough to persuade Donna Esposito to change the date of the christening.

Nonnina turned in her chair slightly and said into the phone, "That's a chance I'm willing to take. This is *very* important to my family." She nodded and smiled triumphantly. "Thank you, Helena, I knew I could count on you."

Nonnina straightened her back as she hung up the receiver. She turned to Mia and said, "Mia, as a member of this family it will be important for you to always pay attention and file every nugget of information you know to be true in a file cabinet in the back of your mind. Knowledge is a powerful tool when it comes to protecting the family." She leaned forward. "But remember, that works both ways. Never, ever share or reveal anything personal to anyone outside of our immediate family. You cannot always trust people, and you must always be guarded with everyone including close family associates and extended family members. Trust can be a tricky thing, it can be the glue that keeps a family loyal, but it can also be the blade that cuts it apart."

Mia nodded, "I understand."

"Be sure that you do. The women of this family are underestimated. We not only have incredible strength and resilience, but we have an enormous power to do *whatever* it takes to protect this family. And very soon, you will be one of us."

Mia pulled in a deep breath and slowly released it as she was led back to the dining room.

AFTER DROPPING RUTH off at home, Mia went straight to Ray and Josie's house. Vicky whipped open the door before Mia got a chance to ring the bell.

"How'd it go? Tell me everything. I hear you're getting married in a few months," she squealed.

"Vick, geez, let her in." Artie came up behind Vicky, picked her up, and placed her to the side. "Hey, babe," he said as he kissed Mia hello.

Mia burst out laughing. "Did you just really pick up your sister and move her out of the doorway?"

"Yes, he did!" Vicky scoffed.

"Sorry, but you guys can talk wedding when the game starts at eight, until then she's mine." Artie put his sister in a head lock and rubbed his knuckles on her head.

"Bite me!" Vicky said as she pushed him off of her. "Okay, we'll talk wedding when the game starts. Besides we only have a few minutes to talk about Matt and Theresa before they get back with the pizza."

"She's here already?" Mia said as they sat at the dining room table.

"She's been here since three," Vicky nodded. "Wait until you see Matt around her. I don't recognize him." Vicky leaned in and looked at Artie, who sat across the table from her. "He's acting like you did when you met Mia."

Artie looked around quickly. "What do you mean?"

"Ha. You were all shy and weird around Mia at first, and when you weren't around her, all you did was talk about her."

"I did not. I mean, okay, I was interested, but I kept it cool. Matt spent an hour and a half in the bathroom before Theresa got here."

"I know. I caught him using my hair gel." Vicky laughed. "That was before he took a bath in that Halston cologne he got at the mall yesterday."

"Cologne? Hair gel?" Mia smiled slyly. "Someone's got it bad. Did he do any of that for Daniella?"

Vicky sat up straight. "Nope. Sometimes he didn't even shower before going out with her."

"I tried to talk to him about that." Artie shook his head. "He just blew me off."

"What's Theresa like?"

"Mee, you're going to love her. She's really sweet, but in a sassy sort of way," Vicky said.

"That's a good way of putting it." Artie agreed. "She seems really nice, but I really can't see her being a pushover."

"Interesting," Mia said. "And she's Angelo's cousin?"

"Yup, so she knows what's what in terms of the family." Vicky raced to the window and pulled back the curtain. "They're back."

Mia looked at Vicky and Artie and said, "Guys, act natural. Don't stare at the door."

Matt and Theresa walked into the dining room laughing, and Mia noticed Matt was beaming.

"Hey, Mia," he said. "This is Theresa, Ange's cousin."

"Hi. Here, let me help you with that," Mia said as she jumped up from the table and took a large bag of food from her hands.

"Thank you," Theresa said. "Congratulations on your engagement."

Mia chuckled and looked at her left hand. "Thanks, I'm still on cloud nine."

"I'm sure you are. Your ring is beautiful."

"Thank you," Artie and Mia said in unison. Artie's face turned red and then he said, "Madone, how much food did you get? I thought we were just having pizza."

"Yeah, but when we got to Paisano's they were making calzones, so I got a few of them too. I figure we'll eat it all." Matt shrugged.

"Theresa, sit here next to me," Vicky said as she pulled out the empty chair. "I'd much rather sit next to you than my brother."

After seeing how heartless Daniella was toward Matt, Mia found herself to be protective of him and wanted to learn as much about Theresa as she could without coming across as nosey. As Matt, Artie, and Vicky were caught up debating which calzone tasted better, Mia saw her opportunity to strike up a conversation.

"Vicky mentioned, you're Angelo's cousin," Mia said as she passed a napkin to Theresa.

"Yes," Theresa said. "Our fathers are brothers. Angelo's father, my Uncle Rocky, actually works for the Bocelli Family, and my father is a cop in Union City."

"I went to school with a girl who moved to Lyndhurst from Union City. Did you grow up there?"

"No. My parents lived there when they first got married, but once my mom got pregnant with my older sister, they moved to Fair Lawn," Theresa said.

"I think we played football against Fair Lawn," Mia said brightly.

"I bet we might've been at the same games," Theresa smiled. "I was a cheerleader and never missed a game."

Mia laughed. "I was too clumsy to be a cheerleader, but my boyfriend, at the time, was a football player, so I never missed a game either."

"So what are you doing now? Mia asked.

"I'm a secretary at a small accounting office in Carlstadt."

"You must be busy during tax season, I bet," Mia said as she grabbed another piece of pizza.

"Tax season is the worst," Theresa waved her hand. "I have to work tons of overtime. But I was able to save enough to buy a new car, so I guess there's a bright side. Matt told me you're an Interior Designer."

Mia sat up straight. "I guess, I am," she mused. "I just graduated school and started my first job at a design firm."

"I knew college wasn't the right choice for me. I did okay in high school, but never had an interest in going to college. I went to secretary school for nine months, and they helped me get my job."

"You know, college definitely isn't for everyone. I'm the first person in my family to have gone to any kind of school after high school. Yet, I'd say they're all doing well for themselves."

"Same with my family. I have a distant cousin that graduated Montclair State College with a degree, but that's about it," Theresa shrugged. "I do like my job and the people I work with."

"That's really important," Mia nodded. She smiled as Matt reached his arm around Theresa's chair and rubbed her shoulder.

"How are you feeling?" He asked her.

"Are you not feeling well?" Vicky looked at Theresa with concern.

Theresa chuckled and shook her head. "I'm not sick, just tired. We went dancing at Butterfield's last night and then to the diner for breakfast."

Vicky smirked at Mia and said, "My brother didn't get plastered last night, did he?"

Theresa looked back and forth between Matt and Vicky. "Who Matt? No way. We only had a couple of drinks."

Matt sat up straight and nodded. "Those days are over for me. No need to get plastered anymore." He looked at Theresa and blushed.

"Really, man?" Artie said. "Good for you. That's really great."

"You are so good for my brother," Vicky said as she squeezed Theresa's arm. "But why didn't you invite Ange and me? We love dancing."

"Next time," Matt said and took a sip from his soda and stifled a burp.

Mia sat back in her chair. She liked Theresa and agreed with Vicky that she was very good for Matt. Mia could see how much Matt liked her, and she sensed that the feeling was mutual for Theresa, as well. There was an easiness between them, and they were very endearing together.

Josie shuffled into the dining room with a large bowl of popcorn. "Here we go. I just popped it fresh with lots of butter," she said as she placed the bowl on the table and started clearing away the remnants of pizza and calzones.

"Thanks, Ma," Artie said as he pushed a handful into his mouth.

"Hey," Vicky scolded him. "Save some for the rest of us."

"What? There's plenty." Artie rolled his eyes.

Matt picked up the bowl of popcorn with his left hand and held out his right hand. "Come on Ter, let's get comfortable on the couch, the game's about to start."

Artie kissed Mia's cheek. "Do you wanna watch the game with us?"

"Not on your life," Vicky answered for Mia. "It's time for wedding talk. Hey Theresa," Vicky called out. "You don't have to hang with them if you don't want. Come back in here and join us for some girl talk."

Theresa popped her head back into the dining room. "I love the Yankees and never miss a game if I can help it."

"We'll have girl talk next time then." Mia smiled. After Theresa was out of earshot, she whispered to Vicky, "She's perfect for him."

Over the next hour Mia told Vicky about the wedding plans, and together they went through Mia's wedding binder and magazines looking for ideas on dresses and flower arrangements. Every so often they would hear either cheers or screams coming from the living room, and they were both amused when Theresa was more animated over the game than Matt.

When the doorbell rang, Vicky said, "That's Ange. Mia, can you let him in? I'm gonna get some more soda from downstairs."

Mia pulled away from the table just as the doorbell rang two more times. "Alright, I'm coming," she laughed as she pulled open the door.

"Hmph." Daniella rolled her eyes as she pushed passed Mia into the house. "I should've known you'd be here."

"Daniella? What are *you* doing here?"

"I'm here for Matt. Oh yeah, I heard about your engagement."

Mia nodded slowly not quite sure what she should say.

"Hey Ange. It's about time you got here," Artie started to say as he walked toward the front door. "Daniella? Did Matt know you were coming over?"

"Hi Artie. I wanted to surprise him. Is he watching the game?" She said as she walked through the house into the living room.

"What's going on?" Vicky asked as she entered the room holding two bottles of soda.

"Daniella's here!" Mia whispered, and the three of them swiftly followed Daniella.

"Hey, honey," Daniella said sweetly. "I've been missing you. I've called you a number of times." She stopped short as she saw

Matt sitting on the couch with his arm around Theresa. "Who the hell is this?" She demanded.

Matt leapt up from the couch. "What are you doing here?"

"Who is this, Matt?" Daniella's voice grew louder.

"Theresa," Matt said and held out his hand to Theresa. "This is Daniella. I've told you about her."

Theresa nodded. "Daniella, right. I'm Theresa."

"What do you mean, you told her about *me*? You didn't tell me about *her*!"

"You two obviously have a lot to talk about," Theresa said as she walked around Daniella and toward the door.

Vicky grabbed Theresa's arm and said, "Oh *no*. You stay."

"Matt, what's going on? I haven't seen you in weeks and you haven't answered any of my calls."

Matt took a deep breath and let it out slowly. "I suppose I probably should've called you back, I thought you would've gotten the hint. I'm seeing Theresa now, and I don't want to hang out with you anymore."

"You're seeing *her*?" Daniella looked at Theresa in disgust. "You don't want to *hang out* with me? That's a good one. We're a *couple* Matt."

"A couple? Really?" Matt's face turned red. "There's been three of us in that couple for at least the past six months. You've been spending more time with Al Moretti than with me."

Daniella shook her head. "I don't know what you're talking about."

He moved in closer to her. "When was the last time you let me take you out on a date? Hmmm?"

She stared at him in silence.

"I remember exactly when it was. You let me take you out to a nice dinner at Romano's for Christmas and happily accepted the gold bracelet I gave you." He shook his head. "That was six months ago!" He shouted. "We're not a couple. We were *never* a couple!"

"Matt," she started.

"What? What Daniella? You think you can come around every so often, act all sweet and then claim we're in a relationship? Everyone knows about you and Al. What? Is he busy tonight and you have nothing else to do?" He pointed his finger in her face. "No! You go wiggle your ass for Al because I'm not interested."

Daniella glared at Matt and said slowly. "You can't treat me this way. Don't you know who you're talking to? I am an *Esposito*."

"Well, Miss Esposito, I believe it's time for you to leave," Josie said sternly as she and Ray entered the room. "You may be an Esposito," Josie put her hands on her hips, "but you are in *Bocelli* territory."

Daniella stepped back and looked at Matt. "You will regret this. There will be consequences."

Ray cleared his throat. "Do I need to get involved? Because I will call your grandfather right now and settle this whole thing."

Daniella rushed to Ray. "But promises were made," she said desperately.

Ray put his hands on her shoulders and said, "That's a thing of the past and isn't binding. It's time for you to move on."

Daniella stood frozen staring at Ray. Mia could see her eyes glass over as she took a look around the room and slowly slunk out of the house.

Matt walked over to Theresa and took both of her hands. "Are you okay? I'm sorry you had to witness that."

"Look, Matt, I like you. I really do. But I don't want any trouble."

"No. I promise you, there will be no trouble."

Theresa nodded skeptically.

"Why don't I drive you home, and we can talk." Matt squeezed her hands.

"Okay, just give me a minute to use the powder room."

Once Theresa was out of the room, Ray pointed to Matt. "Let's play this safe. Tell Angelo to put some protection on her and have the boys keep an eye out. I don't think Daniella will really do anything, but you never know where the Espositos are concerned."

NINETEEN

THE NEXT THREE months went by quickly, and much to everyone's surprise, Daniella seemed to have kept her distance from Theresa, and only bothered Matt with a few emotional phone calls. Mia and Artie had convinced Matt to meet with Daniella to clear the air and make a clean break. They didn't want to have any drama with Daniella at their wedding, and they thought it would be best for Esposito and Bocelli Family relations if there were no hard feelings between them.

All of Mia's free time was consumed with wedding planning, and although it was a tight crunch, everything was falling into place smoothly. She was grateful for her sisters Janet and Nancy who were able to keep her calm and grounded, but she could sense that Tony and Ruth still had reservations about her marrying into the Bocelli Family. In spite of their misgivings, they gave Mia their unconditional love and support, and she would be eternally grateful for that.

When it came time for the engagement party, Mia didn't know how both families would interact together. She especially worried about Tony and Ruth feeling uncomfortable being surrounded by Bocelli Family members and associates. But true to form, the Bocellis embraced everyone from Mia's family and by the end of the night, Tony was arm in arm singing *That's Amore* with Ray. But it was Nancy's catering that was the highlight of the night. Although she stuck to a simple, Italian menu, her presentation elevated the ordinary appetizers and antipasto dishes, and everyone raved about the food. When she was asked for her recipes, she simply said they were family heirlooms handed down by her father's mother. Carla had insisted that Nancy utilize Gina and her daughter Rosie along with other vetted family connections to assist and serve. At first, Mia knew Nancy felt uncomfortable with the arrangement, but she and Rosie had quickly bonded and worked so well together they accepted two other catering jobs from Bocelli Family associates.

Mia and Artie agreed that they wanted a small bridal party, so Mia asked Nancy to be her matron of honor and Janet and Vicky to be her bridesmaids while Artie asked Matt to be his best man and Anthony and Angelo to be his groomsmen. The night before the wedding, as Mia sat in her backyard drinking a wine cooler, she looked around and marveled at how relaxed they all were as they sat together talking and laughing. She thought even Artie looked incredibly calm for a man who was about to be married the next day. Mia was a bundle of nerves. She was worried about everything from standing up in front of a church full of people staring at her, to tripping on her train as she walked down the aisle. She wasn't so much worried about marrying Artie, he was her best friend, and she truly believed he was her soul mate. It was becoming a *Bocelli* wife that had started to unnerve her. Nonnina's words of wisdom shook Mia to the core that day she called Donna Esposito and convinced her to change the date of her granddaughter's christening. Would she, herself, be expected to do whatever it took to protect the family? What did that even mean? Would she really have that type of power? Could she live with herself if she had to wield that power?

She was pulled from her thoughts when Vicky and Theresa sat down next to her. "Mia, your wedding is going to be beautiful," Theresa said as she reached out and took Mia's hand. "I've never been to the Chateau before, but after tonight's rehearsal I can see why it's so exclusive."

Mia shook her head to clear her thoughts. "Truth be told, I've never been there either and never dreamed I would be having my wedding there. Between Poppy and Ray's connections, they were able to make it happen."

"This wedding is going to be tough to beat," Vicky said as she put her arm around Mia. "Even Ange is impressed, and nothing impresses him."

Mia smiled and took a sip from her bottle. "Ugh, this is warm. Does anyone want another wine cooler?" She stood abruptly and started to walk toward the patio when Vicky caught up to her and grabbed her arm.

"Okay. Hang on. What's up?"

"Nothing." Mia forced a smile and looked over at Artie who was in a deep conversation with Anthony.

"Nope. Uh uh. I know you better than that. What's wrong?"

Mia hesitated. "Ok, Nonnina said something to me a while back that I can't seem to shake."

Vicky looked around and then led Mia to a quiet corner of the yard for privacy. "What did she say?'"

"She said that the women in the family are very powerful and pretty much stop at nothing to protect the family." Mia sighed and added, "She made it seem that when I become part of the family, I'll have to defend the family in some way." She lifted her head and looked at Vicky. "I won't have to become a hit woman, or anything will I?"

"A what?" Vicky laughed. "A hit woman? No, Mia, no."

"Am I worried over nothing? Is it just nerves and wedding jitters?"

Vicky took a deep breath to stop her laughter. "Yes, I think you have some wedding jitters, but I also think you've come to the realization that by this time tomorrow you are going to be a member of a very powerful family. But that doesn't mean you'll be expected to do anything illegal or anything that makes you uncomfortable." Vicky put her hands on Mia's shoulders. "It means that you're going to be treated with a lot more respect than you ever have. It means you will become a very influential person and with that influence comes the power. In time, you will have the ability to create and shutdown opportunities that can impact the family. Like when Nonnina casually mentioned Matt and Daniella's breakup to Helena Esposito at that luncheon. All she had to do was mention that Daniella showed up at the house, things got heated, and it would be a shame if anything unforeseen should happen to Theresa or Matt. Donna Esposito got the message and as a result, so did Daniella."

Mia stared at Vicky. "Do you have that type of influence?"

"Yeah, a bit. But I don't let it define who I am. I live my life with the values my parents taught me. I don't take advantage of any situation, and I always try to be kind and use any influence I may have for good things." She waved her hand toward the others. "Artie, Matt, me, and even you, we're the next generation of the family, and as we get older that power and influence is only going to grow. We'll have to learn to be very careful with it. Make sure it doesn't turn to greed, and we don't turn into the people we despise."

"Like the Espositos?"

"Exactly. Look at Daniella. She's a bitch. She uses her influence for her personal gain." Vicky put her arm back around Mia. "You and me, we'll help each other to stay grounded."

Mia nodded. She felt better talking to Vicky and decided she was going to look to her Aunt Carla and Josie as role models to help her navigate her new married life.

Vicky leaned in and whispered, "Speaking of Daniella, I heard she got engaged to Al Moretti."

Mia's eyes widened. "No!"

"Yup!"

"Does Matt know?"

"I'm not sure. I didn't want to mention it to him. Things are going great with him and Theresa."

"Hmm, yeah, I can see that. But somebody should mention it by tomorrow. Daniella's representing her family at the wedding, and that could cause some drama."

"I'll talk to Artie and the two of us will talk to Matt tonight after we drop off Theresa."

"What drama will Daniella be causing tomorrow?" Theresa asked as she came up behind them.

Mia and Vicky exchanged glances.

"Come on, out with it, I need to know so I can help prevent a scene."

Mia looked at Vicky and took Theresa's hand. "Daniella's engaged to Al Moretti. We know how much Matt cares about you, but we don't know how he's going to react to that news."

Theresa blinked at Mia. "No problem there. I already told Matt all about that shrew getting engaged. I wanted it to come from me, and I promise, there'll be no drama over her engagement tomorrow."

"Thank God," Mia said relieved.

Matt put his arms around Theresa's waist and said, "It's getting late, I think we're all going to head out now."

"I'll see you first thing in the morning. Call me if you need anything." Vicky kissed Mia on each cheek and followed Matt and

Theresa to gather their things.

"Looks like I've got to go, too," Artie said as he pulled Mia in for a long embrace. "Are you ready for tomorrow?"

Mia kissed Artie tenderly, "Absolutely!"

TWENTY

MIA CLOSED HER eyes as Ruth draped the locket around Mia's neck and fastened the clasp. Tears formed in both women's eyes as Mia hugged her grandmother tightly. Mia turned and looked at herself in the mirror, gently fingering her mother's locket.

"Beautiful," Ruth said as she put her hands on Mia's shoulder.

"I couldn't bring myself to wear it until today," Mia whispered.

Ruth nodded.

"I wish things could've been different for her."

Ruth nodded again. "Let's just make sure things are different for you. Hmm?"

Mia turned to face her grandmother. "Grammy, I have no doubt they will be. Artie is a wonderful man. You said it yourself, he's nothing like my father."

"That's true. But marriage isn't always easy. In fact, it's probably the hardest thing there is to get right. When you marry someone, you marry their family for better or worse as the vows state." She hesitated. "I need to ask you, are you absolutely sure this is the future you want? Are you sure this is the family and lifestyle you want to commit yourself to and be a part of?"

"I'm sure." Mia had felt better after her conversation with Vicky last night, and her nerves were starting to ease. She was excited to become Artie's wife, and she'd decided not to worry about the rest until if and when she absolutely had to.

Ruth placed her hand on Mia's cheek and said, "Okay then, let's get you married."

"Can I come in?" Tony opened the door slightly and poked his head in.

"Yes, we're just about ready," Ruth said as she opened the door fully.

Mia turned and met her grandfather's eyes. He took a deep breath, opened his mouth, and closed it. "Mia," he managed. "You're stunning. You look just like your mother, may God rest her soul."

"Thank you, Poppy." She rushed to his arms, and they held each other tightly.

"Now I have to tell you something." He pulled back and held her hands. "I've been struggling since you and Artie got engaged, and I've realized that I just can't give you away today."

"Poppy." Mia's face fell and tears formed in her eyes.

"Now, Mia, hear me out." He sat down on the bed and motioned for her to sit with him. "I blame myself for the way your mother's life turned out. The way she ran off and married Dominick. Maybe if I handled their relationship better, they might've both been here for you today. Who knows," he sighed. "I vowed I wouldn't make the same mistakes with you. The first time I held you in my arms, I whispered into your little ear and promised you that I would do better and be better for you. I hope that I've kept that promise."

"Yes, you did. You absolutely did," Mia said desperately.

"Last night I realized there are many reasons why I can't give you away. Mia, you're not mine to give. You're not a possession, you are your own person. *Never* let anyone make you feel any differently." He squeezed her hand. "I will accompany you down the aisle, I will put your hand in Artie's at the altar, and in so doing I will give you both all of my love and my devotion. I will *not* give you away, Mia. You'll always be a part of me, and I won't *lose* you." He shook his head. "No, there will be no loss today. Today I embrace Artie as a member of our family."

"Thank you." Mia cried and laughed at the same time. "This means more to me than you'll ever know." She kissed his cheek and whispered into his ear, "I'll always be a Russo, nothing and no one will ever change that or take it away."

Ruth grabbed a bottle of champagne, opened the bedroom door, and called out, "Girls, come, let's have a toast before we head out to the church."

Janet, Nancy, and Vicky rushed into the room chatting and giggling. "Damn girl, you look amazing," Vicky squealed as she circled around Mia and then quickly covered her mouth, "Sorry Mr. and Mrs. Russo."

Mia delighted as Tony chuckled and waved his hand. "She does look damn good."

"Is this toast only for the girls?" Anthony asked as he entered the room trying to tie his bow tie.

"You're one of the girls, aren't you?" Mia teased.

"Ha ha. I guess I am. Although I would've preferred it if Janet and Nancy would've dressed me up in Janet's polka dot dress rather than her communion dress back when I was four, and Mia, couldn't you have used any other color of nail polish than that hot pink? Do you know how hard it was getting that off completely before football practice?"

"Oh, sweetheart," Ruth said in between giggles, "you were always such a good sport."

Tony poured the champagne and handed everyone a glass.

Janet raised her glass and said, "To our Carmella, may you

have the fairy tale wedding and marriage that you've always dreamed of."

"Wait, Carmella?" Vicky looked around confused.

"Yeah," Tony said. "That's Mia's real name. She was named Carmella after her grandmother, my first wife. Anthony was so captivated by her as a baby, that he insisted on calling her 'My Carmella.' As hard as he tried, all he could manage to say was Mia. It wasn't long before we all started calling her Mia." He shook his head and smiled at the memory.

"I don't ever remember being called by any other name," Mia added. "I only use Carmella on legal documents when I absolutely have to."

"Wow, I never knew that." Vicky laughed. "Does my brother know?"

"Yeah, Artie called me Carmella once to try it out, but he said that Mia was much more fitting."

"Okay, now it's my turn," Nancy sang. "Mia, I wish you and Artie a long and happy life together filled with love. I'm so proud to have you as my sister even though I'm really your aunt."

Anthony looked at Vicky and said, "Did you know Mia's mom, Rena, was really our sister but Mia grew up with us, so we are more like brothers and sisters?"

Vicky smiled and nodded her head, "Yes, that I did know."

"Okay good, just checking." He cleared his throat. "To my Carmella on your wedding day, you are a beautiful person inside and out. May your marriage be long, fruitful, and filled with many blessings, and may you name your first son after your favorite brother!"

"You mean, smartass?" Janet pushed at Anthony with her shoulder.

"Alright now, enough of that," Ruth scolded smiling. "Vicky, it's your turn."

"Mia you've been my best friend and confidant since the first day we met at the beach. I couldn't have picked a better wife for my brother, and I'm honored to now be able to call you sister. May you and Artie be as happy as you are today for the rest of your lives."

Ruth smiled and nodded at Vicky then wrapped her arm around Tony. "Mia, you have been one of our family's greatest treasures and blessings. We all love you and Artie so very much. We'll be at your sides forever, through the good times and the challenging ones as well."

Tony nodded and raised his glass, "Yes! To our family, alla nostra famiglia."

Everyone clinked their glasses and chatted brightly as they drank down the champagne.

"Look at the time, we need to head out," Ruth said as she started collecting the glasses from everyone.

"I'll go see if the limos are here yet," Tony said racing out of the room.

"Can someone please help me with my tie?" Anthony said in frustration heading out the door.

"Forget your tie, do you realize you have different socks on? Blue and black?" Janet said as she shuffled after Anthony.

"I'm going to get the flowers, we can't forget those," Nancy said.

The room was suddenly quiet. "Your family is amazing," Vicky said as she wiped Mia's face with a tissue and started to freshen up her makeup.

"Yeah, they're pretty great." Mia smiled. "But so is yours."

"I was serious earlier, during my toast, you know. I'm so happy you're going to be officially a part of the family." Vicky's eyes welled up. "It wasn't always easy growing up with brothers in a male-centered family. It'll be nice having you around," Vicky said as she wrapped her arms around Mia's waist from behind. She smiled and raised her eyebrows. "Are you ready to become a hit woman?"

TWENTY-ONE

FALL, 1982

"LADIES AND GENTLEMEN please rise as we welcome for the first time, Mr. and Mrs. Arthur Bocelli!"

Mia held Artie's hand as they bopped into the ballroom to thunderous cheers from the close to three hundred guests that were gathered to celebrate their marriage. She couldn't stop smiling as she scanned the crowd and glided into Artie's arms to dance their first dance together as husband and wife. Mia loved how safe she felt as Artie held her tightly and they floated across the dance floor to their song, *Shining Star*.

"This is the best day ever," Artie whispered into Mia's ear.

"It really is." She smiled as she looked into his eyes.

"Have I told you how beautiful you look today?"

"Only about a hundred times."

"Okay, good. I wanted to make sure I got that out of the way."

Mia giggled and playfully stomped her foot on Artie's.

"How does it feel to be Mrs. Bocelli?"

"Best feeling ever, even though I keep thinking of your mother every time someone calls me that."

"I bet you do." Artie twirled Mia around and the guests began to clap.

"You know, I have to admit the receiving line was pretty

overwhelming. I wasn't expecting people to kiss my hand and bow their heads as they greeted me. Even the family members we're close with did that."

Artie pulled Mia in closer to him, kissed her cheek and said, "It's a show of respect. You're now officially Don Bocelli's grand-daughter, which makes you a senior member of the family."

"Oh," Mia whispered as she glanced around the room noticing that everyone was standing watching them dance. She realized that this must be the respect Vicky had been talking about last night, and wondered how long it would take her to get used to it.

At the end of the song, Artie embraced Mia and kissed her as if no one was watching. His tenderness told her he would be her strength as she navigated her new life as a Bocelli. She glowed as Artie hugged Tony and placed Mia's hand in her grandfather's for their special dance and the band began to sing, *Through the Years.*

"It's been quite a day, how are you holding up?" Tony asked as he smiled at Mia.

"I'm doing okay. But it really has been a whirlwind. How are you doing with all this? I know it's not easy for you."

Tony chuckled. "No, easy isn't a word I would use, but I have to admit the Bocellis have surprised me. They really do seem to be different than other families I've had to interact with throughout the years."

"You'll see Poppy, it's all going to be just fine. Better than fine."

Tony nodded and smiled at Mia. "You know," Tony said as his eyes watered. "I never got to dance with your mother on her wedding day." He looked up to the ceiling and then into Mia's eyes. "This dance is one of my life's greatest blessings. I love you and am so very proud of the woman you've become my Mia, Mia, Bo Meena."

"Oh Poppy," Mia said as a tear fell from her eye. "You've given me the greatest life any girl could've ever hoped for. I am who I am because of you." She leaned in and kissed his cheek.

Ruth rushed toward them as the guests cheered and the song ended. Together they walked off the dance floor, exchanged embraces with Artie and Josie, and took their places on the sideline to watch Artie dance with his mother to *In my Life.*

Mia was humbled by the many toasts that were given in her and Artie's honor, but when Matt welcomed her to the family and said he never thought he'd be so lucky to get another amazing sister she was speechless. She sat back in her chair and took a long sip of champagne and thought about how lucky she felt to have fallen in love with someone as kind as Artie and whose family embraced her as one of their own.

"We're sisters now!" Vicky sidled up to Mia as if reading her mind.

"Hey you. Easy with that champagne," Mia said as she took the glass out of Vicky's hand.

"I'm fine, really. I'm just happy." Vicky waved her hand. "How are you doing? Do you need anything?"

"Actually, I need to go to the lady's room. This dress is difficult to maneuver if you know what I mean."

"Gotcha!"

"Oh great. There's Daniella," Mia said as they saw Daniella Esposito entering the lady's room just before them. "I was hoping I would have limited interaction with her today."

"Do you want to wait? We can go get a drink?"

"No, I suppose I need to get this over with," Mia said as she opened the door.

As they entered, Vicky pushed her head toward Daniella who was brushing her hair. "I guess the rumors are true," she whispered.

"I heard that," Daniella said as she slammed the brush down. "Yes, the rumors are true. I'm engaged. You got something to say about it?"

Mia looked directly at Daniella and said warmly, "Congratulations, Daniella."

As Mia leaned in to hug Daniella, she took a step away from Mia and eyed her up and down.

Vicky rolled her eyes, grunted, and grabbed Daniella's left hand. "Whoa. That's quite a rock."

Daniella snatched her hand from Vicky and held out her arm to show Mia the four-carat solitaire emerald cut diamond ring on her finger. "Al and I got engaged last week. It was all very romantic, he proposed over dinner at The Oak Room. You know at the Plaza?"

"Very nice," Mia said humbly.

"Of course, we'll have the ceremony at the cathedral and a *grand* reception at the Rainbow Room."

Vicky and Mia exchanged looks and Vicky said, "Of course."

"That's not to say your wedding isn't lovely, Mia. I like the simplicity of it."

Mia took a deep breath and remembered the cardinal rule of being in the life. She must never reveal her emotions and must always remain dignified. She straightened her back and looked Daniella in the eyes as she said, "Artie and I didn't need a lot of glamour to convince people how much we love each other. In fact, we didn't want anything to detract from our happiness."

Mia could see Daniella was dumbfounded as she stared at Mia silently for several moments before she turned and rushed out of the bathroom.

Vicky tilted her head back and laughed. "Well done! I've never seen Daniella speechless before. Can you believe her? A grand reception at the Rainbow Room. Please!"

Mia felt proud of herself. What she really wanted to do was tell Daniella off and put her in her place. Taking the high road didn't allow Mia to release all of the irritation that swirled within her, but it did give her a strong feeling of elegant satisfaction that she'd never felt before.

"Don't worry about what she said," Vicky said as she bustled Mia's train and helped her into a stall. "She's jealous that Artie loves you, and this wedding really is amazing. Between the ice sculptures, the lobster and caviar, and the champagne fountain I don't know how any wedding of mine will compare. I don't think there are any roses to be had in the tri-state area right now because they're all here for God's sake."

Mia emerged from the stall and smiled brightly. "You're so sweet," She said as she washed her hands. "I love everything about today, and I'm not going to let Daniella's pettiness ruin it."

"Perfect! Now, let's go dance." Vicky grabbed Mia's hand and led her out of the bathroom.

As they walked toward the ballroom, Mia stopped to adjust the train on her gown and noticed Nonnuccio imposingly sitting in a private room with Luca standing behind him, his hands clasped in front. At the doorway, Ray greeted what looked like Artie's boss, Jeffrey Hornstein, with a kiss on each cheek. Hornstein handed a thick envelope to Ray who led him to Nonnuccio while patting him on the back. The door to the room closed swiftly and James and Roberto, Luca's security men, stood guard outside.

"Hey Vick, what's going on in there?"

Vicky shrugged her shoulders and said, "It's probably the tribute."

"What's the tribute?"

"It's when the Don of the family welcomes important associates, and the associates offer a tribute to the Don for the bride and groom as a gesture of respect and loyalty. It's a great privilege and honor to be allowed a private audience with the Don so only the most elite and powerful associates will be permitted."

"Really?! Was that Jeffrey Hornstein, Artie's boss, I just saw go in that room?"

"I'm not sure, I wasn't paying attention, but I'm sure it was."

"But Artie said he didn't work for the family."

Vicky took Mia's hand. "Mia, of course he works for a law firm that's *associated* with the family."

"I didn't know."

"Yeah, in our world, everyone's connected," she said casually. "Now don't sweat it, they're doing the Chicken Dance."

Mia stood staring at the closed door. Her mouth fell open, and her shoulders slumped. *"Everyone's connected?"* Mia repeated to herself, her thoughts swirling. But he worked so hard to get that job. He was so proud when he was offered a full-time position. Did he make it all up? Why didn't he say the firm was connected to the family?

"Hey, Mee, you coming?" Vicky's voice pulled her out of her thoughts. She watched as Vicky grabbed Artie and Angelo, and they joined Matt and Theresa on the dance floor. She slowly joined them, and as she moved her hands and flapped her arms to the music she looked around at the guests. She realized that the Bocelli guests really did seem exceptionally connected. There was a camaraderie among them that was stronger than she ever realized. They were welcoming and inclusive with the Russo guests, but amongst themselves it was obvious that they were a tight knit clan that seemed to share secrets. As she twirled around with Artie, she saw Nonnina hugging her own boss, Carlo. She instantly stopped dancing and stood frozen staring at them.

Artie put his arm around her waist and said, "What's the matter, babe? Are you alright?"

She pointed to Carlo and stammered, "How? How does he know her?"

Artie looked over to where Mia was pointing and said, "Carlo? That's Nonnina's nephew."

"But that's *my* boss!"

Artie shrugged, "Yeah, I know."

"I didn't know he was part of the family."

"He's my grandmother's nephew. What's the big deal?"

"Hey Artie, it's time for some shots!" Angelo and Matt picked Artie up on their shoulders and carried him off to the bar.

Mia's head started spinning, Vicky's words rang in her ears. *"Everyone's connected!"* She thought she was so lucky when Carlo from CL Designs called her in for an interview and hired her on the spot. She assumed the school connected him with her and she sold herself well during her interview. Was that all a lie? When she saw Carlo's name on the guest list, she thought he was invited as her boss, not because he was *family*. Mia shook her head and looked around the reception room. She asked herself, *"What have I married into?"*

TWENTY-TWO

FALL, 1982

AFTER THE WEDDING reception, everyone gathered at the bar of a nearby hotel. Mia had told Artie she was going to go up to their suite while he had a last round with the guys. She was tired in so many ways. She had the wedding of her dreams to the man that she loved but she felt a heaviness in her heart. Was she really that stupid to believe that the family lifestyle wouldn't flow over into her own life? While Mia managed to push down her feelings and enjoy the rest of her reception, she now wanted to reflect on and sort through her unease. As she worked her way toward the elevators, she felt a hand grab her arm and spin her around.

"There's my Mia, Mia, Bo Meena," Tony said with the most genuine smile Mia's ever seen. "Where ya headed?"

"Hey Poppy. I thought I'd go up to the room, I'm exhausted." She managed a smile.

"Nonsense, come have a little Sambuca with us." He pointed to a corner table where Ruth, Anthony, and Nancy were laughing together.

The feeling in her heart lifted slightly, and at that moment, she realized there was nowhere else she'd rather be than with her family. "Okay, you twisted my arm."

"Look who I found," Tony cheered as they approached the table.

Nancy pulled out a chair for Mia as Anthony and Tony went to the bar to get a round of drinks. "How are you feeling Mrs. Bocelli?" Nancy teased.

"Honestly, a little overwhelmed." Mia looked down and tried to stop her eyes from welling up.

Ruth rubbed Mia's back and said, "Weddings can do that." She moved her hand to Mia's chin and lifted her face as if sensing Mia's troubles. "You married a good man."

"But I didn't marry a good family, did I?" Mia whispered.

Nancy and Ruth exchanged glances as Nancy took Mia's hand. "You could've done a lot worse."

"Nancy's right," Ruth chuckled. "Look sweetheart," Ruth said more seriously, "I've come to respect Artie's family very much. It's not always going to be easy, but no matter what happens, know how very much you are loved by us, Russos, and the Bocellis. You can always count on that."

Mia nodded. She too felt that she was loved by Artie's family, but now that she discovered she was working for Nonnina's nephew, she somehow felt like she was betraying her own family. "I was so excited to get married, and I love Artie so much. I think I didn't fully consider what it would mean to be a Bocelli until I saw so many connected people at the reception tonight. It made me think about everything Carmine Esposito did to our family. It hit me how cruel he was, and now I've married into a family just like his." She took a deep breath, "I'm sorry, Grammy." Her breath caught and she helplessly cried into her hands. She cried for every death in her family that she blamed on Esposito. She cried for her mother who lost the love of her life, she cried for her father whose life was cut short too young, and she cried for her great-grandparents who only wanted to make a good life for their family.

"Oh, no," Ruth said shaking her head and took Mia's face in her hands. "Don't do that. Don't you carry any of that with you. Carmine Esposito is an evil, evil man, but I'm not convinced the Bocellis are just as evil. We've made a point of getting to know them, and Poppy even asked around about the family. His connections all said the same thing, the Bocellis make it a point to help the community and are very generous to the needy. Unlike the Espositos, they are well respected. Word has it that Don Esposito's sons are starting to get even more heavily involved in narcotics. The Bocellis are consistent in trying to keep the drugs off the streets, and from what we heard they're rigid about keeping it away from the schools and away from kids. Trust and believe, Mia, your grandfather and I would've put up a much bigger fight if we thought the Bocelli Family was as malicious as the Espositos." Ruth handed Mia a cocktail napkin and she wiped her eyes.

"Did something happen?" Nancy asked gently. "I mean it's been no secret that Artie is a Bocelli."

Mia sighed. "I just realized my boss, Carlo, is Nonnina's nephew."

"And?" Nancy prodded.

"And I didn't know I was working for the family."

"Hmm, okay I get that, but are you *really* working for the family? I mean, since your engagement party, my catering business has started to take off. That doesn't mean I'm working for the family. I'm just making and serving food to hungry people." Nancy shrugged.

Mia sat back and considered her point.

"This is something you need to talk to Artie about. Don't push it aside and don't ignore your feelings. You and Artie need to be able to have these kinds of conversations," Ruth said.

"Dear God, would you look at my husband?" Nancy pointed to Richard who was ingratiating himself into a conversation Jeffrey

Hornstein was having with two other lawyers from his firm. "Richard has mentioned a few times how much he wanted to work for Hornstein, Drakeford, and Brown, and now look at him. I told him not to be pushy with Artie's bosses today." Nancy got quiet when Richard walked away defeated and sidled up to their table.

"It's time for us to turn in," he said flatly.

"Hey, Richard, great timing," Tony said as he and Anthony placed six glasses of Sambuca on the table.

"None for us, thanks. We're going up to our room," Richard looked pointedly at Nancy.

"Can't you stay for just one last nightcap?" Anthony raised his eyebrows.

"It's been a long day, and we're tired."

Nancy looked at Richard and said softly, "Maybe just a toast with the family?"

"Fine," Richard huffed. He raised a glass and looked over at Tony expectantly.

Tony hesitated while everyone took a glass. He looked down for a moment and when he raised his head he said, "Mia, we wish you and Artie a wonderful life filled with love, happiness, and respect. Because without respect you will never have the love or happiness. That is the key to a successful marriage. Respect for each other and respect for family. Marriage is hard." He looked directly at Richard. "But always do the best you can and be the best person you can be. Be mindful, patient, and supportive of each other."

"Here, here," Ruth said as she raised her glass.

Richard swallowed his drink and placed the empty glass on the table. "I'll see you upstairs." He said as he walked away to the elevators.

"What was that all about?" Mia asked.

"Don't mind him," Nancy said casually. "He's had too much to drink." She stood, kissed Mia on the cheek and whispered, "Poppy's toast couldn't be any more accurate." She picked up her clutch and said, "I better go see about him."

Mia looked at Ruth. "Are they having problems?"

"I think so. She doesn't say much, but I can tell something's off."

Tony shook his head, "I still don't trust him."

"Okay, that's enough of that." Ruth stood. "I think it's time we head up for the night also."

"Are you coming?" Mia asked Anthony as she gathered her things and started walking toward the elevator with Tony and Ruth.

"I'm gonna have a last one with Artie." Anthony smiled at Mia. "I'll send him up soon."

Mia let out a long breath as she entered the bridal suite. She was glad for the silence the room held. She closed her eyes and sat in an armchair and tried to sort through her feelings. She didn't know what bothered her more, the sudden realization that both she and Artie worked for firms that were connected to the family or the fact that everyone knew about it but her. Did Artie and the family purposely betray her? Was this how the family really worked, lies through omission? She thought about the times Vicky had said it wasn't easy for a member of the family to work outside of the family and that inevitably they would work somewhere that was associated with the family. Mia scolded herself for not hearing what Vicky was really saying. How naïve could she have been? She never made the connection that Artie would work for a connected firm. She also never considered this would hold true for herself. Maybe if she had gotten her job after she and Artie were married, it would've been clearer to her that any firm she worked for had to be associated. She and Artie weren't even engaged when she was offered the job at CL Designs. Did Carlo have a choice in hiring her or did he do it to appease his aunt? She shook her head.

She looked up as Artie entered the room singing *Shining Star* at the top of his lungs.

"Heyyyy, Stella." His face beamed as he crossed the room and held out his hands to her. She could tell he wasn't drunk, but he was tipsy. "Dance with me one more time tonight." He pulled her up and out of the chair and hugged her tightly as they swayed silently. He kissed her neck softly but pulled back after she stiffened. He studied her face and said, "Come here." Artie took Mia by the hand and led her to the bed. "Honey, what's happening right now?"

Mia burst out crying. "I feel so betrayed." She turned her back on Artie. "You told me you *weren't* working for the family. No one told me I *was* working for the family. We weren't *supposed to be* working for the family."

Artie gently put his hands on Mia's shoulders and turned her around. "I'm not working for the family. What makes you say I am?"

"I saw Jeffrey Hornstein pay tribute to Nonnuccio."

"And?"

"And? And he's your boss. You're working at his firm."

"That doesn't mean I'm working for the family. You know I manage trusts and offer legal advice to organizations. If I were working for the family, I wouldn't be dragging myself into the city every day. I'd be working side by side with my father."

Mia remained silent.

"I thought you understood how things work. We have to be careful who we let into our lives and how much access they have to the family. As a result, if a key member of the family doesn't work directly for the Bocellis, they'll work for a trustworthy associate."

"And my job? Did I only get the job because of my relationship with you?"

"No!" Artie shook his head. "I will admit that Nonnina gave your portfolio to Carlo, but from what I understand, he loved your work and was genuinely interested in hiring you once he interviewed you."

Mia didn't know if she should trust what Artie was saying. He made a good point in that he really wasn't involved in the day-to-day family business, and she could understand how it must be hard to trust outsiders. But she couldn't help feeling deceived. Why didn't anyone tell her?

"Look, I'm sorry if you didn't realize any of this." He shrugged his shoulders. "I thought you knew, but I guess I should've taken more time to lay it all out."

"Yes, you should have! I loved my job. But now I feel like it's not genuine."

Artie ran his hand through his hair. "What is it that you love about your job?"

"Everything. Working with the clients to come up with design ideas, implementing the vision, and then the feeling of accomplishment once the plans come to life."

"How much does Carlo oversee you and change your plans?"

"Almost never. Every once in a while, he'll make suggestions, but ultimately I'm pretty independent."

"Do you really think that if you weren't a good designer, Carlo would trust you with so much responsibility and risk his own reputation?"

Mia hesitated. "No, I guess not."

Artie nodded. "It's the same with me. At my job, I'm learning a lot about legal finance. I'm not being given any special treatment. *Believe me*, no one holds back when they tell me there's a better way of doing things. The way I see it, most people get their jobs because of who they know. That's how life works most of the time. We were blessed to get our feet in the door of some pretty amazing jobs, but now we're working hard to keep those jobs."

"I didn't think of it that way."

Artie took Mia's face in his hands. "I promise you, if the family wants us to work for them, it'll be made clear to us. And if you ever feel like you're in a position or asked to do anything you're uncomfortable with, tell me immediately. We're married now, and we have to trust each other. I'll always protect you!" Mia nodded and Artie kissed her. "You can always trust me. That is my vow to you!"

Mia hugged Artie tightly. She reasoned that he was probably right, most people she knew got their jobs through family contacts. She supposed this wasn't very different, although she wished she knew the full truth up front. She decided that she would trust him, but she also recognized that she needed to be more diligent and aware when it came to the family.

TWENTY-THREE

SPRING, 1983

THEIR HONEYMOON IN St. Lucia gave Mia a fresh perspective and renewed faith in her marriage. When they got home, Artie had told Mia that he was adamant about wanting their marriage to be based on trust not only between themselves but with the family as well. At his insistence, she spoke to Carla and Josie and admitted she felt betrayed when she discovered that she and Artie worked for companies that were connected. She was anxious to have the conversation, and didn't want to cause any hard feelings, but was relieved when they apologized and explained that they didn't intend to be secretive, they just hadn't realized Mia wasn't aware of how things worked. They confessed that they needed to be more cognizant of Mia's feelings and point-of-view being that she wasn't raised in the life.

Mia had also realized she needed to meet with Carlo to discuss her work status and his association with the family. After she pumped herself up for what she expected to be an awkward conversation, she was taken aback when he burst out laughing.

"Mia," he said, "I love my aunt very much, but believe me the Bocellis are not involved in my business practices. Especially who I choose to hire." He shook his head and took her hand. "No, as soon as I saw your portfolio, I knew you were the perfect addition to this firm. Your fresh, modern style was exactly what CL Designs needed."

After Mia had made peace with their work connections, she and Artie settled into a comfortable life together. Mia found she loved married life and took to being an official Bocelli easily. As a Bocelli wife, she was now required to attend many social engagements that she otherwise would have never been invited to. She often thought of her mother, Rena, when she would be at a black-tie ball or fundraiser surrounded by high-level politicians, judges, and celebrities. She remembered seeing Rena's face light up when she would recount how much she, herself, enjoyed attending glamorous parties and meeting influential people. At each event, Mia was sure to sip a Martini in her mother's honor and memorialize the life Rena wasn't able to live.

There were times when the Espositos would attend some of the same social events, but both Carla and Josie made sure that her exposure to Carmine himself was minimal. When she married Artie, she knew that it was going to be inevitable that the Espositos would be a presence within her life, so she would inquire about their attendance before an event so she could mentally prepare herself to be demure and poised. But each time she was in Daniella's presence, Mia found it to be increasingly difficult not to react to her rudeness and contempt. While everyone just passed her behavior off as jealousy, Mia wondered if there was more to Daniella's obvious animosity.

One night as she and Artie entered the grand ballroom of the Waldorf Astoria, Mia let out a large breath to ease her tension. She knew she needed to relax, but a party in honor of Daniella and Al was not Mia's idea of a fun night out. It was an ostentatious event, and the guest list was a who's who among New York dignitaries. As they approached their assigned table, she and Theresa locked eyes, and Mia quickly sat next to her, knowing that Theresa was the only other person in the room that was dreading the event just as much as she was.

"How long do you think we have to stay?" Matt whispered to Artie

Luca looked at Matt from the adjacent table and said, "Be good!"

"I swear Matt," Vicky said, "people down the road could hear you whisper."

"We are all going to remember our manners tonight." Carla said as she stood next to Luca and looked around the table. "I don't care how anyone feels about Daniella, Al, or their families. We are Bocellis, and we will hold ourselves with nothing but dignity."

"Yes, ma'am," Matt whispered while Vicky, and Artie nodded quickly.

Luca pointed toward Joe, Nonnuccio's nephew and most successful Captain, and his wife, Dee, who was carrying two cocktail glasses. "You might want to remind them tonight also."

Matt and Artie huddled together as they tried to stifle their laughs.

"I don't get it," Theresa said.

Vicky leaned in. "Joe and Dee are notorious for their hysterical, but inappropriate behavior. It doesn't take Dee long to get drunk and then the shenanigans begin."

"Remember that time at Cousin Sylvio's wedding," Matt said as he started to laugh. "She grabbed the microphone from the singer in the band and started to sing." Tears started to roll down Matt's eyes.

Artie leaned on Matt as he started to laugh. "She started to kick her legs in time to the music and her shoes flew off her feet."

"Then … she … fell!" Matt managed to say as both he and Artie gasped for breath through their laughter.

Vicky shook her head and giggled. "She didn't spill a drop of her drink, though. Now that's what I call talent."

Matt banged his hand on the table as his laughter grew more intense.

"What did Joe do?" Mia looked at Artie.

"He took one look at her on the floor and stepped over her."

"He didn't help her up?" Angelo chuckled.

Artie shook his head. "Nope. These types of things happen a lot with her, and I guess he was sick of it."

Mia frowned at Artie.

"Don't worry, honey. I'd never step over you." He kissed her cheek.

She smiled and put her hand on his cheek. "You're such a gentleman."

The night turned out to be more enjoyable than Mia had anticipated. To her relief, there were so many people there that she hadn't even had the opportunity to see Don Esposito let alone be close to him.

She noticed Daniella and Al going table to table greeting their guests, and when they were just about to greet their table, Mia took Theresa by the hand and said, "Let's dance." She knew it was not the appropriate thing to do, but as Mia twirled around to the music, she reminded herself that she wasn't being half as rude as Daniella had been every time they were together. When the music ended, Mia followed Theresa back to the table, but accidentally bumped into someone walking toward the dance floor.

"I'm so sorry," Mia said.

Daniella's mother, Antonia, stared back at her. "Mia, right?"

"Yes, that's right. I'm Artie Bocelli's wife."

"I know who you are." She put her hand on Mia's chin and turned her head as she inspected Mia's face. "Hmph. I have to say Rena's child is better looking than she ever was."

Mia shook her head slightly, not sure if she heard Antonia correctly.

She squeezed Mia's arm tightly. "I can see you're just like her though. She always thought she was so special being married to Dominick. But your mother didn't deserve him, just as you don't deserve Artie."

Mia opened her mouth to respond, but she was speechless.

"You see my daughter over there?" She pointed to Daniella who was greeting the guests at the last table. "She should be wearing Arthur's ring. She was supposed to be a Bocelli, not a Moretti," she spat.

"Antonia!" Carla stepped between them and pulled Antonia away. "What a lovely party. Thank you so much for inviting us."

Josie grabbed Mia's hand and led her back to the table and sat next to her.

"Oh, my sweet, I'm sorry you got cornered by her."

"She said my mother didn't deserve my father, and I don't deserve Artie," Mia stammered.

"Don't pay her any mind. She and your father knew each other long before he fell in love with your mother, and quite obviously hasn't gotten over it yet. It's probably why Daniella is always so rude, her mother has a habit of spreading her bitterness."

Mia nodded slowly. "Okay, but then why did she say Daniella was supposed to be with Artie? I remember Daniella said something similar once about promises being made."

Josie took a deep breath. "Many, many years ago when Don Esposito and Don Bocelli were close allies, they talked about joining the families through marriage. If not by their own children, then by their grandchildren." She put her hand on Mia's. "I don't have to tell you that a lot has changed since then, and those intentions could never be realized. My guess is Antonia has held on to the notion that Daniella should be a Bocelli and had instilled it into Daniella."

"But why Artie? She was going with Matt."

Josie rolled her eyes. "She always had her sights on Artie, he was the first born and by rights the initial Bocelli heir." She tapped Mia's hand. "They need to come to terms with reality and move on. I know it's easy for me to say, but try not to let their resentment get the best of you." Josie swung her head toward the sound of Dee's cackling from a nearby table. "Now, if you'll excuse me, I have to yank a drink out of Dee's hand before she starts dancing on the tabletop."

As Mia looked up she saw Artie walking toward the table. He held out his hand and mouthed the words, "wanna dance?"

She eagerly went to him, laid her head on his shoulder, and closed her eyes as they swayed to the music together. The interaction with Antonia had shaken her up. The Espositos were relentless when things didn't go their way. Each generation infuses the next with the same unrelenting, heinous attitudes and behaviors. And although she sometimes understood the source of the maliciousness, it was difficult to endure the wrath. She nuzzled into her husband and reminded herself that she deserved Artie more than Daniella ever could, because she loved him eternally and would stop at nothing to defend what they had together.

Artie whispered into her ear. "Let's go home."

"Do you think we could?" Mia tried to contain her relief.

"They're serving dessert and coffee, it's more than appropriate." He took her face in his hands and gently kissed her forehead. "I'll have the car brought around."

Mia grabbed her purse and started to say her goodbyes.

"We're headed out." She kissed Matt and hugged Theresa.

"If you're leaving, we're out too." Matt hopped to his feet and took Theresa's hand.

"Wait for us," Vicky said as she took a gulp of coffee.

"Artie's already getting the car. I'll see you tomorrow," Mia said as she hugged each of them.

As she entered the lobby, Mia stopped short and gasped. In one swift move, Daniella had pressed herself up against Artie, clutched his behind with her right hand, and with her left, pulled his face to hers, thrusting her tongue into his mouth."

"You bitch!" Mia screamed and lurched at Daniella as Artie pushed her away from him.

"Enjoy your marriage and life as a Bocelli." Daniella laughed. "Because, I promise, it won't last long."

Before anyone could stop her, Mia clenched her fist and swung at Daniella's face, knocking her to the floor.

IN THE LIFE

TWENTY-FOUR

MIA COULDN'T REMEMBER anything after she punched Daniella, but when she tried to open her eyes, the room was spinning. "Get her outta here!" She could hear Artie's yells echoing faintly in the far-off distance. She was hoisted in the air and carried off into a car. Angelo? She thought. Is that Angelo carrying me? Her panic rose as she suddenly felt hands slapping her face. She tried to fight them off, but her arms were being held down.

"Mia? Mia? Come on Mee, talk to me."

"Vicky?" Mia managed.

"There she is. You're going to be okay, we're taking you to Uncle Luca's house."

"What happened?"

"You punched Daniella!" Theresa said as she released Mia's arms and smoothed her hair.

"Yeah," Angelo snorted. "It was great."

"Shut up Ange and drive," Vicky snorted and then chuckled. "It was kinda great."

"My head," Mia said as she reached up to feel the source of the pain.

"Yeah, after Daniella recovered from the shock of your punch, she lunged at you. You don't remember?"

Mia tried to shake her head and groaned.

"She pushed you to the floor. You hit your head pretty hard."

"Artie. Where's Artie?"

Angelo looked to the back from the driver's seat. "He and Matt are still at the Waldorf doing damage control. We're taking you back to Jersey. It's best to get you checked out by one of our own."

"Don't worry, he'll meet us there soon," Vicky cooed.

"Oh my God," Mia said as the memory started to flood back to her. "Oh my God. She was all over Artie, kissing him."

"We saw," Theresa whispered.

"I couldn't help myself. I got so angry. Oh my God."

"Matt and Artie will fix it."

"Oh my God! What did I do!"

As they approached the gate at the bottom of the driveway, James, Luca's head of security, was there waiting for them.

"How is she? Do we need to go to a hospital?" James opened the car door.

"No! No hospital. I'm okay." Mia managed to sit up, but clutched Vicky's hand as she started to sway.

"Maybe just a doctor for now?" Vicky offered.

"Yes." Mia answered. Vicky's concern was evident, but Mia didn't want to bring any more attention to the family than she had already.

"Okay, let's get her up to the house, Gina's waiting."

James got in on the passenger's seat and directed Angelo where to park. Gina darted out of the house as soon as she saw the headlights. She kissed Mia on the forehead and said, "che Dio ti aiuti, God help you."

By the time Mia was settled in the guest room and Luca's doctor was called, Artie and Matt had made their way back to the house. Artie pushed the door open and flew to Mia's side.

"Stella." His voice quivered.

"I'm okay." She put her hand on his cheek. "I'm so sorry."

"Sorry?" He demanded. "You've got nothing to be sorry about." He shook his head.

"I shouldn't have hit her."

"She shouldn't have thrown herself at me. She was completely out of line and inappropriate."

"How mad are the families?"

"Lucky for us, Uncle Luca and Daniella's Uncle Mario saw everything. Both families agreed it was an unfortunate incident but there would be no bad blood between them."

"An unfortunate incident, huh?"

"Mia it could've been much worse. Take it as a win."

Carla tapped on the door and opened it slowly. "Dr. Card is here."

After a comprehensive series of questions and a thorough exam, the doctor determined that Mia had a concussion. He ordered her to get plenty of sleep and to avoid any physical activities for a minimum of two weeks. Artie walked the doctor out while Carla sat on the side of the bed and handed Mia some Tylenol and a glass of water.

"I'm sorry," Mia whispered as tears filled her eyes.

Carla nodded. "I understand your impulse. I do. Daniella has been anything but kind to you, and she really crossed the line tonight. But we've got to start working harder on your temper and impulse control. Particularly where the Espositos are concerned."

Tears streamed down Mia's face. "I don't know if I could've stopped myself."

"Now that I think about it," Carla said as she tapped Mia's hand. "I know someone who might be able to help, Sofia DeGregorio. She's married to Don DeGregorio's son, Giovanni, from Long

Island." She chuckled. "I'll tell you, when she and Gio got married way back when, her temper could rival that of any street thug. The other wives and family members coached her on how to manage her rage and compulsions. Now nothing can ruffle her feathers, she's always as cool as a cucumber, as they say."

Mia began sobbing. "Am I a barbarian?"

Carla handed Mia a tissue and put her hand under Mia's chin. "You are *not* a barbarian. You are a well-mannered, affable woman who has been thrust into a world filled with insolent people. You just need a little coaching on how to react when you're faced with loathsome situations."

"Do you think it could work?"

"I do." Carla nodded and smiled. "Now I think it's best if you and Artie stay here at least for the next few days. We need to wake you up every hour tonight just to be sure you're ok. After that, the doctor wants you to get as much sleep as possible."

"I don't want to be any trouble."

"I insist. Of course, Josie wants you both home with her, but you're already settled, and Gina is at work in the kitchen making a pot of soup. I'd hate to break her heart and not let her feed you." Carla stood, smiled at Mia, and gave a small wave as she left the room.

TWENTY-FIVE

OVER THE NEXT five years, Mia became more comfortable in her role as a Bocelli wife. She met with Sofia DeGregorio a number of times, who was able to give her some good ideas on how to cope whenever Mia felt her temper rise. Sofia's recommended breathing techniques, mantras, and use of humor had worked well for Mia, and she began to flourish within her new lifestyle. She had become confident on how to compose herself whenever she encountered conflict. While apologies were never exchanged, Daniella and Mia managed to be dignified whenever they found themselves in each other's presence. Daniella considerately sent her regrets when it came time to attend Matt and Theresa's wedding, and Mia sent Daniella a generous gift in lieu of attending her baby shower. Although Daniella did attend the christening for Matt and Theresa's son, Mickey, she was under constant scrutiny from both her family and the Bocellis.

Mia's career was flourishing. She was the lead designer at the firm with three associates working for her, and Carlo planned for Mia to run his new Central Jersey office once it opened. While she was happy and content in her career, she occasionally worried about Artie. The long hours he kept at the office, along with the arduous commute began to take a small toll on him. He seemed more and more unsettled and unfulfilled when it came to his career. They spent time curled up together on the couch talking about his options over a few glasses of wine, but they hadn't found anything that excited him.

Mia wondered if he would've felt more fulfilled if he had gone into criminal law like Vicky. Vicky had an office in Hornstein, Drakeford, and Brown's Newark, New Jersey branch and her success rate was quite impressive. Mia knew how hard Vicky had to work to be not only successful but also respected. When Angelo proposed to her, she said yes under the condition that she would not give up her career even if they had children.

Both families had started asking when Mia and Artie would start having kids. Both Ruth and Josie were eager for them to have a child, but it was Nonnuccio who applied the most pressure. "Family is the most important thing," he would say to them every chance he could. "It's time we start expanding the family. I'm not getting any younger, you know." Mia couldn't understand why he was so eager for them to have a child. Matt and Theresa's son, Mickey, had just turned three and Theresa was pregnant with their second child. But Artie explained that he was the eldest grandson and Nonnuccio wouldn't be appeased until Artie produced a child no matter how much he adored Matt's kids.

As she was getting ready to go to their weekly Sunday brunch at Nonnuccio's house, Mia pulled her pocket calendar out of her purse. "This can't be right," she mumbled to herself. "But I'm on the pill. This just can't be right." Her hands started to shake as she shoved the calendar back into the purse.

"You ready to go?" Artie grabbed his keys from the tray on the dresser. "Are you okay? You look like you've seen a ghost."

"Yeah, I'm fine." Mia forced a smile. "I guess I'm not feeling very hungry."

"I'm sure Nonnuccio would understand if you don't come today."

"No, it's alright. I don't want to disappoint Nonnina. She hasn't had us all over in a while," Mia said as she applied lipstick, hoping it would help her complexion.

On the drive over to the house, Artie had told Mia about some investment ideas that he would like Nonnuccio to consider. He was still talking about them as Nonnina greeted them at the door. Mia squeezed Artie's hand in alarm. She could see how tired and worn Nonnina looked in spite of her meticulously styled hair and makeup.

"Hello darlings." She kissed them both on each cheek. "We're just waiting for Vicky and Angelo. I've got brunch all laid out. Go help yourselves."

She led them into the dining room where they found Matt, Luca, Ray and Nonnuccio huddled in a corner deep in conversation and Carla and Josie sitting at the table with their heads together whispering.

"What's going on?" Mia whispered as she sat next to Theresa.

"I'm not sure, but whatever it is, it's very serious. Everyone looks tense."

Mia looked around at the food and considered making herself a light plate when Vicky and Angelo walked in.

"Ciao," Vicky announced brightly. The room became silent as everyone turned to stare at them. "Who died?" She asked.

The silence in the room got deeper as Josie said, "Vicky, don't be so dramatic."

Vicky looked around the room and locked eyes with Mia. She silently mouthed the word, "What?"

Mia shook her head and shrugged her shoulders. She tapped the chair next to her for Vicky.

Nonnuccio cleared his throat and said, "Okay, now that we're all here, let's get started."

He stood at the head of the table while Nonnina, Carla, and Josie filled in the seats to his right. Luca and Ray stood along the back wall with their hands clasped in front of them and Matt, Artie, and Angelo stood behind Theresa, Mia, and Vicky. The room was serious and overwrought.

Nonnuccio looked around and said, "1987 was a good year for us. The Route 78 construction job was completed, we've seen some significant revenue thanks to the ongoing success of our Atlantic City casinos and major events in the Meadowlands, our latest casino and hotel will have its grand opening the end of this month, and we have made great progress in our waterfront development projects." He shifted and continued, "I believe that 1988 will be even more profitable as we will ramp up development in Jersey City, Hoboken, Palisades Park and Newark. Now that the 78 project is completed, our crews will begin work on expanding the Turnpike and various other roads throughout the state."

Mia started to take deep breaths as she fought waves of nausea. She slowly sipped her water wondering if it was the tenseness of the room or a pregnancy that was making her feel sick and anxious. Nonnuccio *never* discussed business with the entire family and as she looked around the room, she tried to read everyone's expressions. The men were silently nodding as Nonnuccio spoke, Josie's eyes were closed completely, and Carla looked down at her hands. Nonnina was as attentive and regal as she ever was.

Nonnuccio continued, "This year also brought us family blessings as we delighted in the news of Vicky and Angelo's engagement and the soon to be new addition to our family with Matt and Theresa's second child. I'm not sure how little Mickey will take to being a big brother, but if he's anything like his father was when Vicky was born, the baby will be well looked after." Nonnuccio smiled, and the mood lifted slightly, as congratulatory chatter ensued.

"Yes, this year is going to be a year of great change. We will all raise a glass and bless our newest family member," he said as he nodded at Matt and Theresa. "And we will dance and celebrate a cherished union," he nodded at Vicky and Angelo. He paused and took a sip of whiskey. Mia noticed his eyes became glassy as he stood up straight and added, "As we honor and cherish these life's blessings, I, myself, will begin to turn the family over to my successor, Luca."

Vicky gasped and the room grew silent once again. Everything started to move in slow motion. Luca stood up straight and met Nonnuccio's eyes, Ray took in a deep breath and shook his head slightly. Josie squeezed Carla's hand and Nonnina nodded.

Artie squeezed Mia's shoulders as he whispered to Matt, "Did you know about this?"

Matt quickly shook his head and said, "Forgive me Nonnuccio, but why?"

Nonnuccio answered as he slowly looked around the room seemingly taking in everyone's faces. "Luca has been well prepared for this, and the time is right. I'll help Luca in the transition to make it smooth and seamless, of course."

Artie looked at Nonnuccio sideways. "Why now? What makes *now* the right time?"

Nonnuccio stood silently before he looked at Nonnina who stood from her chair next to him.

"Your grandfather is having some health issues," she said with her head raised high. "It's time for him to start focusing on what's important."

"What kind of health issues?" Vicky shuddered.

Nonnuccio waved his hand, "It's nothing really, they found a spot on my lung."

"We check into the hospital tomorrow and they'll remove it," Nonnina added. "He doesn't need any stress to interfere with his recovery."

"Tomorrow?" Matt asked, "How long did you know about this?"

"I dunno," Nonnuccio shrugged. "Two weeks, maybe more. I'm fine. We just have to take the necessary precautions in terms of leadership of the family." He pointed around the room. "I don't want anyone on the outside thinking the family is vulnerable."

"I trust that this will stay here in this room. No one beyond these walls will hear of this." Nonnina looked at each of them sternly. "Now there's nothing to worry about. Worrying won't help anyway. Yes?"

Mia could tell that Ray, Luca, Carla, and Josie had already known about his condition, and that the announcement was no surprise to them. She locked eyes with Vicky and wanted to give her a big hug and tell her everything was going to be alright, but she wasn't so sure that it was.

TWENTY-SIX

"WE'VE MET WITH the doctors, and I'm afraid it's worse than they thought," Luca said. It had been over two weeks since Nonnuccio's surgery, and Ray and Luca gathered everyone together to discuss his condition.

Vicky shook her head, her voice quivering. "I had a feeling you were going to say that."

"What did they say?" Artie leaned in.

"They did a lot of scans and biopsies. The cancer has spread to his liver and his stomach."

"Can he be treated?" Theresa whispered.

Josie put her hand on Ray's shoulder, "They said the treatment would be debilitating and would only give him just a little bit of extra time."

"How long?" Matt asked.

"It would only give him maybe a few months more, but he'd be terribly sick from the treatment," Carla answered.

Matt shook his head. "No. I mean how much time do we have left with him!"

Ray shifted in his chair, "They don't know for sure. They're thinking nine months to a year."

Matt jumped up from the table and stormed away.

Theresa looked to Josie who said, "Go to him."

Angelo helped Vicky to the couch, and she curled up in his arms as she cried.

Mia took a deep breath. Her eyes welled up with tears, but she pushed them back and reminded herself that she can have a good cry later. Now she needed to be strong for everyone else. She always found a way to be calm during difficult situations, a trait she learned from everything she went through with her mother.

"How are they handling the news?" Mia asked gently.

"As good as can be expected," Aunt Carla whispered. "Nonnuccio is adamant about not doing the treatment. He wants to spend as much quality time as he can with his family."

Mia nodded, "And Nonnina?"

"She's doing what she always does. Organizing and making arrangements for his comfort and care, trying to stay one step ahead, and prepare for what will come." Josie slowly shook her head.

"He wants to meet with you today, Artie. He wants you to help him put his affairs in order." Ray said.

Artie nodded and his voice cracked. "It'll be my honor."

"MIA, I HAVE to commend you on how well you're taking all of this." Carla said as she put her hand on Mia's face. Mia was glad that she and her aunt stayed back at the house while the others went to Nonnuccio and Nonnina's. She was sure Ray and Luca would be part of Artie's meeting with Nonnuccio, and Nonnina would appreciate visiting with Josie, Theresa, and Vicky. Mia couldn't remember the last time she and Carla had gotten to spend some quality time with each other, and she missed their talks.

"What's going to happen with the family once Nonnuccio steps down and Uncle Luca becomes Don?"

"To start, the infrastructure will need to be reorganized. Uncle Luca will need to appoint an Underboss. It'll most likely be Nonnuccio's nephew, Joe. And Matt, of course, will become Captain and take over for Joe."

Mia nodded slowly.

"Uncle Luca plans to run the family just as Nonnuccio has, maintaining the same ideals and goals, but there are some who think Nonnuccio was too soft at times and wasn't open to making big changes. I'm sure they'll try to convince Uncle Luca to expand the family in size, territory, and ventures."

"Do you think Uncle Luca will want to do that?"

"There are some avenues that Uncle Luca will just not consider." Carla sighed and hesitated. "But Mia, I'm afraid now that the Don of our family is sick, and Uncle Luca will be appointed as the new Don, there will be some changes."

"What sort of changes?" Mia raised her eyebrow.

Before Carla could answer, their quiet visit was turned upside down as Mickey toddled over to them followed by the others just back from Nonnuccio's.

"How'd it go?" Mia asked Artie as she picked Mickey up and nuzzled his neck.

"As good as can be expected," Artie said solemnly. He reached over and took Mickey from her arms and raised him up in the air above his head. He made funny faces at his nephew making Mickey laugh. "But this one sure does know how to lighten a mood."

"I'm sorry to say, Uncle Artie, but it's time for this one's nap," Theresa mused as she took Mickey from Artie. She stopped and met Mia's eyes as she noticed Mia subconsciously put her hand on her stomach. Theresa cocked her head, gave Mia a knowing smile, and giggled as she took Mickey out of the room.

Vicky flopped on the couch next to Mia. "This is really hard."

"How'd he look?" Mia asked.

"That's the thing. He looks just fine. He seemed a little tired, but if I didn't know better, I'd think nothing was wrong." She shrugged. "I'm glad we went over there today. Of course, all the guys were huddled in Nonnuccio's office, but it was nice to see Nonnina laugh at Mickey as he was running around."

"Children have a great way of making everyone laugh," Carla said as she crossed the room to join Josie in the kitchen.

"Who would've thought five years ago that Matt would be married and expecting his second child," Vicky giggled.

"Right?" Mia agreed

"I'll tell you what, thank God Matt didn't marry Daniella. She has no control over her kid, Rocco. When we were at that luncheon last month, he was a terror, and she just let him run around wild."

"Sounds like he's a spoiled brat just like her," Mia said and then quickly covered her mouth. "Oops, I'm not supposed to say those things out loud."

The two girls leaned into each other and burst out laughing.

"Oh, thank you for that," Vicky said as she wiped her eyes. "I needed a good laugh. So seriously, what about you and Artie? Isn't it time for you to start having kids?"

Mia felt herself turn red, and for the second time in the day, she instinctively put her hand on her stomach. "Yeah, I think we'll be starting a family soon."

"Come on everyone, let's eat," Josie called as she and Carla carried trays of food to the table.

Josie stood with her hand on her hip and smiled lovingly as everyone took their seats around the table. "We're going to need a much bigger dining room for family meals, I'll tell you that."

"Yes!" Carla agreed, "With a fireplace. I've always loved a grand fireplace in a dining room."

"That would be beautiful," Josie said as she sat down. "I think we need a professional chef's kitchen for Gina. She would like that."

Vicky, Mia, and Theresa exchanged glances. "What's happening here?" Vicky said waving her fork.

Luca leaned in. "As the elders of the family, we've decided it's time to combine our resources and build an estate for all of us."

Matt looked around. "Say, what now?"

Ray nodded. "The family is only getting bigger, and we'll need a place where we can be safe and secure together while having our own private spaces. We just acquired thirty acres in Bernardsville."

Carla and Josie smiled as they continued eating while Artie, Vicky and Matt stared at each other in disbelief.

Josie looked at her children and shrugged. "We're running out of room here. The baby'll be here in a few months and Matt and Theresa will need more privacy, Artie and Mia are living in that tiny guest house, and where will we put Vicky and Angelo after they get married?"

"It's an investment, really," Carla added.

"Besides, security will be much tighter and more manageable with all of us living within the same grounds." Luca nodded.

"Plus, it'll be much easier to take care of Nonnuccio and Nonnina and see to their needs." Carla took a sip of wine. "Yes, this is most definitely for the best."

Mia cleared her throat. "What did you have in mind in terms of the dwelling?"

Luca smiled. "Right now, we're thinking of a main house with common areas for everyone, a wing built out for Ray and Josie, a separate wing for Carla and myself, and of course a comfortable living area for Nonnuccio and Nonnina."

"Each of you will have your own four or five-bedroom cottages, for lack of a better word, that you can design and decorate as you see fit." Ray nodded.

"You mean, you'll build us our own houses?" Theresa asked in disbelief.

"Yes, of course, sweetheart," Josie said as she took a piece of garlic bread. "That's what families do."

Angelo chuckled, "My family would never do that, even if they could."

"Are you absolutely sure about this?" Artie said as he leaned in. "I mean this'll be quite a venture."

Carla looked around at her nieces and nephews adoringly, "We've all discussed it, and are in agreement. What good is the family wealth if we can't share it while we're alive."

"Yeah. It's really best for everyone. I'll feel better having everyone close together," Luca said and then winked at Vicky. "Besides, I like the idea of having two lawyers on the property."

Vicky sat up straight and stared at her uncle. As her eyes grew wide, her face lit up with a smile so bright, it lit up the room.

"Mia, we thought that you and Carlo could manage the project?" Ray said. "Of course, we'll pay you and the firm just as any other client would. I know having your design talents would make all of our homes extra special."

Mia put her hand to her chest, "I'd be honored."

"Alright! This'll be new for all of us, so we'll need you to guide us through the design process," Carla said excitedly.

"Absolutely."

"This is good," Luca said. "I'm temporarily pausing most of our construction jobs and putting the majority of our men and resources into this project. Mia, let's you, me, and Ray meet with Carlo tomorrow and go over blueprints and logistics. I want everything done so we can move in by the end of July."

"*July?*" Mia's eyes grew large. "That's only about five months away. I'm not sure we can have a mansion and three cottages built and ready to move in by then."

"Actually, it'll be four cottages and a smaller guest house," Ray said.

"Four?" Mia asked looking around counting.

"Yes, Gina and James have agreed to move on to the property. They'll have their own cottage. I want the head of our security living onsite and the guest house will accommodate the crew to rest and freshen up when need be." Luca looked Mia in the eye. "I have no doubt you'll be able to make it happen," Luca raised his eyebrows.

Mia's breath caught in her throat. She'd never seen her uncle so adamant and serious before.

He waved his hand. "There were existing structures on the property so the primary plumbing, utilities, and whatnot shouldn't be a problem. We're just about finished with demolition, and I have every man on our crew and every expert in their field ready to begin work. We're talking more manpower than you've ever dreamed of."

Mia looked between Luca and Ray her mouth hanging open.

"I've got some ideas of how the cottages can be situated. Why don't we talk details after dinner?" Ray nodded at Mia.

Artie squeezed Mia's hand and whispered, "Are you okay with all of this?"

"This will be the biggest challenge I've ever faced." She stared at him blankly.

TWENTY-SEVEN

"WOW, WHAT A DAY," Mia said as she kicked off her shoes as she and Artie returned home to the guest house.

Artie shook his head, "You're telling me. Listen, there's something I wanna talk to you about."

"That's funny, cause there's something I need to talk to you about too."

They sat down on the couch. Mia pulled her right leg under her and leaned in toward Artie. "Who goes first?" She beamed.

"When I met with Nonnuccio today, he asked me for a personal favor," Artie began. "I couldn't say, no."

"What favor?" Mia asked slowly.

"He requested that I serve as a consultant to the family." He looked down.

"What does that mean?

Artie let out a long breath. "It means I'll start working closely with my father."

"Working with your father?" Mia's eyes got wide. "That means you'll be working for the family!"

Artie nodded slowly. "But I'll be consulting. Nonnuccio has been impressed with my ideas and solutions over the past few years, and he said the family will need my levelheadedness. Especially with the change of leadership."

"Consulting?" Mia rolled her eyes. "That's quite a fancy way of saying you're going to be a working family member. What will they open the books for you also? Make it all official?"

"Mia, come on. It won't be like that."

"Won't it?" Mia sneered. "You're being groomed to take over as Consigliere!"

Mia saw a slight smile cross his face.

"Oh my God! You're happy about this! You *want* this! Was this your plan all along?"

"No." Artie raised his voice, "But I will say to be asked personally by the Don of the family to step up and contribute in a role as important as this, is not only an honor, but it's the ultimate sign of respect that a Don can bestow."

"He's your grandfather. Of course he respects you. But you were adamant when we were married you had no intention of working for the family. You *said* you had no interest, and you had the Don's *blessing.*" Mia stood and started pacing the floor.

"First of all, lower your voice. There's no need to shout."

"No need to shout?" Mia could feel her vocal cords straining. "You've gone back on your word without even discussing it with me." She flailed her arm. "How could you? How could you so easily agree to this knowing how *I* felt?"

"Because, Mia, this really isn't about you." He stood and put his hands on her shoulders. "This is about loyalty to the family."

Mia shrugged him off. "What about loyalty to *this* family?" She put her hands on her stomach.

He stared at her and took a step back. "You mean?"

"Yes," Mia spit. "We're having a baby."

"I thought you were on birth control." He tilted his head.

"Doctor said it happens sometimes." She turned her back. "I

guess we're both full of surprises today."

Artie shook his head and wrapped his arms around Mia's waist cupping his hands on her stomach.

"This is the best news," he whispered in her ear and kissed her neck.

Tears filled her eyes as she squeezed them shut. She wanted so much to love this moment. This was supposed to be one of the happiest moments of their life together.

"Is it?" She managed.

"Stella! Yes of course." He turned her around and put his hands on her cheeks. "I love you so much."

"So much that you changed the rules of the game?" She pulled back wiping the tears that escaped.

He stared at her. "I really didn't have a choice."

"I think you did. I think this is what you want."

Artie sighed and ran his hands through his hair. "Come on, let's sit down and talk this out." He took Mia's hand and led her back to the couch.

She stared at him blankly.

"Okay, you're right. I'm thrilled that Nonnuccio has asked me to do this. You know I was struggling with my career."

"Struggling?" She asked flatly. "It's very convenient that you started talking about being restless at work just before Nonnuccio asks you to work for him."

"You think I was making that all up? Advising clients on the best legal ways to manage their money became redundant. It was the same thing over and over again. Then, over time, I started *really* listening to the conversations Dad and Uncle Luca would have about family concerns, and I started weighing in with my opinions. It turned out I had some good insight and solutions."

"Why didn't you tell me this is what you wanted instead of

letting me sit there with you coming up with career ideas?"

"Because I didn't know myself." Artie took Mia's hand. "I didn't plan to change things up like this. When Nonnuccio asked me to step up I felt an exhilaration that I haven't felt in a long time."

Mia shook her head as she pulled her hand from Artie's. "I thought we were in this together. You told Nonnuccio yes without even talking to me first, let alone taking my feelings into consideration." Tears started streaming down her face again.

"How could I say no to my grandfather's dying wish? I'm a Bocelli."

Mia sighed, "When we got married, I hated the Bocelli Family business, but I accepted it because you weren't a part of it all. You were different. You were innocent. But now, knowing everything that's happened to my family at the hands of the Espositos, I just can't believe how easily and happily you joined the life."

"But that's the thing," he implored. "I'll be in a position to ensure that the Bocellis *don't* become the Espositos. Nonnuccio, himself, said that my values and composure are essential to keep the next generation of family leaders from turning the family into the menacing, malicious entity that the Espositos take pride in."

Mia stared at him.

"When a new Don is installed into any family, the family automatically becomes vulnerable. For example, other families may try to move in, or existing Captains may try to pressure the new administration to allow changes in business and policies. You get the idea." Artie leaned in. "Nonnuccio asked me to help maintain his legacy, to make sure the family can still be successful without becoming tyrannical."

Mia's eyes softened.

"Stella, I know how terrible the Espositos were to your family. But I also know your great-grandfather was Nonnuccio's greatest resource and advisor. I feel like I can honor both of our grandfathers by advising the Bocelli Family with integrity and benevolence."

Mia nodded slowly and stood. "I suppose I don't have a choice in this matter." She got herself a glass of water, handed Artie a pillow and a blanket, and locked herself in the bedroom for the rest of the night.

TWENTY-EIGHT

WINTER, 1988

THE NEXT MORNING, Mia was up and out of the house before Artie. She hadn't slept all night, and when she finally heard him start to snore at five a.m., she quickly showered and snuck out. They had never had a disagreement as emotional as last night's and she felt cornered. Was it too much to expect her husband to keep his promise and not work for the family? She thought maybe Artie might find some new inspiration within his career if he changed his focus to family law or estate planning, but she wasn't expecting him to be so eager about working for the family.

She picked up a bagel and herbal tea before going to the office and found Carlo already seated at his desk.

"Good morning," Carlo greeted her as she walked in. "It sounds like we're about to embark on the biggest project of our careers."

"That's an understatement," she chuckled.

"I realize this is your family, so I'm not going to sugar coat this. We'll need to be diligent and stay on top of every last detail. Each dwelling will be built concurrently, and a lot could go wrong."

Mia held her breath and nodded slowly. Although she had been awake all night, most of her thoughts were on her marriage and pregnancy. The magnitude of the project came rushing back to her all at once.

"With that said, you and I will take the lead and be the principal supervisors and managers. Everything will go through us, and we will direct and oversee everything. I don't want even a nail put in place without one of us authorizing it. After our meeting with Luca and Ray, let's map out a schedule, padding it a bit for unforeseen delays." He took a sip of his coffee and leaned in. "Mia, are you alright? You look a little pale?"

"I'm fine." She waved her hand. "Didn't get much sleep last night. I'm going to get things ready for our meeting. Do *you* need anything?"

"Nope. I'm just fine knowing you'll be on this project working at the top of your game."

As she started to make her way to her own office, Mia felt a sudden wave of nausea, clutched her stomach, and ran to the lady's room. "Oh, great," she cried as she slunk to the floor hugging the toilet bowl.

After her meeting with Carlo, Ray, and Luca, Mia felt eager and energized to get started. There were going to be many facets of the project that would challenge her, and her mind was reeling with ideas. She spent most of the day sketching various concepts for each of the dwellings and organizing questionnaires, designs, and samples. She reasoned that the more systematic and structured the early design process was, the more efficient the implementation would be. She had made the decision to not allow the significance of the project to overwhelm her, and she would be as regimented and sensible as possible to facilitate a smooth endeavor.

Mia worked long into the night to complete all of the preliminary work so that she could meet with the family in the morning to explain the process and get design feedback. When she became too exhausted to think straight, she knew it was time to go home. She couldn't avoid Artie any longer.

As she entered their home, she was greeted with a beautiful bouquet of tulips and a fluffy teddy bear along with a note that said, *As long as I got you and our little peanut, that's all I need.*

She found Artie sleeping in their bed, left her clothes in a heap next to the bed, and crawled in beside him cradling the teddy bear beside her. As she ran her fingers through the soft fur, she wondered what would happen if she put her foot down and insisted Artie not work for the family. He said all he needed was Mia and the baby, but she thought about how disheartened he had been lately because of his career. It was subtle at first, but she could see he was becoming more and more frustrated, complaining that his work was predictable and meaningless. One of the things she loved about her own job was that it was anything but mundane. Each new client came with their own unique set of needs and desires, and she cherished her ability to start with a blank canvas and create something new and exciting. She hadn't seen Artie so animated about work for well over a year. Would he eventually resent her if she insisted he didn't work for the family? Being the wife of an active member of the family was not in her life plan, but the one thing she knew was that she loved Artie too much to make demands on his choices. She rolled over and pressed herself against his back wrapping her arm around him and kissed his shoulder.

"Hey," he turned to face her.

"Hey," she said softly.

He rubbed his thumb along her cheek. "I love you."

"I love you." She kissed his finger.

"Are we good?"

"We will be," she said flatly. "I don't love this choice, and I'll need time to wrap my head around it."

TWENTY-NINE

OVER THE NEXT week Mia and Carlo worked long hours nailing down floor plans, layouts, design features, and blueprints. She was amazed at how everything was falling into place, although she knew that the contractors Luca assigned to the project had ways of opening doors and ensuring a quick and smooth project. All construction permits were issued within a day, inspectors were on call and waiting for each phase to be completed, and the excavation on the property had already been finished. Mia feared her greatest challenge would be getting the family to choose their own design elements in enough time to meet the tight schedule.

Mia still felt numb over Artie's career decision and found that she had become emotionally distant when they were together. She wasn't trying to punish him, she was trying to sort through her own feelings about it. The fact was the estate project took up all of her thoughts and time and she didn't have the energy to face the reality of all of the changes that were happening within her life. If it hadn't been for morning sickness, she might've even forgotten she was pregnant altogether. But the morning sickness turned into evening sickness, and although Mia suffered for a good two hours each night, she was pleased that she could focus hard on the property development just so long as she was able to satisfy her craving for hamburgers.

As she entered Bella Cucina, one of the many trattorias in North Jersey owned by the Bocelli Family, Mia was greeted by a young waitress as she struggled with two large binders and her bulging briefcase.

"May I help you with those, ma'am?"

Mia looked around to see who the waitress was talking to and cocked her head when she realized the 'ma'am' was her. "Yes, please," she said as she handed over her binders and placed her briefcase on the chair next to her.

The waitress handed Mia a menu and placed another at the empty seat across from her. "Can I get you anything while you're waiting?"

"She'll have a Cabernet," Vicky announced as she breezed toward the table. "And you can get me an Old Fashioned."

"No thank you. I'll just have some water with lemon," Mia said feeling slightly irritated.

"Water?" Vicky said as she sat down. "Since when do you drink water?"

"I read an article that we should drink eight glasses of water a day. It's good for us."

"Yuck, I'll pass," Vicky said as she opened the binder with her name on it and started flipping through it. "Wow. There's a lot to go through in here."

"I know. We don't have a lot of time, so I put together samples and design ideas based on what you and Angelo said were your needs, wants, and wishes."

"Ange doesn't really have many opinions about how the house should look or be set up. All he wants is a room of his own where he can have the guys over, watch games, and play cards. You know I'll be the one decorating that room. He'd hang a set of velvet pictures of dogs playing poker if I'm not careful."

"I keep telling ya, Vick, those things are gonna be worth money one day," Mia said scootching her chair closer to Vicky. "In the folder are renderings of your floor plan, design layout, and personal modifications just so you have them to refer to if needed. The binders are broken down into sections, flooring, cabinets, counter tops, paint colors, fixtures, etc. I picked out the samples based on your questionnaire answers, the pictures you sent me, and of course availability. Pick out what you like and let me know if you have other ideas or questions."

Vicky's eyes grew wide. "This is so exciting."

"It really is. It's the biggest project and tightest schedule I've ever worked on. I find it exhilarating."

"I feel bad that you have to do this with all of us. Let me guess, Mom is the most difficult, Aunt Carla is the most eccentric, and Theresa is the most scatter brained."

Mia burst out laughing. "I wouldn't call her *difficult*, per se."

"Are you ready to order?" Mia's head snapped toward the waitress. There was something about the squeaky sound of her voice that grated on Mia's nerves.

"I'll have the Cobb Salad," Vicky said as she put the binder aside and handed the waitress the menu.

"And I'll have the Deluxe Cheeseburger with fries, please."

"Yes, ma'am." The waitress nodded.

"Would you *please* stop calling me ma'am?" Mia barked.

"I … I'm sorry, Mrs. Bocelli," the waitress whispered and scurried away.

"Whoa." Vicky said dramatically looking around. "Who are you, and what did you do with Mia?"

Tears filled Mia's eyes, "I'm sorry. I just get emotional so quickly these days. I should apologize. I'm going to apologize," Mia looked around the room as she stood.

Vicky jumped up and gently eased Mia back to her seat. "*What* is happening to you?" She looked at Mia's flushed face. "Oh my God, you're pregnant!" She squealed.

"Shh," Mia urged. "Lower your voice. We haven't told anyone yet. How'd you know?"

"Because I know you!" Vicky said triumphantly. "You never go from exhilaration to annoyance in thirty seconds. Only horomones'll do that. How far along are you?"

"I'm just entering my second trimester."

"This is amazing." Vicky clapped and then leaned in. "Isn't it amazing?"

"I suppose."

Vicky eyed her suspiciously. "Okay, Mee, talk to me."

Mia took a deep breath. She didn't really want to share all that was making her anxious, but she couldn't stop herself from blathering, "I'm happy. I really am. This pregnancy was a surprise. We were on birth control. I'm not prepared. Nonnuccio asked Artie to work for the family. Artie had to say yes. I wasn't expecting it. I'm trying to come to terms with it. Artie says he'll make sure the Bocellis don't turn into the Espositos. I'm trying to figure out what that really means. Can he even do that?" She grabbed her glass of water and took a large gulp.

Vicky blinked quickly. "Okay, okay." She put her hand on Mia's arm. "I'm guessing the biggest thing for you right now is Artie working for the family?"

Mia nodded slowly.

Vicky hesitated and chose her words carefully. "Did you never think that was a possibility?"

Mia shook her head.

"I know my brother always said he didn't want to work for the family. But I have to admit, I'm not surprised that he changed his mind."

"Really?" Mia leaned back in her chair and her shoulder fell.

"This thing of ours is magnetic. It draws people in. Having grown up in the life, I'm surprised it took Artie this long."

"He said he didn't consider it until Nonnuccio asked him."

Vicky grinned. "He doesn't want to let our grandfather down."

"He said Nonnuccio wants him to help the family maintain respect."

"If anyone can do that, it's definitely Artie."

"He says it's his calling."

"Yeah, in a way it is. That's how it is with Dad too. He takes a lot of pride in having a hand in guiding the family away from the most depraved ventures. Artie's just like him."

Mia looked down and slowly shook her head.

Vicky tapped her arm. "It's not the end of the world you know. Artie's a lawyer. He'll learn how to handle, manage, and steer the business to be as philanthropical as he can. Dad and Uncle Luca will see to that, I can assure you." She held up her drink and added, "It'll be alright, you'll see."

Mia wished she had the same levelheadedness over the Bocelli Family business that Vicky had, but she knew there were some things that Artie and Vicky would never understand. Their upbringing and life experiences were completely opposite. She understood the level of loyalty they both had toward the Bocellis because she had the same loyalty to the Russos. She couldn't help but feel that if she came to peace with Artie's role in the Bocelli Family, she would be disloyal to her own family.

"When are you going to tell the family your good news?" Vicky gushed.

"Next weekend. We're telling my family on Saturday and then your family on Sunday."

"Good. How's it feel to be pregnant?"

Mia looked up. "It's kinda weird, you know. The idea that you have a living being floating around inside of you. That you're making an actual person! A little human made from you and the person you love most in the world, and you will be responsible for this little person's physical and mental wellbeing." She took a sip of her water. "And then at ten o'clock every night you're racing to the bathroom to get sick." She shrugged.

"Sounds like fun." Vicky rolled her eyes. "So, I got news." Vicky took a long sip of her drink and sat up straight smiling broadly.

"You're pregnant too?"

"Bite your tongue! Ange and I decided we're going to move the wedding up. We wanna get married in the beginning of May."

"*May?*"

"I know, I know. It's not much time, but if anyone can pull together a wedding in such short notice it's Nonnina and Mom." She looked down. "I really want to dance with Nonnuccio at my wedding and I want him to be able to enjoy it as much as he can."

"I totally get that. A wedding will be good for all of us."

"Will you be my matron of honor?"

Mia's voice caught in her throat. "I'd be honored, but are you sure you want an emotional pregnant woman standing up there with you?"

Vicky grabbed Mia's hand and said, "I want my sister standing up there with me."

ON SATURDAY AFTERNOON, Artie pulled Mia into his arms. "Before we leave, I think we need to talk. I hate this distance between us."

"I know." She blew out a long breath of air as her shoulders slumped.

"I hate that I'm putting you through this. I'm just asking you to see it through my eyes. My grandfather asked me to help guide the family through grave situations. He asked *me*, Stella. He said the family needs *me*."

"It's those grave situations that's the problem."

"I know. I know. But you have to understand, the Bocelli Family is not your typical family. Our New Jersey territory is small, but it could be very lucrative for the Espositos and other New York families. We don't utilize the ports and waterways the way they would for drug trafficking and God knows what else. The other families see us as weak because we won't get into those modes of business, and we try to negotiate rather than jump to violence as a means of gaining power and settling our disputes."

Mia cocked her head and saw the passion in her husband's eyes, something she'd never seen when he was talking about his work at the firm.

"I'm not going to sugar-coat the situation with you. This change of leadership for the family will make us vulnerable, and there's a good chance the Espositos will want to make some moves. I need to ensure our family is safe." He placed his hand on her stomach. "This family, the three of us. I cannot protect us by sitting in an office in New York advising people on the legalities of their investments. I *have* to do this. For us and quite honestly for all that your grandparents endured and the memory of your great-grandparents. But I can't do it without you, Stella. You ground me and inspire me, and I need you. The Espositos cannot win. We cannot let them!"

Mia surrendered. She'd always appreciated the fact that the Bocellis had a line they wouldn't cross. If it meant that Artie needed to be a working member of the family to keep the Espositos at bay and protect them, then she decided she would endure it.

She pulled him in close and wrapped her arms around him tightly. "Okay. I think I'm starting to understand now. I still can't promise you that I'm going to love it."

"Thank you, baby."

Mia nodded and he pulled her in for a long kiss. "I love you."

She felt like a small weight was lifted from her shoulders. On the drive over to Tony and Ruth's house she enjoyed laughing with Artie as they tried to remember the words to the nursery rhymes they used to sing as kids.

"Hello," Mia called out as they entered the house. "We're here."

"What's this?" Ruth delighted as she hugged and kissed them and noticed a gift bag in Mia's hands.

"Just a little something I saw that I thought you could use." Mia waved her hand. "Where's Poppy?"

"Out in the yard. It's such a nice day he thought he'd take a look around to see if there's any damage from all that snow we got this year. Artie why don't go out and tell him it's just about time for dinner."

"Where is everyone?" Mia asked looking around.

"Gabrielle caught that stomach flu from Julia, so Janet and them can't come, Nancy and Richard should be here soon, and Anthony is having dinner with Susan's parents, but they'll be here for dessert."

"Oh," Mia looked down.

"What's wrong?" Ruth pushed Mia's hair away from her face.

"Nothing. I just wish everyone were here tonight. That's all."

"Did you want to catch that stomach bug? Because from the way Janet described it, it doesn't sound like the kids are having a good time with it."

"You're right, I was just looking forward to spending some time with the kids." Mia loved her niece and nephew, and she was hoping that spending time with them would help calm the fears of motherhood that started to crop up.

"You'll see them next week, I'm sure. Come help me get the food out of the oven. I've made a roast chicken."

As Ruth and Mia placed the food on the dining room table, Nancy and Richard arrived. Mia could see by the look on Nancy's face they had been fighting. She used to think Richard was such a great guy, but things had changed, and Mia hated how condescending and arrogant he'd become.

"Hello, Richard," Mia called out sarcastically as he sat on the couch and turned on the television.

"Don't mind him," Nancy scoffed. "Work's been really busy, and he's been in a mood."

Mia gave a slight smile and nodded while she bit her tongue and didn't say what she was really thinking about her brother-in-law. She felt Artie's arms wrap around her waist from behind and she thought about how thankful she was that they had talked before heading out to her grandparents' house. She didn't want her relationship with Artie to become like Nancy and Richard's, always being cranky and sarcastic with each other as if they both had resentments pent up. She reminded herself to always make sure she and Artie continued to compromise, support, and respect each other the way they did now. She squeezed Artie's arms as he nuzzled her neck.

Anthony and Susan arrived just as they were clearing the dinner dishes, and Mia was getting anxious to share their pregnancy news. She knew this baby would mean the world to her grandparents, and although they adored Janet's kids beyond comprehension, Mia knew that her grandfather carried the loss of his first-born daughter, Rena, with him every day. She hoped that perhaps Rena's grandchild would help to heal his heart.

"Should we do it now?" Artie whispered in Mia's ear. "I don't know how much longer I can keep it in."

"I know. At least three times I had to stop myself from talking about my evening sickness."

"What are you guys whispering about?" Anthony teased.

"Well—" Mia put her hand on Artie's arm to stop him from talking.

"Grammy," She called. "It's time to open up your gift.

"Now? I'm putting coffee on," Ruth said exasperated.

"Ah, the coffee can wait." Tony smiled at Mia. "Let's see what Mia got you."

Nancy caught Mia's eye and gave her a questioning look and Mia raised her eyebrows.

"Alright, I'm here," Ruth sat in her seat at the head of the table.

Mia placed the small gift bag in front of her. "I hope you like it. I think you will. You'll get some use out of it. I think. But we can get a different one if it doesn't work right."

Artie put his hand on Mia's. "Go ahead, Grammy. Open it."

Ruth pulled the tissue paper out and frowned as she looked in the bag. She pulled out a baby's bottle and inspected it carefully.

"I don't understand. Oh my! Are you? You're pregnant?"

Mia nodded quickly as tears streamed down her and her grandmother's faces and the two ran to each other and embraced.

"Ha ha ha." Tony pounded the table and jumped to his feet. "Congratulations! Now that's some great news." He grabbed Artie and gave him a big bear hug. "We need to celebrate. Anthony, go get the Sambuca. I'm gonna be a great-grandfather!"

After toasts were given, calls were made to Janet, and everyone had their fill of dessert and coffee, Mia and Nancy went out on the front porch and sat on the rockers.

Mia hesitated. "How's things with Richard?" She noticed a

distant look creep into Nancy's eyes that worried her.

"Good. Fine. Whatever."

"Whatever?

"They're fine. We've been trying to get pregnant and he's working a lot, so we've got some stress. Nothing to worry about." She forced a smile at Mia. "What about you? Other than being pregnant, of course. How's Artie's grandfather?" Nancy's changing the subject was a red flag and Mia suppressed the urge to push her more on the topic. In time, Nancy would open up. Mia was sure of it.

"He's hanging in there. He looks good and seems really upbeat, all things considered."

"What's going to happen? You know, with the family once he passes?" Nancy hesitated. "Can I ask that?"

"It's complicated, there'll be some changes. I can't really talk about details just yet."

"Gotcha! Can you tell me about the estate? It sounds incredible."

Mia brightened. "It will be. This is the most amazing project. I never thought I'd be part of something this huge." Mia leaned in and whispered, "You have to promise me you won't tell anyone."

Nancy moved closer. "Of course, I promise."

"All of the structures are being made with bullet proof glass, hidden rooms, bunkers, soundproof offices, and are being wired for all types of security that I've never even heard of before."

"Wow!" Nancy shook her head quickly. "Is that normal?"

"I don't know. I mean, maybe." Mia shrugged. "I never noticed anything like that in the current homes, but I guess you're not supposed to notice it."

"How do you feel about that?"

"I'll be honest, I was freaked out at first. But when Uncle Luca said it was all just a precaution and probably unnecessary and that he wanted to spare no expense to keep the family safe, I started to like the idea of it all." She reached out and touched Nancy's arm. "You can't tell Grammy or Poppy."

"Are you kidding? That'll kill them. Nope. My lips are sealed."

"How's Artie doing with all of this? What with his grandfather being sick and a baby on the way."

"It's been a tidal wave of emotions," Mia said as she looked down.

"Everything alright?"

"Yeah. He's going to take an office at Hornstein, Drakeford, and Brown's Newark branch."

"That actually sounds like a great idea. Newark's better than working in the city. He'll be closer to you and the baby." Nancy said as she started rocking the chair. "Will he be working with Vicky?"

"No." Mia took in a deep breath. "His father."

Nancy stopped rocking and stared at Mia. She lifted her eyebrows and moved her head forward. All Mia could do in response was nod.

"Then." Nancy reached out and squeezed Mia's hand. "We'll just keep that between us as well."

THIRTY

"YOU'VE MADE A VERY old, very sick man happy." Non-nuccio embraced Artie tightly and kissed him on each cheek. He turned to Mia, and with watery eyes, he gently kissed her forehead and folded her into his arms. Mia took a deep breath sucking in his familiar scent of cigars and his favorite Paco Rabanne cologne. She never wanted to forget that smell.

There wasn't a dry eye all evening as the family reveled in Mia's news, Vicky's upcoming wedding, and Theresa's impending delivery. This was what family was all about. The coming together to celebrate new beginnings in the face of inevitable conclusions. Mia noticed Josie sat at the head of her dining room table next to Nonnina beaming all night, and for the very first time, allowed Carla and Vicky to do all of the serving and cleaning.

"Come, Mia, let's you and I have a talk," Nonnina proclaimed as she led Mia into Josie's sitting room. They sat together on the small couch in silence while Nonnina ran her fingers along the edges of her favorite scarf. Mia had always admired that scarf and noticed Nonnina wore it to every event where she served the family in her role of Donna Bocelli. The beautiful deep red color brocade with flowered paisleys in rich gold, blue, pink, and beige suited her skin tone perfectly.

She gingerly handed the scarf to Mia. "I'm not good with designing and decorating houses. Quite frankly, I have no interest, as I'm sure you can tell from our home that hasn't changed since we built it. But I know how important it is for us to pick and choose how we want our new living spaces to be adorned in a timely manner. If you don't mind, I'd rather leave that decision-making up to you. You are an expert in your field with impeccable taste."

Mia felt her face flush and she broke out in a sweat that radiated down her back. She tried to speak, but found she had no words. Nonnina wasn't one to offer compliments freely, and to allow Mia to design their living space was a huge honor. But that honor came with trepidation over the huge responsibility of creating a living area that they would be happy with.

As if she sensed Mia's fears, Nonnina tilted her head and said, "All I want is for Nonnuccio to have a place where he can feel comfortable and at peace. You've done a wonderful job with the layout of our wing, and I appreciate the bedroom being large enough for us to fit a hospital bed alongside our bed when that time comes. Use this scarf as inspiration for your choice of color schemes and whatnot." She ran her fingers along the scarf again. "Bear in mind I don't want to live in rooms with red walls, of course."

Mia chuckled slightly and bit the inside of her cheek. "What if I put together some ideas and we can go through them together?"

"No need, Dear. I trust you."

"I'll try to do my best." Mia felt her right eye twitch.

"I've never told you the story of this scarf, have I?"

Mia cocked her head. "No. You haven't. I just thought it was one of your favorites."

"It is *the* favorite. When Nonnuccio and I were first married, we started with very humble beginnings. Back then we lived in New York, and he was working as a bricklayer. We couldn't afford to go anywhere, so our honeymoon consisted of an afternoon walking around Manhattan." She smiled and leaned back into the couch. "It was the most magical day I've ever had. We ate hot dogs and peanuts from sidewalk vendors and walked through Central Park. We came upon this little shop that sold fashionable hats, gloves, and scarves. My eyes must've lit up when I saw this scarf in the window." She shook her head. "Nonnuccio took one look at my face and marched right into the shop. I don't know what he said to the clerk, but he was very animated and when he pointed to me standing outside, I saw compassion in the clerk's eyes. Nonnuccio emptied the little bit of money he had out of his pocket and the clerk only took a dollar. He wrapped up the scarf, shook Nonnuccio's hand, and mouthed the words, 'Congratulations, may God bless your marriage,' to me through the window."

"That's an incredible story."

"This scarf means more to me than any piece of jewelry that Nonnuccio has ever given me. I wear it to feel close to him and as a reminder to remain humble, kind, and compassionate. It's the foundation that Nonnuccio and I built the Bocelli Family on, and that's the inspiration I want you to utilize when decorating our new living space."

Mia smiled, and a warm, light feeling spread throughout her. "I will."

"I understand Artie has spoken to you about Nonnuccio's request for him to work with his father."

"Yes, he did. I struggled with it at first, but I think I'm okay with it now."

"I appreciate your uncertainty, I really do. Unfortunately, the time has come for the next generation of Bocellis to step up and maintain our principles and assets. Nonnuccio had hoped it wouldn't come to this, but it's becoming clear that the family must present a united front against those who might try to creep in and claim what we've built."

"You mean the Espositos."

"Primarily." Nonnina nodded.

"But I thought the Espositos were loyal to the Bocellis. Didn't Don Esposito pretty much *give* his territory to Nonnuccio?"

"Aah, yes. But that was a long time ago, I'm afraid. A lot has happened since then. Just like Nonnuccio, Don Esposito is aging and he's mentoring his own successor. But when the time comes, and leadership changes, you can't be sure that the next generation of Espositos won't be so inclined to honor the old family loyalties."

"The Bocelli Family must not only be unified, but we must also be prepared for whatever scenarios that might pop up."

"That's daunting," Mia said as she subconsciously placed her hand on her stomach.

Nonnina closed her eyes and when she reopened them, they were filled with fire. "That's why we must be ready." She took Mia's hand. "And Mia, you will have a very important role in our family structure. A role that will be important and crucial to the Bocellis."

"*Me*? What can I do?"

"It is my desire that you will eventually become one of the most powerful women in this family."

Mia's eyes grew large.

Nonnina turned her ruby ring around her finger. "I will mentor you, integrate you into our society, and teach you how to not only navigate and control situations, but help you to become influential."

"What about Vicky or Theresa?"

"Have no doubt they have their own roles they must play as well. Mia, you have a natural inclination for social communication and persuasion. Vicky's strengths lie in her legal mind and problem solving and will be mentored by Aunt Carla. Of course, Theresa is much like Josie in that she excels in planning and organization." She held out her right hand and gazed at her ring. "The three of you will become part of the *Bocelli Sorellanza*."

"Bocelli Sorellanza?" Mia cocked her head and leaned in.

"Surely, you don't think Aunt Carla, Josie, or I are the type of wives to just sit back and let life happen around us?" She leaned in closer to Mia. "Together, we found that we were quite a force when it came to looking out for family members and assisting our husbands in ways only we could. We made it official and formed La Sorellanza, The Sisterhood, back in 1960."

"How do you help your husbands? I thought business was never discussed with wives."

"Typically, that would be true. But, Mia, the Bocellis are not the typical family. That's not to say that Nonnuccio, Ray, or Luca will sit down and discuss the fine details of the business with us, but they are well aware of our respect and pull in the community and they tap into our abilities to influence other wives or businesses to open doors or achieve their goals."

"I never realized that."

"That means we're successful at what we do. I've told you this before Mia, knowledge is power, and that works both ways. The best way we can help defend the family from the likes of the Espositos is through what *we* know and what *they* do not know." She tapped her finger on Mia's arm. "I will guide you on how to achieve this successfully."

Mia touched her heart. "I'm honored."

"You have your great-grandmother's class, temperament, and loyalty, and unfortunately, you also have first-hand knowledge of what the Espositos are capable of. You've lived it and you've grieved it. Now you must utilize it to protect the family."

Mia sat up and straightened her back. "I won't let you down."

THIRTY-ONE

VICKY'S HAPPINESS AND love for Angelo shone brightly on her wedding day making her one of the most beautiful brides Mia had ever seen. Everyone had told Mia she glowed on her big day with Artie, but she didn't really understand what they meant until she saw Vicky. Mia's heart was bursting with so much elation for her best friend-turned sister that the stress of the huge estate project diminished for the day.

After they entered the reception, Artie, Mia, and Matt were surprised to see that Vicky and Angelo were going to be seated alone at a sweetheart table at the head of the ballroom, and they looked around the room for a table where the bridal party was to be seated.

Theresa waved her hand and caught Matt's attention. "We're over here," she mouthed as she shrugged, and her eyes grew wide.

Matt tapped Artie and said, "Look, we're at the *family* table."

"That can't be right. Only senior members of the family sit with the Don." Artie continued to look around the room.

"Nonnina is motioning for us," Mia said as she took Artie's hand and led him to the table.

"Come, Darlings, sit down. Mia, you sit next to me, Artie you're between Mia and your father, Matt you'll be between Theresa and Uncle Luca, of course."

Each of them nodded and quickly sat down as directed, and it was clear that the seating arrangements were carefully planned. The rest of the Bocelli Family and their associates would see that the next generation of Bocellis were moving up within the family.

"Very good," she said nodding her head.

"Luca," Joe bellowed as he held his arms out spilling drops of whiskey out of the glass he held in his right hand. "There must be a mistake." He eyed Matt and Artie. "The Underboss always sits at the table with the Head of the Family at these things."

Luca nodded slowly, "*I* am sitting with the Head of the Family."

"I mean, Dee and I should be at this table too," he protested. "After all, you did say you were appointing me as your Underboss."

Nonnuccio approached the table and stood next to Joe. "Yes, Joe, in the future you will be at the family table. But as of this moment, I am still the head of this family," he tapped his own chest with his pointer finger, "and I am sitting with my heirs tonight." He raised his eyebrows as he stared into Joe's eyes. "Is there a problem with that?"

"No, Don Bocelli," Joe said humbly. "I apologize."

"Dee," Nonnina interjected. "I've seated you and Joe at the table just next to us with the other Captains and their wives." She raised her head slightly. "I'm sure you understand."

"Yes, of course." Dee nodded quickly, took Joe's hand, and led him to the other table.

Nonnina nodded and whispered to Mia, "That's your first lesson for tonight. Seating arrangements and appearances are very important in social events. Only the Don's closest, most trusted associates have the honor of sitting with the Don at his table. Everyone will see that Matt and Artie are now considered to be part of the inner sanctum of the family, and that they deserve the same kind of loyalty and respect as the Don. Likewise, by positioning you directly next to me, we are showing that you are also an important figure within the family and must be held with the level of esteem befitting a high-ranking wife."

"So, that's what that was all about with Joe and Dee?" Mia mused.

"Yes indeed. Joe has always considered himself to be a high-ranking family member being the Don's nephew."

"I gather Nonnuccio—"

"We are in public dear, it's Don and Donna," Nonnina corrected.

"Right, sorry," Mia began again, "I gather Don Bocelli doesn't see it the same way as Joe does."

Nonnina sighed. "It's complicated. Joe is a good Captain and handles his territory well for the most part, but he's been anxious to move up within the family for a while now, and he hasn't quite learned yet that bloodline alone does not guarantee a promotion."

Mia thought about her own father, Dominick, and how Luca said he was eager to move up within the Esposito Family. "Advancing within a family isn't easy?"

"To protect the family, every Don has a succession plan. People do move up but only after they've proved themselves to be loyal, sincere, and able to successfully navigate the intricate methods of establishing and maintaining relationships with associates and other families. Acquiring these skills can take decades of trials, tribulations, and tests. Unfortunately, not everyone is suited to be considered a senior member of a family." Nonnina leaned in and whispered. "Joe and his wife Dee are lacking in the sophistication that's essential to be successful." She rolled her eyes. "Uncle Luca and Aunt Carla say they can help smooth out the rough edges, but I'm not completely convinced."

"Maybe they *can* help. I had quite a few rough edges when I first came into the family."

Nonnina smiled broadly and tapped Mia's hand. "The sophistication I'm referring to is innate. Your grandmother has it and your great-grandmother had it also, and Mia, you're just like them." She shifted her chair slightly. "It's time for your second lesson for the day. Come sit here in Don Bocelli's seat so you can have a clear view of everyone."

Mia hesitated and then moved into the Don's seat. Although it was the same type of chair as all the others, making the move made her feel like she had just ascended a throne.

"Always, always read a room," Nonnina began. "But never, never let anyone know you're observing them. You must take in every detail discreetly. Pay attention to facial expressions and body language when people are engaged in conversations and are unaware they are being watched."

Mia looked around the room and briefly wondered what her own facial expressions and body language had said about her in the past. There was a lot to take in and she wasn't sure what she was supposed to be looking for.

"Look at Joe and Dee standing over by that table. What do you see?"

"Well, they're talking to another couple. It seems to be a good conversation because Joe is laughing."

"Yes, that's right. Watch Joe's hands every time he laughs."

Mia leaned in and her eyes grew big. "He ran his right hand down that woman's shoulder and back."

Nonnina nodded. "Now look at Dee, what does her face and body tell you?"

"She's smiling, but tightly and she shifts her legs and drinks her wine every time she looks at Joe. She knows what he's doing and she's definitely not happy."

"Precisely. You have a good intuition. I will tell you that Joe has a wandering eye and likes the ladies. Dee is fully aware of his behavior and is quite unhappy as a result. Now, look at your grandparents on the dance floor. Do you see how Tony holds Ruth close to him and sings in her ear as they dance? Do you see her eyes are closed and her face is peaceful? I don't have to tell you what their body language says. Quite a contrast from Joe and Dee, huh?"

"Yes," Mia said with a spark in her eye.

"Now look over at Donna and Tina huddled together at the table across the room. What's your impression?"

"I can see they're very friendly, maybe even close friends. They lean in toward each other and tap each other on the arm and hand."

"Good. Always keep a tally in your mind of close friendships, jealousies, rivalries, and acquaintances. This knowledge is power, and it will be very beneficial when you need allies or need to assert your influence. But always remember, friendships can change suddenly, so always observe even the slightest changes in facial expressions and attitude."

Mia continued to look around and noticed a difference in Artie and Matt's demeanor. They were no longer the crazy guys who took over the dance floor and drank shots at a wedding. They were more composed and self-assured. They smiled and greeted associates as they stood tall and shook hands seriously. They sipped whiskey, and while they smiled and laughed at the appropriate times, they maintained a dignified composure. When Mia caught Artie's eye from across the room, he smiled warmly and nodded. A wave of pride washed over her, and she realized she liked this sophisticated, authoritative Artie. Mia felt confident and poised as Nonnina stood and announced she wanted to bring her around and show her off.

Mia was sure to watch Nonnina's mannerisms and tried to mirror her disposition as she engaged with various associates and their wives. She hoped that she was successful in coming across as dignified yet genuine, but she was well aware that she would never live up to Nonnina's regal image. Maybe someday Mia would have the same refined aura, but for now, she focused on developing confidence in her own style and grace. She quickly learned to restrain herself whenever Nonnina gave her a slight, sideward glance. This disapproval only happened twice, when she had become too animated and chatty.

"Behavior and appearances are everything," Nonnina whispered. "You will only gain someone's respect if you command respect." She put her hand on Mia's shoulder. "I'm not telling you to change who you are. We can be as vivacious as we want in the comfort of our home surrounded by those who love and accept us unconditionally. But in public, everything we do and say is judged, and we must never provide the fuel for the fire if we can help it."

Mia understood that the family matriarch wasn't criticizing her personality, but was teaching her how to develop her public persona. In no time, the sideward glances transformed into nods of approval, and Mia basked in every one she received.

When the time came for them to greet Daniella, Mia squared her shoulders and swallowed the lump in her throat.

"Daniella," Nonnina said as she kissed each side of her face. "You have our sincere condolences on the loss of your grandmother. Helena was a cherished woman that I admired. The services were just magnificent, very befitting."

"Thank you," Daniella looked down as her eyes became glassy. "She was my greatest supporter."

"How is Don Esposito doing? They'd been married over fifty years, isn't that right?"

"Fifty-two last month. You know my grandfather. The only emotion I've ever seen him show is anger, but I know he's deeply sad."

Mia reached out and took Daniella's hand. "I really am sorry also.

I didn't know her well, but I could tell how much she cared about you." Out of the corner of her eye, she saw Nonnina's slight nod.

"Thank you," Daniella said before she muttered, "Congratulations on your pregnancy." She quickly turned to Nonnina. "I understand we'll be somewhat neighbors soon."

"Oh?" Nonnina tilted her head.

"Yes, Al and I are buying a home in Mendham."

Mia felt her mouth fall open and knew she deserved the side-eye glance Nonnina threw her way.

"That's just lovely," Nonnina cooed.

"Congratulations," Mia added.

Mia couldn't believe what she just heard and couldn't understand why Daniella and Al would move to New Jersey. Al was a Captain for Don Esposito in New York, and it didn't make sense why he would move away from his territory.

Nonnina gently guided Mia out of the conversation and toward the garden where private family photos were being taken.

As they returned to their table, Mia whispered, "I apologize for my reaction when Daniella announced she was moving to New Jersey. I immediately felt my facial expression, and I will most definitely try to learn how to manage that."

Nonnina waved her hand. "No worries. It took me quite a while to be able to control my facial expressions every time Helena Esposito dropped a bomb on me."

"I thought you two were good friends."

"Friends is not the word I would use," Nonnina chuckled. "Adversaries is much better suited."

"Really?" Mia shook her head. "I really do have a lot to learn from you." Mia leaned in. "Why do you think Daniella and Al would be moving to New Jersey."

"I've been pondering that myself, and I don't like it. We'll have to keep a close eye on what they do here, paying close attention to who they socialize and do business with. If there's one thing I know for certain it's that the Espositos do everything for their own benefit. Rarely will they do something for their community, and if they do, it's because they get an even bigger benefit out of it."

Their conversation was interrupted as the band leader announced, "And now ladies and gentlemen, if you would please find your seats, it's time for a special dance between the bride and her grandfather, Don Bocelli."

Nonnuccio kissed Vicky on the cheek, took her hand and led her to the middle of the dance floor. Carla quickly sat next to Nonnina and held her hand as the band began to play, Paul Anka's, *The Times of Your Life.*

Mia had heard that song many, many times but it wasn't until she felt the deep emotions that flowed through the ballroom that she understood the magnitude of the lyrics. She felt Artie's hands on her shoulders, but she was unable to see clearly as the tears flowed down her cheeks and she silently gasped trying to contain her composure. She wiped her eyes with her napkin, and through her tears, she could make out Vicky's head leaning on Nonnuccio's shoulder with her own tears flowing down her face. Mia had never seen Nonnuccio look so peaceful as he held his granddaughter tightly and swayed to the music with his eyes closed.

Mia glanced at Nonnina and Aunt Carla who sat with their heads held high clinging to each other as they held hands under the table. Ray stood behind his mother with his hands folded in front of him, his glassy eyes contradicting his stalwart stance. He looked at Mia and nodded slowly sharing the heartache that consumed her.

As the song came to an end, Nonnina stood and strode onto the dance floor joining her granddaughter and husband in a long tight hug. The room exploded in applause and cheers, and knowing how to lighten the mood, the band segued into the song, *Celebration* from Kool and the Gang.

"Let's dance," Artie said as he grabbed Mia's hand and led her to the dance floor followed by Matt and Theresa.

Vicky, Angelo, Josie, Ray, Carla and Luca joined them on the dance floor where they formed a circle, dancing and hugging each other. Mia closed her eyes and sang to the music getting lost in the lyrics. When she opened her eyes, she raced off the dance floor, grabbed Tony and Ruth's hands, and dragged them into the circle where Carla put her arm around Ruth, and Luca and Tony exchanged pats on the back. *Now, this is a celebration!* Mia said to herself.

Theresa and Matt were the only ones from the family circle who stayed on the dance floor with Mia and Artie after the song ended. Together they sang and danced through another three songs releasing the bittersweet emotions they all felt after watching Nonnuccio dance with Vicky. But when the band started to play the song, *Shout*, and they started to bounce around the dance floor to the music, Mia noticed a strange look on Theresa's face. Theresa grabbed her stomach and buckled over in obvious pain as a sudden gush of liquid spilled to the floor. Mia quickly grabbed Theresa's arm and called out to Matt who had left the dance floor and was talking to Nonnuccio.

"Oh my God," Theresa shrieked.

"It's okay, you're okay," Mia soothed. "Artie, can you give me a hand?" She scolded as she turned toward Artie who was standing in the center of the dance floor staring at Theresa.

Vicky ran over, "What's going on?"

Theresa looked up at her and burst out crying, "I'm so sorry. My water just broke."

Vicky blinked quickly, turned, and ran to Matt who hadn't heard Mia's calls over the music.

Within seconds, Nonnina, Carla, and Josie were at Theresa's side as Josie calmly directed Artie to bring the car to the front entrance, and for Matt and Mia to get Theresa to the hospital with Artie. Mia knew that she needed to remain calm, so she took a deep breath, grabbed her and Theresa's purses, and waved at Tony and Ruth as she took Theresa's arm and helped her to the car.

As they were leaving, Ray cut off the band and announced, "I apologize for the commotion everyone, but I'M ABOUT TO BE A GRANDFATHER."

THIRTY-TWO

"CAN YOU *PLEASE* drive faster!" Matt yelled from the back of the car in between Theresa's groans.

"I'm going ten miles an hour over the speed limit," Artie barked back.

"For God's sake, we've got connections in every police department in the state. Speed up will ya!"

"How are you doing, Theresa?" Mia turned to see Theresa staring down at her legs squeezing Matt's hand.

"Fanfreakingtastic! How do you think I am?" Theresa growled.

Mia quickly turned back in her seat and saw Artie shake his head at her as his eyes grew wide. "We're almost there," Mia whispered trying to be reassuring.

Theresa's moans were jolting and petrifying. *Is this what I have to look forward to?* Mia thought to herself as she squeezed her eyes and tried to think of anything to distract her from Theresa's distress.

"Okay, this is it," Artie said as he pulled the car up to the Emergency Room entrance.

Matt and Mia jumped out of the car and led Theresa into the hospital as Artie sped off to park the car. By the time he found his way to the waiting room, Matt and Theresa had been admitted and were led into a delivery room. Artie ran his hands through his hair as he slumped into a chair. "Wow."

Mia let out a long sigh, "I know."

"*Wow*," Artie repeated.

"*I know.*" Mia put her head on Artie's shoulder.

"We're not gonna be like them when it's our turn." Artie shook his head. "They were unbearable."

Mia pulled her head up and turned to Artie. "Really?" she said. "We're probably going to be worse."

"Nah." He shook his head. "You and me, we're good under pressure."

Mia nodded, "How do you think you're going to react when you see me in that much pain?"

Artie raised his eyebrows. "Okay, you might have a point there." He took her hand. "Only three more months until we get to meet our little peanut."

"Yeah," Mia sighed.

"What's wrong?"

"Nothing."

"Something's wrong. What's going on?"

"Do you think we're going to be good at it? Being parents?"

"Of course." He kissed her head and pulled her into him. "You're going to be an amazing mother, and I'm going to be a very involved father. Just you wait and see."

"I wish I had your confidence on that."

"You don't believe I'm going to help?" He huffed.

She rubbed her hand on his thigh. "I have no doubt you're going to be the best father ever." She stopped talking and stared down at her hands.

"Listen to me, Stella. You've got this. You're going to be a great mother."

"How do you know? My mother thought she was going to be

a great mother when she had me, and you know what happened there." She turned and looked at him holding her breath.

"You can't compare yourself to your mother." Artie took Mia's face in his hands. "She had it tough. You're not like her."

"But what if I'm bad at being maternal like she was?" She whispered.

Artie shook his head vigorously. "Nope, not gonna happen. I know you! When you love, you love deeply. That's just who you are." He pulled her in and kissed her tenderly.

"She threw me out!" Matt bellowed as he stormed into the waiting room.

"What?" Artie looked around.

"Theresa threw me out of the delivery room. She said I was annoying her."

Artie and Mia caught each other's eyes and burst out laughing.

"What?" Matt glared at them.

"Nothing, man. Come here, sit down." Artie moved over to let Matt sit between him and Mia.

Matt let out a large breath as he sat down. "I hope you're ready, Artie. Everything changes once the kids come along."

"I'm looking forward to it."

"It's pretty great, but sometimes I miss the old days. You know, bonfires on the beach, hanging out in clubs all night, drinking shots until you have to close one eye to see."

"That sounds like fun." Mia pushed her shoulder against him.

"It was, back then." Matt shrugged.

"A lot has changed since those days," said Artie.

"Yeah," Matt leaned forward and put his head in his hands. He then stood and started to pace. "I hate not being in there with her."

"I'm sure she's alright," Mia soothed. "Artie, why don't you get Matt some coffee."

"You want anything?" He asked as he stood and kissed Mia's cheek.

"No, honey, I'm good."

After Artie was out of earshot, Mia gently led Matt back to his chair. "Are *you* okay?"

Matt turned and looked at Mia, his eyes softened. "Yeah, thanks for asking." He leaned back and looked up at the ceiling. "That's gonna be you soon, you know."

"I know." She hesitated, "I just hope I can be half as good a mother as Theresa is."

He looked at her for a long moment and chuckled. "She does make it look easy, but between you and me, she has her moments." He shrugged. "We all do as parents. You just do the best you can and pray."

"Mr. Bocelli?" A nurse rushed up to Matt. "Your wife wants you back in the delivery room."

"Whelp, gotta go." Matt hopped to his feet. "Wish me luck."

"Shouldn't we be wishing Theresa luck?" Mia asked as Artie joined them with two cups of coffee.

"Nah, she's got this, I'm going to be the one she curses out to help her get through the pain."

Mia and Artie's mouths fell open as the nurse led Matt back to the delivery room.

"We are definitely *not* going to be like them." Mia shook her head

They made themselves as comfortable as they could and passed the time discussing baby names. Mia wanted a fresh modern name like Nicole, Tiffany, Ryan, or Zach, and Artie was set on classic Italian names like Angela, Maria, Marco, or Vincenzo.

"Okay, I draw the line at Whitney." Artie threw up his arms and burst out laughing. "I know she's an incredible singer, but I'd prefer not to name my daughter after her."

"Any news yet?" Josie raced toward them like a tornado still wearing her gown from the wedding, her arms full of bags.

"Ma! What are ya doin?" Artie jumped to his feet and took the bags from her.

"I had them box up the leftovers from the reception. We can't let all that good food go to waste." She pulled out a small box and a plastic fork. "You've got to try the cake, it was wonderful."

"Madone, Josie," Ray snorted as he bounded into the waiting room toting more bags. "Let's say hello before you start serving up cake."

Josie waved her hand. "Are there any updates?"

"Nothing yet," Artie said as he pushed a large forkful of cake into his mouth.

"The waiting is the hard part," Ray said shaking his head.

"The hard part is the delivery," Josie countered. "I was in labor for over twelve hours with this one," she said pointing to Artie. "And Matt, he slipped out within two hours. You just never know. Now your Aunt Mary? Her boy, Bobby, was breach! That was a nightmare."

"Breach?" Mia's eyes grew large.

"You won't have to worry about that these days," Josie said. "Now they do that Cesarean delivery where they can just cut you open and take the baby out. Mary had to push Bobby out feet first. And he was close to eight pounds. Just about killed her."

Mia caught Artie's eyes in a panic. She needed the conversation to end before she ran out of the room in hysterics.

Artie nodded at Mia and managed to change the subject, "How was the rest of the wedding?"

Mia was never more thankful for her husband than she was at that moment. She pushed aside all of her stress over giving birth and being a mother, indulged in a piece of cake, and delighted in hearing all of the wedding gossip. It was close to another two hours before Matt appeared in the waiting room.

"It's a girl," he said simply with tears in his eyes.

Josie gasped and put her hands to her mouth. "How are they?"

"Theresa's exhausted, but they're both doing great."

"Ha Ha!" Ray exclaimed, "I'm a grandfather! To a girl!"

"Do you have a name yet?" Mia asked.

"Jodine Marie Bocelli" Matt answered proudly. "But we'll call her Jodi."

"That's a beautiful name," Mia whispered as she hugged him tightly.

"Look, I know you all want to see her, but it's late and we're pretty tired. Why don't you all go home and get some sleep? You can visit tomorrow."

"That's a great idea," Artie nodded and hopped to his feet.

"Not so fast," Ray said as he shuffled through one of the bags. "We're not going anywhere until we toast our new family member." He held up a bottle of champagne and a sleeve of plastic cups in each hand.

THIRTY-THREE

SPRING, 1988

MIA SIPPED HER lemon water as she waited for the other Bocelli women to arrive at Bella Cucina. She checked her watch for the third time in two minutes, anxious to get back to work. She only had about a month before the estate was scheduled to be completed and everyone moved in. While there hadn't been many major issues crop up with the project, there were a number of items that remained to be completed, appliances to be installed, and furniture to be delivered. She would've preferred to skip lunch, but Nonnina insisted that she, Vicky, and Theresa meet with La Sorellanza at that very place, time, and date.

"Ciao," Vicky sang as she and Theresa were led to the table.

"Look at you!" Mia rushed to Theresa with her arms out. "You had a baby only a month ago and somehow you look thinner than you did before getting pregnant."

"She looks great, right?" Vicky added as she kissed Mia on the cheek.

"Well, I'll tell you, I definitely don't feel as good as I look." Theresa removed her sunglasses. "Look at these eyes! You can go away for a month with these bags." She slumped into a chair. "I miss sleep."

"Mia, I've gotta say. You're looking pretty fantastic too." Vicky grabbed her arms and swung her around. "You don't look six months pregnant at all."

Theresa took a big gulp of coffee. "You really are carrying small. How do you feel?"

Mia squeezed her eyes as she and Vicky slid into their chairs. The truth was she hadn't realized she was carrying small until her doctor mentioned it at her exam the week before. She advised Mia to slow down on her working hours and make sure she ate a good, hearty, and balanced meal at least three times a day. She hadn't mentioned the doctor's concerns to anyone, not even Artie. For now, she was trying to be better at eating healthier meals, but she knew her work schedule wouldn't slow down until the middle to the end of July. She didn't really know how she was *supposed* to feel being six months pregnant, but other than a bit of heartburn, exhaustion, and her body aching by the end of the day, she thought things were going well.

"I feel really good." She forced a smile and tried to change the subject. "How's my goddaughter?"

"Jodi has become quite a spoiled princess." Theresa laughed. "She's got the guys wrapped around her finger. Both Matt and Mickey run to her every time she makes a noise."

"Wait. What's *happening*?" Mia pointed to the door where every staff member had lined up.

"They must be here," Vicky said.

As Mia watched them enter, she felt the tingle of goosebumps flow down her arms. Her mouth fell open slightly as every staff member and patron bowed their heads when Nonnina, Carla, and Josie drifted through the restaurant to their table in the back corner. For the first time, she had felt the magnitude of respect that these women commanded.

"Hello, darlings." Nonnina greeted them with a kiss on each

cheek and took her seat at the head of the rectangle table with Carla and Josie filling in the other empty seats. "I know how terribly busy you all are, and I thank you for joining us today." She held out a hand to the hostess who was headed in their direction and slightly shook her head.

"As this is a business meeting, I won't take up your valuable time with catching up and small talk, we'll have that opportunity during brunch on Sunday. I trust you are all well?"

Mia, Vicky, and Theresa looked at each other and nodded quickly.

"Very good." Nonnina continued. "Let's get to it. Each of you has begun being mentored for your roles as senior Bocelli wives and I'm proud to say you all have been remarkable in understanding the significance of your positions and honing your proficiencies." She nodded to Carla and Josie. "We all agree that it's now time that the three of you start becoming more involved with our philanthropic endeavors and begin incorporating the La Sorellanza engagements into your schedules." She waved her hands around. "First and foremost being our weekly luncheon."

"Weekly luncheon?" Vicky asked with a slight headshake.

"Yes, that's right," Carla said. "Each week we dine in one of the family's restaurants. It's how we keep in touch with the community."

"Keep in touch with the community?" Theresa's eyes widened.

Carla nodded and leaned in. "It's essential for the principal Bocelli wives to be a positive presence within our neighborhoods. Families must be able to trust and depend on us during both the good and the difficult times."

"Of course, during most of the year we focus on the Northern New Jersey communities, but once summer comes and we're living down the shore for the season, we are sure to concentrate on the Southern half of the state," Josie added smiling warmly.

Mia sensed both Vicky and Theresa's displeasure at the notion of traveling around the state each week to have lunch. It wasn't always easy for Vicky to take a lunch break when she was working on a large case let alone leave the office for a few hours. But Mia guessed that the partners at Hornstein, Drakeford, and Brown would have no problem with Vicky taking time out of the office each week to tend to Bocelli Family business. Theresa, on the other hand, surprised Mia. She thought her sister-in-law would welcome the opportunity to take a small break from motherhood each week for an opportunity to benefit the family. Theresa had admitted that she relished the role of mother and wife, but she still called Mia for some adult conversation multiple times a week.

"What do these lunches entail?" Mia cocked her head.

Josie cleared her throat. "Not much really, we enjoy a great meal together and get the opportunity to catch up with people from the community that we've come to know and perhaps helped in the past."

"We also introduce ourselves to anyone who might've recently moved into the neighborhood," Carla added as she looked around at them. "Really girls don't look so anxious, these lunches are quite enjoyable."

Nonnina waved the hostess over. "Camilla," she said proudly. "You remember my granddaughters, Mia, Victoria, and Theresa? They're going to be a permanent addition to our luncheons." She smiled at the girls, and Mia thought she saw Nonnina wink at Camilla.

Mia recognized Camilla as the wife of one of the family Captains, Nico. She always liked Nico and Camilla and got a big kick out of their bickering. They both had strong opinions but big hearts and had no doubt that they loved each other in spite of their banter.

"That's very nice to hear." Camilla beamed. "I'm sure everyone will embrace you warmly."

Nonnina nodded. "What's good today?"

"You're going to love the Scungilli Salad. Chef Bobby tried something new and added artichoke." She tilted her head and nodded. "Really took it to a new level."

"That sounds wonderful, let's get a plate of that for starters, and then follow it up with the Chicken Piccata and Linguini."

"Of course. Family style like usual?"

Nonnina looked at Carla and Josie who nodded in agreement. "Yes, that would be lovely." She leaned closer to Camilla, "How's everyone doing?"

"Fairly well," Camilla smiled brightly. "Tracey Johnson would like to personally thank you for the baby items you sent over; Rose Young has an update on her work situation; and Renee Cook is home from college and would like to stop by and say hello."

"Very good."

As Camilla nodded and retreated toward the kitchen, Mia met both Vicky and Theresa's eyes. It was clear neither of them were expecting this type of lunch, and they were just as perplexed as Mia.

"It'll be nice to see Renee. She was so excited to go off to Rutgers," Josie said as she dipped a piece of bread in olive oil.

"Yes," Carla agreed. "I just hope Rose's job is going well. It had to be hard for her to go to work after Jim died."

"Excuse me, Donna Bocelli?" A young girl tentatively approached the table. Mia knew it was Renee as she was wearing a Rutgers tee shirt. She shifted from one foot to the other as she wrung her hands in front of her. "I'm sorry to disturb you all during your lunch."

"Renee!" Nonnina beamed. "You would never disturb us. How's school?"

"It's great. Thank you again for the scholarship."

"And your grades?" Carla raised her eyebrows as she smiled brightly.

"First semester I made the Dean's list, and it looks like I might again this semester."

Josie reached out and put her hand on Renee's arm. "We're so proud of you. Keep it up."

"I will." Renee smiled broadly as she straightened her back. "I appreciate all of your help with the scholarship and everything, and I thought maybe I could do a little something to pay it back."

"No need, sweetheart." Carla waved her arm. "There are a lot of other expenses related to college besides tuition and books."

"Actually, I was thinking more like volunteering my time during the county's Fourth of July Festival to do some face painting for the kids."

"Now that's a fantastic idea," Josie said nodding her head quickly. "The kids would love it."

Carla smiled pointing to Renee, "I like your way of thinking. We could set up a small tent and set you up with the face paints and maybe some stickers." Carla slapped her hand on the table. "Yes, let's do it."

"I agree." Josie squeezed Renee's arm. "I'll contact you when it gets closer to the event to go over details and logistics." She nodded toward Mia, Vicky, and Theresa. "I don't think you met the other women of the Bocelli Family. This is, Mia, Victoria, and Theresa."

"It's very nice to meet you, Renee," Mia said and extended her hand.

"It's nice to meet all of you too," Renee answered biting her lip.

"What are you studying?" Vicky smiled warmly.

"Actually, I haven't officially declared my major yet. I'm torn between Social Work and Criminal Justice. I'm even thinking about Law School after."

"Good choices." Vicky nodded as she reached into her purse. "Here's my card, please feel free to reach out if there's a need."

Renee's eyes widened as she looked at the business card. "You're a lawyer?"

"She's a great lawyer." Mia leaned into Vicky.

"Thank you so much." Renee's eyes shone, and stepped out of the way as a waitress approached the table. "I'll let you get back to your lunch but thank you all for everything."

"You'll hear from me soon, Renee." Josie sang as Renee bounced away from the table.

Mia caught Nonnina's look of approval as she glanced at Mia and Vicky. But she wondered why Theresa didn't join in the conversation with Renee. Mia found her to be a sweet girl and easy to talk to, yet Theresa remained silent with a bewildered look on her face.

"Good afternoon," the waitress said brightly. "I've got your Scungilli Salad."

Mia noticed it was the same young waitress who had insisted on calling her ma'am the last time she had been there.

"Thank you, Dawn." Nonnina took her hand after she placed the platter on the table. "How's your mother?"

Dawn shook her head. "The doctor says it's Dementia."

"Poor Carol."

"They say it will eventually go into Alzheimer's, but we're not quite there yet."

"How are you coping?" Carla asked.

"My cousin Toni is a home health aide and she's been helping a lot. It's tough for me to get there sometimes what with the kids and all."

"I understand." Nonnina squeezed her hand. "Give my best to Carol."

"Thank you, ma'am."

Mia saw how Nonnina, Carla, and even Josie took pride in being called ma'am and wore it like a badge of honor. She had already felt bad about snapping at Dawn over the term, but now she felt even worse. It was clearly a sign of respect and reverence, and when this young waitress tried to show Mia the same type of respect, she cut her down. She made a mental note to pull Dawn aside and make it right.

"Josie, I think we ought to send over a large meal to Carol each Sunday. Something that can be reheated easily during the week." Nonnina said as she passed the salad.

"I was thinking the same thing. They're going to have a tough road ahead of them." Josie shook her head.

They spent the next hour enjoying their meal and talking with some of the patrons at the restaurant. Tracey Johnson brought her five-month-old to the table and was very thankful for the case of diapers and formula the Sisterhood arranged to have delivered. It turned out, she was a single mother trying to make ends meet since the baby's father moved away and hadn't been heard from since the day she gave birth. Rose Young made a quick stop at the table announcing her recent promotion to Office Manager at the Insurance Agency where she worked. She cried tears of happiness as she explained that when her husband died no one wanted to hire a fifty-five-year-old woman who never worked a day in her life, but the Sisterhood helped her get a secretarial job.

Mia, Vicky, and Theresa were met with warm hugs and nods of appreciation as they were introduced around the restaurant. Story after story of the Bocelli generosity through the years were shared, and Mia had started to see just how much the Sisterhood had done in this neighborhood alone. She knew that the Bocellis did a lot for the community, but she hadn't realized it was on such a grand scale. She had enjoyed hearing how much good the Sisterhood had done and was proud that she was now a part of it.

After lunch, Mia spent the rest of the day at the estate. As she was navigating a golf cart toward the main house, she noticed Artie's car parked in front and marveled at the fact that her heart still skipped a beat when he popped up unexpectedly to pay her a visit at work. She found him inside standing with his hands on his hips as he gazed around the front foyer.

"Do you like what you see?"

"Mia. It's breathtaking." He slowly circled around taking in each detail of the marble columns, the Tiffany skylight, and the grand staircase that split off on the second level."

"The family was quite specific with their desires."

"Has anyone seen this yet?" He waved his hand around.

"They've seen and approved most of the elements separately, but they haven't seen everything pulled together. I'm saving that for the big reveal."

He pulled her in close and took her face in his hands. "You've outdone yourself." He kissed her long and slow.

She melted into his embrace suddenly realizing how much she needed his warm touch. "I'm exhausted," she whispered.

"Whaddya say we get you home and into a nice warm bath."

"That sounds amazing, I do love my baths. But I have to go through today's project sheet to make sure everything was done and done correctly."

He took the clipboard from her hands. "I'll help you. You can give me a tour as we work through it."

Mia raised her eyebrows as she considered his offer. "So, like, you'll be my assistant, and I'll be your boss?"

"If you wanna look at it that way, sure." He shrugged.

"I think I'm gonna like this," she chided.

"Just don't get used to it." He laughed and smacked her butt as she led him through the foyer into the kitchen.

"I had a very interesting lunch today."

"I forgot about that. Was it fun?"

"Did you know that Nonnina, Mom, and Aunt Carla go around and have lunch at various Bocelli restaurants each week?"

"I really never paid attention to what they did during the day."

"Well, they do, and they talk to the people of the community and help people out. You know, with food and stuff if people are struggling."

"Really?" He cocked his head. "I didn't know that."

"Apparently they've been doing this for a long time, and now they want me, Vicky, and Theresa to start doing it."

"Huh. How do you feel about that?"

"I. I. never thought about it. I love the idea of helping people, but I'm nothing like them. They're all caviar and champagne and I'm hotdogs and beer."

Artie tilted his head back in laughter. "I wouldn't go that far. You've got class. Look at this place. If this isn't classy, I don't know what is."

"Give me any home and I can class it up with the best of them, but they have a certain quality that I don't think I have. Like when they enter a room, everyone's breath is taken away just by their presence."

"Hey," he said as he kissed her cheek. "You take my breath away with your presence."

It was clear to Mia that Artie couldn't understand the point she was making. She smiled at him and put her hand to his cheek. He was so handsome and so attentive, yet so clueless when she tried to talk about her own insecurities. Mia decided it would probably be best to suppress her self-doubt for the moment, took his hand, and placed it on her belly.

"Little peanut wants to say hello to Daddy."

"Hey, there it is." He marveled. "Now don't kick Mommy too hard."

She gazed at her husband who was now bent over her belly talking to the baby.

"Come on Daddy, let's get to work so you can take me home and cook me dinner."

"You got it, boss."

THIRTY-FOUR

MIA LIFTED HER face toward the sun and allowed the warmth to soak through her. It burned away the anxiety of the estate project and her concern about her baby being too small. She took deep cleansing breaths and repeated the mantra *breathe in faith, breathe out fear.* Her sister Nancy had taught her that trick when she was going through her yoga and meditation phase, and now Mia found that it actually worked.

"Mia? Are you listening to me?" Vicky poked at her.

"Oh, yeah, Vick, I am." Mia was jolted out of her Zen space. "Sorry. It's so nice today, I was just enjoying the sun."

"Like I was saying," Vicky continued, "It looks like Ange is going to be promoted to Captain and get his own territory."

"Let me ask you something. I know you grew up in this life, but doesn't all of this ever get to you sometimes?"

"What do you mean?" Vicky tilted her head.

Mia hesitated. She'd never had a frank discussion with Vicky about the family business, but she found herself feeling bold. Maybe it was the pregnancy hormones, maybe it was all of the immersion into the Sisterhood, but Mia felt like the time was right to have the conversation.

"I mean, the Bocelli Family is New Jersey's most powerful

family. Does it ever bother you how the family got there?"

Vicky stared out over her parents' meticulously groomed garden.

"I don't let myself think about it," she whispered. "I mean, I know the Bocellis pride themselves on not being as ruthless and violent as some of the other families." She pushed her eyebrows up and shrugged her shoulders. "But there are those times when Ange comes home and takes a long hot shower, pours himself a drink, and sits in the dark for the rest of the night." She shook her head. "Then I know. I know what the family is really all about." She lets out an ironic chuckle. "And, now? Now, I'm proud that my husband is moving up in the organization and running his own territory."

"Do you suppose that's why Nonnina, Mom, and Aunt Carla formed La Sorellanza? You know, to maybe balance things out?"

"Could be," Vicky said thoughtfully. "I'm just surprised that I've never known about any of it until now. Especially with all the good they're doing. Why didn't I know? How did I miss it?"

"You probably weren't looking. You were living life." Mia leaned in. "If they kept this a secret, do you think there are other things we don't know?"

"Without a doubt."

They sat in silence as they took in the sounds of the rest of the family conversing inside the house. From the outside, they appeared like any family that had gathered together for a Sunday brunch. Ray beamed as he held his new granddaughter in his arms. Josie rolled a ball on the floor for Mickey to chase. Nonnina and Nonnuccio held hands as they sat on the couch lovingly whispering to each other. Theresa and Dee shuffled around the kitchen washing dishes. But then reality slinked into the picture as Luca, Matt, Artie, Angelo, and Joe huddled together in a deep conversation that no one would be able to decipher, let alone hear. It was those intense huddles that unnerved Mia the most. They were a reminder that the family she loved so very much was imperfect.

Vicky broke their silence. "I do like the idea of being able to help people though."

"Me too!" Mia nodded enthusiastically and turned to Vicky. "Do you think Theresa is okay with all of this? She was very subdued at lunch."

"I noticed that too. But I don't think she's all that comfortable in the spotlight. Don't get me wrong, she can be quite the spitfire, but she'd been brought up to keep her head down and mind her business."

"Hmm, okay I can see that. I guess that's why Nonnina felt like she was like your mom and organizing things was her strong suit."

"Yeah, probably." Vicky shrugged.

"I hope we can make them proud."

"Make who proud?" Theresa asked as she shifted Jodi in her arms, closed the sliding door, and sat next to Mia.

"Nonnina, Aunt Carla, and Mom. We were just talking about our lunch the other day," Mia said as she took Jodi from Theresa's arms and kissed her head.

"That was something, wasn't it?" Theresa let out a long breath.

"How do you feel about the Sisterhood?" Mia asked.

"Actually, I'm a little overwhelmed by it all."

"I am too, kind of." Mia agreed.

"I think we'll be fine," Vicky said leaning forward. "We just have to get used to it all." She craned her neck as she looked in the house. "Uh oh." Vicky looked at her watch and then pointed inside the house. "Now that's a record. Dee hasn't been here more than two hours and already she's drunk and starting trouble."

Mia could see Dee flailing her arms as Aunt Carla and Josie appeared to be calming her down. She followed Vicky and Theresa into the house and handed Jodi off to Matt, who met them at the door.

"Well, there they are. The three little princesses." Dee pointed to them.

"What's going on?" Vicky looked wide-eyed at her mother.

"I should've been at that lunch this week." Dee pounded her chest. "I've been a part of this family longer than any of you, and I've earned a seat at that table."

"Watch yourself, Dee. This is not the time or place." Carla said putting a hand on her shoulder.

"If I can't talk about it here and now, then when? When does the next Underboss's wife get to have her say? Hmm?" Dee stumbled. "I should be the one. Me. I've given years of loyalty to this family. The girls," She swayed as she pointed toward Mia, Vicky, and Theresa. "They're too young. They don't have experience."

Josie leaned into Dee's face. "You've got to stop this right now."

The room fell silent as Nonnina entered. "Is there a problem?" She stared into Dee's eyes.

"Dee was just questioning her absence at lunch," Carla replied nodding slowly at her mother.

"I see. Well, that is a conversation that should take place in the privacy of Josie's office. I will not have Nonnuccio awoken from his nap over this." She glared at Dee as she led Josie and Carla to the office.

Dee lifted her glass of vodka and orange juice and swallowed it down in one gulp before stumbling after them down the hall.

"What the heck?" Mia whispered to Vicky.

"And she wonders why she's not embraced by the women of the family," Vicky whispered back.

Mia turned to see Luca shouting at Joe out on the patio, pointing a finger in his face. "I'm telling you right now, you've got to do something about her."

Joe shook his head and raised his hands. "I've tried Luca. I don't know what to do."

"This is unacceptable." Luca's face was dark red. "I can't have the wife of my Underboss getting drunk and acting out every time she's in public."

"Okay, okay." Joe nodded in defeat.

"If you don't handle *this*, how can I trust you to handle anything *else*?"

"I'll take care of it."

Luca waved him off and stormed back into the house. He nodded his head toward Ray's office and thundered across the room with Ray, Matt, Artie, and Angelo following closely behind.

"Wow," Mia said as she slunk onto the couch. "I knew Dee liked to drink but I didn't think it was this bad."

"It's gotten worse since Nonnuccio got sick and Joe was told he would be Underboss," Vicky answered as she and Theresa joined Mia.

"Why do you think?" Theresa asked.

"I think she had it in her mind that Joe would become the next Don."

As Josie's office door opened and the ladies began to emerge, Joe blustered in and bounded toward Dee. He grabbed her purse, then her hand, and said, "It's time to go," leaving both the door to the patio and the front door of the house open in their wake.

"Girls, I'm sorry you saw all of that," Josie said as she and Carla sat on the couch and Nonnina sat in the adjacent armchair.

Carla shook her head. "That whole scene was unfortunate and completely uncalled for."

Theresa leaned in. "Was she right? Shouldn't she have been a part of the lunch?"

Nonnina shook her head. "No."

"But she's a Bocelli wife. The wife of the future Underboss."

Josie snorted. "A title doesn't automatically render privilege."

Carla leaned in. "Dee will be the wife of the next Underboss, that's true. But today's spectacle only confirms that she doesn't present herself with the adequate class and dignity that a senior Bocelli wife must present."

Nonnina nodded. "I don't want any of you to give anything she's said today further thought. You are exquisite Bocelli women and you each deserve your position in the family, but more importantly within the future La Sorellanza. I have no doubt the three of you will work together to represent the family with distinction."

"NONNUCCIO LOOKED A little frailer today," Mia said as she put her legs on Artie's lap, and he began to massage her feet.

"Yeah." He sighed. "I noticed that too. But he still has a sharp mind for business, I'll tell ya that."

Mia nodded slowly, her eyes welled up thinking about Nonnuccio. She couldn't imagine what he must be going through knowing his cancer was going to be the death of him. Whatever he was thinking and feeling, he never let on to anyone. He remained the lovable teddy bear that she'd come to adore and the imperial family leader she'd come to respect.

"What was all that with Dee? Luca was beyond furious with Joe."

"Apparently, she feels insulted that she's not a part of the endeavors the Bocelli women oversee."

"I always thought she was a crackpot. I don't know what Joe sees in her."

"They've been married for over twenty years, right? Maybe she changed?"

"Dad and Uncle Luca said she's always been overbearing. She's part of the reason Nonnuccio never even considered Joe to be his own Underboss. It's all about appearances."

"So, I'm learning." Mia bent her left leg so Artie could focus on her right foot.

"I'm just glad I've got you. I know this wasn't our plan, but you and me, we're gonna do good things together. I just know it. Today's drama reminded me how proud I am to have you as my wife."

She reached out and pulled Artie close to her and nuzzled his neck. How does this man always know the right thing to say? She knew she had to tell him the truth about her last doctor's appointment. She didn't feel good about keeping it from him.

She took a deep breath. "Artie, the doctor is a little concerned that the baby may be too small," she whispered.

He pulled away, his eyes grew large. "What does that mean?"

"Nothing yet. She wants me to come in a little more frequently to get checked out. She said it's not time to panic, I just need to make sure I eat right and get a little more rest."

"That's it! I don't want you working on the estate anymore. I want you home taking it easy."

"Well, now, hold on. We only have a few weeks until we move in. The bulk of the project is just about complete. It's only design, deliveries, and landscaping from here on out."

Artie shook his head. "No, you can't keep putting in those long hours. It's not good for you or the baby. Someone else can oversee the design and deliveries."

Mia bit her lip. This is why she didn't want to tell Artie about the doctor's concerns in the first place. How could she possibly walk away from the project now, during the home stretch?

"I feel fine, and I know the baby is doing good too. Little peanut is tumbling around as we speak."

"Mia. I have to put my foot down."

Mia burst out laughing. "Put your foot down?"

"How is that funny? I'm serious."

Mia gulped down her laughter. "It's not funny. I'm sorry for laughing, but, honey, I can't just stop working. The family's depending on me. I've put my heart and soul into this project, and I just can't walk away."

"But when the doctor says you should rest, I tend to agree with the doctor."

"How about a compromise? Maybe I can get an assistant to be onsite and oversee the bulk of the remaining work under my direction. I'll be available if an emergency comes up and will inspect the work at the end of each day. That'll give me all morning and early afternoon to rest."

Artie raised his eyebrows and hesitated. "That could work." He raised his pointer finger. "But if the doctor is still concerned after your next appointment, then you're off the project."

"Deal!" Mia said as she crossed her fingers behind her back.

THIRTY-FIVE

MIA GROANED AS she flung her arm to turn off the blaring alarm clock.

Artie rolled over and swung his leg over Mia's. "Are you ready for your big day?" He asked sleepily.

"It's five a.m., I've had two hours of sleep, and I'm eight months pregnant. I can't wait for this day to be over." She rubbed her eyes. "I need to get up. The movers should be unpacking everyone's things, and I've got a whole crew of people staging each home as we speak."

"Okay." He kissed her cheek. "Let's head on over."

"Oh no, uh huh." She sat up. "You come at three with everyone else."

"No, I'm coming with you to help."

"No, you'll be in the way." She put her hand on his cheek. "I love you, but I got this. I've got seven personal assistants supervising each family member's living space along with a team of people at each dwelling handling all of the unpacking and setup. Carlo will be right by my side all day, and don't forget he's promised you not to let me overdo it." She tapped his cheek. "You can trust him to look out for me."

Artie sighed. "I don't like it, but okay." He jumped out of bed. "I *am* going to make you breakfast before you leave, and I want you to eat every bite."

Carlo met Mia at the front entrance of the main house. "This is it." He kissed each of her cheeks. "I still can't believe we pulled this off."

"You had doubts?"

"Big time." He chuckled. "Not on our talents, but, Mia, I don't think anything this grand and specialized has been pulled off in such a short amount of time."

"I guess we make a great team."

"Undoubtedly. Let me catch you up." He led her through the house, weaving through an array of workers, to the back patio. "We had a few minor issues earlier. The movers started to deliver Vicky and Angelo's things to Matt's house, but Andrea caught it and we're back on track. The truck with the kitchen items arrived late, so I pulled a few of the stagers from your place and assigned them to the kitchen to make up for the lost time."

"Okay, that's not a problem." Mia nodded. "I spoke to Nancy last night and she's going to be here by one with the food and drinks. Maybe I should tell her to come at two?"

Carlo shook his head. "I think we'll be okay for the catering at one. Oh, yeah, and that new intern, Lena, forgot to confirm the floral delivery so I made a few phone calls, woke some people up, and we'll now have beautiful arrangements in place before the big reveal at three."

Mia rolled her eyes. "I warned you about her."

"You did, but I'm thinking she won't make that mistake again. It took a half hour for her to stop crying and for the vein in my forehead to stop bulging."

Mia shook her head, patted him on the back, and started walking toward the golf cart.

"Uhm, where do you think you're going?" Carlo shuffled after her.

"I'm going to each of the cottages to check on things."

"I'll take care of that." He turned her around and led her back toward the house. "Why don't you sit down and oversee the kitchen."

"I'm pregnant, not an invalid."

"I know. But I promised Artie I won't let you overdo it and have no intention of going back on that promise. We'll inspect all of the houses together at noon. I gave everyone a strict deadline to be completed by then."

As Mia made herself comfortable at the dining table in the kitchen, she was grateful that Carlo insisted she sit down. She was exhausted and knew that if she closed her eyes, she would fall asleep right where she was. By noon, all of the assistants had reported that each of the dwellings was completed, and all trash had been hauled away. She was pleased to see that each living space was warm and welcoming and hoped that they met everyone's expectations.

When she returned to the main house, she found Nancy and Rosie busy preparing food and setting up.

"Mia!" Nancy dropped her spoon in the mixing bowl and ran to Mia. "This house is amazing, and that tree-lined drive! What an entrance." She hugged her sister.

"Right? Getting those mature trees wasn't easy, but it was worth it."

"My mother is going to love this kitchen," Rosie added. "I know I'm going to look forward to cooking here every weekend, that's for sure."

Mia turned her head as she heard a commotion in the front entryway. She could make out Josie's distinct voice and Luca's laugh. She looked at her watch. "It's not three yet." She took a deep breath and wrung her hands as she greeted the family.

"You're early." She managed a smile and began hugging everyone.

Artie put his arm around her waist. "Carlo called and said the coast was clear and if we wanted to come early, it would be fine."

"Mia, my sweet." Josie pulled her in for a hug as her eyes welled up. "I can't believe this is our new home."

"I'm going to need a map to find my way around," Ray said as he took in the double staircase leading to the second level.

"Is this an elevator?" Nonnuccio asked as he pressed the button.

"It leads to both the second and the third floors. The third floor is your living space." Mia smiled.

"The whole third floor?" Nonnina asked.

"We wanted you to be comfortable," Luca said as he put his arm around Carla.

"Ciao!" Vicky sang as she, Angelo, Matt, Theresa, and the kids entered the house. "Damn! This is like a museum."

"Would anyone like a cocktail?" Nancy asked as she and Rosie carried trays of champagne and sparkling cider.

Nonnuccio cleared his throat, raised his glass, and said, "Standing here, I see so many blessings that have been bestowed upon our family." He looked at Mia. "You, my dear granddaughter, have helped build a magnificent estate that the Bocellis will call home for generations. I'm proud of you and am honored to live out my last days here." He took Nonnina's hand. "As I look around, I see clearly that it's not the grandeur of the house that reflects the success of my life, it's the privilege of being surrounded by what I love and cherish most in this world. And that is all of you. Here's to our family. Each day I have with you will be my life's greatest treasures."

"Here, here." Nonnina straightened her shoulders, lifted her glass, and nodded.

Luca patted Nonnuccio on the back. "Mia, how about you give us a tour?"

"Sure, I'd love to. Why don't I walk you through the common

areas of the main house, and then you can all explore your own spaces and the grounds at your leisure? Nancy will have dinner ready by six, so we can all sit down together then."

"That's a wonderful idea." Carla squeezed Mia's hand.

After the tour, Carlo gathered everyone outside in front of one of the four-car garages attached to the main house.

"I would like to express my gratitude for allowing CL Designs to build your new estate. It's been an honor and a pleasure working with all of you, and on behalf of the firm, I'd like to present a small token of our appreciation." Carlo pressed a button on the garage door opener to reveal a line of eight golf carts with personalized plates for each of the families.

"This is amazing," Vicky squealed as she jumped into her and Angelo's cart. "Hop in honey, let's take it for a spin." She waved her hand and cried, "Thanks, Carlo," as they sped away.

Nonnina embraced Carlo. "This was not necessary."

"I know," he said. "But this project has catapulted the firm, and I'm having to turn down business because I can't keep up with the demand. Thank you for that."

"That wasn't us, my dear." She kissed his cheek and sat in the passenger seat next to Nonnuccio as he honked the horn and drove off.

"HOW DID YOU ever pull this off?" Vicky put a cup of tea in front of Mia.

"I'm still not sure." Mia sat at her kitchen table with her legs up on one of the chairs.

"You should be so proud of yourself. Ange and I love everything about our house, and I know Matt and Theresa feel the same about theirs. Apparently, Mickey hopped right into his speed car bed and put himself to sleep."

"Now that's the best approval of the day." Mia beamed.

"You know, the boys'll be over there playing pool with Uncle Luca every night. When Ange saw the pool table in his office, he smacked his head and said he should've gotten one for his space."

"It's not too late you know," Mia said as the doorbell rang.

"Sit, I'll get it," Vicky said as she crossed the room. "Nonnina, come in."

"Am I at the right cottage? I was looking for Mia."

"Yup, I made her stay put."

"You don't have to ring the bell," Mia said as she started to stand.

Nonnina waved her hand and sat at the table with Vicky and Mia. "I didn't want to just walk into your house, but ringing the bell did feel formal."

"How about we just ring and walk in? I'll turn the entry light off if we don't want to be disturbed," Mia suggested.

"Great idea." Vicky agreed. "Let's all do that."

"I just wanted to stop by and tell you how much I appreciate your designs and attention to detail in our space. You really captured the essence and significance of the scarf."

Mia closed her eyes and grabbed Nonnina's hand, "Thank you. I'm so happy you like it."

"No, *we* love it," she said. "There are a few business matters I would like to discuss with both of you." She shook her head. "I have it on good authority that Daniella is making herself known within the community. She's joined the Women's League and has started cementing her place among the upper echelon. I don't have to tell either of you how worrisome this can be."

"What are they up to?" Vicky asked.

"They're making connections here in New Jersey. That can only mean one thing."

"You think they'll try to take over our territory?" Vicky asked.

"I think we should hope for the best and prepare for the worst." Nonnina raised her eyebrows. "Vicky, I would like you to be very diligent with your social calendar. Aunt Carla and I are going to do the same, but you have many contacts within the political and legal field that we don't. It's time to tap into your resources and make yourself known."

"Absolutely, I'm on it."

"Excellent. One more thing. Mia, your sister Nancy and I have had the opportunity to chat today, and I'm quite impressed with her. I've always liked her, and after getting to know her more today, I've decided that I would like to help her in her catering venture."

"Nonnina, that's very generous, but you don't have to."

Nonnina raised her hand. "I insist. It's difficult to build a business from the ground up and given the chance, I believe she could be quite successful."

"I, I don't know what to say." The truth was, Mia was concerned about the Bocelli Family investing in Nancy's business. What would be expected of Nancy in return? Will this put her in a precarious position?

"Talk to her. Your sister is very smart, but I get the sense that having her own financial independence might be good for her. Perhaps we could meet with Artie to discuss a business plan and legalities." Nonnina stood, kissed both Vicky and Mia's cheeks, and strode out the front door. They could hear the honk of her golf cart as she departed.

THIRTY-SIX

"WHAT TIME IS the appointment again?" Artie asked as he pressed his foot on the gas pedal.

"It's two o'clock." She shifted in the passenger's seat. She'd been having appointments with her OB more frequently to monitor the baby's growth. "We have plenty of time."

"I shouldn't have met with Nonnina and Nancy this morning. I should've insisted we meet tonight."

Mia put her hand on Artie's arm. "It's fine, we're fine."

"You know I like to be on time, if not early for these things."

"We will be," Mia reassured. Artie had become more and more anxious at each doctor's appointment, and today was no different.

"Tell me about the meeting. When I asked Nancy if she was interested in accepting help from Nonnina, she cried as she said, 'yes.'"

"The meeting went really well. We crunched some numbers and talked about the legalities. It could get tricky, but I wanna protect Nancy and her business as much as possible just in case she and Richard ever decide to divorce."

"Good." Mia nodded her head. "I don't like Richard's behavior, especially lately. I just don't trust him."

"Yup. I'm gonna try to do all I can."

She wanted to protect her sister as much as she could, which meant that she was also concerned about Nancy accepting help from the family. Mia hesitated. "What does Bocelli backing really mean for Nancy?"

"What do you mean?"

"I mean, how much control will the family have over her business? Will she have large loan payments each month?"

Artie looked at Mia. "What do you think she's getting involved with some loan sharks? Nonnina is giving her granddaughter's sister a financial gift. There's no loan and no obligations. Nonnina likes Nancy and wants to help her succeed."

"I didn't mean to imply anything like that."

"I get it," Artie mumbled as he pulled into the parking lot.

Mia began twirling her hair and Artie began pacing as they waited for Dr. Stragazzi to come into the exam room. Both Mia and Artie didn't think she looked much bigger since the last appointment, and they breathed out a sigh of relief when they heard the baby's heartbeat during the ultrasound. Just that morning, Mia had taken Artie's hand and placed it on her stomach so he could feel their little peanut kick, but there was always that moment of apprehension at the beginning of each ultrasound that made them hold their breath as they waited to hear peanut's official heartbeat.

"Good afternoon Bocellis," Dr. Stragazzi sang as she breezed into the room and put fresh exam gloves on. "How are we feeling today?"

Mia liked and trusted Dr. Stragazzi from the first moment she met her. Originally, she wanted to be a patient of Dr. Steiner, who was her sister, Janet's, OB. But Dr. Steiner wasn't accepting new patients and gave a referral to her partner, Denise Stragazzi. She not only appreciated Dr. Stragazzi's warm, personable demeanor, but she particularly loved the fact that when Dr. Stragazzi was in the room, Mia was her only concern. She took extra time to get to know Mia on a personal level and to really listen to and address all of Mia's thoughts and concerns. Never once did Mia feel rushed, dismissed, or stupid for asking her numerous questions. When Artie met her, he was a bit leery about her youthful appearance, but he was soon comforted by the fact that she graduated top of her class from Johns Hopkins.

"I'm feeling alright, I suppose," Mia answered.

Dr. Stragazzi began to examine Mia as they spoke. "Any pain or discomfort?"

Mia shook her head. "No."

"How's your appetite?"

"She's eating well, Doc. I'm making sure of it." Artie said proudly.

"Are you getting rest?"

"Yes. Now more than ever," Mia said. "Since we moved into our new home a few weeks ago, I've been pretty much off my feet. No one'll let me do anything."

Dr. Stragazzi nodded as she took off her gloves and pulled out the ultrasound results. "I'm going to be honest. I don't love how small baby is."

Mia reached out and grabbed Artie's hand.

"I don't want to alarm you, but you're showing signs of Fetal Growth Restriction."

"What does that mean?" Artie looked back and forth between Mia and the doctor.

"FGR is a condition where a fetus doesn't grow to an expected weight during pregnancy."

"Oh my God," Mia cried as she put her hand over her mouth. "I did this. I did this to our baby."

"No, Mia. No, you didn't." Dr. Stragazzi put her hand on Mia's arm. "You don't have any of the markers that are typically associated with FGR such as high blood pressure, major illness, alcohol or drug usage, and you don't smoke."

"What does this all mean?" Artie asked as he gripped Mia's hand tighter.

"It means I'd like to schedule a Cesarian and deliver your baby early."

"Deliver early? Is that safe?"

"There are always concerns under these circumstances, but I'm confident that your baby's lungs and other vital organs will be in good shape if we deliver early next week."

Mia dropped her head into her hands and sobbed uncontrollably. No matter what Dr. Stragazzi said, she felt like she failed her husband and her baby. What kind of mother was she? She couldn't provide adequate nourishment and protection to her child so it could grow into a healthy baby.

"Mia, it's going to be okay," Dr. Stragazzi said.

"I ... put ... the ... baby ... at ... risk," Mia cried.

"No, no you didn't, Mia."

"I ... worked ... too ... much."

"Now Mia," Dr. Stragazzi took Mia's face in her hands. "I monitored you and the baby throughout your entire pregnancy. I knew all the details of your workload, and I assure you, I would've stepped in and ordered bed rest if I thought you were doing harm to your baby." She looked to Artie and then back at Mia. "This is not on you!"

"Listen to the doctor, Stella," Artie said. "She knows better than we do."

Mia took a few deep cleansing breaths, wiped her face with Artie's shirt, and said, "Okay."

"Okay," Artie said as he kissed Mia's head.

"Okay," Dr. Stragazzi said as she opened Mia's file. "My nurse, Lucy, will be in to discuss the details and procedures, but it looks like your little peanut will have Tuesday, August 2nd as their birthday." Dr. Stragazzi smiled. "In the meantime, I'd like you to take it easy, continue to eat healthy, and stay off of your feet."

Once Mia was home and settled on the couch with her favorite blanket and pillow, she called Josie and Ruth, knowing that within minutes they would spread the word about the baby's condition and her impending C-Section. Within two hours, Ruth had shown up with a large pot of her Chicken Soup with Josie, who had a large tray of Gina's Eggplant Rollatini and a tray of lasagne.

"You know, we won't be able to eat all of this food in three days," Artie chided as he led them to the kitchen.

"Nonsense." Josie waved her hand. "We'll go through all of this along with the other trays we have Gina making.

Ruth nodded. "When people visit, you'll need to feed them."

"Visit?" Mia asked.

"Of course. Anthony and Susan said they're going to stop by this weekend, Janet and Ryan will bring the kids over on Sunday, and Nancy said she's thinking about packing a bag to stay with you to help out."

Josie nodded. "Yes, and we'll all be over as well."

Mia and Artie exchanged looks. "You do know Mia is supposed to rest."

"How else will she rest if we all don't come by to look after her?" Josie and Ruth looked at each other and shook their heads.

"You won't have to worry about a thing," Ruth reassured him. "We want to make sure you both have a peaceful, relaxing weekend and neither of you will have to lift a finger or move from the couch."

"Mia, my sweet, when you get tired and feel like a nap, you just let either Grammy or me know, and we'll help you to your room." Josie kissed Mia's head just as she heard a commotion at the front door. "That must be the guys."

Mia looked at Artie and mouthed the words, "The guys?"

Artie shrugged and watched as Josie opened the door for Ray and Tony who were carrying two more trays of food, a large bowl of salad, and three loaves of bread. Just as she was about to close the door, Angelo and Vicky appeared carrying a case of wine and four pitchers of iced tea.

"There's my Mia, Mia, Bo Meena. How are you feeling?" Tony kissed his granddaughter and sat on the adjacent couch.

"I'm okay, Poppy."

"Are you?" He eyed her suspiciously.

"I'm a little scared," she whispered.

Ruth and Josie's ears perked up when they heard Mia, and Josie nodded to Ruth.

"Oh, sweetheart. I can understand that." Ruth sat next to Mia and pulled her granddaughter's legs across her lap. "But we need to trust Dr. Stragazzi, she knows what she's doing. Don't forget I had a tough time of it with Nancy, and she was born much earlier than her due date. There were a lot of concerns about her lungs, and we both had to stay in the hospital for over a month. But everything turned out just fine."

"You have to think positive thoughts," Tony said as he pointed his finger.

THROUGHOUT THE REST of the weekend, Mia didn't have a moment to worry about the baby. She and Artie had a never-ending flow of visitors dropping by. It took a lot, but they were able to convince Nancy it wasn't necessary for her to stay the weekend. When Sunday evening rolled around, Artie insisted that everyone go home and get some rest. He wanted to spend the night alone with his wife before they checked into the hospital Monday afternoon.

She lay in his arms as he ran his hands over her baby bump.

"Artie, what if?"

"No, uh huh, no what if's. Only positive thoughts."

She took a cleansing breath. She lifted her head urgently. "A name. We don't have a name."

"You mean we can't call him peanut forever?"

"No, we can't call *her* peanut forever."

"Hmm. Okay, let's start with boy names. My favorites are Rocco, Dario, Silvio, and Bob."

Mia looked up at Artie. "Bob?"

"Yup, Bob."

She stared at him for a long moment and realized he was serious. "My favorites are John, James, and Edward."

"Edward is too formal."

"We can call him Eddie."

"Eh, I like Bob better."

"What about Armando?" She raised her eyebrows.

"Armando?"

"Yeah, after Nonnuccio."

"I like that. Armando Arthur Bocelli."

"Yes!" Mia nodded in satisfaction.

"Now for girl names. I really like Maddalena," Artie said.

"Maddalena? That's beautiful. You never mentioned that name before."

"I just heard the name the other day, and it kinda stuck in my mind."

Mia smiled. "I love it. Maddalena Rose Bocelli."

"Rose?"

"It was my mother's middle name."

Artie squeezed Mia tightly and whispered, "Then Rose it is. She'll be our little flower."

THIRTY-SEVEN

"HOW LONG WILL she have to be in the NICU?" Mia asked as she clung to her baby girl.

Dr. Stragazzi looked up from Mia's chart and said, "We'll run some tests to make sure her organs are as healthy as they seem, but we're probably looking at a few days. We need to monitor her blood sugar levels, and I would ideally like to get her weight up a bit. Four pounds three ounces is a good weight for an FGR baby, but I'd feel more comfortable if we can get her closer to five pounds."

"But we can visit her, right? In the NICU?" Artie sat on Mia's bedside with his right arm around his wife and his left hand on his daughter's head.

"Yes. The nurses will be in to go over all of the protocols and procedures. Mia, you'll be in some pain from the C-Section, so I'd warn you to be extra careful." Dr. Stragazzi looked over at the nurse and nodded. "I'm sorry, but we really need to bring Maddalena to the NICU now."

"So soon?" Mia cried.

"The sooner the better. You're one of the lucky ones. Some mothers don't even get to hold their FGR babies right after giving birth."

"We understand." Artie kissed Mia's forehead. "We'll go see

Maddie as soon as we can." He leaned over and kissed Maddie's head.

"I love you my little peanut," Mia said as she gave her daughter a final squeeze and handed her to the nurse.

"This is so hard," Mia sobbed as Artie held her tight.

"Mia?" Ruth whispered as she and Josie softly entered the room.

Josie looked at Artie with wide eyes.

"They just took Maddie to the NICU," Artie said. "The good news is that the doctor said on the surface she seems healthy, but they want to do some tests to make sure."

"It'll all be alright. You'll see," Ruth said.

Artie's voice cracked. "She's so small."

"Maddalena Rose is half Russo and half Bocelli," Josie said proudly. "She's a fighter."

"Where's Poppy?" Mia asked.

"He and Ray insisted on escorting the nurses and the baby to the NICU." Ruth let out a nervous chuckle. "They're not going to let anything happen to her."

"Good," Mia whispered as her eyes shut.

Mia fell into a deep slumber and when she opened her eyes two hours later the room was quiet and Artie was fast asleep, reclined on the chair next to her bed, his head back, and mouth open. The door swung open with Uncle Luca struggling to carry a dozen helium balloons.

"Congratulations, Momma," he beamed as he crossed the room and tied the balloons to a chair.

Mia chuckled, "Thank you."

"How ya feeling?"

"I'm fine," she sighed.

"No, you're not. But that's okay." He squeezed her hand.

Artie sat up quickly and ran his hand through his hair. "Hey,

Uncle, I must've dozed off."

"How are *you* doing?" Luca nodded to Artie.

"Good, good."

"You're not very convincing either." Luca raised his eyebrows. "Why don't you run over to the house and get yourself some food and a hot shower? I got things here."

Artie looked at Mia and she smiled and nodded at him.

"Okay but call me if you need anything." He leaned over, ran his hand along Mia's cheek, and kissed her tenderly on the lips. "I love you."

"Your father would've been over the moon with pride today. Your mom, too." Luca smiled.

Mia sat silently for a long moment. "Yeah, although if my mom was still alive, I'm not sure she would've been in any condition to be a good grandmother."

"That might be true. Try to remember, hers was not a peaceful life."

"No, I suppose it wasn't. Maybe I just don't understand her as well as I thought I did. When they placed little Maddie in my arms, an overwhelming surge of love came over me. I knew instantly that I would fiercely protect and nurture her with every ounce of my being. No matter what." Mia looked down. "I wish I could say my own mother felt the same about me."

"Mia, your mother loved you immensely."

She shrugged. "Then why couldn't she be the kind of mother she should've been? Why couldn't she get clean and sober? Do you know she couldn't get it together to come to any of my school pageants or basketball games?" Her voice grew louder. "What kind of mother kisses her daughter good night and then washes down pain pills with a bottle of vodka and lets her daughter find her dead the next morning? How could she do that to me?"

Mia clenched her hands into fists. She always had mixed feelings about her mother that ranged from sadness to anger. Often, she would be able to acknowledge her mother was unwell and suffered from depression, and although she had also come to realize that alcoholism was a disease, it didn't make Mia's pain feel any better. All she ever wanted was a mother who loved her and was there for her, not a buddy to watch movies with. She was grateful that her grandmother was there unconditionally and was like a mother to her, and she knew her life could've been so much worse. Yet, Mia felt like she would never completely heal from all the pain she felt from her mother's addictions.

"I'm sorry Uncle Luca. I guess giving birth has opened up some old wounds."

Luca nodded. "I won't even try to say anything to make you feel better because I'm not sure anyone could fully understand everything you've experienced and are feeling. But I can give you a piece of advice." He took her hand. "You can't change events of the past, and I've learned that it's not a good idea to suppress the memories and emotions. I found it's best to acknowledge what's happened, accept that it can't be changed, and learn from the experience to do better and be better. Let yourself feel your emotions from time to time, but don't dwell on them for so long that they overwhelm you and take control of your life."

"I'll try." She sighed. "It really is good advice."

"Oh dear God, what advice is he giving you now?" Carla asked as she breezed into the room.

"I'm sharing the secret of life, my dear," Luca mused.

"If he's shared any good nuggets, please pass them on." Carla smiled. "Meanwhile, Maddie has to be the most beautiful baby I've ever seen." She lowered her voice. "Don't tell Matt and Theresa I said that."

"You got to see her?" Luca stood up quickly.

"Josie snuck me in. We couldn't stay long, but I got a chance to lay eyes on my grandniece, and she is just precious." Carla's eyes welled up.

"Why are you crying?" Mia shifted herself to sit up.

"No, no. Everything's good. You know how we felt about missing out on so much of your childhood, and now I'm just so happy that I'll be able to watch this little angel grow up."

Luca handed Carla a tissue and put his arm around her. "I have a feeling our little Maddie is going to be one of the most cherished Bocellis yet. And don't tell Matt and Theresa I said that either."

THIRTY-EIGHT

MIA AND MADDIE were released from the hospital after only a week and a half. The doctors were pleased that she had gained some weight, and her overall health was good. On the way home, Artie serenaded his daughter over and over again with the song, *You Are My Sunshine.*

"Uhm, you got any other songs to sing to your daughter?" Mia chided.

"Don't you worry, I've got a whole album in my head ready to go."

"Thanks for agreeing to Grammy and Poppy staying for the first week we're home."

"Are you kidding? I love the idea. I'll feel better having Grammy on hand to help with Maddie, and I need to win some of my money back from Poppy."

"He really does love playing Chess with you."

"Chess? Uh uh. We're planning a poker tournament up at the main house. Uncle Luca and Dad have the game room all set up."

Mia chuckled and looked out the window. This was it she realized. Her life was completely changed forever. From the first moment Mia held Maddie, she fell in love with her daughter deeply and vowed she would do everything in her power to protect her and make her life a happy one. Yet, she was still insecure about her own motherly instincts. She was now a mother responsible for the smallest human being she'd ever seen, and she didn't know what to do. She was relieved when Ruth offered to stay at the house to help with her. Mia's always heard people say that babies don't come with a handbook, and if she could ever use a list of instructions now would be the time. Ruth had a lot of experience raising kids, and Mia was ready to take all of the help she could get.

"Are you nervous at all about bringing Maddie home?"

Artie drummed his fingers on the steering wheel. "Yeah," he whispered so low that Mia wasn't sure she heard him correctly.

"Me too."

"But we got this." He nodded. "We'll figure it out."

"We'll certainly have a lot of help that's for sure."

"That's true, But Mee, if the family becomes too overwhelming, you gotta let me know."

"Okay."

"I mean it. You promise."

She squeezed his hand. "I promise."

"Do you think it'll be safe for her to be around everyone?"

"I already discussed it with her pediatrician, Dr. Gordon. She said it'll be fine, but we should make sure everyone washes their hands, and if anyone has a cold or feels sick, we should keep them away."

As they drove down the long tree-lined drive to the main house, Mia could see every family member including Gina the housekeeper, her husband James, and Rosie their daughter waving and craning their necks to see them. She was especially touched to see all of the Russos amongst the crowd. She knew Nancy and Rosie were going to help Gina with the food, but she wasn't expecting to see Janet, Anthony, their spouses and their kids to be standing alongside Tony and Ruth.

"Overwhelmed yet?" Artie shook his head as he parked the car. He jogged over to the back seat and said, "Okay, okay everybody, let's give Maddie some space."

"I want to see my great-granddaughter," Nonnuccio demanded. He moved forward slowly his hands gripped on his walker as his nurse hovered beside him.

"Here she is. Maddalena Rose Bocelli," Artie said proudly as he held his daughter close to Nonnuccio.

"Bellissima." Nonnuccio nodded as his eyes became glassy. He looked up at Mia and repeated, "Bellissima."

"Okay everyone, let's head in. Gina, Rosie, and Nancy have fixed us a feast," Carla sang.

Vicky wrapped her arm around Mia's waist. "You did good. She's perfection."

"Thanks," Mia answered as they leaned their heads together and walked into the house.

"Now I want everyone to wash their hands every time you want to touch her. The doctor said it's important and we don't want Maddie catching any germs," Artie announced as he placed his daughter in the bassinet.

Mia sat in one of the oversized upholstered chairs and let everyone wait on her. Josie brought her a plate of fruit, Ruth gave her pain medicine and an iced tea, Matt made a sausage sandwich for her, Anthony made sure she got two cannolis that had extra filling, and Mickey handed her his favorite dump truck to play with. While she enjoyed talking with everyone, she never took her eyes off her little Maddie.

"Yup, I was just like you when we brought Mickey home," Theresa said as she and Vicky sat down on the couch next to Mia's chair. "I was like a lioness protecting her cub. To tell you the truth, I didn't want anyone holding him." She chuckled, "But when Jodi came home, I was only too happy to pass her around. With the second one, you have a lot more experience and confidence, that's for sure."

Mia noticed Theresa's comfort and ease as she held Jodi. She did remember how both Matt and Theresa hovered every time she or Artie held Mickey and realized they were far more relaxed when it came to Jodi. Mia hoped she would be as comfortable holding Maddie as Theresa was with Jodi. But Maddie was significantly smaller than Jodi who was only three months older. Although Dr. Gordon had insisted that Maddie was healthy, and would probably always be petite, Mia still worried about her delicate little peanut.

"Yeah, I remember," Vicky rolled her eyes. "Hey Mick, come here to Aunt Vicky," she called out to Mickey who was standing behind Matt staring at Maddie.

"But you're okay with it now." She laughed as she swooped Mickey up, tossed him in the air, and caught him. Mickey's laughter filled the room.

"I hate when you do that," Theresa said trying not to laugh. "One of these days, I'm afraid you're going to drop him. He's getting so big."

"That's why I have to do it as much as possible now. Here," Vicky said holding out her hands toward Jodi, "give her here. Let me give Jodi a turn."

"Are you *crazy*?" Theresa laughed.

"What's going on over there?" Mia pointed to Luca and Joe who were involved in an intense conversation.

"Probably another problem with that new casino they're building down in A.C." Theresa waved her hand. "I've heard there's been nothing but problems lately."

"Problems? What kind of problems?" Mia asked.

Vicky leaned in. "Permits and inspections aren't getting approved like they used to, and supply deliveries are delayed."

"Really? That's unusual, isn't it?"

"Yeah, it is," Theresa said. "Matt's getting concerned."

"That can't be good," Vicky said as she nodded toward Joe, Ray, Matt, and Artie who followed Luca into his office.

Luca's rage exploded, and they could hear him shouting through the closed door. "Joe, I'm telling ya right now, you better well fix this! Moretti's gotta be stopped."

"Daniella's husband, Al Moretti?" Mia asked with surprise.

"Yup, Matt said he's been trying to cozy up to everyone and anyone who's influential. Apparently, he and Daniella had dinner with Senator Robinette and his wife at the Bernard's Inn just this past weekend."

"You're kidding?"

"Nope. They are definitely starting to make some moves." Vicky said shaking her head.

THIRTY-NINE

WINTER, 1989

IT HAD BEEN six months since Maddie was born. Mia was back at work with CL Designs and becoming more active taking on tasks for the Sisterhood. Like Matt and Theresa, she and Artie had hired a nanny, Jenn, to help with Maddie's care. Mia struggled with the idea of having a nanny at first, but she soon valued Jenn's flexible schedule, and the comfort Mia felt in knowing Maddie was being well cared for. Artie insisted that he have Daddy and Maddie time together every Saturday morning, which enabled Mia to meet with her Uncle Luca every chance she could for pancakes and opera. One of the things Mia loved best about living on the estate was how easy it was to spend time with the family. She cherished her relationships with both her Uncle Luca and her Aunt Carla. They had become like parents to her, and were sensitive to her insecurities over motherhood, supportive of her career, and mindful of her fears over the Bocelli way of life. There was nothing she wouldn't do for them, and she knew there was nothing they wouldn't do for her.

"Good morning," Mia said brightly as she tapped Luca on the shoulder.

Luca was waving his hands and singing to *Figaro's Aria*. "Aah, there's my cuoricina," he said as he grabbed a remote and turned down the volume on the music. "My little heart." He kissed her forehead. "And how's my baby cuoricina? I didn't get to see her yesterday." He chuckled. "I miss her."

"She's sleeping soundly in her bassinet next to her daddy. I swear she only sleeps in on weekends when it's his turn to get up with her."

"She's daddy's little girl. How was her visit with Dr. Gordon?"

"It was good, she gained some weight, and the doctor told me there's nothing to worry about. Although she's tiny for a six-month-old, she's healthy."

"That's what I like to hear."

"Tonight's the big night, huh?" Mia tried to sound casual.

"I'm afraid it is. It won't be easy for any of us." Luca shook his head.

"Aren't you happy to be named the new Don of the Bocelli Family?"

"I wouldn't say happy. I'm honored Nonnuccio respects and believes in me, but I would much rather be Underboss if that meant we could have Nonnuccio around and healthy for some more time."

"Yeah," she whispered. "What will it be like tonight?"

"You know I can't say much, but I can tell you that Nonnuccio will announce his wishes that I be named his successor. There'll be discussions and approvals, and then the Captains will pay tribute and honor Nonnuccio as their Don. It'll be a bittersweet evening, I'm sure. He's very much admired, and his Captains respect him."

Her eyes grew wet. "It's been really hard seeing him get weaker."

"That it has." Luca pulled her in, and his strong arms squeezed her tight giving her peace and comfort. "We're really lucky to have had him with us this long. Every day's a gift."

She nodded and tried not to allow herself to fixate on Non-nuccio's decline. She closed her eyes and brought up the image of his smile and the feisty spark he always had in his eyes. She always looked forward to seeing the content look of happiness on his face when he took his place at the head of the table for family dinner every night. This was her first experience watching someone she loved grow weak from a fatal disease. She appreciated being able to spend as much time with him as she could, but it was overwhelming watching him get sicker knowing he would never recover. The fact that he had set up the meeting to announce his successor made Mia painfully aware that their time with him was limited.

MIA'S EYES FLUTTERED open when she heard Nonnuccio humming an Italian lullaby to Maddie. There he was, sitting next to her bassinet, watching over her lovingly as his soft tune made the baby giggle in delight. "Nonnuccio?"

"Sleep, sleep. I didn't mean to disturb you. I just wanted to see my sweet little princess before I retire to bed."

"Are you okay? Is everything alright?"

"As good as it's going to be, I suppose," he said.

"Does Nonnina know you're here?"

"No. I slipped away from the dinner early to escape from the scrutiny of the nurses. I told Roberto to bring me here, and he'll take me back to the guard after. I just wanted a little time to visit before the others returned from the meeting," he said as he smirked and nodded toward Roberto who was standing by the door keeping guard.

"Would you like me to make you a cup of tea?" Mia sat up and peered over at Maddie who was smiling at Nonnuccio.

Nonnuccio hesitated. "No tea. But you *can* get me a nice glass of chianti."

"Oh. Um. I don't think you're supposed to be drinking."

"Probably not." He shrugged. "Think of it as a special favor, a kindness for this sick old man."

"Well, alright. I guess one glass can't hurt," she conceded.

"It'll be our little secret," he looked down and winked at Maddie.

He continued to sing as Mia poured the wine.

"That's beautiful," Mia said as she handed Nonnuccio the wine and got comfortable on the couch.

"Nonnina's mother sang it to her, and she sang it to Ray and Aunt Carla when they were babies. I'm sure she'd teach you if you asked."

"I'd like that." She smiled and looked down at the baby. "How was your night?"

He took a long sip of the wine and closed his eyes. His look of delight immediately erased all the pangs of guilt Mia had about giving him alcohol.

"Ah, il mio atto finale." He waved his hand. "My final act has brought me much peace." He smiled and held out his pointer finger for Maddie to grasp. "I'm leaving my legacy in good hands. You know, it wasn't easy building the Bocelli Family up from nothing. There were things I've done in my early days that I regret, and I'll no doubt have to answer for in the next life. There were also actions I've had to sanction for the sole purpose of protecting the family. All that I've done in my lifetime has been for them. Now, we're in a good spot, the family is successful, yet respected."

Nonnuccio never spoke about his role in the family, and she wondered if his health along with tonight's meeting made him reflective. She closed her eyes. As much as she liked stepping up as a Bocelli wife and helping others, she was still conflicted over Artie's involvement in potentially nefarious family operations. The truth was she didn't know what exactly the family was involved with or how they made their fortune. She's chosen to believe all that she was told about them being less ruthless and more ethical than the other syndicated families. But deep down she questioned whether that was possible, and now that Nonnuccio was speaking of his regrets, she wondered if she and Artie would also have the same type of regrets someday. She felt like she needed to know more. "How did you get involved in the life?"

"Let's see. When Nonnina and I were first married, I was a very young and poor bricklayer. We lived in a cold water flat and could barely afford our meals. When she got pregnant with Joe, I vowed that I was gonna do all I could to make a better life for us. I made it a point to be the best, most efficient bricklayer there was. I put myself out there and made sure the foremen, supervisors, and anyone who was anyone knew who I was. As I started moving up through the ranks, I met Carmine Esposito."

Mia felt a shiver run down her back. She pulled a blanket over herself and took a long sip of wine.

"I admired Carmine. Success seemed to come easy for him, and he taught me the way of the world. You see, Mia, a bricklayer could only go so far in life. There's a limit to their potential. To truly earn a good living, a man with my limited background had to play the game or get left behind." He shrugged. "I chose to play the game." He took a sip of wine and gazed at Maddie for a long time. "He brought me into the life, introduced me around, and soon I was able to provide nicely for my family. That felt good, but truth be told, I've got great sorrow for some of the things I did early on for Carmine. Malice that just about tore me up." He grew quiet as he looked down at his hands.

Mia walked over to Nonnuccio's side and placed her hand on his shoulder as she leaned over to adjust Maddie's blanket. When he looked into Mia's eyes, she could see all of the pain and regret he must've been living with through the years. She kissed his cheek, and he squeezed her hand.

"By that time I was good friends with your great-grandfather, Sal." Nonnuccio shook his head. "What a great man he was. He filled a room with joy, always held his head high, and would give a stranger the shirt off his back if they needed it more than him. He knew all about my ties to Esposito, and he could see how conflicted I was between my success and offenses. We spent many a night talking together at a corner table in our favorite bar. He knew all about the life and had offered some great advice. Of course, at that time I didn't know about his past experiences back in Italy."

"I wish I could've known him," Mia said softly.

"You would've been the apple of his eye." He chuckled and looked down at Maddie. He straightened his back and cleared his throat. "I knew Carmine was in a tight spot with the New York families. I didn't know all the specific details, of course, but I'm certain his ruthlessness got him in deep trouble. He wanted the Commission to break up his territory and allow me to run his Jersey and Pennsylvania terrain. The only way they would agree to that is by removing his influence completely and making me Don. I figured they wanted to rein in his power, so when they offered me the opportunity, I jumped at it. After all, one man's trouble is another man's opportunity. I wanted to be a Don more than anything. It was the power and prestige that had me hooked in spite of the transgressions. Nonnina stood behind me every step of the way and helped me to become distinguished." He shook his head and sighed. "She's a marvel, I'll tell ya that. But it was really Sal's intelligence that enabled me to attain success without being unreasonably dangerous or ruthless. You see each Don has his own way of conducting business and his own set of tenets. Some are more malicious, others are more benevolent. You've heard the saying 'You attract more bees with honey than vinegar'?" He held up his pointer finger. "Sal managed to help me make that saying a reality.

Between our unique business interests and management, the Bocellis created a nice niche for ourselves. We've always respected the other Jersey factions and interests as they do ours."

Mia took in the details of his face as he gazed at Maddie. She could see that this conversation was important for him, and that he wanted her to understand the story of the Bocelli Family, *his* story, just as much as she needed to.

He swallowed the last drop of his wine. "I'm sure Carmine thought the Commission would return his territory back to him when everything was settled in his world, but I worked hard to cultivate relationships and distinguish our family apart from the others. When it came to it, the other families appreciated us as an ally rather than a threat. Carmine was loyal to our friendship and put his efforts into building his New York territories rather than try to take back ours. You know, this thing of ours is a conundrum, we do what we gotta do to be lucrative. Sometimes it's good, sometimes it's not so good. But if we don't do it, somebody else'll come in and take it for themselves." He looked at Mia. "It's true I loved the thrill of being a Don, but I also knew that if Carmine came in and took back control, there'd be more drugs on the streets and shortcuts would be taken with construction projects." He shook his head. "One of the reasons why the Bocellis are successful is because we're conscientious. I wouldn't be able to live with myself if a tragedy occurred due to shoddy construction or cut corners just to save a buck. And I will not have any child die of a drug overdose at the hands of a Bocelli. Men in power have said time and time again how they appreciated the Bocelli standards." He shrugged his shoulders. "Standards within a crime family, pretty ironic, huh?"

Mia offered to refill his wine glass, but he shook his head and took her hand. "You see, Mia, this is why I need Artie to work for the family. I'm looking to the future. The reality is Uncle Luca and Ray won't live forever, and Matt'll need an anchor to keep him levelheaded as he grows within the organization. He's got a great mind for business and he's doing well developing meaningful relationships and affiliations. But Artie, like his father, and much like your great-grandfather, as a matter of fact, is a voice of reason and a man of integrity. He'll ensure that success can be maintained while upholding the beliefs that the Bocellis have always held. Mia, I know I gave you and your family my word that Artie wouldn't be required to be a part of the Bocelli business, and I'm honoring my promise. Artie isn't obligated in any way to work for the family."

Mia sighed. "I understand, but Nonnuccio, he wants to now." Her voice cracked. "And sometimes that scares me. I don't trust the Espositos. Who's to say what they'll do if they decide they want their region back? There are times when I feel empowered that I can stand behind him and help him like Nonnina did for you, but sometimes I feel inept."

"You're right. No one can predict what the Espositos may do. But I know Uncle Luca won't allow anything to happen to anyone in this family. He's smart, he's shrewd, and he's an excellent negotiator. Put your trust in him. He knows how to manage the Espositos."

Mia nodded quickly. "Okay," she whispered as she squeezed Nonnuccio's hand.

He pulled his walker to him, slowly stood, and placed his hand on Maddie's chest. As he whispered to his great-granddaughter, Mia couldn't stop the tears from streaming down her face. He turned to her and placed his hand on her cheek.

"No tears." He kissed her forehead. "You have no need to be sad or afraid. I promise I'll always be at your side protecting you and Maddie." He waved Roberto over and as Roberto helped him to the door, he stopped and smiled at Mia. "It's gonna be nice to see Sal again."

FORTY

"HONEY, WAKE UP." Mia felt Artie's hand on her shoulder, and she knew. She knew that Nonnuccio was gone. Nonnina said when he got home Saturday night after his visit with Mia and Maddie, he sat with her, and they reminisced about their life together. She said she had a feeling that when he kissed her goodnight and got into bed, he wouldn't ever get back out. During the next three days, the family kept vigil at his bedside as his body began to shut down and his spirit prepared for his next great adventure.

"Nonnuccio?"

Artie nodded. There was nothing more to say.

The main house was filled with visitors paying their respects. Artie had helped Nonnuccio pre-plan his funeral so there wasn't much to do except grieve and cry. While Mia had found peace in the fact that Nonnuccio died on February 7th, what would've been his eighty-fifth birthday, his passing opened up the wound of losing her mother and she found her sorrow to be deep. She was always able to pull herself up and swallow her emotions, but this time she found it difficult to be the tower of strength for everyone else. She was relieved when Tony and Ruth agreed to come and stay at the house until after the funeral. Having them close gave her comfort, and she could tell the family appreciated their warm presence as well. She found Tony and Nonnina sitting together talking quietly, and he reached out and held her hand as she began to cry. Ruth was especially comforting to Carla and Josie, and she took over the role of ensuring all of Nonnuccio's wishes were carried out to the letter.

On the day of the funeral, Mia was caught off guard by the huge number of people who came to say goodbye to Don Bocelli. The cathedral was filled with state dignitaries, politicians, judges, lawyers, police chiefs, and community leaders not to mention the Dons and Captains of the New York families, their New Jersey faction leaders, along with their wives. Mia marveled at Nonnina's composure throughout the services but found herself weeping and squeezing Artie's hand as she watched Nonnina whisper something to Nonnuccio, kiss his forehead, and place something in his hands. She then straightened her back and glided elegantly to her seat, caressing her cherished scarf that hung around her neck.

Mia, Vicky, and Theresa walked together arm in arm behind Carla and Josie as Luca, Ray, Joe, Artie, Matt, and Angelo served as pallbearers and carried Nonnuccio's coffin. It seemed as if the entire state of New Jersey had come out to pay their respects, and the streets surrounding the cathedral were lined with people waving and throwing kisses as the long procession of cars and limousines followed the police-escorted hearse to Gate of Heaven Cemetery in East Hanover.

At the cemetery, Artie held Mia's hand tightly. She shared his sadness and already longed to look into Nonnuccio's eyes one more time. Her heart felt empty knowing she wouldn't be able to sit next to him and sneak him an extra sweet treat or wake up to find him singing a beautiful lullaby to Maddie ever again. She somehow thought his death would've been easier to bear than her mother's because she thought she had time to prepare for the inevitable. But she realized it wasn't easier. The loss was just as profound, and the emotions were just as deep. As the priest recited the final prayers, Mia looked up and saw a cardinal sitting on the roof of the private Bocelli mausoleum. She locked eyes with the bird and a wave of peace drifted through her. Just after the priest sprinkled holy water on the casket, the cardinal took flight. It flew gracefully over the crowd of mourners and ascended high disappearing behind the soft, billowy white clouds. Mia smiled and whispered, "I love you." She locked eyes with Tony and he nodded at her.

After the funeral, the family invited everyone to join them at their catering hall for a reception in honor of the Don. Throughout the afternoon, there were many stories shared, and toasts given, praising him for being incredibly benevolent and revered. Mia's pride in being part of the Bocelli Family grew with every account of kindness, goodwill, and virtue that was shared by dignitaries and the syndicate alike. It was amazing to see everyone from such diverse worlds come together and share their grief over a man they valued so highly.

Carla stood next to Mia wrapping her arm around Mia's waist. "Pretty incredible, huh?"

"I knew he was well respected, but this is really amazing," Mia said.

"Take this in and never forget it. We must ensure that our family honors his legacy."

Mia looked around the room and observed Josie and Nonnina as they warmly acknowledged the guests. They held their heads up in pride and reverence, remaining dignified – the epitome of class and grace. Her attention turned to Luca who stood at a prominent location at the head of the room with Joe and Ray standing at attention behind him. One by one men ceremoniously bowed in respect to Luca. In turn, he nodded, firmly grasped their hand, and kissed them on each cheek. She then noticed how distinguished Artie and

Matt were as they spoke with various notable figures introducing Vicky as their sister, Victoria. Vicky worked the room with confidence and authority, giving Mia hope that maybe she would be able to someday work for the family like she so very much wanted.

But when her eye caught Tony involved in a conversation with Don Esposito, Mia's breath caught in her throat. She grasped Carla's hand and nodded in their direction. "Should I go over there?"

"Give it a minute, let's see how it plays out. Their facial expressions are not alarming just yet." Carla squeezed Mia's hand. "Would you look at that, they've shaken hands."

Mia waited a few minutes for Tony to get settled in his seat before she approached him. She wanted to remain poised, but she couldn't stop the trembling that flowed through her body.

"Poppy, is everything alright? I saw you talking to Don Esposito."

Ruth pulled the chair next to her out from the table and gestured for Mia to sit. "Everything's fine," she said before she glanced over at Esposito.

"This is the first time in many, many years that I've been in the same room as Carmine Esposito," Tony said as he casually sat back in his chair. "I felt it was time to finally let go."

"Let go?" Mia was confused.

"Yes. You know how much bitterness and resentment I've carried all these years? Well, Mia, look at him, he's an ailing old man who can barely sit up in his wheelchair."

Mia looked over at the Esposito table. It was true, Don Esposito had aged significantly since she'd seen him two summers ago. He was frail and could barely lift his fork to his mouth without shaking. She wouldn't be surprised if they got news of his death within the next year.

"That man is going to meet his maker someday, probably

sooner than later. I know I'm never going to see him again, and your grandmother encouraged me to talk to him so I can release the crushing weight of hatred I've felt all these years."

"You, you did?" She looked at Ruth who sipped her tea and nodded her head.

"What did you say?" Mia was worried on so many levels about what Tony could've said to Don Esposito. If he insulted the Don, he could've put himself and the Russo family in danger or he could've put the Bocellis in a difficult position.

"Don't worry. I know how to handle myself with Esposito." Tony waved his hand.

"No really, Poppy, what did you say?"

"To start, I had to introduce myself because he didn't recognize me. Once he remembered me and all the circumstances that occurred between us, I told him that I understood everything that transpired was just business decisions for him, but for me and my family those decisions were traumatically life changing."

Mia leaned in. "And what did he say to that."

"He stared at me for a few seconds, and then he said, 'I now understand that.' He then said he regretted the pain he's caused. And that was that."

"That was it? Nothing else?"

"No, that's all I needed to hear. I shook his hand and said a silent prayer for him."

"You *prayed* for him?"

"I did. I have a feeling he's gonna need all the prayers he can get."

THE FAMILY AND most of the Bocelli associates returned to the main house after the reception. Tony and Ruth offered to relieve Nanny Jenn and look after Maddie for the rest of the night so Artie and Mia could unwind with the family. The mood was lighter than it had been over the past few days and the sound of laughter was a welcome relief.

"How are you doing?" Mia asked Vicky.

"I'm just glad today is over. I'm gonna miss him, though."

"Me too," Mia agreed. "I don't know how Nonnina held it together like she did. I would've been a mess."

"I think because she's spent most of her life wearing a mask in public that it's natural for her now."

"You're probably right. I almost lost it completely when she said her final goodbye."

"Are you kidding? I had to bury my head in Ange's shoulder because I was crying so hard."

"What do you think she put in Nonnuccio's hand?" Mia asked.

"His good luck charm, I'm sure."

"Good luck charm? I didn't know he had a good luck charm."

"Yup. It's a coin he's carried with him every day since he met Nonnina. Apparently, he was coming out of a coffee shop and bent over to pick up a coin. As he stood, she was right in front of him waiting to enter. He said he took one look at her and fell in love instantly."

"That's how they met?"

"Yeah, It's quite a love story. Nonnuccio was smitten from the first moment he laid eyes on her and was never without that coin ever since." Vicky shrugged.

"I love that story!"

Vicky's eyes grew wide. "And here we go." She nodded to Dee who was pouring herself a glass of wine. "Now watch, she's going to look around, gulp down half the glass, and then refill it again."

"I think she's really got a problem," Mia said with concern.

"She definitely does. Joe has tried everything. He talked to her, pleaded with her, and even threatened her. The problem is, she doesn't think she has a problem." Vicky tapped Mia's hand. "Here she comes."

"Hello ladies, mind if I join you?"

"Of course not, Dee. How are you?" Mia said as she shifted in her chair.

"I'm doing just great. That was some reception today, huh? It was nice to sit at the head table for once and rub elbows with the elite."

"It was a beautiful tribute to my *grandfather*," Vicky said brusquely as she jumped to her feet, shook her head, and stormed away.

Dee leaned in closer to Mia. "I had a lovely conversation with Diane Rosetti, you know the Chief of Police in Jersey City's wife? She runs a fabulous yoga studio and told me to come on in any time I wanted." She took a sip of wine. "I'm really enjoying being the wife of the Underboss."

Mia stared at her and was speechless. She had never seen anyone be so entitled, rude, and oblivious. She tried to formulate how she should respond to her, but Luca and Joe walked over to them just in time. Luca congratulated Joe on doing such a great job in sorting out all of the trouble they were having with the Atlantic City construction project. Joe not only managed to get the materials delivered, but he negotiated a significant credit due to the inconvenience. He worked tirelessly with the inspectors and licensing officials to get back on track and restore good faith between them and the Bocellis. No one admitted that the Espositos were behind the recent trouble at the work site, but Joe said he had his suspicions and was doing his own investigation.

"Dee, your husband really came through for us," Luca said as he patted Joe on the back. "This is exactly why I made you Underboss."

Joe nodded his head humbly.

"Now that everything is said and done, I wanna go ahead and take care of some renovations on your house," Luca said as he sat down.

"Renovations? What do ya mean?" Joe asked.

"As Underboss you need to have the same level of security that we have here. I'm gonna meet with Carlo to get to work as soon as possible. We'll need to pretty much overhaul the whole thing. Of course, we'll do an expansion and add on a nice office for you."

"Does this mean I get a whole new kitchen?" Dee squealed in delight.

"Yes, Dee, I suppose we can make that happen. Now it'll take a bit of time from start to finish, so you can stay at the Alpine house until you can move back in."

"Luca, I don't know what to say." Joe shook his head in disbelief. "Thank you."

"Mia, can I count on you to oversee the project with Carlo? I'm going to want the same type of attention and diligence on this project as you put into our estate here. It'll probably be a little easier because you already have many of the specs when it comes to security and whatnot."

"Of course, Uncle Luca."

"Good, then plan to meet me Monday morning at Carlo's office. Joe, start packing up your stuff and move your essentials to the Alpine house, and when we have the blueprints and plans drawn up, we'll go over them together."

"What about me?" Dee looked around. "Don't I get a say?"

"Of course," Luca appeased her. "You'll work with Mia to decorate your house just as you want it.

Dee perked up and clapped her hands. "Mia, how exciting. I'm gonna get a bunch of magazines first thing tomorrow. Isn't this exciting?"

Mia forced a smile. "Yeah, exciting."

FORTY-ONE

WINTER, 1989

TWO WEEKS LATER, Vicky and Theresa waited for Mia at Bella Cucina for their Sisterhood luncheon. They all had become so comfortable in their roles that Nonnina, Carla and Josie had been able to take a step back. Carla was the Chairman of New Jersey's top nonprofit Down's Syndrome organization, and she started spending more of her time raising money and advocating for services to help children and their families with Down's Syndrome. Josie was very active in supporting the local animal wellness center and started to spend more time working with the animals and organizing fundraising events. Nonnina informed the Sisterhood that she was going to start taking a step back now that Nonnuccio was gone, but she made it a point to meet every Thursday evening with the Sisterhood to discuss and weigh in on important Sorellanza matters.

As Mia walked through the restaurant, she noticed a number of the patrons and wait staff had bowed their heads as she passed the same way they always did whenever they saw Nonnina, Aunt Carla, or Josie. She smiled and nodded back and found herself overcome with pride over their show of respect.

"I'm so sorry I'm late," she said as she slid into a seat between Vicky and Theresa. "Dee had me on the phone for over an hour. She just couldn't accept that the budget wouldn't allow for an imported Italian mosaic to be brought in. I told her that if it was important to her, she and Joe would have to pay for it themselves. And then she started to insist that their entire yard be redesigned and landscaped complete with a brand-new patio, hot tub, gazebo, and flower garden. Even though the house renovations didn't impact their current yard design. And don't get me started about the new heated driveway she wants."

Vicky and Theresa locked eyes and fell into each other roaring with laughter. "I … knew … she … was … gonna … be … demanding," Vicky managed to say between squeals.

"You don't know the half of it," Mia said as their waitress, Dawn, approached the table. "Dawn! How are you today, it's nice to see you." Mia had come to appreciate Dawn in spite of her insistence on calling her ma'am.

"Good afternoon, ma'am. I mean Mrs. Bocelli," Dawn said softly. "Will anyone else be joining you today?"

"Not today. It'll just be the three of us." Mia put her hand on Dawn's arm. "Is everything okay? You look like you've been crying."

Theresa quickly became serious and looked up while Vicky drank a few sips of water to regain her composure. Theresa looked deep into Dawn's eyes and said, "What's going on?"

"Is it your mother?" Vicky added.

Dawn looked up to the ceiling and took a few deep breaths. "I'm sorry," she managed to say. "My mom now has full-blown Alzheimer's, and I can't care for her any longer." She wiped her eyes with a tissue she pulled out of her pocket. "She needs to go into a facility, and," She took a few more deep breaths. "We don't have the money."

Mia looked at Theresa, whose eyes had become glassy. Theresa's mother had passed away last year from Alzheimer's, and Mia remembered how debilitating the disease was not only for her mother, but for the whole family.

Vicky cleared her throat. "I really don't want to be nosy, and please tell me to mind my own business, but I remember your father had left your mother a very substantial inheritance only five or six years ago."

The tears streamed down Dawn's face with speed. "He did, but now it's gone." She covered her face with the tissue and whispered, "Stolen."

"I'm sorry, did you just say stolen?" Vicky shook her head and leaned closer to Dawn.

Dawn nodded her head quickly. Mia stood up, put her arm around Dawn's shoulders and helped her sit at the table. "It's okay. Why don't you tell us what happened," Mia said as she handed Dawn a glass of water.

Dawn drank the water and stared at the glass for a moment after she placed it on the table. "I had hired my cousin, Toni, to be her caretaker. Everything was going great, she was taking good care of my mom and was very patient and attentive during her decline. But then when I tried to get Mom into a care facility, her bank account balance was next to nothing. There should've been plenty of money in her accounts because her monthly expenses were minimal. So, I went down to the bank to look into it." Dawn looked down and let out a long breath. "They showed me her bank statements and there were several large checks made out to Toni from over a year ago before the Alzheimer's really kicked in." She shook her head. "It turned out that Toni brought my mother into the bank and had her sign a form to give her check writing privileges." Dawn looked at Vicky. "And she had been systematically wiping out her account ever since. I was so stupid not to keep a close eye on my mother's account. I never thought my cousin would do such a thing."

"Wait a minute," Vicky said. "Your mother had a debilitating mental illness and couldn't have been of sound mind to make that decision or sign those forms."

Dawn nodded her head. "The bank manager had the documents and said he handled the paperwork himself. It was my mom who was adamant about giving Toni the ability to have access to her account. They went to the bank when she was just a little forgetful – long before Mom had gotten bad. I'm not sure she was even officially diagnosed with Dementia then." She let out a sarcastic chuckle. "All this time, Toni was playing at being a loving niece. She saw the early signs of Dementia in my mom long before I did and set things into motion. She convinced my mom it would be easier on me if she could help out with the banking and errands. I was only too happy to let her help when she mentioned it to me." Dawn put her head down and choked, "I had no idea what she was up to. I thought she was just making deposits and cashing checks my mom had written. How could I have been so stupid?"

Mia shook her head. "What does Toni say about all of this?"

"When I confronted her, she said that Mom had wanted to give her and her husband special gifts. Of course, we really got into a shouting match then, but there was no use. When it came down to it, there was really nothing I could do. The money's gone, and her husband who's a cop said it's all perfectly legal."

Mia, Theresa, and Vicky exchanged looks. "I'm sorry for what you're going through. My own mom had Alzheimer's, and I know the struggle firsthand," Theresa said.

"Thank you." Dawn nodded. "This all came down on me over the last few days, so I'm still feeling pretty raw about it."

"I'm sure you are," Mia said.

Dawn shook her head and jumped to her feet when she saw Camilla, the hostess, glaring at her. She cleared her throat and said,

"Can I bring you your usual salad and maybe an order of today's special for the table? It's Veal Parmigiana."

"That sounds lovely," Theresa said and shook her head in disbelief as she watched Dawn walk toward the kitchen. "There must be something we can do?"

"As soon as I get back to the office, I'm going to look into this whole thing. Something doesn't sound right," Vicky said.

Mia nodded. "I'll also make a few phone calls. Maybe Hospice can help?"

"Yes!" Theresa said. "That's a great idea. I'll run it by Mom and Nonnina tonight too when I pick up the kids. Maybe they have some ideas on how we can help."

FORTY-TWO

LATER THAT NIGHT, Vicky called to tell Mia that she looked into Dawn's cousin, Toni, and her husband, Marc. Apparently, Marc was a low-level cop in the Union City police department, but he wasn't known to the Bocelli Family. Vicky assumed that he was the brains behind the theft, and she set up a lunch meeting for the next day so she and Mia could have a chat with Toni to enlighten her on how it would be in their best interests to do right by Dawn.

By the time Mia met Vicky at the newest Bocelli restaurant in Rutherford, she had put in almost a full day's work at CL Designs. She hadn't eaten much all morning, and no matter how starved she felt, she figured this wasn't going to be the type of lunch meeting where they might actually eat. She was the first to arrive and chose a small corner table in the back of the dining room. Vicky was right on her heels and the two of them situated themselves so that they would be facing out and Toni would have no choice but to face the wall and keep her focus on them.

"Here she comes," Vicky nodded toward the door.

Toni was slighter than Mia had expected and looked lost in the baggy scrubs she was wearing. It was obvious that the money she had taken from Dawn wasn't used on herself, as her thin, brown hair was pulled up in a tight bun revealing almost two inches of grey roots, and her sneakers were old and worn.

Vicky gave Toni a slight nod and gestured for her to sit with them. "You must be Toni O'Brien."

"Yeah, I am." Toni rolled her eyes and craned her neck to look around the restaurant. "What's this all about?"

"I am Mia Bocelli, and this is Victoria Bocelli-Rizzi we're acquaintances with your cousin, Dawn." Mia held her eyes on Toni longer than usual, a technique she found was very useful in establishing authority.

Toni shifted in her chair. "Dawn, oh."

"We have come to understand that you've withdrawn so much money from her mother, Carol's, accounts that they are now just about empty," Vicky said as she crossed her legs and slightly leaned forward.

"Look, I don't know what Dawn has told you, but I did *not* withdraw money or empty her accounts."

Mia handed Toni multiple sheets of paper. "How do you explain these?"

As Toni flipped through the papers, Mia could see a quick look of alarm flash across her face. "These checks were gifts Aunt Carol gave to me and my husband. I told her it wasn't necessary, but she insisted." She sat back and crossed her arms. "She said she wanted to see us enjoy the fruits of her labor because she couldn't take it with her."

"I see," Vicky said and stared at Toni. "And the fact that she had dementia leading to Alzheimer's didn't have anything to do with her generosity?"

"Hey, my aunt wanted me to have the money, and I wasn't going to disappoint her."

"Okay, look, we're not going to play this game," Mia said. "We all know you took advantage of Carol and now you have to return the money so she can be cared for properly."

"You can think what you want, but I'm not returning a dime. Besides, I can't. The money's gone." Toni sat up straight and smirked.

Vicky looked around quickly. "What do you play us for? Do you even know who we are?" She shoved another paper at Toni. "You better wise up and quick."

Toni's mouth opened slowly as she looked down at the printout.

"What'd you think? We wouldn't be able to track the money and your actions? You're going to collect all of that money that you tried to hide and return it to Dawn and Carol."

"Or what? You're gonna put a hit out on me? My husband's a cop, and he'll bring down your whole family."

Mia and Vicky looked at each other and giggled. "A hit?" Mia smirked and tapped her hand on Toni's. "Uhm, no. We will not put a *hit* out on you. But perhaps Chief Brown may get wind of this scenario. We know Walter well, and he doesn't condone thievery within his ranks. I would hate to see your husband, Marc, miss out on that very prestigious promotion he's up for due to this, how should we call it? Lapse of judgment on your part?"

Toni looked back and forth between Vicky and Mia and swallowed hard.

"Lapse of judgment, you're being kind, Mia," Vicky said as she leaned in and locked eyes with Toni. "If you don't return that money by the end of the day today, we'll see to it that your husband will work the beat in the streets for the rest of his life. That is, if he's allowed to still *be* a cop. And you? You'll never get a job in any capacity other than bagging groceries, and your life will be a living hell." Vicky shrugged. "I would also hate to have your daughter, what's her name? Jessica? Yes, Jessica! She's a first-year teacher, right? I would hate for Jessica to lose her current tenure-track teaching position and never obtain another teaching job in the tri-state area due to rumors of theft. You know how parents and the Board of Education can react when there's even a suspicion of illegal activity. You'd be surprised how quickly and easily word gets around. Especially when her savings account shows multiple large deposits on a teacher's salary."

"You're bluffing," Toni looked at Vicky sideways.

Mia cleared her voice. "Make no mistake, sweetheart. We don't bluff. Our reach is long and wide. If I were you, I'd convince that husband of yours that it's in your best interests to return the money and stay away from Carol and Dawn. You do *not* want to try us."

Vicky nodded. "Do we understand each other?"

"Yes," Toni whispered.

"Good, we expect to see that money transferred by the end of the day," Mia said dismissively with a wave of her hand.

Vicky and Mia watched Toni as she scurried out of the restaurant. "That went well," Vicky said.

"Agreed. Let's eat. I'm starving," Mia said as she waved over the waitress.

FORTY-THREE

IT HAD BEEN two months since the Sisterhood convinced Toni O'Brien to return all the money she had pilfered from Dawn's mother's bank accounts. Toni had no problem convincing her husband the money needed to be returned. Thanks to an informative conversation Vicky had with Chief Brown, Marc O'Brien had been informed by his superiors that he was the prime person of interest in a number of internal crimes in which money and other valuable evidence had disappeared from the district's evidence room. Marc knew the Bocelli's reputation and processed the transfer within an hour of speaking to his wife. Fortunately for Dawn, Marc moved enough money to cover the amount they had taken plus interest. Unfortunately for Marc, he had been indicted on a number of charges. Some of which he was actually guilty of.

Mia was relieved when the renovations on Joe and Dee's house were completed. Much to Dee's dismay, Mia managed to stay within Luca's budget and was able to give Dee a beautifully modern update to her kitchen and bedroom, but she could not deliver on all of the other unrealistic embellishments Dee had thought she was entitled to. Once the project was completed, Mia made arrangements with Carlo to only work on projects for his high-level clients so she could have more time to embrace and refine her role as a member of La Sorellanza. She and Vicky took the lead on managing situations much like Dawn's and used their influence to help rectify unjust circumstances. Theresa focused more of her time and effort on fundraising and organizing events for charitable causes. She was at her best when she was bringing people together and convincing them to dig deep into their pockets and make donations. Together, under the advisement of Carla, Josie, and Nonnina, they were establishing themselves as esteemed leaders within the community.

Mia had found that her path crossed with Daniella's frequently now that she was attending more social events. She would observe Daniella cozy up to anyone she thought was important. While she never tried to hide her brusque, surly attitude toward Mia, she feigned a cordial manner as she attempted to work her way into social circles that were obviously wary of her and her intentions. Not only did the Bocellis have a longstanding favorable relationship with these people, the Espositos had an ugly reputation that Daniella seemed to be trying to modify. Often, her ignorance and lack of decorum would work against her, and Mia would find herself feeling just a little sorry for her and her social awkwardness. Mia would inevitably be reminded by Daniella's contemptibility that she was not to be trusted, and that Mia could never let her guard down where Daniella was concerned.

Tension began to rise when the Bocellis got word that Don Esposito's health was failing and that he could pass on at any time. His son, Mario, was his Underboss and named successor to the Esposito Family. While Luca maintained a good relationship with Mario through the years, no one could be certain if he would uphold his father's loyalty to the Bocellis. Daniella's husband, Al, had been doing all he could to increase his influence throughout New Jersey, and it was rumored that he wanted to expand the

Esposito territory. Joe was keeping close tabs on Moretti's activity, and he was certain that once Don Esposito had passed, the Espositos would try to take back the Bocelli's terrain.

Mia had hoped that enjoying the spring weather together would help ease some of the anxiety the family was experiencing over the Espositos. It had become rare that they were all home on a Saturday afternoon, and they spent much of the day relaxing and enjoying each other's company.

"Ugh, look at them out there," Theresa said as she scrunched her nose pointing to Matt, Artie, and Angelo smoking cigars on the patio. "I hate when Matt comes in with his clothes and hair stinking of cigar smoke."

"I know what you mean. I make Artie take a shower before coming to bed after a cigar." Mia no sooner got her words out when she saw Joe and Ray rush through the house and wave everyone inside.

"Oh, boy," Vicky said as she, Mia, and Theresa joined everyone in the dining room where Carla was standing wringing her hands.

Luca put both of his hands on the table, leaned forward, and said, "We just got word that Don Esposito passed away last night. He had had a very difficult week and suffered a great amount of pain, but he is at rest now."

Artie moved across the room and put his hand on Mia's shoulder. She knew she was supposed to feel sympathy or even empathy over his passing, but she didn't. A part of her felt vindicated that the man who had inflicted so much pain and suffering on her family had suffered himself in the end. She wondered if his pain could ever equal the amount of pain her grandfather had lived with. She picked up Maddie and held her close.

As she kissed her daughter's cheek and nuzzled her neck, Mia turned to Artie and said, "We need to go tell Poppy."

"I'll get my keys," Artie said without hesitation.

Artie and Mia sat with Tony and Ruth at the dining room table as they broke the news of Esposito's death.

Tony nodded his head, opened a bottle of wine, and took a long sip. "I don't know what happens when we die," he said. "The man I knew was cruel and heartless, yet I feel no joy in the fact that he suffered in the end. Maybe he got what he had coming? Maybe he didn't? Who's to say? I do know that his family is mourning his loss, and for them, I'll say a prayer to ease the pain they feel in their hearts."

Mia wrapped her arms around her grandfather and kissed his cheek, "You're a good man, Poppy."

"Yes, he is," Ruth said as she kissed his other cheek.

"What does this mean for the Esposito Family? Who'll be in charge now?" Tony looked at Artie.

"From what I understand, his son, Mario, has been named his successor. He is to be called, Don Mario to distinguish himself from his father."

Tony nodded, "I remember Mario. He was always serious but seemed levelheaded."

"Yeah, that's been my experience too."

Tony stood, "Art, let's you and me take a walk in the garden."

"I'm right behind you," Artie said and followed Tony through the kitchen and out the back door.

"Your grandfather's worried about what will happen between the Bocellis and the Espositos," Ruth said.

"So am I," Mia sighed. "So am I."

A WEEK AFTER Don Esposito's funeral, Artie and Mia were woken at six in the morning by heavy pounding and the sound of a commotion at their front door.

"This better be important," Artie said as he swung the door open. Mia stood behind him bouncing Maddie in an effort to get her to stop crying.

"Arthur Bocelli, I am Agent Smith with the FBI. We have a warrant to search your premises as well as all of the premises on this estate," the agent said as he pushed past Artie handing him the warrant documentation. Within seconds, a team of agents followed and began to rifle through all of their belongings, dumping items on the floor and searching the house from top to bottom.

"Artie? What's happening?" Mia's eyes were wide.

"Don't worry, honey," Artie said stiffly as he read over the document and reached for the telephone that had begun to ring.

"Uncle Luca, yeah," Artie said into the receiver. "They're here, too. It's legit, I don't know what prompted it. Just tell everyone to cooperate." There was a long silence. "Yup, uh huh," he said. "Okay."

"Agent Smith, can we talk?" Artie said as he pulled the agent aside.

She tried to make out what Artie and the agent were saying, but when her husband locked eyes with her, he shifted so that his back was to Mia. She continued to nervously bounce Maddie in her arms although the baby had stopped crying. As she watched the agents go through their personal belongings, she felt like she was watching a movie. Dozens of FBI agents wearing black pants, white shirts, and windbreakers with the letters FBI on the back filtered in and out of their home. As far as she could tell, they weren't finding whatever it was they were looking for, and within an hour Agent Smith said, "Let's wrap it up," and they were gone, leaving chaos in their wake.

Mia spent the rest of the day shaking as she attempted to put order back into her home while Artie met with Ray, Luca, Matt, and Joe. The entire ordeal unnerved her, and although Carla had told her this type of thing was always a possibility, nothing could've prepared her for the reality of it. When the family gathered to compare notes at the main house, Mia noticed that Theresa and Vicky were perfectly calm, and were even commenting on how good-looking one of the agents was.

"Are you kidding me?" Mia asked. "They invaded our homes and sifted through our personal belongings. Our underwear! Don't you feel exposed?"

Josie hugged Mia tightly and whispered in her ear, "Mia, my sweet, of course we're all feeling like we've been unnecessarily harassed. This wasn't easy for any of us, and I, for one, am feeling just as vulnerable as you are. I think the girls are making light of it as a coping mechanism." She gave her a squeeze and pulled her out to arm's length.

"I'll tell you what, this sort of thing hasn't happened in over twenty years," Nonnina said shaking her head. "Makes you think, doesn't it?"

"What do you mean?" Mia asked.

Carla shrugged her shoulders. "Why now? What were they looking for? Did they take anything from any of your houses?"

Vicky, Theresa, and Mia all shook their heads while Josie and Nonnina locked their eyes with Carla and raised their eyebrows.

Luca poured a double shot of scotch. "Okay everyone, come sit down, I think we should talk about today."

Everyone moved into the family room where Luca stood at the head of the room. Mia noticed how her uncle held himself much like Nonnuccio did when he took command in his capacity as head of the family. Luca's presence made Mia feel safer from the anguish she felt at the hands of the FBI, but she still felt the need to reach out and take Vicky's hand for comfort.

"I know today was traumatic, but I wanna say how pleased and proud I am of all of you. There was no need to be rude or disrespectful, and you stood tall and held yourselves like the distinguished Bocellis we are. We've got feelers out and are trying to get to the bottom of this event."

Joe shifted from side to side, "I'm tellin ya Luca, it's the Espositos. They've got to be behind all of this."

"That could very well be a possibility," Luca said as he narrowed his eyes at Joe.

"They're trying to jam us up with Feds. Next thing you know, they'll swoop in and take over our territory."

Mia squeezed Vicky's hand as the rest of the family started whispering and mumbling among themselves.

Luca stood taller and cleared his throat. "We don't want to jump to conclusions, and I assure you we're doing a thorough investigation to uncover the truth. In the meantime, I don't want you to worry, but I do want you all to be aware. Pay attention to your surroundings and be cognizant of anyone who seems out of place or makes you feel uncomfortable. Let me know if anything seems amiss. In the meantime, I want the word out to all of our Captains, soldiers, and associates. Everything is by the book. I don't want any funny business while we're on the FBI's radar." He pointed his finger and looked around the room, "Capice?"

As everyone nodded and muttered their agreement, Vicky pulled Mia aside.

"How are you holding up? You're shaking." Vicky said as she rubbed her hand on Mia's arm.

Mia let out a long breath. "This morning really did a number on me."

"Don't worry. They didn't find anything because there was nothing to find. These sorts of things happen from time to time, but between my father, Artie, and Uncle Luca, we've got nothing to worry about."

"I wish I had your confidence," Mia said. "I mean, sometimes I wonder, would it really be so terrible if the Espositos took over the Bocelli territory? That could give us all a clean slate."

Vicky stared at Mia for a long time. "A clean slate? What do you think would happen to people like Matt, Ange, and even Uncle Luca? They can't just walk away and start a new life as a regular citizen. They know too much about too many people." She put her hands on Mia's shoulders and looked her straight in the eye. "There's no such thing as a clean slate in this life of ours."

FORTY-FOUR

SUMMER, 1989

OVER THE NEXT few weeks, Mia and Artie didn't see much of each other. Since the FBI raid, Artie had been either sequestered in Luca's office or out until all hours of the night, 'taking care of business' as he would reply whenever she asked him about it.

"Do we really need to go today? I mean, it's only a birthday party for a five-year-old," Mia said as she sat at her vanity applying makeup.

The last thing Mia felt like doing was spending a day at Daniella's home socializing. Sometimes it was so exhausting putting on cordial airs whenever she was around Daniella. Now that they both had become members of the event planning committee for the Elder Care Resolutions Organization, the unpredictability of their relationship had escalated. Daniella often behaved as if they were in competition with each other rather than being aligned on the same goals for the organization and welfare of the community. Daniella would try to subtly undermine her during planning meetings and take credit for various Bocelli Family accomplishments. Mia really wanted a break from Daniella's spitefulness and would much rather have spent the day alone with her family. Artie's mood had been very somber and serious lately and she thought a relaxing day with just the three of them might do him some good.

"We absolutely have to go. It's not just any birthday party. It's

Rocco Moretti's birthday party. We need to keep up appearances where the Espositos are concerned," Artie answered.

"Does that mean we'll have to invite them to Maddie's first birthday party?"

"I would plan on it." Artie shrugged.

Mia sighed. "Vicky and Angelo are the lucky ones getting a pass for today."

"Uncle Luca thought it would be best for only the upper administration of the Bocelli Family to attend today."

Mia perked up. "Wait, wouldn't that mean that only your father and Joe should attend with Uncle Luca? Maybe we really don't have to go after all?"

"Nice try." Artie poked his head out from the walk-in closet. "Matt and I have to go, and you and Theresa have to represent the Bocelli wives. It's protocol."

The party was much like Mia had expected. Daniella went over the top when it came to providing a memorable party for her son. There were jugglers, magicians, balloon artists, face painters, an ice cream truck, and pony rides set up outside for the kids, while the adults enjoyed live entertainment, an open bar, and seafood buffets situated throughout the house. This was the first time Mia had been to Daniella's home, and she found it to be pleasantly understated and tasteful.

Theresa looked at her watch and locked eyes with Mia. They had finished their rounds and made the appropriate small talk throughout the afternoon while Nanny Jenn watched over the kids outside. Mia raised her eyebrows and motioned to a few chairs that were empty in a quiet corner.

"It really is a lovely party," Mia whispered.

"I know, right?" Theresa chuckled. "I don't really know what I was expecting, but I wasn't looking forward to it, I'll tell you that."

Mia tilted her head back in laughter, "Me neither. I kept trying to get out of coming."

"The margarita bar's a great touch," Theresa said as she raised her glass.

"Hello, ladies. Are you enjoying yourselves?" Daniella smirked as she approached them.

"We are," Theresa nodded her head. "It's a great party. Thank you for including us."

"Of course," Daniella said as she looked around the room. "I wasn't so sure you would've been able to come though, what with all of that FBI trouble and all."

Mia tilted her head. "You must be mistaken, Daniella, there's no FBI *trouble.*"

"Mia, there's always trouble when the FBI raids your home. At least that's what I've been *told.*"

"It was just a misunderstanding," Mia waved her hand. "It won't be happening again anytime soon."

Daniella chuckled, "I wouldn't be so sure of that. Enjoy the rest of the party."

"And *that's* why I wasn't looking forward to this party," Theresa squeezed Mia's knee as they watched Daniella saunter away.

"You girls alright?" Ray asked as he and Luca walked past Daniella.

"Yeah, we're fine," Mia said as she let out a long breath.

Luca leaned in and whispered to Mia. "Don't let her get to you."

"Easier said than done," Mia mumbled.

"I think we're going to say our goodbyes. Ray and I are gonna hit the road and head down to Mantoloking from here," Luca said as he leaned in and kissed Mia and Theresa. "Aunt Carla and Josie are expecting us for dinner."

"Have a safe trip," Theresa said. "I think we'll round up our kids and fellas and head out too. I've got a little more packing to do before we head down tomorrow morning."

Mia and Theresa walked out to the yard where they found Artie and Matt kicking a large ball around the grass with the kids.

"Uncle Luca and Dad just left, why don't we head home too?" Mia said as she lifted Maddie.

"Alright," Artie began when shots rang out from the front of the house and a woman's scream pierced the air like a sharp blade.

"Protect the kids," Artie yelled at Nanny Jenn as he and Matt ran through the yard.

Mia thrust Maddie into Jenn's arms as she grabbed Theresa's hand and followed their husbands. As they ran, the woman's wrenching screams continued to bellow. They immediately came upon a swarm of armed guards that had formed a barrier around Mario Esposito, Al Moretti, Luca, Ray, Artie, and Matt. Mia craned her neck as she tried to make her way closer.

"Mia, that's Daniella!" Theresa stopped and pointed.

There was a break in the crowd and Mia saw Al bent over grabbing Daniella's shoulders in an effort to try to pull her off the ground. She pushed his hands away as she wailed and screamed, "Nooo!" She pulled her mother, Antonia's, lifeless, blood-soaked body up to her and rocked back and forth.

"What happened?" Joe tried to catch his breath as he ran up to Mia and Theresa.

"I think Antonia was shot," Mia said numbly.

"*Antonia?* Are you sure?" Joe pushed his way through the Esposito guards and Mia could make out the look of shock on everyone's faces.

As the police sirens grew louder, much of the crowd and party guests disappeared from the premises leaving the Esposito and Bocelli families frozen in place. Luca ran his hands through his hair, paced back and forth, then bent over pressing his palms into his legs. Artie and Ray were involved in a deep conversation with Mario and his Consigliere, Nico, while Joe stood in shock staring at Antonia's body.

Matt caught Theresa's eye and hurried over shaking his head.

"What *happened*?" Theresa ran into his arms.

"I want you and Mia to take the kids home right away. Call Mom, Aunt Carla, and Vicky and tell them everyone needs to return to Bernardsville immediately."

"Matt! What happened?"

"Someone tried to hit Uncle Luca but got Antonia Esposito instead."

FORTY-FIVE

THERESA HELPED NANNY Jenn get the kids to sleep at her house while Mia called Angelo at the shore house. She thought it would be best to tell him what happened first so he could organize the security details and ensure everyone returned safely. Within two hours Carla, Nonnina, and Vicky came bustling in while Angelo met with James, their head of security before driving out to the Moretti house.

"This is crazy," Theresa repeated over and over again as the family gathered in the main house waiting for the guys to return home.

"Now let's all keep our heads about us," Nonnina said. "We don't know any of the details yet, so nothing good will come of getting ourselves worked up."

"I'm sorry, but I just can't get the images out of my mind," Theresa said as she pulled her legs up on the couch and rocked back and forth.

"Josie, bring over that bottle of bourbon I like and five glasses," Nonnina said as she wrapped her arms around Theresa. "I think we could all use a drink."

The women sat up all night waiting for their husbands to come home. They drank bourbon and tried to eat some of the ziti Gina had put out for them, but no one had much of an appetite. Mia figured everyone was thinking the same thing, and no one was saying it out loud. What if Uncle Luca had been shot and more importantly, why would someone want to kill him? Finally, at four in the morning, the front entrance opened, and Carla threw herself into Luca's arms.

"Tell us everything," Nonnina said in her most authoritative voice.

Luca shook his head and sat next to her and took her hand. Artie sat next to Mia while Matt stood with his arms around Theresa and Angelo stood behind Vicky with both of his hands on her shoulders. Mia looked across the room and saw Josie put the back of her hand against Ray's forehead as they huddled together whispering. He looked very pale and had deep dark circles under his eyes. He kissed her cheek and took a seat next to Nonnina as Josie shared a look of concern with Carla.

"It all happened so fast," Luca began. "Ray and I were walking to the car. There was security everywhere. Little Rocco ran up ahead of us and Antonia was following close behind trying to get him back to the party." Luca closed his eyes and shook his head. "I heard a shot come from the wooded area off to the side. Ray was so fast! He threw me to the ground and covered me with his own body." Luca's eyes were glassy as he looked over at Ray who was nodding slowly. Josie squeezed Ray's hand and kissed his cheek. "I owe you my life," Luca said.

Ray shook his head and waved his hand.

"I heard a little voice say, 'Nonna?' Just as light and innocent as can be. When we got up, we saw Antonia just lying there. Blood was all pooled around her." Nonnina handed Luca her glass of bourbon and he drank it down in one gulp. "By that time it was nothing but chaos. Esposito's men were all over the place searching the woods, cars, and everyone who was there."

"Who do you think was behind it?" Carla asked.

"I dunno," Luca looked at Ray, who nodded slowly looking down at his hands.

"Could it have been the Espositos?" Nonnina asked.

Matt shook his head. "If it was them, their plan went terribly wrong."

"They found a rifle just where the woods started. Looks like someone was waiting there. The ground was disturbed all the way down to the road, so they could've had a car parked nearby and took off."

"Luca, this is very serious," Nonnina said as she squeezed his hand.

"I know, Momma, I'm gonna do my own investigating. In the meantime, I want everyone to stay here on the estate. The security is much tighter, and I don't want to take any unnecessary chances."

"Agreed!" Ray stood and looked at Josie. "If you don't mind, I'm going to go get some rest. All this excitement's got me exhausted."

"Good idea, let's all get some rest, and for God's sake, stay on the grounds until I get some answers." Luca kissed Nonnina's cheek and took Carla's hand as he led her to their rooms.

FORTY-SIX

THE BOCELLI MEN huddled in Luca's office over the next few days with the family Captains coming and going at all hours of the day and night. James had stepped up the security and there were more guards surrounding the houses and escorting everyone who came and went.

A heaviness filled the air, and while the family shared their meals, silence echoed throughout the main house. Mia and Theresa tried their best to act casually and continue a normal routine, but the kids could sense the adult's anxiety and had become moody themselves. Mia braced herself when she received Ruth's inevitable phone call to inquire about Antonia's murder. She and Artie had discussed how much they would tell her grandparents about the events of that day, and agreed it was best for everyone if they didn't know the truth. The story was all over the news, and Mia knew it would only make her grandparents even more troubled over her life as a Bocelli if they knew the bullet was intended for Luca. Mia had hoped she was successful in sounding casual when she told Ruth she didn't know anything about what happened and that none of the Bocellis were even at the party.

On the day of Antonia's funeral, the security detail was so tight, Mia couldn't properly pay her respects to the family or greet any of the other attendees. Representatives from all of the New York and New Jersey families were in attendance, surrounded by a tight circle of guards. When Daniella walked past Mia as she was leaving the church, Mia impulsively set aside her personal feelings, reached out, and squeezed Daniella's hand. They shared a brief, warm acknowledgment as Daniella nodded her head slightly. Mia knew Daniella's pain over losing her mother, and if she could have said something comforting, she would have, but in a flash, the Esposito and Bocelli guards formed a barrier between them.

Only Luca and Ray, along with their security, were permitted to pay their respects to the Espositos after the funeral. While the immediate family grieved together over a luncheon at the Esposito estate in New York, all the family heads sequestered themselves in an unknown location in an effort to resolve Antonia's murder.

When the family returned home, Gina had prepared her own feast at the main house. After they fixed their plates, Artie, Matt, and Angelo joined Mia, Theresa, and Vicky on the patio.

"Matt, really?" Vicky said as she rolled her eyes and pointed to his plate that was overflowing with food.

"What? When I'm stressed, I eat!" Matt said as he took a large bite of a meatball sandwich.

"Here, give me some of those ribs. You don't need all that," Artie said as he grabbed food off of Matt's plate.

"Get your own," Matt said, and as he swatted Artie's hand, crumbs of food sprayed out of his mouth.

"Thanks for the beer, bud. I forgot to get myself a drink," Angelo said as he winked at Matt, grabbed his bottle, took a big chug, and gave it back to Matt.

"Ugh. You gotta keep it now. I don't want your backwash."

They all had a good laugh, and as Mia looked around the table, she couldn't remember the last time the six of them sat around laughing and teasing each other. This was exactly what she needed to help her cope with the reality that someone had tried to shoot her Uncle Luca. She realized how much she had come to love her life and the people in it, and she didn't know how she would possibly be able to cope if something happened to any of them.

"How'd it go?" Carla asked as Luca and Ray returned home looking tired and weary.

Luca shook his head. "I dunno. Ray and I were just saying that it's pretty clear the Espositos are under the impression that we staged the whole thing."

"You mean to tell me that they seriously think the Bocelli Family would purposely *kill* Antonia? For what? What's there to gain?" Carla's voice grew louder.

Ray waved his hand in disgust. "They didn't come out and say as much, but Moretti wouldn't stop alluding to it."

"What about the Commission leaders? What'd they say?" Matt asked.

"They were levelheaded as expected. We've got friends there, but Moretti seems to really have it in for us," Luca said.

"Do you know how much influence Al Moretti really has with the Espositos?" Josie asked.

"It's hard to tell," Ray said as he rubbed his chest. "He's never been the smartest of Captains, but he *is* Daniella's husband."

"What happens now?" Carla asked.

Luca drew in a deep breath. "Now we wait, prepare for the worst, and hope for the best."

Mia looked around in confusion. "Prepare for the worst?"

"Yeah, retaliation," Artie said as he put his arm around her.

"Josie," Ray coughed suddenly. He reached out for her as he fell to the floor.

"*Ray!*" Josie cried and ran to his side. "Someone call 911."

"I ... I ... can't ... breathe." Ray rubbed his chest as he struggled to speak.

Mia stood frozen. She could see Carla shouting into the phone and Josie and Luca kneeling next to Ray, but she was paralyzed. Her ears were ringing so loud she couldn't hear, she couldn't move, and she couldn't speak. She looked around and saw Theresa run to the internal house phone and wave her hands as she yelled. Angelo held Vicky up as she became weak with tears. Mia's heart was racing, and a cold sweat ran down her arms and legs. She could make out Matt and Artie as they met the security team at the door and rushed toward Ray.

As Ray was being lifted onto a stretcher, Mia rushed to his side and squeezed his hand.

"I love you," she leaned over and kissed his cheek.

"I'll be alright," he whispered and tried to squeeze her hand back, but it was weak and limp.

Luca took charge as the paramedics were preparing to take Ray out to the ambulance. "Josie, you go with Ray in the ambulance. Artie, I'm going to have Roberto bring the car around and take you, Matt, and Vicky. Aunt Carla and I will be right behind you with James and some of the guys, but we'll need to go up and break the news to Nonnina first. Ange, I'm going to need you to keep a close eye on things here. Let's keep everyone else in the main house with the remaining security to keep watch."

Mia rushed over to Artie and squeezed him tightly. "Please call me with updates."

"I will." He kissed her forehead. In a flash, he was out the door, and the ambulance took off down the long driveway, its siren piercing the silence.

Theresa wrapped her arm around Mia and led her to the couch. They watched as Uncle Luca took Aunt Carla's hand and led her up the stairs toward Nonnina's rooms. Within fifteen minutes they re-emerged with Nonnina following behind, looking like she had aged twenty years.

FORTY-SEVEN

SUMMER, 1989

WHILE THEY WAITED to hear news about Ray, Theresa and Mia huddled close together on the couch wrapped up in a blanket. Angelo spent most of the time on the phone updating the other Captains, consulting with the security men that stayed on the estate, and pacing from room to room alternating between looking at his watch and looking out the windows. After a few hours, he rushed toward Mia with the cordless phone pressed against his ear.

"Yeah. Yeah. Okay. Got it," he said into the handset. "Mia it's Artie," he said as he got to the couch.

Mia grabbed the phone from Angelo's trembling hand, "Hey, what's going on, how is he?"

"He's in surgery," Artie's voice was weak. "The left main artery needs a bypass."

"Oh, honey," Mia's voice quivered. "What can we do?"

"Just say some prayers. Joe and the Captains'll be coming by later. Luca wants to have a meeting with everyone as soon as we know more about Dad."

"How's Nonnina and Mom holding up?"

Artie let out a long breath. "They're okay. We're all doing the best we can. How's everything there?"

"Quiet. The kids should be waking up soon. We're going to

have Nanny Jenn keep them occupied today," Mia said softly.

"Good. I don't have to tell you to stay aware," Artie said firmly. "We still don't know who's after Uncle Luca so it's best just to stay put for now."

"I agree," Mia squeezed her eyes shut. "Give my love to everyone."

"Alright gotta go. I'll call back with updates."

Mia tossed the phone on the cushion next to her and rubbed her hands over her face. "He needs surgery."

Theresa blew out a rush of air and said, "Oh, boy."

Gina rushed into the family room from the kitchen. "Any news?"

"He's in surgery. We don't know anything more."

Gina walked over and squeezed Mia and Theresa's hands, "He'll be alright," she said and moved her right hand up to her heart. "I can feel it."

"Thank you," Mia whispered. She always appreciated Gina's love and loyalty to the family. "Uncle Luca's calling a meeting with the Captains later, so I'm afraid we're going to have a houseful."

Gina nodded quickly. "Good," she said firmly. "I'd better get started preparing some things. But first, I'll make some breakfast. You all need to keep up your strength too. How does French Toast Casserole sound?"

"Gina, that would be fantastic," Theresa said rubbing her stomach and looked over at Angelo who was nodding in agreement.

At eight thirty Joe bounded into the house. "How's everyone here?"

"Where's he been?" Theresa whispered to Mia. "Dad went to the hospital nine hours ago. Now he shows up all concerned?"

"Maybe he was at the hospital?" Mia breathed through the corner of her mouth as she watched him fill up a plate with the breakfast casserole.

"Any news from the hospital?" he asked, scooping a forkful of food into his mouth.

"He's in surgery, we're waiting to hear more," Mia said flatly and rolled her eyes at Theresa.

"Damn. I'm telling ya it's all that stress from the Espositos. That's what did it to him. First, they wanna start pushing in our territory and then that attempted hit on Luca," Joe said shaking his head.

Mia sat up. "What do you mean they wanted to start pushing in our territory?"

"Yeah, Moretti offered to cut us in if we let his dealers do some business, but Luca and Ray were adamant about blocking it." He pushed food around his plate. "I told them last night it had to be Moretti who put out the hit."

Angelo entered the kitchen and twisted his neck to release his tension. "Uncle Luca just called with an update. The bypass was successful, and they had to put a stent in his right artery. Everyone's headed back to the house."

While Mia was relieved to hear that Ray made it through the surgery, the idea of Al Moretti wanting to sell drugs in the Bocelli territory terrified her. She knew this could be the beginning of a fierce battle, and she feared that the Esposito heirs may not hold the same loyalty to the Bocellis as Carmine did. It was ironic that she felt more fear toward Carmine Esposito's family than she did toward Carmine himself. Joe was right. She wouldn't be surprised if Al wanted to kill Uncle Luca to improve his own reach, and if that idea made Mia tremble, it certainly could've triggered Ray's heart attack.

WITHIN TWO WEEKS, Ray was discharged from the hospital and was back home to recover. Mia tried the best she could to hide her emotions when she saw how thin and frail he looked. She had wanted to visit him at the hospital, but Luca wanted everyone to remain on the estate unless it was absolutely necessary to leave.

There was nothing pressing for Mia to tend to, and she hated the idea of being surrounded by a team of bodyguards, so she made the best of the situation and fell into a daily routine on the estate. Each morning, she and Maddie would meet Carla on the patio of the main house for breakfast. Carla fussed and cooed over Maddie as she and Mia chatted. Sometimes they discussed La Sorellanza business, sometimes the latest gossip, and sometimes Carla would reminisce and retell stories about Mia's mother and father. By now there was nothing new that Carla could tell Mia about them, but when she heard the same stories over again, it made them feel real and close and not the ghostly shadows they had become. After Mia put Maddie down for her nap, she let Nanny Jenn take over her care for the rest of the day. She would then head over to Nonnina's rooms and the two of them would share a pot of tea. This quickly became Mia's favorite part of her day, as she loved reliving the events of Nonnina's life and learned a lot from every conversation they shared. Mia felt like Nonnina was trying to counsel and prepare her for situations that could arise as a Bocelli wife through the accounts she told of her own experiences. Each anecdote ended with Nonnina detailing the lessons she learned, the successes she achieved, or the things she would've done differently.

She made sure to stop in and visit Ray and the two of them would sometimes play a couple of hands of Gin Rummy if he felt up to it. Each day it seemed like his color was improving, but he was still weak. The doctors said it could take upwards of three months for him to start feeling like his old self, and they warned that he could experience some feelings of depression and anxiety. Mia had noticed that he had become more introspective.

One day he looked up from his cards and asked, "Mia, how do you feel about being a Bocelli?"

"How do I feel?" She hesitated because in the seven years she'd been married to Artie, Ray had never inquired about her feelings on being a Bocelli. From the beginning, he had embraced her as a daughter and treated her with so much kindness and care, making her feel like she had been a Bocelli all of her life.

He nodded. "This life of ours is not easy, especially on the wives."

"I'm fine. I worry like everyone else, but I'm doing okay."

"You know, my father did the best he could. He wanted a good life for us, a life filled with opportunities, but sometimes those opportunities don't always come easy," he said casually as he drew a card. "All the same, we've been lucky."

Mia nodded. She was at a loss for words and wasn't sure what her father-in-law was trying to say.

"But now it's time for us to look forward, and Mia we must protect the family." He leaned in. "At all costs."

She reached over and put her hand on his arms. "What are you trying to tell me?"

"Change is going to be inevitable, decisions will have to be made, and we'll all have to play our part. But always remember it'll all be for the protection of the family."

He put a card face down on the table and spread out the rest of the cards in his hand. "Looks like I got Gin."

FORTY-EIGHT

WHEN THE FAMILY sat down for dinner, Mia noticed that in spite of Ray's joining them at the table for the first time since his heart attack, the men were extremely serious. Theresa and Vicky chatted on like usual with Aunt Carla, but Nonnina seemed to be especially quiet as she surveyed the conversations at the table. Even Artie had been more distant, and when she sat next to him, he pulled his arm away after she brushed against it.

Luca tapped his hand on the table. "There are a few things that we need to address as a family."

Everyone fell silent and turned their attention toward him. He looked down at his plate and then across to the other head of the table directly at Nonnina who nodded at him. "Ray," he said.

Ray sat up straight and looked directly at Luca. "I've made the difficult decision to step down as the Bocelli Consigliere. I can no longer serve the family in the capacity that is necessary at this crucial time. It's been an honor and a privilege to serve under my father and Luca and to work together to achieve all that we have and protect all that is dear. I, now, must focus on gaining my strength and maintaining my health."

Josie squeezed Ray's hand as everyone nodded and began whispering their agreement. But Mia's throat closed, and her hands began to shake. She knew what was coming.

Luca tapped his hand on the table once more. "Artie has stepped up in his father's absence and has been exceptional in every aspect of the family business. He is an integral leader in the Bocelli Family, and I'm proud and honored to announce that tomorrow evening, he will be ordained as our new Consigliere." Luca held up his wine glass and said, "To Artie."

Ray raised his glass and with glassy eyes, added. "To Artie, may God guide you, enlighten you, protect you, and give you strength and courage."

Everyone raised their glasses and repeated, "To Artie."

As Carla raised her glass with her left hand, she squeezed Mia's leg with her right. Mia stared at her wine glass in a trance. Heat flowed from her head down her body and her heart began to race. She recognized the anxiety that was quickly attacking her body, and all she could do was look down and wring her shaking hands together. Deep down she always knew Artie would eventually become the Bocelli Consigliere, but now she had to face the reality.

AFTER THEY PUT Maddie to bed, Artie turned to Mia and said, "You've been quiet tonight."

Mia put her shaking hands on her hips. "Can you blame me?"

"I don't understand."

"Artie, I never wanted to be the wife of a top-level Bocelli executive."

"Are you kidding me right now with this?" Artie raised his hands in the air.

In a flash, Mia's fear and anxiety morphed into anger. The reality of the recent events felt like a harsh punch that she couldn't prevent or control. "Everything I've been afraid of has happened. Someone tried to kill Uncle Luca and Antonia Esposito died as a result!"

"Uncle Luca's fine," Artie said calmly.

"But Antonia is dead! And your father—"

"What? What about my father? He risked his own life and his health to make sure Uncle Luca is alive today!"

Mia took a deep breath and looked at Artie closely. Something about him had changed. It wasn't his appearance, but his demeanor. He'd become guarded and closed off. "I'm just saying that I never wanted this type of danger for us."

"You know, you can't have it both ways, Mia," Artie said as he began to undress. "You thrive on the power and notoriety of being a Bocelli wife. But I got news for you, that type of prestige that enables you to do what you do with the Sisterhood comes at a price."

Mia stared at her husband.

"There's a lot you don't know, and the family's counting on me." He sat down on the side of the bed and looked up at her. "Let's say I back out and walk away from the family like you want. What happens then? What'll happen to everyone else? Have you even thought about that? This is not just about us."

She sat next to him. "I understand that. I do. I just didn't think things would escalate the way it has."

"This life has risks, there's always going to be risks. When we got married, we were young and naïve, but this is our life now. In an ideal world, we could all just walk away and live different lives, but that's not how this works." He shrugged. "Besides, this life is in your blood. You couldn't walk away if you wanted to."

"In my blood?" She stood up and felt her face turning red.

"Yeah, look at your parents. Your father was entrenched in this life. His very existence thrived in it. If I would hazard a guess, I'm thinking your mother enjoyed the life he provided her, kinda like you do."

"And there's my point!" She waved her hands. "My father was killed in prison because of this life, and my mother's life spiraled out of control as a result."

Artie shook his head. "You missed *my* point. The point is you can't help but be drawn to the thrill and the power of this life of ours. But what you need to understand is that your father's recklessness and temper was his fatal flaw, and I'm *not* your father." He brushed past her as he moved toward the bathroom. "And, I've also got news for you, you're *not* your mother."

FORTY-NINE

SUMMER, 1989

MIA COULDN'T SLEEP. She dug deep into the closet and pulled out her sketchpad and pencils, put on sweatpants and tee shirt, and went to the main house where she was sure she wouldn't disturb anyone. After she made herself a cup of tea and curled up on the couch, she spent most of the night releasing her emotions and thoughts through her drawing. When her hand had cramped so much that she could barely hold the pencil anymore, she tossed it aside, leaned back, and fell into a dreamless slumber.

When she started to stir, she found that her legs were stretched over Josie's lap who was sitting on the couch next to her flipping through a book with Mia's sketchpad nearby.

"Good morning, my sweet," Josie said.

"Good morning, what time is it?"

"It's not yet six," she replied as she picked up a pen and wrote notes on a pad that was next to her. "Did I wake you?"

"No. Not at all." She crossed her arm over her eyes "What are you doing up so early?"

"I find I haven't been able to sleep much lately. I came down to warm up some milk and sneak a few chocolate chip cookies, and I found you and your sketchpad. I hope you don't mind that I took a look?"

"I don't mind. I'm not even sure what I drew last night. My mind was racing, and I find that sometimes when I draw to calm it down, I don't always have a plan. The final outcome is often a surprise." Mia sat up and looked over at the pad.

Josie tilted it so Mia could see it better. "It's incredible. I remembered I had a book on symbols, so I thought I'd look up the meaning of your images."

"I'm sure it doesn't have any meaning. I was tired and Artie and I had." Mia stopped short of telling her mother-in-law she had a disagreement with Artie. She didn't want Josie to get the wrong impression about how she felt about Artie becoming Consigliere, when she, herself, wasn't sure about it after everything Artie had said.

"You and Artie had words? I'm not surprised. Last night's announcement had to be jolting. That's a tremendous change for both you and him."

"It's not that I don't support him or the family. I just don't know how to put it into words."

"You had no choice in the matter," Josie said shrugging her shoulders.

"Exactly," Mia said, realizing that maybe she would be more at peace if she and Artie had made the decision together.

"Many husbands and wives make major decisions that impact their family together, but unfortunately, in our world, it's not always the case. And it's often not easy."

"How did you do it? How did you live your life every day knowing how much danger your husband was in?"

"I didn't fixate on the danger. I concentrated on his intellect and his astuteness. My husband is a master chess player, just like Artie."

"*Chess?*" Mia tilted her head.

"Yes, indeed. A successful Consigliere must possess and constantly hone the very same skills that it takes to be a master chess player. Like for instance, problem-solving, patience, remaining calm under pressure, and creativity."

"I never thought about it like that. Artie really is good with all of those things."

"Mia, both Artie and Ray's strengths lie in their ability to discern patterns and clues. They have strong instincts to calculate and predict their adversary's strategy and their future actions. Their persistence and memory enable them to understand what motivates their rival, and as a result, are very successful at counseling and advising their Don."

"Hmm," Mia whispered.

"No one else is better suited to advise Uncle Luca than Artie. But do you know why?"

"Because he's a skilled chess player?"

"That, plus he is exceedingly motivated to keep this family safe and uphold Nonnuccio's principles."

"Everything you've said makes sense, but the fact that Uncle Luca was almost killed, and Dad's stress led to a heart attack *terrifies* me."

"Mia, my sweet, now I'm not minimizing your feelings, but you can't live your life in a constant state of distress, or else you'll miss out on all the greatness life has to offer. I realized long ago I had two choices. One was to let myself get paralyzed by fear and grow to be bitter and resentful and the other was to embrace my life and do the best I can with what I have."

"You make it sound so simple."

"Oh, it's not simple, nor is it easy. Your fear and anxiety will kick up, it's only natural. But try to learn how to acknowledge it, accept it, but don't let it take root. Don't let it eat away at you or distract you from all the good that you could accomplish as a result of being Arthur Bocelli's wife."

Mia nodded, "I'll try hard to reconcile this in my mind."

"It looks to me like your subconscious might've already embraced our way of life," Josie said as she held up Mia's sketchpad. "Look at what you've created. You drew a butterfly which according to this book represents the fragility of beautiful new beginnings. But within each of the four corners of her wings, you've added a dog, a dove, a lion, and an elephant with various hearts filling in the empty space. What do you think each of these images represents?"

Mia held up her sketchpad and studied it. "The hearts are obvious, and dogs are very loyal to their owners, so I would say the dog could mean loyalty. Doves are known for signifying love and peace, and lions are fiercely strong and protective, but I'm not sure what I was thinking with the elephant."

Josie chuckled. "I had to look that one up. According to this book, elephants are highly intelligent animals that maintain strong family bonds. So much so, that they remember and mourn those who have died."

"Really?" Mia asked as she took the book from Josie.

"Mia, your sketch is the epitome of who we are as a family. I'm certain these were not random doodles, but your mind's way of telling you it's safe to embrace this life of ours."

Mia was quiet as she studied her drawing. She didn't want to live her life filled with dread, and she hated the distance that was growing between her and Artie. Mia made a conscious decision that she wouldn't let fear take root in her mind, and she would support her husband's role in the family. "I think I'm going to make some pancakes. Would you like some?"

"Maybe I will have some," Josie said as Mia swung her legs around and began to stand. "Before I forget, our La Sorellanza induction will be this evening. Be sure to dress formal, and there will be a family dinner following."

"Induction?" Mia asked.

"Of course. Just as Artie will have a ceremony inaugurating him as Consigliere, you girls must be instated into The Sisterhood of the Bocelli Family."

"I GOT YOU something." Mia tentatively handed a small, gift-wrapped box to Artie.

He put his tie down and said, "What's this?"

"It's just a little something I got for you. For you becoming Consigliere."

Artie raised his eyebrows and unwrapped the box. He squinted his eyes as he opened it to reveal a gold horn pendant on a gold rope chain. He looked at her and shook his head.

"It's just like the one Aunt Carla gave Uncle Luca on their wedding day. He's worn it every day for protection. I got one for you to wear, you know, for protection also."

His eyes softened and he pulled her in for a warm embrace. "Stella," he whispered as he nuzzled her neck.

"It's silly, I'm sure. But I figured it couldn't hurt."

"I love it," he said. "Help me put it on." He bent over and Mia fastened the chain behind his neck. He turned to look in the mirror, kissed the horn, and said, "You don't know how much this means to me."

"I don't know if I'll ever be able to not worry, but just know that you have my support and love." She kissed his cheek.

"What's changed since last night?"

"This." She showed him her sketch.

"It's nice, but I don't understand," he said shaking his head.

"It's all symbolic. I drew it after our conversation without even thinking about it. Your mom saw it and realized that it represents all of the love, loyalty, and strength that make up our family."

He nodded his head. "I'm not real good at all that artsy symbolic stuff, but it makes sense."

"Back when you told me you were going to work with your father, I knew I didn't have a choice. The family needed you and it was what you wanted. It wasn't really a surprise that this day would come, but I wasn't expecting it to happen so soon. I thought we'd be much older, and the circumstances would've been more peaceful. I thought I would've had more time to wrap my brain around your position in the family, and I guess I got scared. But your mom gave me some good advice on how to manage being a Consigliere's wife, and after talking to her I feel more at ease." She buttoned up his shirt, slipped his tie around his neck, and began to tie it. "This afternoon I decided you needed a horn just like Uncle Luca's, not only for protection, but to remind you how much I love you."

"Wait a minute, you ventured off the grounds to get me this today?"

"Yup. Me and my entourage. Louie drove, and Roberto and Frankie were at my side the entire time."

"You're something else, my Stella Splendente." He kissed her long and deep. "It's time to go," he whispered. "But let's pick this up later."

Mia took a last look in the mirror, fluffed her hair, and applied lipstick.

"You look gorgeous," Artie said and playfully tapped his hand on her bottom.

Together they walked hand-in-hand to Luca's office in the main house. Joe, Ray, Matt, and all of the Captains formed two lines outside the door with Luca at the head in the doorway. As Artie walked past, each man bowed their head and tapped him on the shoulder. Luca kissed each of his cheeks and led Artie into his office with the rest following closely behind. Mia held her breath as the door closed.

"Please be safe now and always," she whispered softly.

She felt a hand on her shoulder and turned to see her Aunt Carla at her side. "Come on, Mia, it's time."

Carla smiled broadly as she took Mia's hand, and they walked together to her large office. Throughout the room, there were at least one hundred candles glowing softly. Nonnina stood tall in front of a small round table draped with a burgundy cloth embroidered with gold beaded medallions and fringe. Centered on the table was an exquisite floral arrangement filled with pink roses, peonies, hydrangea, and eucalyptus, a dark mahogany box, and six crystal champagne flutes. Josie came up behind them holding both Vicky and Theresa's hands.

Nonnina held out her arms and motioned for the three girls to stand before her as Carla and Josie took position to her left and right side. Although she wore the same navy beaded gown she wore to Vicky's wedding, Nonnina had a warm glow emanating from her, and Mia had never seen her look more elegant or regal. She gave each of them an approving nod and smiled. She closed her eyes for a few moments, and when she opened them, she raised her head and pulled her shoulders back.

"La Sorellanza, the Sisterhood," she began, "came to be out of our desire to serve our communities. It has grown and evolved into a covenant based on loyalty, honor, and respect."

Carla and Josie stood tall and nodded in agreement.

"As senior Bocelli wives, you have power and privilege that is second only to the Donna of the family." She held up her pointer finger. "Use it wisely. You can change lives with your influence, control circumstances with your sway, and set a trajectory that would impact the future for many."

Josie nodded. "You must only use your authority to honor the family. Every action you take and every word you speak is a reflection of the Bocelli name and reputation."

Nonnina nodded. "We are a sisterhood that upholds the ambitions of the Bocelli Family while assisting and strengthening the women of our associates and community. We utilize our strength and resilience to succeed in the most challenging circumstances. We do not tolerate suffering, harassment, victimization, or maltreatment, and will tenaciously persevere to improve another's plight and circumstances." She smiled and looked at each girl lovingly. "Together you have exceeded not only our expectations, but the doctrine upon which La Sorellanza was built." She took Carla and Josie's hands. "We are so very proud of each of you and are honored to receive you into our Sisterhood."

Carla stepped forward. "Do you agree with the principles of the Sisterhood of the Bocelli Family?"

Vicky, Theresa, and Mia looked at each other and said, "Yes."

Josie moved next to Carla. "Are you committed to serve and uphold the ethics of the Sisterhood of the Bocelli Family?"

"Yes," they said in unison.

Nonnina took a step forward. "Are you concerned with the needs and welfare of the women within the Bocelli Family and all Bocelli communities?"

"Yes," they said firmly.

Nonnina nodded. "Let us all join hands and form a circle. Victoria, Theresa, Mia, please repeat the pledge after me: I promise to be faithful and loyal to the Bocelli Family. I pledge to respect and honor the women of our family and community through the Sisterhood of the Bocelli Family principles. I promise to defend and assist those in need with integrity, character, and trust."

Mia's eyes grew wet as she recited the pledge alongside Vicky and Theresa. She was honored to be part of La Sorellanza and would uphold her promises with pride.

Nonnina moved away from the circle and opened the wooden box on the table. She, Carla, and Josie removed three ring boxes. "These rings are symbols of your commitment and loyalty to the Sisterhood of the Bocelli Family."

Josie stood before Theresa, Carla before Vicky, and Nonnina before Mia. When Nonnina opened the box, Mia recognized the ring as the very same one that Carla, Josie and Nonnina wore every day. She now understood that the 'family ring' they wore represented La Sorellanza.

Josie held up the ring and said, "We've had these rings custom-made by a family jeweler in Italy. The large center ruby represents loyalty and honor, with its oval shape reflecting balance and harmony. The two princess-cut rubies on each side signify confidence, while the twelve round opals that surround the center ruby represent clarity and truth. The baguette diamonds along the shank of the ring indicate strength and stability. The uniqueness of these rings highlights the traits that each of us possess as members of La Sorellanza."

"Wear these rings in good health, faith, and trust as loyal wives and members of the Sisterhood of the Bocelli Family," Carla said as she placed the ring on Vicky's right hand, ring finger.

Josie placed the ring on Theresa's finger and said, "May you continue to be the beautiful, compassionate, and selfless women you are."

Nonnina straightened her back and with glassy eyes said, "I could not hand-pick anyone more faithful and trustworthy to carry on our legacy than each of you." She placed the ring on Mia's finger, nodded her head and kissed each of her cheeks.

"Now we celebrate!" Josie sang as she pulled a bottle of champagne from the ice bucket and began to pour the bubbly liquid into the champagne flutes.

"Well done girls," Carla said as she held up her champagne.

"I just still can't believe you kept La Sorellanza a secret all these years," Vicky smiled widely.

"It's a secret well worth guarding," Josie said.

"These rings are gorgeous," Theresa said as she held out her hand.

"It suits you," Nonnina said as she beamed at Theresa.

"Nonnina," Mia said. "What will Artie's ceremony be like?"

"Oh my dear, that is a sacred ritual that I'm afraid only very few are permitted to witness. I couldn't even begin to tell you anything about it. In all of our years together Nonnuccio would never divulge any details for any of the installation ceremonies."

Carla put her champagne glass on the round table. "Ladies, it's time for dinner," she said and led the way through the house and out to the patio.

Mia was speechless as she looked around. The patio had been transformed into an eloquent paradise. Strings of lights illuminated a long banquet table that was set with fine white china, crystal glasses, and gold cutlery. Candles and flowers were arranged down the center, and around the perimeter. As they approached, multiple servers in black tuxedos were lined up waiting to serve the food. She heard laughter, and when she looked up Artie was approaching her smiling with pride.

"Hey you," he said.

"Hey," she replied and threw herself into his arms. She had never felt more connected to him than this very moment. That somehow being initiated into La Sorellanza at the same time he was installed as Consigliere had united them on a deeper level.

"Get a room," Vicky laughed as she brushed past them and kissed Angelo's cheek.

The family indulged in a four-course meal fit for royalty. At the end of the feast, Nancy had emerged in her chef's jacket, and when the family applauded her talents, she bowed. Mia sat back in her seat and reflected on how much had changed over the past nine years. Nancy was now a talented chef and caterer, and it wasn't lost on Mia that much of her success was attributed to the Bocelli Family. They not only gave her a chance, but they appreciated her talent and invested in her. Nonnina's generosity gave Nancy confidence and, more importantly, choices. Mia didn't trust Nancy's husband, Richard, and she knew that Nancy would be just fine if she chose to leave and start a new life without him. This was the very thing that La Sorellanza stood for. As she spun her ring around her finger, Mia smiled at Nancy and recognized that her life wasn't what she had planned back when she married Artie. It was better.

"This was a fabulous night," Mia said as she looked over at the guys smoking cigars by the firepit.

"Agreed," Vicky said and held up a glass of wine.

"These types of events are few and far between. They unite us as a family, and remind us to take pride in our legacy," Carla said.

"You sound like your father," Nonnina mused. "I do miss that man."

"We all do," Josie said as she squeezed Nonnina's hand.

Nonnina looked up at the sky, nodded her head, and said, "I am going to have another piece of that cannoli cake."

"Another? You've had two already!" Carla said. "I don't think that's such a good idea."

"It's a perfect idea," Nonnina said with determination. "Theresa, would you be a sweetheart and get me a nice big piece?"

She looked at Carla who shrugged back at her. "Sure. Can I get anyone anything?"

"Get everyone a healthy piece of the cake. Tonight is a night for celebration, and I would like us all to enjoy it."

As Theresa handed everyone a piece of cake, Nonnina said, "Always remember to appreciate the little things in life that make you happy. Those are life's true blessings and never take them for granted."

"Well said." Carla nodded and closed her eyes with delight as she took a bite of cake.

Mia smiled to herself. Her grandmother, Ruth, often said the same thing about appreciating the little things in life, and Mia decided she would try to remember to do that when life became hectic and stressful.

As the night wound down, Mia could see that both Vicky and Theresa appeared to be just as tired as she was, but didn't want the night to end. It was Josie who broke the reflective silence they had all fallen into.

"I'm sorry to say, but I think Ray and I should call it a night."

"I'll go up with you," Nonnina said as she stood. "Good night, girls. It's been a splendid evening."

Josie made a waving gesture to Ray, and they walked with Nonnina back into the house.

"Tonight was one for the books," Luca said as he held his arms out and Carla curled herself into him. "I'm one damn lucky man."

Artie put his arm around Mia and whispered in her ear. "Whaddya say we pick up where we left off earlier?"

Mia gave Artie a large smile and took his hand.

"Where are you guys going? Let's have a nightcap," Vicky said.

"We're getting a room," Mia said as she looked over her shoulder and led Artie home.

FIFTY

TWO WEEKS AFTER the installations, Artie burst into the bedroom. "We did it!" He announced.

"Artie, it's three o'clock, you're going to wake Maddie," Mia groaned as she pulled the comforter over her head.

"Mia, wake up," he said and sat down next to her. "We came to an agreement with the Espositos."

"Really?" Mia threw the comforter off and bolted upright. "It's over?" Over the past month, she felt overwhelmed with the limitations that had been imposed on the family members for their safety. Just when things looked like they were getting better, Joe raced over to the house announcing that word on the street was the Espositos were going to retaliate for Antonia's murder. He, Luca, and Artie had spent day and night trying to negotiate with Don Mario Esposito while investigating who wanted to kill Luca.

"Yes, Joe's connections identified the head of the Clinton Kings, Jose Diaz, as the one responsible for the shooting. Apparently, he sent a couple of his goons to take out Uncle Luca because he wouldn't open Bocelli territory for his drug trade. We had a sit-down with Don Mario and came to an agreement."

"An *agreement*? What type of agreement? Our family did nothing wrong."

"It's not as simple as that. Moretti is eager to expand the Esposito business throughout New Jersey. Particularly their drug trade. If we hadn't been standing in the way, the hit wouldn't have gone out on Uncle Luca and Antonia would still be alive. Not to mention the amount of revenue Moretti feels he's losing because we won't partner with him."

"What's the agreement?"

"I can't get into specific details. Let's just say the Espositos will now have access to New Jersey ports, for a fee of course, but must honor our territory when it comes to distribution."

"Won't that increase the drug supply in New Jersey?"

"It will increase the Esposito profits without a war. It's the best we could hope for."

"What about Jose Diaz? What'll happen to him?" Mia's eyes grew wide.

"Mario wants to handle it himself."

Mia knew exactly what that meant. She hated the man for trying to kill her Uncle Luca, and a small part of her was kind of glad he wouldn't have the opportunity to try again. She shook her head to dismiss the guilt she felt. "Does this mean I can leave the house without a security detail?"

"There's gonna be a formal dinner meeting tonight at Santorini's to lock in the contract, but yes, I suppose it does."

"Good," Mia breathed. "I'm going to Grammy and Poppy's for dinner. I've run out of excuses of why I couldn't see them, and now I don't have to come up with a story as to why I have security guards following me."

"MIA!" RUTH MET Mia at the front door and pulled her and Maddie in for a long embrace. Maddie giggled and pulled at Ruth's hair as Ruth took her great-granddaughter from Mia's arms.

"There they are!" Tony bounded over and kissed Maddie all over her chubby cheeks. "How's everyone feeling over there? It must've been some kind of summer flu to keep you quarantined for so long." Tony said as he raised his eyebrows.

"We're good. Much better now," Mia said as she brushed passed her grandparents.

"How's Ray feeling?" Ruth asked and handed Maddie to Tony.

"He's getting stronger every day," Mia said trying to think of something to change the subject. She thought she was being brilliant with her story of a bad summer flu going through the estate, but it was clear that her grandparents saw right through it. At least she didn't have to lie about Ray's health. Since he stepped down as Consigliere he did seem to have improved significantly. His demeanor was calm and upbeat, and she was sure she'd never seen him so relaxed. "What's for dinner?"

"We're having a Russo feast just like the old days. Everyone's coming."

"Even Richard?" Mia couldn't help but be sarcastic.

"Hmph, we'll see if he decides to grace us with his presence," Tony said as he sat on the floor with Maddie and rolled a ball to her.

"Before I forget," Ruth said, "I've been doing some cleaning, and I found this box of pictures and things that were your mother's. I thought you might like to have them."

Mia took the box and tentatively opened the lid. She remembered looking at these pictures as a kid, and her eyes lit up when she pulled out old pictures of Ruth and Tony, Rena, Janet, Nancy, and Anthony as children, and a few pictures of what she recognized as her own great-grandparents, Sal and Anna. She dug through the box and found a few pictures of Rena and Mia's father Dominick.

"Grammy, thank you. I forgot about these."

"Pictures keep our loved ones and memories alive," Ruth said and kissed Mia on the head as she went into the kitchen.

The evening flew by quickly and Mia felt almost like a kid again as she joked around with Anthony and reminisced with Janet and Nancy. It felt good to spend time with her family and eat her grandmother's cooking. When it was time to go home, Anthony carried a sleeping Maddie out to Mia's car.

"Everything good with Artie?" He asked after putting Maddie in the car.

"Yeah, he's good. At a work function tonight." Mia waved her hand.

"You know he knows, don't you?"

"Who knows what?"

"Poppy knows Ray stepped down and Artie moved up within the family."

Mia felt the blood drain from her face and had to grab the car door to keep from falling. "How?"

"Have you forgotten he manages *Villa Roma*? He knows people. People tell him things."

"Oh my God," she said as she looked up at the house. She saw Tony lifting Janet's daughter, Julia, up in the air. "What do I do? Should I talk to him?"

"Probably, but not now. Wait until it's just the two of you out in his garden and be open and honest. He knows there's nothing he can do to change it, and he loves Artie like a son, so he's accepting it. But you and Artie could do a lot to give him peace of mind if you both talk to him."

Mia nodded. "And Grammy?"

"How do you think he's come to accept it?"

"Right." She took a deep breath.

"Come here," Anthony said and pulled Mia into his arms. "We all love you and accept you and Artie unconditionally. There's no need to hide your true selves from us."

She squeezed Anthony tightly. Guilt flowed through her, and she hated the fact that her grandparents knew she had lied to them. They even helped her perpetuate it by acting like they didn't know. She wanted to march back into the house and sit down with both of them now, but she knew Anthony was right. She couldn't have those conversations with anyone else around, and Artie needed to be a part of them. She knew it would be a relief once she was able to apologize and clear the air. Not many families would be as forgiving as hers was.

Mia tried to stay awake until Artie came home. She figured it would be a late night, but she couldn't keep her eyes open any longer, and when she last looked at the clock at one-thirty, she surrendered to sleep. When Maddie's cries woke her up at eight a.m., Mia was panicked when she realized that Artie hadn't slept in the bed.

She ran to Maddie's room where Nanny Jenn was dressing her daughter expecting to see her husband. "Jenn, have you seen Artie?"

"No. Not this morning. I let myself in with my key, but he wasn't here."

She ran to the kitchen to check the coffee pot, but it hadn't been on, and Artie's cup was in the drainboard not in the sink ready to be washed like he left it every morning. The house felt still and quiet. Too still and quiet, and there was no evidence that Artie had been home since he left for the Esposito meeting. She grabbed the phone and called her Uncle Luca's office, but he didn't answer. She then dialed Matt.

"Hey Mia," Theresa sang when she answered.

"Hey. Is Artie over there?"

"Are you okay?"

"Theresa! Is Artie there?"

"No, he's not here."

"Where's Matt? I need to talk to Matt!"

"Mia, you're scaring me. You sound hysterical."

Tears poured down Mia's cheeks, "Artie didn't come home last night."

"Hang on," Theresa whispered.

"Hey, Mia, what's going on?"

"Matt, do you know where Artie is? He didn't come home last night?"

Matt's silence was deafening.

"Matt!"

TRUTH &
CONSEQUENCES

FIFTY-ONE

MATT HESITATED. "I left the dinner early. Jodi had a fever and Theresa needed help. Let me make a few calls. Uncle Luca and Aunt Carla were going down to the beach house early this morning, maybe something came up."

Within fifteen minutes, Vicky and Theresa were sitting next to Mia holding her hand.

"Everything is fine, I'm sure," Vicky said.

"Matt'll find him," Theresa added.

Mia did her best not to lash out and release the compilation of fear and anger that was pulsing through her brain.

"Uncle Luca said he was going to have one last drink with Joe," Mia said flatly. "Joe was home by two."

Mia could see Vicky and Theresa exchanging looks. There were two possibilities that could've happened to Artie that Mia could think of. He either hooked up with some broad and stayed out all night or something devastating happened that prevented him from coming home. Her faith in her husband and their wedding vows made her feel helpless and she started to prepare herself for the worst possible outcome.

All three of them jumped when the phone rang, and Vicky pounced on the receiver. "Matt?" she said. "Hang on let me put you on the speaker."

"Matt?" Mia said desperately.

"I found him. He's here at Santorini's."

"*Santorini's?* What's he still doing there?" Vicky asked.

"Is he okay?" Mia said quickly.

Matt chuckled. "He'll be fine. That is after he washes a bottle of aspirin down with a pot of coffee."

Theresa and Vicky rolled their eyes at each other and Mia said, "What?"

"Our boy must've had one too many tequila shots last night. I found him passed out in a lounge chair in the bar of the restaurant." They could hear Artie moaning in the background. "Whoop gotta go, he needs a bucket."

Vicky disconnected the call as they heard Artie retching in the background.

"That's just not like him," Mia shook her head. "You know Artie, he doesn't drink like that, and I've never known him to drink Tequila."

"I guess there's a first for everything," Vicky shrugged.

The front door opened and Josie, Ray, and Nonnina flew in. "Is there any news?" Josie rubbed her hands together.

"He's fine," Vicky walked over to Josie and hugged her mother while Mia and Theresa motioned for Nonnina and Ray to sit on the couch. "He must've drank too much last night and passed out at the restaurant. Matt's bringing him home now."

"Artie?" Ray asked in disbelief. "I would expect that from Matt, but not Artie."

"Hmm, that is uncharacteristic of him. But these have been trying times. Ray, maybe you should talk to him about it later," Nonnina said as she looked deep into Ray's eyes.

"I'm going to put on a pot of coffee and start some breakfast.

He'll need to eat something when he gets home," Mia said.

"I'll help you," Theresa said and squeezed Mia's shoulders while they walked together into the kitchen.

When Matt finally managed to get Artie home, Vicky needed to help him get Artie into the house and up the stairs to the bedroom.

"He doesn't look good," Vicky said as Mia wiped his face with a cloth. All at once, Mia was transported back to the countless times she had to clean up after her mother when she would be in one of her own drunken or high stupors.

"He'll be alright," Matt said and held him upright while Mia coaxed him to take the aspirin and drink some water. "I'd keep a bucket by the bedside though and try to make sure he drinks a lot of water. That'll help."

"Yeah, I know," she said flatly.

"Stella?" Artie slurred. "Is that you? You're my shining star." He reached out for Mia, but his arm fell limply off the side of the bed.

"Okay," she said as she put his arm back on the bed. "It's time for you to get some sleep."

"Matt, help me roll him on his side."

Artie put his hand on Matt's cheek and mumbled, "I love you, honey," as they rolled him over.

"Yup," Mia said and rolled her eyes. "Let's go eat. I'll check on him in a little while."

MIA SPENT MOST of the day at Artie's side, and when he finally woke up coherent enough for a conversation it was past nine p.m. He turned to look at her, his eyes bloodshot and his skin pale.

He slowly looked around in a daze, "What happened?" He attempted to sit up and groaned as he reached for his head.

"You don't remember?" Mia stared at him. "That's just great.

I'll tell you what happened. You got yourself so drunk that you blacked out at Santorini's and never came home."

"I did? I don't remember that."

"Of course you don't remember that Artie, you were drunk!"

"I remember Al Moretti handed out shots of tequila to toast our settlement."

"I guess you had a few too many then, didn't you."

"I guess I did," Artie said rubbing his hands on his face. "I don't usually drink tequila."

"Perhaps you shouldn't drink it again."

"How'd I get home? I don't remember getting home?"

"Matt had to go searching for you. He brought you home and then your family's been here most of the day helping me look after you."

"I'm sorry," he reached out and put his hand on hers. He looked so pitiful that it made Mia start to cry.

"I can't do this again, Artie," she sobbed. "I spent the first half of my life taking care of my drunk mother, and I don't have it in me to spend the next half of my life taking care of a drunk husband."

"Oh, Mia, oh, God. No," he pulled her into him. "I promise you this will never happen again. I don't know how I got so drunk last night, but I do know I'll never do this to you again."

She curled up into him and sobbed. She relived every painful memory of her past with her mother, and when the memory of finding Rena dead, slumped on the floor in a pool of her own vomit reared its ugly head, she howled. Artie held her tight, kissed her head, and cried alongside her.

FIFTY-TWO

FALL, 1989

OVER THE NEXT few weeks Mia, Vicky, and Theresa found they had a lot of things to catch up on with the Sisterhood. Since Uncle Luca wanted them to stay on the estate during the trouble with the Espositos, they hadn't been able to make their weekly lunch visits and check in with the communities. When they started up again, they became energized, and they provided much relief and assistance to women who had started to feel hopeless.

Vicky was helping a woman get full custody of her kids from their abusive father, Mia had helped a homeless woman get a job and an apartment after she lost both due to an accident that prevented her from working, while Theresa had helped a single mother bury her child due to a drug overdose. When the girls realized there were quite a few families that could use some help making Christmas merry, Theresa made up her mind to organize a luncheon for the families where Santa would arrive and hand out toys to the children, and the parents would receive a box of food complete with a ham and side dishes to take home and prepare for their Christmas feast.

Mia enjoyed the return of their weekly Sisterhood evenings. Carla, Josie and Nonnina offered their support and guidance over dinner, and the rest of the night was spent laughing and catching up.

"Mia, how's Artie doing since the incident?" Carla asked as she sipped her tea.

They had just finished discussing La Sorellanza business and had settled back in their chairs to enjoy 'the little things in life' as Nonnina liked to call her sweet treats. They took turns choosing the delicious delicacy and this week, Mia chose a moist yellow cake with chocolate icing. Gina had gone out of her way to make it thick with icing just as Mia liked.

"He's fine. Back to his normal self. I don't know what got into him that night, but I'm glad to have him back."

"I agree, that really wasn't like him at all. Let's hope that doesn't happen again," Josie said as she raised her fork.

"It's funny, because Matt was always the party guy, and he barely drinks like he used to," Theresa mused.

Nonnina smiled, "I think it's because you give his life meaning and stability. You're a very good match together. Mia, keep a close eye on Artie. Be sure he's all right. He tends to hold his emotions in, you know."

Mia smiled and touched Nonnina's hand. "I will."

"Vicky, I know you don't like to speak of it, but I predict you'll be a mother within a year or two," Nonnina said nodding at her granddaughter.

Vicky dropped her fork. "I hope you're right." Her eyes got glassy as she smiled hopefully at Nonnina.

"I might not have been very active with La Sorellanza recently, but you know I've been keeping a close watch on everything. I'm very proud of the three of you and all you've accomplished. But I'm even more proud of how devoted you are to each other and the family. That's a blessing far greater than any amount of money."

"Thank you, Nonnina, that means a lot," Vicky smiled.

"It means a lot to all of us," Mia agreed.

Over the next few hours, they played cards, gossiped, and laughed. Josie told stories about when she and Ray were just starting out, Carla reminisced about meeting Luca for the first time, and Mia, Theresa, and Vicky talked about all of the crazy situations they had found themselves in when they were teenagers.

After the cards were put away and dishes were cleared, Nonnina yawned and stood from the table. "Thank you, my dears, for a lovely evening," she said and put her hand on Mia's cheek. "Now it's time for me to rest."

The next morning, Mia and Artie woke up earlier than usual, and she thought about Nonnina's advice. She curled herself into him and placed her head on his chest.

"How's life as Consigliere?"

"Not bad," he said and kissed her head.

She needed to figure out how to check in with his emotions without sounding like she was prying. "Is it a lot different than before your father stepped down?" She ran her fingers through his curly chest hair trying to sound casual.

"Well, yeah," he pulled away just slightly. "Dad was doing the brunt of the work, and I was just helping and offering suggestions. Now I'm the one on the hot seat."

"You know, you can talk to me about anything."

"Mia, what's this all about?" She could tell he was losing his patience.

"Nothing." She turned to face him. "Look, I know you usually don't like to talk about things that bother you."

"I don't like to worry you or burden you. There's a difference."

"Still, it's not healthy to hold everything in. Look at your dad."

"You think I'm going to have a heart attack?"

"Artie, no. I'm just saying, we're a team and I'm an impartial ear if you ever need to release your stress." She leaned up to him and started kissing his neck and tugged at his ear with her lips. She could feel his tension loosen. She pulled herself up and straddled him as he ran his fingers down her back and grabbed her hips.

"I like your way of helping me release stress," he said and pulled her face close to his. Their lips brushed and Mia teased him with her tongue. Just as he groaned with delight, the phone rang.

"This better be good," Mia said as she answered.

"Mia?"

Mia could barely make out Vicky's voice. "Vic, what's the matter?"

"Nonnina," she whispered.

FIFTY-THREE

FALL, 1989

MIA GRABBED ARTIE as the room began to swirl. "We're coming," she managed to say and threw the receiver.

"What's going on?" Artie grabbed Mia and helped her to sit on the edge of the bed.

She jumped up and started to dress. "Nonnina." The only word she was able to say.

Artie ran into the main house before Mia as Angelo swung open the door. Ray sat on the edge of the couch with his head in his hands, and Josie was holding Carla who was sobbing mournfully. Vicky raced into Mia's arms as streams of silent tears flooded down her face. Just behind Mia, Matt and Theresa arrived with Mickey and Jodi.

"Mia, our nanny is sick today, can Mickey and Jodi go by your house with Maddie?"

Mia stared at Theresa for a long moment trying to comprehend her question. Her head was in a fog, and nothing seemed real.

"Of course, Nanny Jenn won't mind at all," Artie answered.

"I'll bring them over," Angelo offered as he took Jodi from Theresa's arms and held out his hand for Mickey.

"Thanks, man," Matt said as he tousled Mickey's hair and nodded at Angelo.

"What happened?" Artie asked as he looked around the room.

"Nonnina didn't join us for breakfast as she always does," Josie whispered. "Aunt Carla went to check on her." She gasped. "She must've gone in her sleep." She looked at Artie and Matt, her face wet with tears and her eyes almost swollen shut. "Uncle Luca's up there with her and Dr. Harrison. We're waiting for Gustano's funeral home to arrive," she choked.

Artie and Matt rushed up to Nonnina's rooms as Mia and Theresa helped Vicky to the couch. Gina set out a tray of coffee and hot tea along with a few pastries. She looked over to Carla, sorrow filling her face, and squeezed her eyes shut before slowly retreating into the kitchen.

"It looks like Jimmy Gustano and his guys just pulled up," Angelo announced as he came back in through the patio door. "I'll show them up."

"Thank you, sweetheart," Josie said as she rubbed Carla's back.

Mia felt lost and helpless. All she could do was rub her fingers on Vicky's hand and squeeze gently as she cried. Did Nonnina know it was her time? She thought as she remembered the words of wisdom and encouragement she had given them the night before. She realized Nonnina was so happy and serene when she stopped at the foot of the stairs and looked back at her before she went up to her rooms.

Dr. Harrison slowly walked into the room. "It's time for them to take her. Would anyone like to go up and have a few moments with her before they do?"

Everyone looked around the room at each other. Ray stood and held out his hand to Carla who needed Josie's help to stand. The three stood together and embraced just before Josie said, "You two go."

Josie moved to the couch and sat between Vicky and Theresa. She put her hand on Theresa's cheek and looked into Mia's eyes.

"She loved you girls so very much."

"We loved her back," Theresa said softly.

Mia was still at a loss for words, and all she could do was nod.

The elevator pinged and they all stood as the doors opened. Mia squeezed Vicky as they rolled the gurney that held Nonnina's body out the front door with Luca following close behind.

Jimmy Gustano, stood before them, bowed his head, and said, "I'm so very sorry for your loss. Donna Bocelli was a grand lady."

"That she was," Ray said as he shook Gustano's hand and led him to the door.

Luca had called in every one of his security guys to keep a close watch over the house as it was filled with many friends, relatives, and associates paying their respects throughout the day. Representatives from all of the New York, Pennsylvania, and New Jersey families along with their wives had made a showing, and Mia was surprised to see that most of New Jersey's elite had come as well. At one point, the patio was filled with the Dons and Captains of the other families while police chiefs, judges, and the governor were in the dining room.

Mia took a deep breath to ground herself as she watched Don Mario arrive with his wife, Elena, along with Daniella and her husband, Al. Joe and Dee rushed over to greet them at the door, and Mia was relieved when Joe led Mario and Al over to Luca while Dee escorted Elena and Daniella toward Carla and Josie. Mia didn't mind meeting and greeting most other people, but today she felt like her emotions might get the better of her if Daniella was her usual snarky self. After a few hours had passed, she felt a hand on her shoulder. "I'm sorry for your loss," Daniella said flatly. "Donna Bocelli was kind."

Mia felt her grip on the wine glass she was holding tighten. "Yes, she was."

There was an awkward silence between them, and when Mia was about to excuse herself, Daniella smirked. "I guess we're both up for Morris County's Humanitarian of the Year Award."

"I. I didn't realize that." She shook her head. Nonnina's death was still very surreal to her and the humanitarian award was the furthest thing from her mind.

Daniella leaned in and whispered, "What? Do you think you corner the market on doing good things? My work at the hospital and cancer center far exceeds anything you've done all year, I'm sure."

Mia opened her mouth to respond, and she could immediately see the look that Nonnina would've given her if she were there. She swallowed her breath, shook her head, and said, "I guess we'll find out soon enough," in the most endearing voice she could muster.

"Yes, two weeks from Friday. Don't feel like you have to attend, although it would be a pity if you missed my acceptance speech."

"You know what Daniella," Mia sneered. "I can't do this with you right now. There's a time and a place for everything, and this is not it." She slammed her wine glass down on the dining room table, pushed her way through the guests, and found a quiet spot in the sunroom.

She let out a long breath and put her face in her hands.

"Want some company?" Artie sighed as he sat next to Mia. He put his arm around her shoulder and pulled her close to him.

"You've got great timing," Mia said as she allowed tears to run down her face.

"I can't believe she's gone," he whispered.

"I know, I feel like the hole that I have in my heart from Nonnuccio just tripled in size. What am I going to do without her?"

He kissed the top of her head, and they sat in silence. "I know how hard this is on you. I'm glad Grammy and Poppy will be staying with us until the services."

"Me too. They both loved Nonnina, but Poppy especially has taken this hard."

"I can understand why. Nonnuccio and Nonnina reminded him of his own parents. They helped to keep their memory alive."

Mia sighed. "Yeah."

They sat together in silence while Mia watched the visitors come and go. So many of them with tears in their eyes, and she thought about what an incredible woman she was.

Artie broke the silence as he said, "Did I see you talking to Daniella in the Dining Room?"

The tension she was able to let drift away careened back into her shoulders and she sat upright. "Yup." She couldn't hide her disgust.

He leaned forward and squeezed his eyes. "Everything alright?"

"She just couldn't resist gloating that she's up for the same humanitarian award that I've been nominated for. She even went so far as to say I might as well not attend the awards dinner because she's going to win."

"She said that?" Artie stood up quickly. "To you? In our home? The day our grandmother died?" He clenched his fists, and his face turned bright red.

Mia thought of Nonnina and how she would hold herself up with class and dignity if she were the one in Mia's position. Mia took both of Artie's hands.

"She did indeed," she said calmly. "But that just shows you the kind of person she is. I'm going to go to that awards ceremony and hold Nonnina in my heart with my head held high. I intend to enjoy the evening, and if Daniella wins, I will sincerely congratulate her. I don't need the award to make me feel good about myself or prove that I've helped people. Winning the award would be an honor, but it's not important. Continuing the work in Nonnina's memory is what's important."

Artie stared at her for a long moment and shook his head slowly. "And that's why I love you so much." He kissed her warmly and tenderly. "*We* will attend that dinner together with pride."

FIFTY-FOUR

FALL, 1989

OVER THE NEXT few days, the estate had become very sad and quiet. Everyone walked around in a fog unable to have any conversations of substance. Carla spent her time up in her rooms, and Josie and Ruth worked together to organize Nonnina's services. Mia really appreciated her grandmother and how easily she and Poppy had integrated into the Bocelli family. Every once in a while, she'd notice one of them cringe if a sensitive topic came up in conversation, but all-in-all, she knew they'd grown to care about the Bocellis as much as she did.

Luca called a family meeting in the main house on the third afternoon and insisted that Ruth, Tony, and all of the children attend. Mia looked around the room, and she could see that everyone was just as grief-stricken as she was by their drawn faces and demeanor.

After Carla shuffled to a chair and let out a long sigh, Luca began. "Losing Nonnina is one of the greatest traumas this family has had to endure. I can say without a doubt that she was the backbone of this family, and we're all feeling pretty lost without her." He took Carla's hand. "But she wouldn't want us to fall into a black hole of despair because of her."

Ruth reached out and squeezed Mia's hand and tears streamed down both Vicky and Carla's faces.

Luca continued. "She navigated her life with dignity, grace, and style, and there was nothing she loved more than her family." He shifted. "Well, maybe she loved her desserts just as much, but I'm pretty sure her family ranked higher."

Josie stifled a laugh, and in that instant, Mia felt the heaviness of the room begin to lift.

Luca looked directly at Carla. "A part of me believes she was at peace and maybe was ready to join Nonnuccio. A few days before she passed, she had told me that she felt her job mentoring the next generation of Bocelli wives was complete and she couldn't be happier."

Vicky, Theresa, and Mia exchanged looks and smiled at each other.

"I do want to thank Josie and Ruth for all of your patience, determination, and attention to ensuring that every one of her final wishes were carried out. Her services will be beautiful, I'm certain."

Ray kissed Josie's cheek and Mia squeezed Ruth's hand, who nodded with appreciation.

"At this point, I would typically pass around some booze and make a toast, but the other day I got a better idea when I realized that Nonnina loved life and would want us to celebrate and remember her with excitement and energy." Luca looked over at James, the head of his security team and nodded.

James quickly went toward the kitchen and in a few moments returned with his wife, Gina, holding four standard poodle puppies with large red bows tied around their necks. Mia looked at the puppies and joined everyone else as they gasped, laughed, and admired them. Luca handed the smallest puppy to Carla, and said, "Meet the newest member of our little family." Carla laughed and cried as she hugged the puppy, and it began licking Carla's face. "This one is the most mellow of the group," he said. "I thought we could let the kids have the ones with all the energy."

"I love her," she exclaimed.

"Vicky, Mia, Theresa, the other three are for your families. Go ahead and pick the ones you want."

"What about you, Mom? Don't you want a puppy?" Vicky looked over at Josie.

"Hell no," Ray answered. "When Uncle Luca told us what he was doing, we both agreed we don't need to start chasing after a puppy at our age." He chuckled and rubbed the belly of the all-black puppy that threw himself at his feet.

Mia looked over at Artie. "Did you know about this?"

"Yeah." Artie smiled as he brought Maddie over to pet the all-white female pup. "Uncle Luca asked me, Dad, Matt, and Ange if we minded before he got them. I couldn't say no."

Tony looked up at Artie as he was petting the puppy with Maddie. "Smart man."

"It looks like they chose their families," Ruth said to Josie and put her arm around her shoulder.

Josie laughed. "I think you're right. That apricot one has been following Mickey around since he laid eyes on him, the all-white one is quite taken with Maddie, and Vicky hasn't let go of the black one since he started nibbling her toes."

"Luca, are they all from the same litter?" Tony asked as Maddie's puppy pounced on his foot.

"Yup. They're all standard poodles from a breeder up in Hackettstown. Their mother was white and apricot, and their father was all black. He's a retired show dog, won best of breed, and this was the last litter for the mom."

Throughout the rest of the day, everyone's mood lifted as the puppies crawled their way into their hearts in spite of house-training accidents. It wasn't hard for anyone to name the puppies. Mickey decided his pup should be named Charlie because it was a cool name, Vicky named her boy Marley after the singer, Bob Marley, Carla named her sweet girl Lily because it was Nonnina's favorite flower, and Mia landed on the name Whitney for their puppy, because if she couldn't name her daughter after one of her favorite singers, she would name her dog after her.

"Where should we set her up for the night?" Artie asked nodding toward Whitney as he carried Maddie into the house.

"You might want to consider the laundry room," Tony offered.

"Nope, she'll sleep with us," Mia said as she squeezed the dog in her arms.

Artie's eyes grew wide, and Mia saw the look of concern he shared with Ruth. "What about in your master bathroom? She'll be close to you, and yet if she has any accidents throughout the night, it won't be in the bed," Ruth suggested.

"I agree with Grammy. Let's get her potty trained and then we can decide on permanent sleeping arrangements.

"Alright," Mia said reluctantly and kissed the top of Whitney's head. "She's no replacement for Nonnina, but I love her already."

FIFTY-FIVE

FALL, 1989

IT HAD BEEN two days since Luca had brought home the pups, and Mia was grateful for the distraction. Whitney was a perfect fit for her family, and she seemed to know when to be playful yet gentle with Maddie and affectionate with Mia and Artie. But even Whitney couldn't prevent the sadness that flowed through her as Mia woke up in the morning knowing she would be saying good-bye to Nonnina that day.

Carla gathered Mia, Vicky, and Theresa together before they left for the funeral. "Before we head out, Nonnina had left instructions that each of you were to receive these gifts in her memory. She said they were some of her most valued treasures, and she wanted you to think of her as you wear them," Carla said as she and Josie handed Mia, Vicky and Theresa small gift bags.

Vicky opened her gift bag first and gasped as she pulled out a marcasite and diamond bracelet, tears streaming down her face. "This was always my favorite. I remember being really little and running my hand on it when I sat in her lap." She held out the bracelet to Josie who clasped it on Vicky's wrist.

Theresa gingerly reached into her gift bag and pulled out a black velvet box that contained the antique broach Nonnina wore on special occasions. "I. I. don't know what to say," Theresa's eyes were glassy as she looked at Carla.

"She wanted you to have it," Carla said and wrapped her arms around Theresa.

Mia took in a deep breath as she reached into her gift bag. As soon as she felt the soft silk her heart felt like it skipped a beat. She pulled out the scarf that Nonnuccio had given Nonnina on their honeymoon and brought it up to her face. She closed her eyes and breathed in Nonnina's scent.

"A scarf?" Vicky scoffed. "She left you a scarf?"

"Vicky!" Josie admonished.

"I'm sorry, but Theresa and I got two of her most valuable pieces of jewelry and Mia got a scarf!"

"This is the best gift she could've ever given me." Mia cried and smiled. "I will cherish it always," she said as she wrapped it around her neck.

Carla and Mia shared a meaningful look. Mia knew the scarf meant more to Nonnina than the jewelry, and she was overcome that Nonnina wanted her to have it. As Carla put her arm around her and led her toward the car, Mia whispered, "Are you sure I should have it?"

Carla nodded and kissed her cheek. A tear fell as she said, "Absolutely. I can't think of anyone else who would honor and appreciate it more than you."

Nonnina's funeral was the most beautiful service Mia had ever attended. She was in awe of the abundant flower arrangements and swarms of people who attended. While they didn't line the streets as they did for Nonnuccio, Mia recognized countless people from the communities who showed up to pay their respects.

After the services, they gathered at Nonnina's favorite Bocelli restaurant for a luncheon in her honor. She had requested that Nancy manage the entire affair and serve Nonnina's favorite dishes. Mia didn't hold back, and let herself indulge in the stuffed shells, short ribs, and risotto, but she was sure to save enough room for cannoli cake and pistachio gelato. While her stomach felt full, her heart still ached for the woman who had become her beloved grandmother.

"Artie, did I notice you walking funny?" Mia's brother, Anthony, asked as he handed Artie and Mia glasses of wine.

"Yeah," Artie rolled his eyes. "My sock has a hole near my big toe, and it grows with every step I take."

Anthony roared with laughter. "Are things so tight that you have to wear socks with holes in them?"

"Listen, smart ass. I had to wrestle my sock away from Whitney and I didn't have time to grab a new one." Artie took a large gulp of the wine.

Mia tried hard to hold her laughter, but she couldn't contain it any longer. Between giggles, she said, "Throw them out when you get home, and I'll make sure to get you some extra pairs."

"What's so funny?" Angelo asked as he and Vicky joined them.

"Whitney chewed a hole in Artie's sock," Mia mused.

Vicky's eyes went wide, and she quickly shook her head to Mia.

"You got off lucky!" Angelo fumed. "Our little terror chewed up my good black shoes."

Everyone looked down and burst out laughing when they saw Angelo was wearing blue and tan loafers with his black suit.

"Listen," Vicky said. "Theresa and I are gonna head home. Looks like things are thinning out here and she wants to get back to check on Jodi's cold, and I'm mentally and physically exhausted."

Mia breathed a sigh of relief, and the idea of going home eased her thoughts and emotions. "Do you mind?" She asked Artie.

"No, you girls go ahead. We'll stay," Artie said as he kissed her cheek.

"Great, I'll grab my purse and tell Grammy and Poppy."

AS SOON AS they got home, she changed into her favorite pair of shorts and sweatshirt and brought Maddie and Whitney outside to frolic and play with Mickey, Jodi, and the other pups while Ruth took a nap. Although Mia tried to convince Ruth to go back home with Tony after the luncheon, she was happy that Ruth wanted to stay a few extra days. She didn't need to lean on Ruth as much as Nancy and Janet did for emotional support, but she had to admit that Ruth's calm and loving demeanor was exactly what Mia needed.

"Lookout!" Vicky yelled as her dog, Marley, bounded across the lawn and knocked Mickey down showering him with kisses.

Theresa laughed. "I think you got the craziest one of the bunch."

"I *did*," Vicky said. "Although Ange loves dogs, and I can tell he loves Marley to death, he's starting to lose patience with the puppy antics. For some reason, he only chews up Ange's things."

"Same here. Whitney latches on to Artie's socks like they're Filet Mignon."

"All Matt has to do is give Charlie a look and that dog just drops whatever's in his mouth. I don't know how he does it, but it's working so far."

"He's got to teach Artie and Ange the look, otherwise I think we're going to have a tough road ahead of us," Mia laughed.

"Hi, James!" Mickey stopped running and waved his hand.

"Uh oh," Vicky said. "This can't be good."

"Uhm, I'm going to have to ask the whole family to relocate to the main house for the time being. Mia, are your grandparents still here?"

"My grandmother, she's taking a nap. What's going on?"

"It's just a precaution, but I'm going to need you to wake her and gather your Nannies immediately."

"James, what's happened?" Vicky stood directly in front of him with her hands on her hips.

"All I can say is there's been some trouble after the luncheon, and I've been ordered to gather everyone into the main house. The rest of the family will fill you in as soon as they return."

"I don't like this," Theresa said as she lifted Jodi.

Mia rushed into the house and alerted Nanny Jenn to gather some of Maddie's things and bring her to the main house immediately. She took a deep, calming breath and lightly tapped on the guest room door.

"Grammy," she said trying to muster a soothing voice.

"Mia, did I sleep too long? I feel like I just shut my eyes."

"You did. I'm going to need you to get dressed and come over to the main house. You can finish your nap in one of the guest rooms there if you want."

Ruth sat up quickly, "What's wrong?"

"I don't know. Nothing, I'm sure everything's fine."

Mia knew she couldn't hide the fear that was all over her face, and Ruth was able to see through her.

"Okay, let's go," Ruth said calmly and nodded her head.

As they approached the back patio, Mia noticed that there were security guards surrounding the entire house.

"James, when will everyone return home?" Vicky was asking as Mia and Ruth entered the family room.

He shook his head, "I'm not sure."

"Isn't there anything you can tell us?" Theresa asked.

"I'm sorry." He shook his head again slowly and said, "I'll be in the security office if you need me."

They sat quietly in the family room, trying to be patient. Mia knew that Vicky and Theresa were thinking the same thing she was. The last time they were instructed to stay in the main house was when someone had tried to shoot Uncle Luca. After three hours had passed, they all stood anxiously staring at the front door when they heard the cars pull up.

The door swung open, and Ray and Josie entered holding Carla up on each side. Her legs were limp, and her head bobbed back and forth as she wailed.

Vicky was the first to move and she raced to the door to help her parents carry Carla in.

"What? What happened?" Vicky whispered.

"LUCA!" Carla screamed. "My Luca!"

"Uncle Luca?" Vicky asked her mother who turned her tear-stained face away. She turned her head to Ray who shook his head slowly. She made a retching noise as she grabbed her stomach and ran from the room.

Mia gasped and reached out for Ruth before she collapsed on the floor. She felt Artie's strong arms pull her into his chest, and they sat together on the floor rocking back and forth.

"What happened?" She managed to croak. She looked around the room and saw Ruth had joined Josie and Ray at Carla's side. Angelo folded Vicky into him as they stood nearby, and Matt rubbed Theresa's back as she sat on the couch bent over covering her head with her arms. The hysterical moans and wails pierced the air.

"WHAT HAPPENED?" Mia screamed. "TELL ME! YOU'VE GOT TO TELL ME!"

Artie continued to hold her tight and kissed her head over and over as the hysteria filled the room.

After what seemed like an eternity, the cries and screaming were replaced with moans and weeping, and Matt stood and cleared his throat. Mia stared up at him but couldn't make him out through her tears.

"As we were leaving the luncheon," he said tentatively, "a car approached." He paused. "Shots rang out." He swallowed hard. "And Uncle Luca was hit."

Carla moaned, "All the blood. There was so much blood."

Ray turned to Josie and Ruth, "She shouldn't be here for this. Let's get her up to her rooms."

The room stood frozen as Ray, Josie, and Ruth carried Carla toward the elevator. As the doors shut, her wails cut through the house only dissipating after they heard Josie close the doors to her wing on the second floor.

"Matt, tell us the rest," Vicky clung to Angelo. "Tell us he's okay."

He shook his head. "We raced him ourselves to the hospital. It was only five miles away." He bent over and put his hands on his legs. "This never should've happened," he said and stood up. "IT SHOULDN'T HAVE HAPPENED!"

They all turned their heads toward the front door as Joe raced into the house. "I just heard. Oh my God, I just heard."

Matt turned to Joe. "I'm gonna get the son-of-a-bitch who did this, and I promise you, he'll be sorry."

Joe nodded and put his hand on Matt's shoulder. "Come on, let's gather ourselves and talk strategy." He pushed his head out toward Artie and Angelo, "Let's go to Luca's office. We'll have to inform the other Captains."

Artie kissed Mia's head, whispered, "I'm sorry," and stood up to follow Joe into Luca's office.

"I guess he's the new Don," Vicky whispered and sat next to Mia on the floor.

"Who do you think's responsible?" Theresa asked as she joined them.

"The Espositos," Mia said with contempt. "That family has caused nothing but heartache and pain to my family." Her eyes glazed over. "I have no doubt they did this, and I'm telling you right now if Matt doesn't see to it they're held accountable. I will."

FIFTY-SIX

MIA LAY IN bed staring at the ceiling. After it was decided that it was safe for everyone to return to the individual homes, she put Maddie to bed, kissed Ruth goodnight, took a long bath and retreated to her bed. She looked at the clock when she heard Artie enter the room and saw that it was after five a.m. He quickly changed his clothes and pulled her toward him as he got under the sheets.

"I'm sorry, honey. I'm just so sorry." He squeezed her tightly.

"This is a nightmare," she whispered.

"You don't know the half of it."

"What do you mean?" She looked up at him.

He let out a long breath. "Joe's jumping into his new role as Don with both feet. He called a meeting with all the Captains tonight and he's setting up sit-downs with the other families already."

"Isn't he supposed to do that? I mean, didn't Uncle Luca do that after Nonnuccio passed?"

"Yeah, I suppose, but everything's moving quickly, and I'm still trying to wrap my head around all that happened only hours ago."

"Who does the family think ordered the hit?"

Artie shook his head, "We've got our suspicions, but we've got to get some solid proof."

"I should hope the Espositos are on the top of your list." She sat up and looked him in the eye. "Whoever did this, must be punished."

"Don't worry, honey, we're gonna handle it." He kissed her head.

Mia laid her head on Artie's chest. She felt her emotions ebb and flow between anger and rage and grief and sadness all night. It was sad when Nonnuccio and Nonnina died, but she knew that was part of life's cycle and they lived long, happy lives. But her Uncle Luca didn't deserve to be gunned down outside of a restaurant on the day of his mother-in-law's funeral. Whoever was responsible was ruthless and callous. She squeezed her eyes shut. In the past, she could never imagine a circumstance where she would condone violence, but now the only thing she knew would ease her pain was vengeance that was equivalent to her Uncle Luca's cold-blooded murder.

"How's Grammy doing with all of this?" Artie broke into her thoughts.

"She's been really quiet."

"This is going to be hard on both your grandparents, you know. Under the circumstances, I'm sure it's going to open up a lot of wounds."

Mia sighed. "I know. I think it'll be best not to talk to them about specific details as they come up."

"Yeah," Artie yawned.

Mia could feel his arms around her loosen as he fell into his slumber. As she rolled over, she felt the tears flow like a river down her cheeks. She hugged her pillow and closed her eyes, her emotions alternating between deep sorrow and profound fury.

The next morning everyone gathered at the main house for breakfast. Vicky and Theresa's faces mirrored her own, and each of their voices was raspier than the other from spending the night crying. Gina kept herself busy in the kitchen cooking a feast, and when Mia moved in to hug her, she squeezed Mia tightly and sobbed into her shoulder.

Mia fixed herself a small plate and had to turn her head each time the pancakes came into her line of sight. It was only two days ago that she and Uncle Luca met up in the wee hours of the morning and made their usual pancakes while singing their favorite arias. She didn't know if she'd ever be able to eat pancakes again.

As Ruth sat next to Mia she said, "You know, sweetheart, I've been thinking. What if we let Maddie have a little fun time and stay with her Aunt Janet and cousins Gabe and Julia for a few days? There's a lot going on here and it may be good for her."

Artie leaned in and said, "That really is a good idea."

Mia squeezed her eyes shut and consented. "Yeah, I think you're right."

"I'll give a call over there. I'm sure Poppy'll lend a hand."

"You know, I like that idea too," Theresa said. "Matt, what do you think if we have Mickey and Jodi spend some time over at my sister's?"

Matt considered it. "Yeah, okay. I just don't want them eating Oreos for breakfast again this time."

Josie slid into a chair and took a long sip of coffee. "I'm really worried about Aunt Carla. She screamed and wailed most of the night and now she's just sitting staring into space rocking back and forth hugging the dog."

"I called Dr. Harrison," Ray said as he entered the room. "She's on her way over." He ran his hand across his face as he sat in a chair.

"How are we going to handle all of the visitors today?" Vicky sighed as her eyes filled up. "I just feel like I can't do it all over again."

Matt shook his head. "No, uh-uh. That was one thing we stood firm on with Joe. Artie and I thought it was better not to open the house today under the circumstances. Joe thought we should. He didn't want to offend any of the other families, but we wouldn't budge. I'm sure they'd understand."

"Thank you," Vicky said as she hugged her brother.

"That must be Dr. Harrison," Ray said as he heard James at the door. Josie jumped to her feet and followed her husband as they led the doctor up to Carla's rooms.

"What about the arrangements?" Theresa asked Matt.

"They want us to hold off on anything for now until they do some investigating. Artie and I are working real close with our associates in the department, so the quicker we can get some answers and take some action, the better it'll be for everyone."

"In the meantime, it would be best to follow the same protocol we used the last time," Artie added. "Don't leave the estate unless you absolutely have to and then always have security with you."

Everyone agreed and broke off into their smaller conversations. Mia and Theresa discussed packing up the kids, while Vicky and Ruth talked about making homemade bread together later in the afternoon to help work out their emotions.

Ray and Josie saw Dr. Harrison to the front door and looked worn and weary as they approached the table.

"How is she?" Mia asked.

"The doctor said she's in shock. Witnessing her husband get shot right after burying her mother was quite traumatic for her," Ray said.

Josie put her hand on Ray's shoulder. "She wrote a prescription for Xanax to calm her and recommended that we take her away to somewhere quiet so she could get some rest. We've decided to bring her down to the Mantoloking house. It'll be nice and quiet there and the ocean will be soothing for her."

"What can we do?" Mia asked.

"Nothing. Be there for each other and draw on your Bocelli strength. We'll get through this together as a family," Josie said. "I'm going to talk to Gina, I think it would be best if she came with us. No one can help take care of Aunt Carla the way Gina can." She looked over at Ruth. "Ruth, would you mind helping me pack up some things for Carla?"

"We'll need to bring the dog too," Ray said scratching his head. "Don't forget to pack up Lucy's things too."

"*Lucy?*" Vicky's eyes widened. "Who's Lucy?"

"Aunt Carla's dog." He shrugged.

"It's *Lily*," Vicky rolled her eyes.

Matt stood and patted Ray on the back. "Let's go meet with James about the security. We need to make sure both houses are secure,"

They could hear Ray mumble, "I thought her name was Lucy. I like the name Lucy," as he followed Matt to the security office.

FIFTY-SEVEN

FALL, 1989

RUTH HAD INSISTED on staying indefinitely, and over the next week everyone was trying to find a new sense of normalcy. Sending Maddie to Janet's gave Mia the chance to grieve freely, and she alternated between bouts of hysterical crying and angry shouting. Throughout it all, Ruth had become a strong anchor for not only Mia, but for Vicky and Theresa who were also struggling. Ruth always knew the right response to any of their emotions. She would sit and hold their hands when they reminisced, she would hug them tightly when they found themselves caught up in tears, and she would back off when the anger would rise, and they needed to scream and shout.

Josie called to check in and provide updates on Carla each afternoon. It seemed that she was making small improvements, but was still grieving deeply, and would wake up screaming from nightmares every night. Josie didn't know when they would be returning and thought that the beach was soothing for Carla. Mia wished she could be at the beach house with her aunt, but knew it was better if she stayed on the estate.

Artie and Matt were in and out of meetings with Joe all day and sequestered themselves in Luca's office throughout most of the night. When Mia did get to see Artie, he was short-tempered and irritable. She knew he was burying his grief and shock, and she worried about what all the stress and anxiety were doing to him mentally and physically. He had developed deep black rings under his eyes, and she noticed his right eye had developed a consistent twitch.

"Are you just getting up or coming to bed?" Mia asked Artie as she rubbed the sleep out of her eyes.

Artie leaned over and kissed her forehead. "Sorry, I'm just getting up."

"I didn't feel you turn in last night."

"Yeah, I didn't want to wake you."

"It's fine, I like to feel you next to me when you slip into bed." She reached out to him, but he stepped away.

"We need to talk about the awards ceremony Friday night," he mumbled.

"Yeah, I don't think I wanna go."

"Actually, Joe insists that we should go. He thinks it'll be good for the family that we show our resilience and strength."

"I'm not feeling very strong," Mia said as her eyes got wet.

Artie sat next to her on the bed. "I know you don't, but I actually agree with Joe on this one. Both Nonnuccio and Uncle Luca would've done the same. It's important that the community leaders and the Espositos see that nothing can tear us down. Even if we're feeling weak inside."

"Alright," she consented.

"Good." He looked down at her for a long moment.

Mia slipped out of bed and took a long look in the mirror. *Ugh, I've got three days to get rid of these bags*, she said to herself.

That afternoon, Ruth encouraged Mia and Vicky to spend the day pampering themselves. After getting manicures, pedicures, and facials, they had a light lunch, and then went shopping in their favorite boutique to get dresses for the awards dinner. Mia still felt like she was carrying a boulder in her heart, but the weight of it seemed to have gotten a little lighter.

"This was a good idea," Vicky said and slipped her arm through Mia's as they walked down the street.

"It was." She smiled and turned her head to Roberto, one of the four security guards that surrounded them. "Don't you think this was a good idea, Roberto?"

"Yeah, great," he mumbled as he scanned the street.

"I feel like our world has crumbled around us. Nothing feels real anymore," Vicky said.

"I know what you mean. Sometimes I feel so devastated and hopeless, and sometimes I get so angry I just want to hit something."

"I hit Ange," Vicky admitted.

Mia stopped short and turned to Vicky. "What do you mean?"

Vicky chuckled. "It's not what you think. The other night was a really rough one for me. I was hysterical and when he tried to hug me, I pushed him away. He kept coming closer and I kept pushing him, and he finally said, 'let it out.' I started pounding my fists on his chest." Vicky shrugged. "He kept saying 'do it again' and 'let it all out.' So, I did, and it actually felt really good."

"You didn't hurt him, did you?"

"Of course not," Vicky waved her hand, and they continued walking. "Have you noticed the muscles on my husband? My little fists probably felt like annoying little gnats bumping into him."

"Wow, can you imagine if I did that to Artie?" They both looked at each other and burst out laughing.

"I'll tell you what, the sex after was amazing," Vicky raised her eyebrows.

"I didn't realize how much I missed this. Missed us palling around like this," Mia said as she smiled.

When Mia arrived home, Whitney greeted her at the door and started jumping and biting at the bottom of her garment bag. "Oh, no. This dress is not a toy. Here Whit, play with this," Mia said as she grabbed a ball and threw it. She chuckled as Whitney followed her up to the bedroom and entertained herself with the ball as Mia sorted through her shoe collection looking for the new Kenneth Cole black velvet pumps she had been saving for a special occasion.

"Here they are," Mia said as Whitney chased the ball into her closet, knocking over a small stack of shoe boxes. As Mia collected the shoes that were strewn throughout the floor, she noticed the contents of the box Ruth had given her with Rena's things had been scattered as well. She sat on the floor and looked at each picture and memento Rena had saved. She chuckled when she found an old newspaper clipping with a picture of Mia and her Brownie troop marching in the Memorial Day parade. Mia's breath caught when she turned an envelope over and saw her name written on it in her mother's handwriting. She ran her fingers over it taking in the familiar swirls that she hadn't seen in years. Inside the envelope, she found a letter:

My Dearest Mia,

As you read this, I want you to know that you have been my life's greatest blessing. I wish I could've been a better mother, and please know that I tried. Each and every day I woke and told myself today's the day I'll conquer my demons and make things right. But I just couldn't. There was nothing I could do to atone for my sins, and now it's time you knew the truth.

I loved your father with every inch of my being. In fact, you could say, I loved him too much. He was a complicated man who insisted on doing things his way. Just before I found out I was pregnant, I discovered he was having an affair with Antonia Esposito. He said he got close to her in an effort to get her father, Carmine's, respect and to help himself move him up through the ranks of the family. Once we discovered I was pregnant with you, he said he'd end things with her. The day you were born was the best day in both of our lives. Dominick was so proud. He put you up on a pedestal and held you there for the rest of his days.

I was blissfully happy with our little family, and I let myself believe the affair was over. Until one day, I caught your father and Antonia snuggled up together in a café downtown. I flew into a rage and made quite a scene right there in the restaurant. But when she stood up and Dominick put his hand on her stomach, I went numb. I knew I was losing your father to Antonia who was pregnant with his child.

Mia, I was utterly and completely devastated. I pray you never experience the same type of demoralizing betrayal in your life. It could cause you to make rash, destructive decisions as I did. I had become so desperate to keep our family together, that I did the unthinkable. I anonymously tipped off the police and had Dominick arrested for distribution of drugs. I thought he would see how loyal I was when I stood by him and got him released. I thought if I could manage to get the charges dropped he would realize we belonged together.

But my plan backfired in the most horrific way. As you know, he was killed in prison before I could make things right. On that very same day, Antonia married Paul Matino. Four months later she gave birth to a daughter she named Daniella. Although I have my suspicions that either Matino or the Espositos organized his murder, I am the one who was responsible for your father's death.

There are no words that could truly express how very sorry I am for taking your father from you and hindering your life with the effects of my own intense guilt. I know I'm completely undeserving of your forgiveness, but I ask you, my darling daughter, to find it in your heart to forgive me, as I have never been able to forgive myself. Don't carry my sin with you and let it be a burden for the rest of your life. Always know your father and I loved you so very deeply. I beg you, Mia, release all the pain from your heart and live your life filled with peace and love. Be happy. Please, be happy.

Until we meet again,
Mom

Mia gasped and re-read Rena's letter over and over again. Her fury growing with each pass, until she was in a frenzy. She finally knew the truth. Her poor mother carried this burden for so long, and it destroyed her. Rena wasn't just a depressed addict, she was paralyzed by guilt. She found herself in a position where she did what she felt she had to save her marriage from Antonia Esposito's wicked manipulations. No, her mother wasn't to blame. Mia blamed the Espositos, who, in her mind, kept taking and taking from the Russos.

"Damn them!" She spit as she jumped to her feet and charged out of the room.

FIFTY-EIGHT

FALL, 1989

MIA GRASPED A COPY of her mother's letter in her fist as she strained her neck to look out of the back seat window.

"How much longer, Roberto?"

"We'll arrive at Mrs. Moretti's home in just a minute," Roberto answered as he looked in the rear-view mirror. "Are you absolutely sure you want to go there? You seem upset."

"I am *quite* upset, Roberto, and no I don't *want* to pay Daniella Moretti a visit, but I *have* to." She glared at his eyes in the mirror. "And let's not call Artie, Matt, or anyone else while I'm there. I'll tell them all about this visit when I return."

He nodded as he pulled the car up to the security gate.

Daniella stood in the doorway with her arms crossed over her chest waiting for Mia to exit the car. "What's this all about? I'm quite busy you know, and don't appreciate drop-ins."

Mia stared at Daniella's face searching for Dominick's characteristics, and when she looked closely, she saw Daniella had his eyes and nose. She never would've figured it out had she not known they shared the same father, but now it was very clear and distinct.

Daniella pulled her head back. "You look disgusted, Mia. This ought to be good," she said as she opened the door fully and waved Mia into her home.

"Did you know? All this time? Did you know?" Mia was shaking and couldn't control her harshness.

"Know what?" Daniella sighed.

Mia glared at her. "We are sisters!"

Daniella's mouth fell open, and then she tilted her head back in laughter. "Oh, that's rich. *We're* sisters?" She straightened her posture and glared back at Mia. "You're delusional, just like your mother."

Mia snapped. "Don't you dare call my mother delusional! If it wasn't for your whore of a mother, both my parents would still be alive!"

"Excuse me? You can't come in here and throw insults at my mother. Who the hell do you think you are?"

"*I* am your sister! That's who I *am*!" Mia waved the copy of her mother's letter in her face. "Your mother was sleeping with my father *knowing* he was married to my mother. She let herself get pregnant with *you*! Your family has shattered my family's lives over and over again. Is there no end to your cruelty?"

Daniella scoffed. "Your family did enough damage to themselves, they didn't need us to help them." She looked down at the letter. "This is your proof? A bunch of dribble written by a psychopath?"

Mia was pushed too far. She felt intense heat radiate down her head to her toes. Her head pulsated and everything she'd ever learned from Sofia DeGregorio and Nonnina on how to control her temper and remain stoic, dissolved. She lunged at Daniella and screamed, "All of you Espositos are evil! You're pure evil! I could kill you!"

Mia pinned Daniella on her back and squeezed her fingers around her throat while Daniella coughed and scratched at Mia.

"What the hell?" Al rushed into the foyer and pulled Mia off of Daniella. "I don't know what this is all about, but it was a *big* mistake!" he said and pushed Mia out the door.

"WHAT WERE YOU thinking?" Joe was pacing. "We have a good relationship with the Espositos. I mean, we *had* one, that is, until this little stunt."

"I wasn't thinking," Mia admitted. "With everything my family had suffered at the hands of the Espositos, I couldn't take it anymore." Mia had no excuse for what happened.

"You should've come to one of us," he said and waved his hand toward Artie and Matt. "We would've handled it for you."

Mia lowered her head. "I am so sorry my anger got the better of me, and I apologize if it's caused tension with the Espositos. I'll apologize and make it right." She felt ashamed that she had dishonored Nonnina's memory by letting her emotions set off a blinding rage. Nonnina's lessons rang through Mia's brain, *never show your emotions, always remain dignified, everything you do and say is a direct reflection of the Bocellis,* and Mia didn't know how she was going to make this all right.

"That'll be a good start, but we have more damage control to do," he scoffed.

Artie raised his hands in protest. "Okay, Joe, I understand you're upset, but all things considered, Daniella had it coming. She's been nothing but offensive and spiteful toward Mia since the day they met. I think you would agree that we've all been under a lot of stress since the trauma of Uncle Luca's murder. Now I'm not making excuses or sweeping it under the rug, but I'm sure our relationship with Mario will not suffer at the hands of his sister."

"Mario?" Joe waved his hand. "We've got business with Al, and now's not the time to be hauling insults at his wife."

As Mia raised her head, she caught Artie and Matt exchange a quick look.

"Why don't we have a drink and talk this out," Artie patted Joe on the back and motioned for Matt to follow them into Luca's office. He turned and met Mia's eyes and blinked once slowly. She nodded back and knew that Artie had her back and would try to smooth things over.

"I heard everything," Vicky whispered as she tip-toed toward the table and sat down next to Mia. "Oh my *God*!"

"I know. I really screwed up," Mia said as she rubbed her face with both of her hands.

"Damn, I wish I had been there to see you strangling that wench."

"You know, Vick, I'm not sure I would've stopped. So much wild rage flooded through me." Mia looked into Vicky's eyes. "I don't even know who I am anymore. I'm just so angry, and all I want is retribution so the Espositos can suffer for what they've done to my parents, my great-grandparents, and probably Uncle Luca."

"I get it. But be very careful not to go down a road of no return. Because once you go there, you'll forever be changed, and not for the better."

"How do we go on living like this?"

"I don't know," Vicky said as she hugged Mia. "I guess we have to find a different way of living."

"But how do we do that?"

"I don't know," Vicky said as the two girls sat together silently wiping away the slow trickle of tears that ran down their faces.

Deep down Mia knew Vicky was right, but she wished she knew how to cope with the emotions of the past couple of weeks. After saying goodnight to Vicky, she walked slowly through the grounds to her own home. She appreciated the silence of the night and thought maybe she would take a bath and try to do some sketching, although she was wary of what dark images she might involuntarily produce.

"Hey, Grammy." Mia found Ruth lying on the couch looking

through the contents of Rena's box.

"Mia," she said, and Mia had never seen her eyes look so sad. "I couldn't help but read the letter. Are you alright?"

"I don't know," Mia wailed and threw herself into her grandmother's arms and cried like she was five years old again.

They sat together while Mia cried the last of her tears and Ruth stroked her hair. "Did you know about all of this?" Mia asked as she wiped her face with tissues.

"No." Ruth shook her head. "But I wish she had told us. We would've done anything to help her with the burden of her guilt." Her voice cracked. "Maybe things could've been different."

"I think you would've been able to help her. I see how you are with all of us, and I know how much your being here has helped Vicky and Theresa just as much as it's helped me. You always know the right things to say and do, and I don't know how to thank you."

Ruth put her hand on Mia's face and smiled. "You would actually have to thank your great-grandmother, Anna. She had more compassion, concern and empathy in her little finger than most people have in their whole being. I learned a lot from her, and during tough times I try to think about what she would do."

"I wish I could've known her."

"You two would've loved each other." Ruth smiled and slowly shook her head. "But Mia," Ruth said seriously. "I'm worried about *you*. Your deep sadness and anger are only natural given all of the loss you've experienced, and your mother's letter was yet another devastating shock. But losing control with Daniella today, that's got me worried."

"I know. I'll be honest, my rage scared me too."

"You're a lot like Poppy in that respect, and if you're not careful it could lead to a terrible downfall."

Tears slid down Mia's cheeks. "I don't know how to be anymore.

I can't stop myself from crying, and when I'm not crying, I just want to lash out. I feel like I'm going to explode."

"Then explode, sweetheart. Go outside into the woods and scream or go to the gym and pound on a punching bag. Do something, anything to release your tension and emotions."

"Do you think that'll work?"

"It can't hurt." Ruth shrugged. "But Mia, that's only the first step. You're going to need to find a way to forgive and move on."

"Forgive? Who? The Espositos?"

"Yes, actually. The Espositos, your mother, your father. Deep down, people are human, and they make mistakes, but if you dig really deep into your heart and find a way to absolve them, you'll finally be able to release your anger."

Mia looked at her grandmother as if she had gone mad. "If Antonia Esposito didn't sleep with my father and gotten pregnant, my mother wouldn't have been compelled to go to extremes to save her marriage. My father wouldn't have died in prison, and my mother wouldn't have become an alcoholic and an addict from all of her remorse. How do I forgive that?"

Ruth nodded her head. "Yes, but you can't honestly think that Antonia was solely responsible for what happened to both of your parents. Everyone involved made their choices. It would do you a world of good to acknowledge how egregious some of those choices were and leave them in the past while you forge ahead becoming a better person by learning from their mistakes."

"I don't know how to do that, and I'm not sure I can."

"What I do is try to see the circumstances through the other person's perspective. Try to identify what drives them and what their motivation is. Some people are driven by greed, some by honor, some might've been raised with certain beliefs that might not align with yours, while others may actually have mental illness and can't help themselves. This doesn't make the wrongdoing right, but I will say if I can try to understand someone's motivation, it helps me to let go of the hurt and pain sooner and make room in my heart for more love and happiness."

"You make it sound so easy."

Ruth shook her head and squeezed Mia's hand. "It'll probably be one of the hardest things you'll ever do in your life. It'll take time, but I do think it's worth trying. For your own mental health and well-being."

Mia sat in silence pondering her grandmother's advice. She didn't know if she could possibly find a way to forgive all the wrongs that had happened to her family, but she knew that she couldn't carry the heaviness in her heart forever.

Ruth stood and handed Rena's letter to Mia. "Read your mother's letter again. But this time don't focus on Antonia's role in the situation, pay attention to your mother's last request of you." Mia took the letter, and after taking a long, hot bath where she pondered her grandmother's advice, she picked up Whitney, curled up in bed, and re-read the letter three more times.

"I forgive you, Mom," Mia whispered. "And I promise, I'll release all the pain I'm carrying in my heart." Mia saw it clearly for the first time. She couldn't change any of the tragedies that had occurred, but she had to move forward and do her best so she wouldn't spiral down a black hole of madness.

FIFTY-NINE

FALL, 1989

"MIA, YOU look beautiful," Ruth beamed at her granddaughter.

"You do look stunning," Artie said.

"I feel grounded and calm for the first time in weeks." Mia squeezed Ruth tightly and whispered, "Thank you," in her ear.

Mia took Ruth's advice and spent the last few days focusing on herself through meditation, yoga, and a particularly strenuous kickboxing class she joined in the gym. Whenever her mind started to go dark, she repeated the mantra, 'Let it go,' and she was beginning to feel hopeful that the small bits of her calm composure would continue to grow.

Artie looked at his watch and said, "Everyone's going to meet at the ceremony, and if we don't leave soon, we're going to hit traffic on Route 287." He handed Ruth her shawl and quickly opened the front door leaving Ruth and Mia in his wake.

"Maybe you should bring him to that meditation class you started going to," Ruth whispered as she and Mia locked up the house.

As they entered the banquet hall, Mia caught sight of Daniella and told Ruth and Artie she would meet them at the table. She smoothed her dress and gingerly approached Daniella, tapping her lightly on the shoulder.

"Mia," Daniella said softly.

Instantly, Mia felt like her younger self as she began prattling on like she used to. "Look Daniella, I'm so very sorry for everything that happened the other day. I handled everything poorly. I should've stopped myself from becoming unhinged. I never should've attacked you. I just miss Nonnina so much. And Uncle Luca—"

Daniella reached out and put her hand on Mia's. "Mia, it's fine. I was going to seek you out tonight, too." She led Mia over to a quiet corner. "There's so much I need to say. I've been nothing but cruel to you all this time, and you really didn't deserve it.

"Why *did* you hate me so much? You didn't even *know* me."

"You're right, I didn't know you, but I thought I knew the type of person you were. You see, I grew up with an overbearing mother who convinced me that it was my destiny to marry Artie Bocelli. Apparently, our grandfathers joked about it a thousand years ago when they were friends, and my mother wouldn't let it go. When you came into the picture, she was furious. She said all sorts of terrible things about your parents. She led me to believe that they were vile, and you were just as loathsome." She looked up to the ceiling and wiped her eyes. "I became really jealous. Everything seemed to come easily for you, and you were so personable, and everyone liked you. I tried everything to get Artie's attention including sleeping with his brother. But it was clear how much he loved you, and my mother tormented me over the fact that Artie chose you over me."

Mia braced herself against the wall and Daniella shook her head as she continued. "Look, I'm not making excuses, I'm really just trying to explain myself." She took a deep breath. "The past few days, I've been doing a lot of thinking, and I realize that I grew up with parents who were never kind to anyone, let alone their own daughter. That mentality got in my head, and I obviously became just like them." She shook her head. "I was never close with my father, hell I didn't even have his last name." She chuckled sarcastically. "That should've told me something right there. Throughout my whole life, he was always distant and cold. For the life of me, I couldn't understand what I had done to make him hate me so much. I began to believe that something had to be wrong with me if my father wanted nothing to do with me, and I wasn't ever good enough for my mother." She wiped another tear from her eye and waved her hand. "Maybe all that doesn't matter. After you left, I sat down and read the copy of your mother's letter you gave me. I realized my whole life was built on a lie. I confronted my father, or I should say, the man I thought was my father. At first he tried to blow me off, but I was persistent in my attack. He finally acknowledged everything except the part about having Dominick killed. He swore he didn't know anything about it."

"Wow," Mia whispered. She didn't have any words. She'd never heard Daniella sound so sincere, yet broken, and Mia's heart ached a little for her.

"Mia, it's all clear to me now that the truth's come out. I am *so* sorry for everything. The way I behaved toward you was unconscionable, and I've spent the last few days re-evaluating who I am. It's abundantly obvious that I've got a lot of work to do on myself and have actually set up an appointment with a therapist. I know it's going to take a lot of time and work on my part, but I really would like to try to make amends. There's no reason in the world for you to trust me and, or, give me a chance, but I'm hoping someday maybe we'll be able to get together for some coffee and maybe try to get to know each other. You know, maybe after I figure out who I am?"

Mia took a deep breath, and everything Ruth had told her about understanding another person's perspective and forgiveness ran through her mind. She reached out and squeezed Daniella's hand and said, "I'd like that."

As Daniella's face brightened, Al rushed up to her, grabbed her hand, and said, "Get a move on, the ceremony's about to start." Mia's mouth fell open as she watched him pull her gruffly into the banquet room.

"How's it going?" Vicky whispered through the side of her mouth as Mia took her seat. "I was ready to jump in if you started strangling her again."

Mia chuckled. "No need. Everything's fine. I'll fill you in later."

Artie draped his arm along the back of Mia's chair, and she noticed the twitch in his eye was more pronounced, and he had now started frequently biting his lip. She placed her hand on his leg, and he looked at her in surprise.

"Are you okay?"

"Yup, just fine," he said and took a large gulp of water. "Here we go. They're about to announce the winner."

Vicky grabbed Mia's hand as the announcer said, "This year we've had a number of wonderful candidates for our humanitarian award. Each of you has made our county proud through all of the hard work and dedication you've given to not only help those in need, but to make Morris County a better place to live. I am proud to announce that the winner of this year's Humanitarian of the Year Award is Denise Coppola. Ms. Coppola has spent countless hours educating our young people on the dangers of drug use, organizing educational sessions for parents and guardians, lobbying to crack down on drug distribution in our school districts, and fundraising to subsidize the building of our brand-new treatment center. She is responsible for helping many of our young adults to get the treatment and services they needed to become clean and sober. Ms. Coppola has helped to save lives, she has offered support and counseling, and she has made a true difference in our community. Please join me in a round of applause for Morris County's 1989 Humanitarian of the Year, Denise Coppola."

Vicky groaned. "Well, crap."

Mia smiled and clapped loudly. "She deserves the honor. I've met her. She's sincere and genuine."

Joe smacked his hand on the table and grunted. "Go figure."

Artie gave him a long sideways glance and put his hand on Mia's leg. "Sorry, babe," he whispered.

"I'm fine, really," Mia announced to the table. "Actually, I'm relieved that I don't have to get up there and give a speech."

Matt raised his wine glass. "Here's to Mia, and all of our wives, actually. You are the true stars of our family."

"Here, here," Ruth said as she sipped her wine.

"Yes, here's to us wives," Dee said loudly as she swallowed her full glass of wine and refilled it quickly. "We're the ones filled with decency."

Vicky leaned into Mia as she watched Joe grab Dee's arm. "I think she drank a whole bottle already, and she showed up pretty wasted. This is new, even for her."

Mia noticed Joe's face grow red as Dee hurled insults at him. But when she said, "You're not a real Don," Joe slammed his fist on the table.

"That's enough! Someone get her outta here."

Everyone at the table stared at each other in silence. Matt leaned in and whispered in Theresa's ear, and she nodded.

"I'll drive her home," she offered. "I'm sorry, Mia."

Mia waved her hand and blew her a kiss.

"Mia, if you don't mind, I think I'm going to go with Theresa and lend a hand," Ruth said placing her napkin on the table and standing. She went around the table to hug Mia and whispered,

"Dee's really drunk, and I'm worried about letting Theresa handle it alone."

"Thank you, Grammy." Mia kissed Ruth's cheek and gave Theresa a look of concern. Theresa nodded quickly, and with Ruth's help, she led Dee out of the banquet hall.

"Wow," Vicky said slowly. "Maybe we should try to have a heart-to-heart talk with Dee. I mean she is the new Donna and all."

"You're probably right let's invite her to lunch next week," Mia said.

As she looked up, she saw her sister Nancy whisper in Matt's ear just before she drew Mia in for a big hug. "Hey, I'm so sorry you didn't win."

"Maybe next year," Mia smiled. "Is everything okay? We don't usually see you this early in the night when you're catering an event."

"Yes, just fine," Nancy said quickly. "I've got to get back, love you."

Mia watched her sister carefully and noticed she and Matt locked eyes and gave each other a slight nod. Matt excused himself from the table and approached Don Mario who was sitting at the adjacent table with his niece, Daniella and Al. As Matt whispered in his ear, Don Mario threw his napkin down, grabbed the Martini glass Daniella was about to sip, and said, "Enough's, enough." He stood up abruptly. "Let's not make a scene," he said sternly. "Al, Daniella join me in the empty banquet room down the hall. This is *not* a request." He turned to Matt. "Matthew, bring *all* of your people as well. This ends now!"

Matt moved to Artie's side and gestured with his head toward the door. Artie stood and said, "Matt, not the wives."

"It's best if they come," Matt said firmly.

"What's this all about?" Joe jumped to his feet

Matt put his hand on Joe's shoulder and leaned in toward the table. "I'm sorry to have to break up the party, but we all need to join Don Mario in the other room." He locked eyes with Angelo who stood, moved toward Joe, and walked with him and Matt out of the banquet room.

Artie let out a long breath, "Let's go," he said and held out his hand directing Vicky and Mia to follow him.

SIXTY

VICKY AND MIA held hands as they followed Artie into the other banquet room. Don Mario waved them in, and Mia felt her shoulders tense when she noticed that both Esposito and Bocelli guards were stationed outside of the room and a number of them lined the perimeter of the interior room as well.

"Now I've had about enough of these accusations being hurled against both families, and it's time we get down to the business of setting the record straight," Don Mario started. He held up Daniella's Martini glass. "Al, I would like you to drink this."

Al looked around the room and put up both hands. "No, thanks. I don't drink Vodka."

"This was not a suggestion." Don Mario held the glass out to Al.

"I don't understand, what's this all about?" Al put his arm around Daniella's waist.

"There was a witness who claims they saw you pour a substance into the glass when you were up at the bar," Don Mario said.

"I don't know who this witness was, but I certainly didn't spike my wife's drink with anything." He scoffed and snapped his finger. "In fact, Mia, you were standing next to me at the bar."

"Me?" Mia felt her face flush. "I didn't do anything." She

looked over at Daniella who was staring at her with contempt growing in her eyes.

"I had to stop you from strangling my wife just three days ago. I believe the words you were screaming were, 'I could kill you.'"

Daniella gasped, "You did, you said that."

Mia looked around the room, "I didn't do anything, I didn't try to poison anyone."

Artie put his arm around Mia as Matt started to say, "Don Mario, no disrespect, but—"

Don Mario waved his hand at Matt and sighed. "Al, go ahead and empty your pockets and Mia, if you wouldn't mind emptying your purse, we can get to the bottom of this much quicker."

"This is ridiculous," Al sneered as he emptied a handful of change, his wallet, and half a roll of Life Savers onto the table.

"Artie," Mia whispered as her shaking hands placed a lipstick, a compact, folded tissues, a change purse, and a pre-written acceptance speech on the table.

Matt nodded at Angelo, who along with both an Esposito and Bocelli security guard left the room. While another Esposito guard stepped forward and inspected Al and Mia's belongings.

"It's all clean, Boss."

"Don Mario," Joe started, "I apologize on behalf of my family. I'm not sure what's gotten into them, but I assure you I will get to the bottom of all of this, and it will *never* happen again."

Don Mario nodded slowly. "I take attacks on my family very seriously. Whether they be accusations or physical, and I have to say," he waved his hand around, "this does *not* make me happy."

Joe stood up straight and buttoned his suit jacket. "I agree. I'm not happy either. I promise you, there *will* be consequences. I value our relationship and will do all that I must to ensure that our business interests are not compromised due to the recent irrational events."

Don Mario nodded slowly again.

"I believe it's time for us to leave," Joe said as he scowled at Matt and Artie.

"Don Mario, if you don't mind indulging me," Matt said as he turned his head toward the Don. "In regard to our conversation this afternoon, I've brought along that proof you had requested." He motioned for Angelo, who had just returned carrying a briefcase.

"Conversation? You met with Don Mario without my permission?" Joe fumed.

"Very well," Don Mario said and held his hand up to Joe.

Matt opened the briefcase and took out a cassette player along with one of at least two dozen cassette tapes.

"My Uncle Luca could read people really well. He was always a good judge of character," Matt said as he put a cassette in the recorder. "As a result, he always knew who he could trust and who he could not." He pressed the play button and smiled at Joe.

Joe: *"Yeah, hey, it's me."*

Al: *"What the hell happened?*

Joe: *"My guy had a clean shot before she got in the way."*

Al: *"A clean shot? Your guy's incompetent."*

Joe: *"I don't know what to say, it was an accident."*

Al: *"Your accident's gonna cause a war between the families. I mean, personally, I'm not gonna miss that contemptuous she-devil of a mother-in-law, but the rest of the family is pretty upset over losing their beloved Antonia."*

Joe: *"Don't worry, I got a plan. I'll pin it on the Clinton Kings. I've got an old beef with Diaz anyway, and it's time for some retribution. In a couple months, we'll get the job done right."*

Al: *"You better. Every day we're not distributing in Bocelli territory is a financial loss for both of us."*

Joe: *"Don't worry about it."*

Al: *"And use a different guy next time. The sooner you're Don and have your own people at the top with you, the better."*

Joe: *"Yup."*

Matt pressed the stop button on the recorder as silence rang through the room. "Luca suspected Joe was behind the first hit attempt. He knew the Espositos wouldn't arrange a hit at a family function. Particularly their own family function."

"He was correct. You know, I've always honored and respected the Bocelli Family, just as my father had." Don Mario said solemnly.

"This is ridiculous," Joe sneered. "It's all a sham. I don't know how you did it, but that was not me on that recording."

Artie turned on his heel and leered at Joe. "Cut the crap already, Joe! When Uncle Luca arranged for your house to be renovated, he had recording devices installed. We've got videos too. He never trusted you, and obviously, he was right."

"I offered him the world!" Joe exclaimed. "He turned down millions of dollars all because he was so righteous. He might've bought into Armando's antiquated morals, but I saw opportunity."

"So, you had him killed?" Matt stepped in front of Joe and pushed his face forward almost touching Joe's nose. "Come on, admit it out loud. The sooner you do, the easier it'll be on you."

Joe took a step back and raised his hands. "It was Al's idea. He knew as well as I did that Luca would never consent to partnering with him and opening our territory for distribution."

"Shut up you imbecile!" Al moved to punch Joe, but the Esposito guards held him back.

Joe looked desperately around the room. "Check his pockets again, you'll see. He was gonna poison Daniella and pin it on Mia. He didn't like how she changed over the last few days, talking about doing the right thing and all."

"Pat him down," Don Mario commanded.

"This is ridiculous," Al boomed. "You can't believe this little weasel." Al tried to push away the Esposito guard.

"Al," Don Mario said calmly. "We can do this the easy way, or the hard way. Either way, it's getting done. I suggest you start cooperating."

Al took a step back and held up his arms. The guard ran his hands up and down Al's legs, across his back and chest, and finally over his stomach. He pulled an empty vial containing white residue from Al's vest pocket.

"You tried to kill me?" Daniella said in disbelief. Her eyes grew wide, and she lunged at her husband. "You son-of-a-bitch!"

The guard pulled Daniella away from Al while Mia stepped forward and wrapped her in her arms.

Don Mario straightened his back. "I believe it's time for the women to take their leave." He approached Mia, squeezed her hand, and bowed his head. He then kissed Daniella's cheek and said, "I'll meet you at your home a little later."

Daniella nodded quickly as tears streamed down her face. Angelo nodded to Vicky who helped Daniella out of the room, while Mia walked over to Joe and slapped his cheek so hard, he lost his balance. "I hope you rot in hell!" She said and spit in his face. She then reached out and squeezed Artie's hand before leaving the room with her head held high.

SIXTY-ONE

FALL, 1989

AS MIA OPENED her front door and dragged herself inside, Ruth put the book she was reading aside and raced over to her.

"What's happened? Where's Artie?"

"He's taking care of some business and won't be home for a while," Mia said flatly. "Joe had Uncle Luca killed." She squeezed her eyes shut. "It all came out tonight."

"Oh, sweetheart," Ruth gasped and hugged her granddaughter. "I'm at a loss for words."

"I know," Mia sighed.

"How about I make some tea? Something soothing to calm your nerves."

Mia nodded, "That'd be great." She kicked off her heels and slid into a chair at the table. She didn't want to talk about what she was sure was going to happen to Joe, and by the look on Ruth's face, Mia knew she didn't want to hear it either.

"Daniella and I spoke before the dinner," Mia said hoping the change of subject would be sufficient conversation to justify not addressing the elephant in the room.

"And how did that go?" Ruth's demeanor softened.

"Actually, Grammy, I took your advice. After I awkwardly tried to apologize for attacking her, I really listened to everything she had to say. I think I have a better understanding as to why she'd been so mean to me so long."

Ruth nodded.

"She admitted she was jealous of my relationship with Artie, and she said her mother had said some pretty mean things about me and my parents."

"That doesn't surprise me. Her mother must've been carrying around a lot of baggage due to her getting pregnant by your father. I'm not sure compassion is a strong trait within some of the Espositos."

Mia took a long sip of tea and pondered how so many members of a family could be devoid of the kindness trait. She thought about what Daniella said about wanting to work on herself.

"Do you think people can change? Like can they learn to be kind?"

"I do. I think if someone wants to change badly enough they can. Of course, I think it would require someone to be sincere in their intents."

"Daniella said she's going to see a therapist and she really wanted to change. I hope she's serious."

"Seeing a therapist is a huge leap in the right direction. It'll help her determine who she really wants to be."

Mia squeezed her eyes shut. The way Daniella described her relationship with her parents haunted Mia. She couldn't imagine growing up feeling unloved. No matter how badly her mother spiraled with her addiction, she knew Rena loved her, and there was never a day she felt otherwise.

"Gram, can you get Maddie and bring her home tomorrow? I think it's time."

"Of course," Ruth said. "I'm sure you miss that little peanut around here."

"I do," Mia said as the front door opened and Artie wearily walked in.

Ruth grabbed her teacup and put it in the sink. "I'm going to say goodnight." She kissed Mia's cheek and gave Artie an extra-long hug. She cupped her hand on his cheek and nodded at him before she walked to her room.

Mia ran to her husband and whimpered as she plunged into his arms. They stood holding each other in silence, and Mia could tell Artie didn't want to let go any more than she did. She was the first to pull away.

"Do you want some tea?" She whispered.

"No." He shook his head. "I need to scrub myself down in a hot shower."

"Okay," she said and took his hand, led him up to their bathroom, undressed him, and turned on the hot shower. She waited in bed for him to finish, and as he laid down facing her, Whitney jumped up and curled herself into the bend of his knees.

"About Joe," he said carefully.

She put her pointer finger on his lips. "I know," she said placidly.

"We're going to need the Sisterhood to look after Dee. She's got a sister in Clearwater so get her a nice place down there and set her up with a monthly living allowance."

"Okay. Consider it done." Mia looked at Artie closely and read his expression. He was all business on the outside, but she could see from the look on his face that the night's events traumatized him.

"Matt and I stopped over there on our way home. She wasn't surprised. She found out what he'd done. When she got to the awards ceremony tonight, she had asked Matt if she could meet with us tomorrow. She was going to tell us what she overheard that morning when Joe was on the phone."

"That must've been so hard for her." Mia whispered.

"It wasn't easy for any of us."

Mia wanted so much to ease Artie's burden. As she ran her fingers through his hair, she realized that she felt strangely at peace. She thought that she should've been feeling angry, hateful, or even regretful that another man most likely lost his life in an act of retribution, but a tranquil stillness flowed through her.

"How long did you know about Joe?" She asked.

"We suspected right from the start. Even before Nonnuccio died. That's why Uncle Luca wanted to take care of the renovations on his house. He had Carlo set up the recording devices so we would have absolute proof of his betrayals. But it took us some time to go through all of the tapes and the video footage. Turns out, our suspicions were right. He was the one behind everything, the construction delays, the FBI raid, all of it."

"You're kidding?" Mia said in disbelief.

"Nope. He had gotten obsessed with being Don. Thought he should've been Nonnuccio's Underboss the whole time. We even suspect he slipped something in my tequila that night I passed out. He never came out and said it directly on the tapes, but reading between the lines, it was clear that he wanted his own people in place with him at the top."

"He could've killed you!"

Artie cupped his hand on Mia's cheek. "He tried." He shook his head. "Thank God he was completely inadequate and wasn't able to pull it off."

Mia leaned in and squeezed Artie tightly. She needed to feel his heartbeat next to hers.

Artie yawned and ran his fingers through Mia's hair. "When we met with Don Mario and laid it all out, he said he wanted to do his own investigation and wanted to see our proof. I suppose I could understand his reservations. Al's been a part of the Esposito

Family forever, not to mention he's Daniella's husband. But when Nancy told Matt that the bartender saw Al put something in Daniella's drink, Esposito knew he had to act sooner rather than later."

"And Al?" She asked.

He shook his head. "He might not have ordered the hit on Uncle Luca himself, but he both suggested it be done and condoned the action. Uncle Luca was a Don, and in this thing of ours, you can't play any part in a Don's murder, or attempted murder, like he did without approval from the Commission. Not to mention, it was pretty clear he tried to poison Daniella. Family member or not, you can't get away with trying to kill a Don's sister."

Artie pulled Mia in close to him and began shaking. She held him tight trying to will all of the tension, anxiety, and despair out of him.

"I never thought something like this would ever happen. I never thought I would directly, or indirectly, play a role in someone else's demise. But there's rules, there's honor, and there's loyalty. This is the very element of our family lifestyle that you always fought against. This is why you didn't want me to work for the family. I get it now. But I had no choice. Tonight, there was no choice."

"Artie, honey, Joe made his decisions and took his actions knowing full well what would happen to him."

"I know," his voice cracked. "But that doesn't make it any easier on the rest of us.

"It's okay." She held him tight. "It's all going to be okay."

"We've got to do something. We've got to make it okay."

"We will," she assured him.

"I'm so sorry, Mia," he whispered. "For all the secrets. There were so many secrets."

"Shh, I know." She kissed him. "Go ahead and sleep. We'll finish talking tomorrow."

Mia held her husband. She comforted him, soothed him, and held him in her arms feeling the tears fall down his face until he fell asleep. She kissed his cheek, closed her eyes, and drifted into a deep slumber knowing she had no more tears left to release.

SIXTY-TWO

THE NEXT MORNING, Mia woke up early like she used to on weekends. She felt refreshed and lighter than she had in weeks. She didn't want to wake Artie, so she got dressed and made her way to the main house. There she played her Uncle Luca's favorite arias as she gathered the ingredients to make pancakes. She had decided it was time for the family to heal and for life to move forward. She couldn't think of a better way to make that happen for herself than to continue her tradition of singing opera and making pancakes in her uncle's honor.

She was just about to pour her first batch of pancakes when *Figaro Aria* began to play. She stood at the stove waving her hands and singing loudly just like he used to do so many times in the past. Her eyes welled up with tears and as she sang, it was as if she could hear him singing along with her.

"You might want to turn that flame down."

Mia's heart skipped a beat, and she felt lightheaded as she spun herself around.

"Uncle Luca?" She stared at the man who was standing behind her. The man who looked exactly like the uncle who had been like a father to her. But his hair seemed slightly grayer, and his left arm was held up across his chest with a sling."

"Aah, Mia. Come. Come, give your old uncle a hug."

Tears flowed down her face. "Is it really you?"

Luca's voice quivered. "Yes, my cuoricina, it's really me."

She dropped the spatula and ran to him, she threw her arms around his waist and inhaled sharply. She wouldn't believe it was really him until she smelled his Polo Cologne. She hugged him and sobbed uncontrollably until the kitchen filled with smoke and the fire alarms went off from the burning pancakes.

"See, I told you, you should've turned down that flame," her uncle laughed as he sniffled and dried the tears that had run down his cheek.

"What's going on down here?" Aunt Carla said as she entered the kitchen and started opening the sliding doors and windows. "The fire alarms are blaring throughout the whole house." She walked to Luca and wrapped her arms around his waist.

Mia looked back and forth between them and reality hit her. "We were told you got shot and killed." She waved her hands. "I grieved for you. I couldn't function for close to two weeks. I almost choked Daniella Esposito to death."

"You what?" They both said in unison.

"She's fine and that's not important right now." Mia put her hands on her hips. "Why would you put us through that?" She whispered.

"Come, sit down," Carla said, took Mia's hand, and led her and Luca to the table.

"It tore us up, having to put you all through that. But we felt like we didn't have a choice," Luca said and took Mia's hand. "We suspected Joe was behind the first shooting, but I couldn't act upon a suspicion. No one ever thought he would've tried again the day of Nonnina's funeral, so I suppose we let our guard down a little when we were leaving the luncheon. But he did try again, and lucky for me, the goon he hired was a bad shot and missed my heart."

"Hmph, by inches." Carla shook her head and ran her hand down Luca's back. "He was in bad shape for a while, and in reality, it was touch and go in the beginning."

"You knew that whole time he was alive?" Mia leaned in closer to Carla.

"I did, but I wasn't acting. I really was in shock. Nonnina's death crushed me, it was so sudden and unexpected, and then to see my husband get shot and bleeding all over the sidewalk was horrifying. They said he might not make it, and I really couldn't cope with the idea of losing him." She shrugged her shoulders. "Ray, Artie, and Matt had collectively made the decision that it would be best for everyone's safety if Joe thought he had succeeded. It also bought them time to prove Joe was responsible."

"We had to keep it on the down low. Joe was very cunning, and if he even suspected that I was still alive, he would set out to get the job done himself," Luca said.

"I could've kept the secret," Mia said defiantly.

Both Carla and Luca stared at her.

"Okay," Mia relented. "I suppose you're right, my face would've given it away."

"Not to mention Vicky's attitude and Theresa's emotions." Luca raised his eyebrows.

"Where were you?" She asked Carla.

"Ray and Josie did take me to Mantoloking. Ray had Luca transferred to a hospital near there once he was stable, and when he was released, he recovered with us at the shore house."

"Unbelievable," Mia shook her head. "You guys are something else," Mia chuckled.

"Do you forgive us?" Luca asked.

"You're alive! I think I can find a way to forgive you."

They all turned their heads as Artie and Ruth entered the room.

"Luca," Ruth said and gave him a tight squeeze. "It's so good to see you at last."

"Wait, Grammy, you *knew*?"

"Of course, I knew," Ruth rolled her eyes. "You girls needed a mother figure looking out for you while Josie was looking out for Aunt Carla and Uncle Luca."

"Unbelievable," Mia repeated in shock. "And I'll talk to you about this later," she said as she teasingly pushed Artie.

Within minutes Josie and Ray, along with Matt and Theresa, had arrived in the kitchen. Lucky for Theresa, Matt was able to tell her about Luca before they arrived at the main house. She squealed in delight as she raced through the door to greet him. When Angelo came in, he looked more worn than either Matt or Artie.

He nodded to Luca and shook his hand. "It's good to have ya back, Boss." Luca pulled him in for a large man hug and nodded back to him. The look in their eyes said more than any words could have.

"Where's Vicky?" Mia asked Angelo as she looked around.

"She went to church," he said as he sat down and rubbed his hand over his face.

"I understand," Josie said solemnly and walked over to Angelo. She pulled him up and gave him a long squeeze. "You're a good man," she said and kissed both of his cheeks. He nodded quickly and slumped back into the chair.

By the time Vicky arrived home from church, the initial shock of Luca's arrival had worn off, and the entire family was enjoying a large breakfast of pancakes and eggs with bacon, sausage and mimosas. She walked into the kitchen, took a long look at Luca, and screamed at the top of her lungs.

"Are? Are you a ghost?" She said pointing to him.

"I am not. I'm the real deal," Luca beamed.

"Oh my God," she said as she made the sign of the cross.

"Come on, sweetheart, you, me, and Aunt Carla need to have a little talk as you change out of that black dress," Josie said.

Carla grabbed three glasses of champagne and turned to Ruth. "What's with the long, black veil she's wearing?"

Ruth shrugged, "Beats me."

CARLA AND JOSIE decided to have a huge open house to celebrate Luca's return to the living. Throughout the day, the house was filled with associates, friends, and various members of the other families congratulating Luca and wishing the Bocelli Family well.

Mia took great comfort when she saw Luca and Don Mario warmly greet each other, and whisk Matt and Artie to Luca's office for a private meeting. She no longer felt contempt for the Espositos as she realized Mario was not much like his father, Carmine, and Daniella had been genuinely warm and personable in spite of everything that had happened the night before. She even asked to be introduced to the rest of the Russos, and she spent much of the afternoon sitting in a circle with Janet, Nancy and Anthony getting to know them and making a great first impression.

After greeting most of the guests, Mia found Theresa and Vicky in a corner watching the kids run around in circles.

"Hey, there you are," Mia said as she lifted Maddie high in the air. She nuzzled her neck and kissed every inch of her face before putting her daughter down to join her cousins.

"Talk about an emotional roller coaster, huh?" Vicky said as Mia sat next to her.

"I've been saying it all day, unbelievable." Mia held out her glass of champagne for Vicky to sip and she waved Mia away.

Theresa took Vicky's hand. "How's Ange holding up?"

"He'll be alright." Vicky nodded. "He'll spend a couple of days at the gym and work out the emotions and tension."

"How are *you* holding up?" Mia asked.

"You know, I grew up with Joe. He was always around, always with us. Every holiday, every Sunday he was there. I just can't understand how Nonnuccio's nephew, whom he treated like a son, would do this. For what? Money? Why would he throw away all that we were to him? We were *family*. You should be loyal to your family."

"You know, it's funny. I've never felt prouder to be a Bocelli than I do now. It's crazy, but everything that happened has really put it all in perspective for me. I couldn't love you guys more if we were all blood-related sisters," Mia said as she reached out for both Theresa and Vicky's hands.

"I feel the same," Theresa said.

"Loyal to the end," Vicky said.

After the party, Tony and Ruth sat with Artie and Mia in their kitchen drinking coffee and eating leftover cake.

"You know, we would love it if you both stayed a little longer," Mia prodded.

"No, sweetheart, it's time for me to go back home with your grandfather tomorrow morning."

"I miss my Ruthie," Tony winked at Ruth. "But before we turn in for the night, I've got some paperwork I'd like you to take a quick look at if you don't mind, Artie?"

Tony handed Artie a manila folder containing various papers.

"This is a deed to a restaurant in Brooklyn, Salvatore Bruno's." Artie looked at the papers closer. "It looks to me like Carmine Esposito signed all rights and ownership to you before he died."

Tony nodded, "That's what his lawyer said too. So, it's

legitimate? Salvatore Bruno's is legally mine?"

"It most certainly is," Artie looked up at Tony. "Congratulations."

"Poppy, that's the restaurant you opened with your father, right?"

"And my cousin Frank," he said with pride and squeezed Ruth's hand. "I wound up selling it to Esposito long ago."

"It says here that Carmine expressed his wishes that it be returned to the rightful owners, the Russos."

"I'll be damned," Tony said shaking his head.

"Are you going to run it again?" Mia asked.

"No, I'm too old to start all that over again. But Artie, I would like you to do something for me. I'd like to put ownership in Janet, Nancy, Anthony and Mia's names. I had already told the others about this, and they requested that if it was, in fact, legitimate, they wanted Nancy to have 70% ownership and have full reign to run it as she likes. If that's alright with you, Mia."

"Poppy, I'd happily give Nancy my share. She deserves this."

"No, no. I don't have much to leave you kids, and it would make me happy knowing all of you would own even a little piece of your family's legacy."

"Okay, I understand."

"That's easy enough to make happen. I'll get the paperwork started first thing Monday morning."

"But there's something else. Nancy's husband, Richard is out for himself, and I have it on good authority that he's caught up in some illegal funny business. Can you make it so if anything happens, Richard can't get her share of the restaurant?"

Artie sat back and let out a long breath. "Yes, I can do that. In fact, as long as Nancy's in agreement, I think it would be a good idea to also amend her will and write up a post-nuptial agreement. We can further protect what happens to her assets upon divorce or God forbid her death. I think the bigger problem might getting Richard to agree to signing it."

Tony nodded his head slowly and raised his eyebrows. "I'm sure *you* can find a way to persuade him."

"I'm sure *I* can," Artie reached out and shook Tony's hand.

Artie shifted in his seat. "Uhm, there's something Mia and I have wanted to talk to you both about for quite a while. The timing never seemed right." He started to shake his right leg. "It's about my role in the Bocelli Family."

Tony raised his hand. "No need." He stood, reached out his hand to Artie, and pulled him in for a hug. "I understand. Just promise me to honor your grandparents and Mia's great-grandparents who lived their lives with integrity and compassion."

"I will, I promise."

SIXTY-THREE

TWO MONTHS LATER, Artie was able to draw up the legal papers for Tony concerning the ownership of the restaurant. Nancy's husband, Richard, however, was being more difficult about signing the post-nuptial agreement than anyone had anticipated. Artie decided he, Matt, and Angelo needed to have a sit down with him to explain what his options were concerning his future. The night they took him out to dinner, Mia brought Maddie and Whitney over to Vicky's place so the dogs could play, and Aunt Vicky could get her Maddie cuddles. Vicky seemed to glow as she held Maddie in her lap and sang Maddie's favorite song about monkeys jumping on a bed.

Mia pointed to her and said, "You're pregnant!"

Vicky quickly looked up, and with perfect timing, Maddie started clapping. "What gave it away?"

"Your face. You look so serene and happy."

"And how does my face usually look?" Vicky raised her eyebrows at Mia. "Never mind, I already know the answer to that."

Mia raised her hand to her chest. "I'm so happy for you. How are you feeling? What's the doctor say?"

Vicky's smile lit up her face. "I'm almost through the first trimester, and Dr. Stragazzi said everything's looking good so far. I'm feeling pretty good, too." She hesitated. "We aren't going to tell people outside the family until I'm into the second trimester, so could you do me a favor, and avoid seeing people for a few weeks? Your face is a dead giveaway."

"Pff." Mia waved her hand. "I'll keep your secret, I promise."

Vicky stared at Mia, and they both burst out laughing.

"I'll try to keep a low profile." Mia rolled her eyes.

"So, Mee, I don't know how to thank you for convincing Artie to bring me in on family business." Vicky's voice cracked. "How did you do it?"

"Don't give it a second thought." Mia waved her hand. "After Uncle Luca named Matt as his Underboss, I felt the time was right. I reminded Artie that you had a great mind for both the law and business, you understood how the family ran, and no one was as loyal as you. Of course, he said the typical jargon that many associates wouldn't respect you as a female, so I suggested that they start small and slow." She shrugged. "Besides, if any of the old timers have a problem, they should take it up with Uncle Luca. You know he's completely on board, thanks to Aunt Carla's persuasion."

"I'm just so glad that they're starting to let go of that old-fashioned, patriarchal way of thinking," Vicky said and handed Maddie to Mia. "So you're going to be super busy soon, huh?"

Mia put her daughter down on a blanket and handed her a teddy bear. "I feel like it's the calm before a major storm strikes." She shook her head. "Nancy wants to hold off on renovating the restaurant until Richard signs the postnup, and your parents are still working with Carlo to determine if they want to tear down that house they bought in Palm Beach and rebuild, or just gut the inside and renovate." She put her hands on her hips. "Either way, I'm going to be taking a whole lot of trips out to Brooklyn and down to Florida."

"I'm exhausted just thinking about it. How are you and Artie doing, by the way?"

"That trip we took to Aruba, just after Uncle Luca returned, turned out to be the best thing we could've done for our marriage. We both needed that time to decompress and reconnect. It was great seeing him return to his old self as his demeanor softened and his sense of humor came back."

"It sounds like it was an amazing trip," Vicky nodded.

"It really was. We spent our days soaking up the sun and our nights falling in love all over again. We slow danced in the moonlight and took long walks on the beach," Mia said dreamily. "That's when we came up with the idea for Nonna's House."

"That's that new project you and Artie started working on, right?"

Mia nodded. "That situation with Joe really changed Artie, and he decided that the only way he could continue to play a major role in the Bocelli Family, was if he played an equally major role in helping people who didn't have the resources to help themselves. He said he had admired how much the Sisterhood was able to do all the good they did for the community, and he became driven to do his part."

"I can see that," Vicky said. "Artie is far more tenderhearted than most Consiglieres, and I think it'll be good for him to be able to balance his conscience by becoming more philanthropical."

"Exactly!" Mia straightened her back and smiled broadly. "So, we came up with our Nonna's House idea. It's going to be a facility designed to help people in crisis. We're going to be offering assistance and shelter for the homeless, medical and counseling services for those without insurance, a food bank, and educational and training resources to assist people to not only earn their GED, but to become successfully employed."

"Wow, Mia. That's a huge undertaking." Vicky raised her eyebrows.

"We're still in the planning stage. There's a whole lot that has to be done before we can even find a location or break ground, and each component will be rolled out in phases."

"Mia, that is really an incredible thing you and Artie are doing. You know, you've got my full support. Whatever you need, I'm your girl."

"Thanks," Mia said as she reached out and took Vicky's hand. "I may need you to talk me off a ledge before this is all over."

"No problem, I'll stand in the street and talk you down with a bullhorn. This way everyone can hear your business," She chuckled. "Speaking of ledges, what's happening with Daniella?"

"I actually had lunch with her the other day, if you can believe that."

"Get out! Was there a food fight?"

"No." Mia rolled her eyes and waved her hand. "She just got back from spending a month at a wellness center in Arizona. I've got to admit, she seems like she's really putting in the work. Her attitude and overall manner have changed. She bought a townhouse not far from where she and Al lived, and said she wanted to continue her humanitarian work here in New Jersey. She said she's set boundaries with her family and doesn't want to be consumed with the harsh way of life she had before."

"Good for her," Vicky said as she shrugged. "I guess time will tell if she really means it."

"Yup," Mia agreed. "I'm cautiously optimistic."

As Angelo came through the kitchen, Mia looked at the clock and noticed it was past nine.

"Hey, Ange. Is Artie home too?"

"He's home waiting for ya," he said and put his arm around Vicky.

"Vicky told me the good news. Congratulations, Papa."

"Yeah, thanks," he blushed and looked down.

"Hey, Mee. Why don't you leave Maddie and Whitney here

for the night? They're both sound asleep and I hate for you to have to spend a lot of time getting Maddie back down if she wakes up. Besides, it'll be nice to have a sleepover."

"You don't mind?" Mia looked back and forth between Angelo and Vicky.

"Nah, you can leave her here," Angelo said as Vicky nodded vigorously.

Mia didn't waste any time leaving Vicky's house for fear they would change their minds. She practically ran home anticipating a long hot bath and curling up with a good book. As she walked through the door, she noticed multiple candles lit throughout the living room, a bottle of chilled champagne on the table, soft love songs playing in the background, and Artie standing in the center of the room smiling sheepishly.

"What's this all about?"

"I realize life is going to start getting crazy soon, so I thought it would be nice to spend a romantic evening together."

"I like your thinking," she said as she melted in his arms and kissed him warm and tenderly.

They snuggled on the couch and sipped champagne while they admired the fire burning brightly in the fireplace.

"How'd it go with Richard? Or should I not bring it up?"

"Let's just say, he signed the papers, and I'm confident he's going to both be kind to Nancy and be on the straight and narrow from here on out."

Mia turned her head toward him and snorted. "What did you guys do?"

"We *did* nothing, but we made it very clear that he would be ruined financially, professionally, and socially if he didn't sign the paperwork and get his act together."

"And that worked?"

"Yeah, it did. Richard's only goal in life is to make as much money as he can by doing as little as possible. He's caught up in stature and power, so we hit him where we knew it would hurt and threatened to destroy his career and his reputation. Such as it is. He signed immediately. He knew we had the connections and the means to ruin him."

"Good," Mia nodded her head. "Good."

"Hey, that's our song," Artie sat up as the song *Shining Star* began to play. "Care to dance, my Stella Splendente?"

Mia took Artie's hand and closed her eyes as they swayed to the music.

Artie brushed his thumb over Mia's cheek and whispered, "You are my everything."

Mia kissed him gently and replied, "Forever and Always."

SIXTY-FOUR

MIA PUT HER right arm around Nancy's waist while she placed her left hand on her own protruding belly. "It's gorgeous. Poppy's gonna love it."

"You're an amazing designer," Nancy said.

"Nope, I just gave you options. You had the vision and made all the choices."

"Don't sell yourself short. I know you put your all into renovating this place while renovating Ray and Josie's winter house in Florida, too. I just don't understand how you managed to get pregnant in the process."

Mia chuckled, "Artie and I made the best of the little time we had together."

"What are we laughing about?" Janet asked as she and Vicky joined them.

"Mia's sex life," Nancy bounced on her toes.

"Nice to hear someone has a sex life these days." Vicky rolled her eyes. "Ever since Joanie was born, it's tough to find a time when we're both not exhausted."

"It'll get better, I promise," Janet said. "But I'll let you in on a little secret. Get the grandparents to take the baby for a weekend. They love that, and it'll give you and your husband time to sleep, get reacquainted in bed, and sleep some more."

"She's not wrong," Mia agreed.

Nancy took a glass of champagne from the server who approached them. "Listen, Kevin," she said to him. "I want you to make sure that everyone in this room is treated like a VIP all night, no matter how crowded we get. They're all family, and no one gets better service than family. You got it?"

"Yes, ma'am," he bowed his head and filtered through the rest of the room offering champagne to everyone who was milling about.

"Oh, Nancy," Vicky touched her heart.

"I wouldn't be half as successful as I am if the Bocellis didn't treat me like family, look out for me, and help me to get my start," she said as she looked around the room.

"Yeah, I consider you all my close family too," Janet said as she reached out and hugged Vicky.

"What's happening over here?" Artie asked as he and Anthony walked over.

"We were just saying how much we love the Bocellis," Nancy said.

"Well, *yeah*, they're family," Anthony said shaking his head in confusion.

Artie walked over to Mia and kissed her cheek as the others followed a waiter who walked by with hot hors d'oeuvres.

"Should you be sitting?" Artie asked, looking around the room for an available chair.

"I'm six months pregnant, I'm not an invalid."

"This is true, but wasn't it just last Sunday you were on the couch with your feet propped up on a pillow begging anyone who walked by to give you a foot massage."

"Oh, very funny," she jabbed him in the side.

"You know what *is* funny? Ten years ago, we couldn't imagine a day would come when we would be gathered together, with both families, at the grand opening of Russo's Ristorante."

"Ten years ago, I was afraid for you to meet Poppy," Mia smiled as she scanned the room and observed Josie hugging Nancy, Matt and Anthony sitting together discussing the Giants, Carla, Janet, and Theresa sipping wine and giggling. "And now look at us, we are so very lucky."

"I guess Operation Family Unity was a bigger success than we thought," Artie chuckled.

"They're pulling up," Theresa announced as she looked out the window.

"Wow," Anthony whistled. "Nice limo."

"We thought they should arrive in style. Besides, we had to get a big one to fit all six of them when they go to the airport later." Mia shrugged.

"Airport?" Anthony's wife, Susan asked.

"Yeah, Mom and Pop are going with Ray, Josie, Carla and Luca to christen Ray and Josie's new Palm Beach house," Anthony said. "I'm sorry, I thought I told you about it."

"Okay, yes, you did say something about that. I just didn't realize they were going tonight."

"Yup," Mia nodded. "They're leaving right after the grand opening and staying for a week."

"Here they come," Anthony said and opened the door.

Nancy held out her arms. "Welcome to Russo's," she said, her voice cracking as Tony and Ruth slowly walked in.

Ruth put her hand over her mouth and gasped. She looked at Tony, who stood as still as a statue, seemingly overcome with emotion. He made his way to the middle of the dining room and put his hands on his hips, while he slowly turned around.

"We kept the original woodwork and chandeliers," Nancy said proudly.

"My father chose that woodwork," Tony said softly.

"And your mother and I picked out those chandeliers," Ruth said as a tear fell down her cheek.

"This is amazing," Tony managed. He looked at the bar and noticed the small picture gallery Nancy and Mia had hung just that very morning. "What's this?" He asked as he took Ruth's hand, and they walked over to it.

Together they gazed at an assortment of pictures that were taken almost forty years earlier at the original Salvatore Bruno's Restaurant.

"Tony, look," Ruth said in amazement as she pointed to a picture of them with his parents, Sal and Anna, and his cousin, Frank on opening night. "That feels like it was just yesterday, yet it was a whole lifetime ago."

"Luca come on over here, have you seen this?" Tony called out and pointed to another picture from opening night featuring Anna and Sal sitting at a table with Carla's parents. "I knew them as Manny and Ella, my parents' nearest and dearest friends."

Luca shook his head and patted Tony on the back.

"Mia and I wanted to honor every special person from the past and left some space so we can add pictures from tonight to celebrate every special person who's here with us now," Nancy said.

"It's fantastic," Ruth said as she wiped her nose with a tissue she pulled out of her purse. "Where did you ever get these pictures of Rena as a teenager, and Janet, Nancy, and Anthony all dressed up eating spaghetti and meatballs?"

Janet and Anthony joined them and said, "We can be resourceful when we need to be."

Tony turned and looked at his children, a tear fell down his cheek as he said, "I'm overcome. I never thought I'd see this day."

"How about a toast before we officially open?" Nancy motioned for the wait staff to re-fill champagne glasses.

Tony shook his head slightly, took a deep breath to compose himself, and straightened his back. "If you had told me thirty years ago I would be standing right here today, I would've said you were crazy. Life is difficult and challenging, and it's amazing and joyous. I've learned through the years, that the love and loyalty of family is the one true constant through both the good and the bad times. Looking at all of you here today, I thank you for that love and loyalty and for being there through the good and the bad memories. Here's to many more years of family love, loyalty, and memories. To our family, alla nostra famiglia."

THE END

AUTHOR'S NOTE

Dear Reader,

Thank you so much for reading *In the Name of Loyalty*. I have lived with the Bocelli and Russo families in my head for a few years, and they have become like members of my own family. In writing this story, I realized that every family has flaws and secrets, and it's unfair to make judgments based on perceptions or rumors. I have come to believe that most of us try to do the best we can with what we have.

If this is the first book of mine that you've read, please consider reading the prequel, *In the Name of Family*. It was through this book that the Russo family came to life, and I fell in love with each and every one of them. I promise jaw-dropping twists and turns that you won't see coming.

I learn a lot when I receive thoughts and feedback from people who've read my work. I would love to hear from you and would value anything you have to say. You can send me an email through my website: http://cynthiacoppola.com, connect with me on Facebook: https://www.facebook.com/cynthia.coppola.author, or follow me on Instagram: www.instagram.com/cynthiacoppola.author

It's difficult for new authors, such as myself, to be noticed and appreciated. So if you've enjoyed *In the Name of Loyalty*, please consider writing a review on Goodreads or on the retail site on which you purchased the book. Every star and comment helps significantly.

Thank you again for your support.

ACKNOWLEDGMENTS

Thank you to everyone who has shown up for me. Your acceptance, support, and enthusiasm has touched my heart and has been my greatest inspiration. I love you all.

I would most especially like to thank:

Deborah Brown – My one and only – None of this would've been possible without your unwavering love, understanding, and encouragement. You are all I need in this life.

Denise Fedorchak – My beautiful sister – You've helped me more than you'll ever know. You've given me comfort whenever I needed it, criticism whenever I deserved it, and praise whenever I earned it. Thank you for sharing the laughter and wiping the tears.

Robin Brown – My sister in love – Thank you for all of your love, wisdom, and praise. You make life so much brighter.

Nancy Maldonado Harrison – My true-life Vicky and cherished friend – There are not enough words to express how much I appreciate you. You are one of my life's greatest blessings. Thank you for always being in my corner.

Jodi Sheridan – My dear friend – Thank you for being an amazing cheerleader and advocate. Your reassurance whenever the self-doubt creeps in means the world to me. Life is sweeter with you in it.

Cara Stevens, Elina Vaysbeyn, and Ian Koviak – My amazing professional team – Thank you for your incredible talent, attention to details, encouragement, and professionalism.

Julia Harrison – My up-and-coming superstar artist – Thank you for your design inspiration and for your talent. I know we will do great things together on future designs.

Denise Stragazzi – My student-turned friend – Thank you for being such a source of inspiration. You've helped me to be successful in so many ways. Thank you for being you.

ABOUT THE AUTHOR

CYNTHIA COPPOLA is the author of *In the Name of Family*. She was born and raised in New Jersey and holds a BA in English and an MA in Education. She has spent much of her career teaching High School English and now lives in Michigan with her wife and two dogs. She is grateful to have the opportunity to tap into her creativity and do something she loves…storytelling. Visit her website at http://cynthiacoppola.com